THE WORLD'S ROOM

A NOVEL

THE WORLD'S ROOM

TODD LONDON

DISCARD

STEERFORTH PRESS
SOUTH ROYALTON, VERMONT

CHESTERFIELD COUNTY LIBRARY
VIRGINIA

Copyright © 2001 by Todd London

ALL RIGHTS RESERVED

For information about permission to reproduce
selections from this book, write to:
Steerforth Press L.C., P.O.. Box 70,
South Royalton, Vermont 05068

Library of Congress Cataloging-in-Publication Data

London, Todd.
The world's room : a novel / Todd London.— 1st ed.
p. cm.
ISBN 1-58642-022-4 (alk. paper)
1. Children of divorced parents—Fiction. 2. Loss
(Psychology)—Fiction. 3. Suicide victims—Fiction.
4. Brothers—Fiction. 5. Grief—Fiction. I. Title.
PS3562.O4882 W67 2001
813'.54—dc21

00-012130

This novel is a work of fiction. Names, characters, places, and incidents are either
products of the author's imagination or are used fictitiously. Any resemblance to
actual persons, living or dead, is entirely coincidental.

"The Dream," copyright © 1955 by Theodore Roethke, from Collected Poems of
Theodore Roethke by Theodore Roethke, is used by persmission of Doubleday, a
division of Random House, Inc.

"The Messiah of Stockholm," by Cynthia Ozick, is used by permission of Alfred A.
Knopf, a division of Random House, Inc.

"Bullet Park," by John Cheever, is used by permission of Alfred A. Knopf, a division
of Random House, Inc.

The excerpt from Madame Bovary, by Gustave Flaubert, was translated by Francis
Steegmuller and is used by permission of Random House, Inc.

"Last Train to Clarksville," words and music by Bobby Hart and Tommy Boyce.
Copyright © 1966 (renewed 1994) SCREEN GEMS–EMI MUSIC, INC. All rights
reserved. International copyright secured. Used by permission.

FIRST EDITION

Bernie and Rudi
in memory

Juanita and Guthrie
in life

I'm grateful to the many friends and colleagues who offered help, support, and insight during the writing of this book. They include Michael Forman, who said the right things and never too much, Bill Bly, Jan Cohen-Cruz, Jim Peck, John Istel, Dean Fortunato, Nan Gatewood, Debra Nystrom, Judi Forman, Carolyn Clement, Laurie Liss, Mac Wellman, Neena Beber, Barry Jay Kaplan, Jim O'Quinn, Catherine Filloux, Gino DiIorio, Candice C. Baugh, Kate Robin, and Jan Cooper. Thanks also to Sara Jane Kasperzak and the Lake Placid Institute of the Arts and Humanities. On a daily basis, I'm indebted to and inspired by the writers, staff, and board of New Dramatists. My deepest thanks go to Alice Martell, for doing business from the heart; Robin Dutcher, whose precision, insight, and generosity help keep the art of editing alive; and, foremost, Juanita Brunk, who got me into this, set an impossibly high standard, and then stuck by it and me.

And the days are not full enough
And the nights are not full enough
And life slips by like a field mouse
Not shaking the grass.

— Ezra Pound

I

MY BROTHER'S NAME

When my brother hanged himself in a shower stall at St. Elizabeths, I took his name. My family, with only slight hesitation, called me by the name I'd chosen. We all behaved as if nothing unusual were taking place. No one openly expressed concern, disapproval, or fear, though all these feelings ran on currents under their conversational voices. I listened at once to both registers, attuned as I had always been to the harmonics of the family distress. I absorbed their uncertainty through my skin. I was twelve then. Now, sixteen years later, I still go by the name of Erich.

No one who knows me now would doubt that Erich is my name. It's been the name on my license and my leases. My family — what's left of it — gives no indication of remembering that I was, from birth, called otherwise. Bosses, friends, teachers, women I've had sex with — they've all known me only by my brother's name. My name. He gave it up and I chose it.

Something unnatural happened in the exchange. When I think of myself as Erich or am called Erich, I still experience a doubleness. Part of me takes this address as my own; another recalls his face — usually as he was in 1969, the summer he died. His looks were puffy and pale, nondescript, the way something is when it's unfinished: vague blue eyes, hairless snowball cheeks with skin almost translucent so you became aware of the blue of his veins, sand-colored sprouts of lashes, and sandy hair — not wild, but undomesticated — tufting out in several directions at once. His face was comfortable, cushy. His moonish features lit up from that wacky, chip-toothed grin. You had to laugh.

I loved no one more than him, except my mother. Erich was my brother, protector (though he couldn't have beaten a cow to the punch), and my only friend. My mother was a beautiful distant planet I'd glimpse through a powerful telescope.

Taking his name was easy. I asked to be called Erich as part of a conspiracy to keep him alive. I joined the conspiracy by offering a trade, me for him. I couldn't have put it into words, but I knew I was expendable in a way that Erich was not. "Erich is the fuel," my mother once said, and I agreed.

"The fuel on the hill," Erich said when I reported this back to him. Then he farted in the crook of his arm and drag-raced around in a figure eight.

My mother called me by his name almost from the day he died. She leaned over to tuck me into my grandmother's pullout couch. Then she smiled and said, as if some living form of him had stepped into her line of vision, "Goodnight, Erich." She caught herself. She stared into the space between us, where no one was, and then looked back at me. For a moment she saw me — me as me. Finally, she repeated, "Goodnight." No name attached. That kind of thing happened many times.

My mother's mother, my Oomie Doris, had been doing it, too. We stayed with her for two weeks after the funeral. Her slips were comically obvious. In her fierce determination to avoid all mention or thought of suicides, funerals, or the dead himself, she consistently misapplied the name of her departed firstborn grandson to her living last-born one. She would hold out my chair, saying, "Erich, you sit here." She'd arrange for my sister and Erich (me) to stay home with Papa, while she and Mom went to the beauty shop. She'd call me into the kitchen for a snack, using the name of the deceased. This confusion of identities didn't seem nearly as odd, under the circumstances, as the fact that she never noticed or corrected it.

With Oomie, though, it wasn't personal. She didn't mean anything by it. She refused to talk about what was on everybody's mind, and, so, the subject forced itself to her lips. My mother, on the other hand, had rarely called me by name before all this happened, as if the

nameable fact of my existence were distasteful. When Erich died I
became unspeakable. I knew she was thinking, "Why couldn't you
have been the one to die?"

So, when I said, "Call me Erich," she looked deep into me and
let out a long breath.

"Yes," she said, "we always meant that to be your name." Then,
for the first time I could remember, she kissed me. A benediction.
It was this simple.

That night, as I lay on the sofa bed, eyes closed and awake, I
heard Mom talking to my sister Deborah. "It's what he wants. Let
him have it," my mother whispered. "It won't last forever."

"I think it's sick," Deborah spit back.

Mom was silent. I imagined her fixing Deborah with a look that
said "I understand you, but I'm deeply disappointed." Finally, she
explained, "He's a young boy. His brother died. He wants to keep
him alive."

"He's twelve years old. That's not so young. And my brother
died, too. It's still sick. He's not so young; he knows what he's doing.
You've said so yourself. He always knows what he's doing."

"Meaning what?"

"You know what. As if everything that happens, happens only to
him. He didn't die. Erich did."

My mother stopped her. "He knows that, we all know that."

"It's morbid and perverted."

Mom started crying. Deborah whispered to soothe her. I strained
to hear but couldn't. I fell asleep.

For some days afterward, Deborah tried to avoid me. We were
thrown together, though, in a two-bedroom condo with the usual
decisions to make: what to watch on TV, when to take Papa for his
walk. Before long, the ordinary subsumed all that was jarring in our
lives, including Erich's death and my name. Deborah didn't care
enough to fight it. She didn't fight for anything, not even for the
close companionship she and Mom, until Erich's death, had shared.
Deborah hung back, loitering on the periphery of the family as if
watching us through a window from the street. So, I became Erich.

When I spoke to my father on the phone, it was clear he'd already been spoken to.

"Your mother tells me you want to be called Erich," he said.

"Yes."

"She believes we should respect your wishes."

"Yes."

"Is that what you want?"

"Yes."

"Can you tell me why you want this?" His tone carried more distress than curiosity. It was a troubled version of his philosopher's voice: measured, logical, verging on rhetorical but shy of demanding, and world sad.

"No."

I was trying to piece together my father's features. We'd left him only days before, standing beside a car at the cemetery where we'd buried Erich. I couldn't assemble his face in my mind. I could see the ridge that outlined his pink lips like a raised seam, could see the way he pursed those lips, both wise and worried. I could see the brown plastic of his glasses, the creamy white of his bad eye — but not the man.

"Was this your idea?" he asked.

"Yes."

"Don't you like your own name?"

"Yes. No."

"Yes or no?"

"Yes and no."

"But you like 'Erich' better."

"Yes."

He knew better than to disapprove. He was entitled to ask, to press even, but he'd given up the right to an opinion. He'd given it up by giving me up, only days before. We both knew it, but were too polite to say. However violently he wanted to stop what was happening, he'd condemned himself to the role of pained observer, lobbing questions from the back of the room.

"Have you always liked that name better?"

"Yes."

"Always?"

"Yes."

"Are you sure this was your idea?

"Yes. Who else's would it be?"

His silence told me whose he thought.

"This is what you want," he said.

"Yes."

"Just for now, right?"

"Yes. Just for now," I agreed.

The rest was even easier. When we returned to California, school had already begun. We had only arrived in Venice Beach that spring and I didn't know anyone. At school I was the new kid, the one whose brother had died. That information, having mysteriously preceded us, was common knowledge. As for my name, I could have been Astro or Porkchop for all they cared. What mattered most, at least to the kids my age, was the means of my brother's demise.

"How'd he do it?" was the first thing anyone said to me after the school secretary had ushered me to my locker.

"Bedsheets," I said. "Hung himself."

The kid put his hand to his neck and shook his head, before ambling off to report the fact to a couple of wriggly guys down the hall.

Later, another boy, peeing next to me before gym, sought confirmation. "Your brother really lynched himself?"

"No," I shrugged. "He shot himself in the brain."

I told one kid that "He went for the Gillette" and another that he'd smashed a stolen vw van into a gas pump. It didn't matter what I said. As long as the gossip mill stayed greased, I was in. So I did my best to sustain the group fascination. Erich lived on and his nameless older brother died all sorts of spectacular deaths.

This is the way you get used to things:

First, things are one way. A family of five lives in a small ranch house outside the city. Things are as they should be. Then gradually,

one of the family — in this case the mother, being restive and imma-
ture, maybe even crazy — begins to move toward another way of
being. Everyone feels this happening and for a while tries to insist
that things remain the way they are. After a bit, though, this pulling
feeling coming from the mother starts to seem commonplace. What
was once odd and uncomfortable is now the way things are.

Soon, however, this state of affairs yields to another, more
extreme. The tugging transforms into tearing, and, in one fell
swoop, the mother, like a daring, diving bird, snatches her children
in her mouth and carries them away from all the things they know.
Now nothing is as it was.

The feeling is so strange: flight, unfamiliarity. Crazy landscapes
shoot past. The father who was with them is no longer with them.
The place that they were part of is no longer theirs. And, for a time,
it seems that everything will remain uncertain, painful. Slowly,
though, this family begins to conceive of a life without the father.
Slowly, it dawns on them that movement, like stasis, can be a constant. The unimaginable becomes the ordinary. The ordinary — the
idea of home, for instance — assumes the lost logic of a dream. And
so on, as each state of difference and confusion comes to feel, in contrast to the state that supersedes it, painless, status quo.

You get used to things when they begin to look less awful than
the alternatives. Anything short of adaptation — total integration
with the new — will result in the most difficult state of all: hunger
for what you can never have — that is, what was.

It happens in language, too. Your words mean less and less, until
you come to expect no meaning from them at all. You get used to
the emptiness of words, the game of language. You construct (with
words, sentences, syntax) worlds whose meanings are self-contained,
in which the concepts of truth and untruth have no relevance. Who
is responsible in a world of "plausible deniability"? What is family in
a world of flight? Who is Erich?

And so, you get used to things. Almost everything.

I am Erich now. It's too late to return to what I was, even
though I hunger for my old single self. I've grown used to this

strange double being, to this name, which, even as it identifies me, raises the specter of my brother, a puff pastry of a boy who strung himself up when he was little more than half my age. He haunts me and I haunt his memory.

I have become so unlike him. I am longer — at five feet eleven inches the tallest in my family by four inches — and thinner, even gaunt. I have never really assumed my body, or maybe I should say my body has never assumed its designated space in the world. I hunch over, gesture tentatively, live up in my head. My facial hair, which I rarely shave, grows in patches that never fill in. The passage of time further distorts my relationship to Erich: Now I am his senior. He is still and forever seventeen. I am steadily growing older. He no longer wants anything. I want out.

2

MY FATHER'S BLIND EYE

If my father hadn't been blind in one eye, if his eye hadn't been murky and off-kilter in the milk of its own almost total deadness, he never would have been caught off guard. He would have seen it coming, seen the suitcases, the pleated skirts and penny loafers flying, the tugged arms, slamming doors, passports. He might have pictured Deborah running down the walk to where Mom was pulling me; might have anticipated Erich's hesitation in the doorway, the apathetic look on his doughboy face, glancing back as if to add a rhetorical, "What can ya do?"

Or if it had been the other eye — right eye, left brain — if the eye that knows the odd, irrational, inchoate impulse, the half-baked, whimsical, muttering, bat-out-of-hell choice had been the sighted one, he wouldn't have bothered trying to make her see reason. Reason wasn't what she saw. Ever.

Nor were words any help, which is where, I believe, my father's dependence on language derailed him. All those years vacuuming letters off pages, as though the good eye had to take in twice as much to compensate for the dead one. I picture him as a young boy, an adolescent, a graduate student, a newly appointed assistant professor, always standing (walking slowly or shifting from one foot to the other), book in hand pressed up close to his face, covered by the shadow of his head. In the tight, musty corridors of booksellers, in the towering stacks of libraries, this short, gnomelike man stares with Cyclops' eye at a page as if to look through it. His single window is doubled by the thick lens of his tortoiseshell glasses. What a deep belief in the word he's nourishing.

No wonder my mother blindsided him.

Maybe, if he'd thought of her as music, everything would have been different. He wouldn't have relied on words. My father knows that words bastardize what music does, that they get it all wrong. He'll lift his head out of a book and start explaining, querying, arguing, but when he shuts an orchestral score or turns off the stereo, he goes silent to his corner chair and a glass of Jameson neat.

With this woman, his wife, however, he never made the connection. She might have been the *Goldberg Variations* or Fauré's *Requiem*, Bartok or James Brown. Was that the groan of a double bass or the pulse of a kettledrum? He was as tone-deaf to her as he was blind — at least half — so he would never know.

At night, after we'd gone to bed, they'd read or listen to the console stereo in chairs about a yard apart. He pointed his knees toward her; she tucked her legs up. Lorna would fall asleep. Willy would remain awake. As she drifted, he'd stare across at her, his inexplicable gift.

Seven years her senior, he seemed even further removed. He was a father, scion of an old world of bad teeth and physical deformity, of milky eyes and twisted spines. He had grown up in the shadow of this world, as though living in color backgrounded by a black-and-white photo of fin-de-siècle Hungary and Austria. His parents, as far as I can tell, had kept a discreet, brittle distance from him. They grew old, as Old World parents do, having always seemed old, until they died, leaving him yellowing albums of posed photos, a watch with a hunter cover, a good head on his shoulders, and furniture that they'd lived among for decades (which he donated to a socialist charity). My father bore the stamp of their delicacy. It was bred into his soft hands, his fingers stubby, but graceful, almost feminine. They smoothed his wide brow, four fingers pulling from the left and the thumb from the right until they met in a meticulous point in the center.

So different from Mom's hands. Hers were thin and athletic — midwestern doer hands. The nails were curved and short, whereas Willy's were a touch too long, a bit too shiny. They'd invented slacks for women like Lorna, those fifties gals with chestnut hair in short

ponytails, outfitted in men's Oxford button-downs by day, moving
beyond housewifery by dint of graduate degrees in English, sociol-
ogy, art history.

She had been his student. Sometimes she'd fall back on the role.
We'd pop up at his department, after a day of chasing her through
the city, and she'd demand, in her most stagy voice, "Take us out to
dinner or I'll tell everyone how you kissed me during office hours!"
He'd beam. ("Tell, tell," I could hear him think.) I guessed at their
early teacher-student conferences, the thrill of shared research that
drew her to him, making him feel the glow of his newborn author-
ity. He knew things. He would lift her out of her life and set her
down in the life of the ages.

When Mom slept, Dad studied her. I'd watch them from my spot
in the hall. I shared Dad's wakefulness, and, so, when Erich dropped
off, I'd creep out of our room to a place where I could see her, coiled
in the chair next to my father's. I'd crouch on the carpet, in the unlit
passage, head leaning slightly back. There wasn't much to see and
even less, other than quiet music, to hear, but there was her tanned,
angular face, floating. Dad was a picture of fascination, pensive
devotion. Like him, I loved her madly, with the blindest of eyes.

He always had a book in his lap, open or not. It would take him
a moment to remember it — to remember himself, I think. In time,
though, he would notice the book and then, finally relinquishing my
mother to whatever currents she was sinking through, he'd notice
me. Night after night, without urgency or surprise, he'd set the book
aside, pad over to me, and place his hand on my head. My mother
was curled in a world of her own dreaming. My father helped me up,
led me back to bed.

He'd pull the thick, folded covers up to my chin and sit on the bed's
edge. Erich would snort and wheeze from a few feet away. And then
my father, who'd kept a strict silence till now, would tell me a story.

"Once, long ago, in that part of Spain know as the Alhambra,
there lived an adventurer by the name of Dos Es Ulalingua." Dad
would spin his midnight tale of this elfin hero with giant glasses and
a gargantuan nose, whose exploits were only half as fabulous as his

pidgin English. He would improvise me to sleep with a "shaggy-coyote" story fashioned from B-movie plots, arithmetic lessons, word play, and wacky history. Volcanoes were "lava-tories," hankies were "schnoz linen," and the moon a woman in head scarves named "Madonna Luna Mia." The midget Ulalingua peopled our private nights, making the world safe for the timid, happy for the dull, and paradise for the brainy. "And cchwat docs dey call me, hugh ahsk?" I'd hear as I drifted. "I ees Dose Es Uuuuulaleeengua!"

My mother had threatened to leave him many times. I'd hear her muffled contempt, the gunfire bursts of her impatience, through their bedroom door. "I'm so bored; you bore me, Willy!" The reasonable singsong of his appeal would follow, then the fury of her tears — a woman trying to rip herself out of herself. The lull of his words again, tamping her down, soothing her. And the respondent roar of her silence, bent under his words.

Everything fell out according to Mom's usual design: sudden, casual, no going back. He hadn't seen it coming anymore than I had.

I was the last one out of bed. Deborah and Erich were already dressed and fed. It was too early for anything to be happening in our house, but something was definitely happening. Mom was stuffing my clothes into two suitcases. Erich was tossing his things into a third. Deborah wafted in and out, asking questions: "Will I need the green dress?"

To which Mom responded, "Everything, sweetheart, everything."

Dad was there, too, hands in the pockets of his bathrobe, saying, "You can't mean this, you can't mean this."

They were all whispering. I woke to this manic hush.

"It's time to get up, " Mom said over me. "Dad's gonna make you some breakfast."

"Where're we going?" I asked.

"It's a surprise," she said. "A big, absolute, total surprise."

"Lorna, you don't want to do this," Dad said, still whispering.

"Your dad'll make you breakfast. Please make him some breakfast, Willy."

My father and I toddled off to the kitchen, him in full morning dress — pajamas, slippers, robe, hair brushed back off his forehead — me in a pair of underpants. He poured me a glass of milk and another of apricot nectar. He cracked two eggs in a skillet, but forgot to turn the burner on. He held a spatula in one hand, while he massaged his forehead with the other. When he realized the eggs weren't frying, he gave up on them, reached into a basket on the counter and grabbed a banana, which he set down on a plate in front of me. He handed me a knife and fork and sort of patted my hair. Then he walked out, in the direction of my room. I drank the milk and followed him.

"May I please have a moment alone with you," Willy was saying.

Erich was still packing. Mom was scanning the room.

"Go wash up and get dressed," she told me. I went into my drawers, but they were empty. There was an awkward moment, as she had to heave one of my suitcases back onto the bed, unlatch it, and get me something to wear.

"Damn this," she said, glaring at me.

"Just a moment alone," Dad said.

When I was finished in the bathroom, I went back to the bedroom. They were all gone. I could see them out the window: Lorna loading the car, Deborah standing around, toying with her hair. I didn't know where Erich was. Willy, a gentleman to the end, couldn't resist helping his wife lift one of the heavier bags into the trunk. Mom stepped back and watched him position the suitcase. She shook her head, as if to say, "Well, doesn't that just say it all?"

The next thing I knew, doors were slamming and she was leading him up the walk to the house. Deborah stood by the car for a second, with both hands on one hip and one knee bent, as though impatient for her date to get back with the burgers. Then, after checking to see that no one was watching, she dashed after them.

Mom stormed inside the house and down the hall to the bathroom. She plucked four toothbrushes from the holder and passed them over Dad's head to Deborah, who, with me, was crushing in behind them.

"Here, guard these with your life," she said.

Sliding past her soon-to-be-former husband, she added, "We're taking the toothpaste, Willy." With that she headed for the door, my hand in one hand and a tube of Pepsodent in the other. Deborah chased behind, toothbrushes raised up like the Olympic torch.

"I would never imprison you," my father called after her. And then he added, with a strange emphasis that made the corners of his mouth cinch up, "It was never my intention to imprison you."

Mom spun around with a kind of floppy insolence. "Well, isn't that sweet?" she cooed, a woman rattling her chains to a Christmas tune. She pushed me out the door ahead of her. Deborah followed. Dad hit a force field at the open door — couldn't get past it.

Erich stepped out of somewhere. He paused at the threshold of the house, face-to-face with Dad. Dad put his hand to Erich's hair, on the side of his head. His mouth was moving, but I couldn't tell if words were coming out or if he was stammering. Then Erich said something. "You try and cross that river on a chicken and you'll find out why a duck," I imagine him saying, a teenager's version of consolation for the incomprehensible. And he left Dad.

Mom sat behind the hard black steering wheel, key igniting the works, with my sister riding shotgun to navigate, me slammed in back with the stuff, and Erich lumbering down the walk, at his own sweet leisure. We all watched him.

Everything stopped for a moment. My mother's hyped-up determination abated. She swung her graceful legs out of the car and circled around to the passenger side. She kissed her firstborn on the top of his head. He just looked at her, blank, no big deal, this shit happens all the time. She opened the door for him. Something a chauffeur might do. Her gaze panned to my father staring from beside the screen door. She flashed a smile, and I could see the slight flare of her nostrils.

Erich didn't look back. He squeezed behind Deborah's seat and plopped down beside me. In a snap, Mom had taken the wheel. The front was alive with anger and purpose as the "girls" got the show on the road. Erich and I were the silent sentries of the backseat. My father's face at the half-open door was owlish, blinking, a smart man struck dumb. The car screamed south.

How long did Dad stand on the front stoop? In my mind he became a snapshot: the father at the door. He stands watching, in a paralysis of thought, philosopher Dad, faced with a will more determined than his own. He blinks. He thinks. His mind is a courtroom of ifs and thens, therefores and howevers. And as he stands — not idly, but ponderously, by — his family races off. He calculates the distance between Lorna's car and the front step. When the car pulls out, he begins to calculate its speed.

Mom began to sing show tunes almost as soon as we hit the highway. She was Nellie Forbush the cockeyed optimist, the queer one Julie Jordan, Annie "anything you can do" Oakley. She was "Whatever Lola wants, Lola gets" Lola. And we were her fans. It didn't stop. She felt pretty, enjoyed being a girl, called herself the "Wild Spanish Rose."

I can't tell you how long the first leg of our rolling hootenanny lasted. In fact, every leg until we hit Nuevo Laredo blurs into versions of this same scene, my mother never running out of songs — Broadway, opera, pop standards, vocalizing exercises. She was our radio. She was our movie score, moon hitting the sky like pizza one day, longing for a place over the rainbow the next, winding up lost in the stars.

No one but Lorna knew where we were going. Erich stared out the window and I stared at the back of his head. I hummed along with Mom. Erich played the air guitar and the headrest drums. Deborah pored over maps and chattered to us. We didn't cry, we didn't question, we didn't call Dad from the road. More than once a day, every day, I would lean forward, resting my head against Deborah's bucket seat and say to the singing driver, without irony or ambivalence, "You have the most beautiful voice in the world."

Erich would groan, Deborah would mumble assent, and our mother would sing on, louder and lovelier.

3

My Mother's Songs

We settled in California the spring before the summer Erich died. It was the end of our two-year vagrancy in Mexico, the last stop on Mom's flight away from life with our father. We were driving north, headed home — which to me meant Dad's house in New Jersey, but to Mom meant anywhere else in North America — when she took her hands off the steering wheel and covered her eyes.

"I see vast ocean. I see palm trees and houses perched on the edges of cliffs. I feel salt air. There're vineyards, orange orchards, coastal highways. Wait! Who's that? Oh, my god, I see — you'll never guess — it's Rock Hudson!"

Deborah had, meanwhile, grabbed the wheel. The needle shimmied at seventy-five.

She and I tried to laugh. Then Erich said, "ok. Rock Hudson it is." Mom opened her eyes and headed for "the Coast." Deborah gradually ungripped.

Mom launched into a medley of songs about California: "California, Here I Come," "California Dreamin'," "I Left My Heart in San Francisco," "Coming into Los Angeles," "Oh, Susannah" (with California replacing references to Carolina), and "California" (to the tune of "Oklahoma").

California in the spring of '69 was at least twenty years removed from our life in Maplewood, New Jersey. Pulling into Venice Beach, however, it felt as though the time spent crossing those years had been a blink. We'd gone to sleep one night and Rip-van-Winkled through the transition. The streets were explosions of color: psychedelic beachfront boutiques; painted buses; slow-moving pop-up figures in floral belts, tapestry vests, and eyeglass shards of church windows, all crystalling in the glare of sun off water. "We have left *drab* behind," she said as we drove through the phantasmagoria. "Ting tang walla walla bing bang," Erich mumbled, looking out the car window.

She had dreamt us there. And the painful drift of the past couple of years seemed to have had a purpose all along. We had left behind the dreary Garden State and wound up in the garden of love. That night Deborah wove our mother's hair into a flow of braids.

Erich saw the disparity between the place as it was and as Mom imagined it in a way that I, eager to view the world through her brightening eyes, didn't. The whole place made him inarticulate. In public, he appeared to have traded in words for a series of grunts of mockery. He'd walk past the ranks of surfers, run his hands over imaginary muscles and mumble, "Oooo-aaah," like Narcissus in a sudsy bath. In crowds of hippies he'd scratch his armpits and make quiet chimp sounds. He found similar sub-verbals for the groaning bucks of Muscle Beach, the sweaty cops, the dolled-up middle-aged ladies. The whole squalid place incited him to orgasms of mugging. He sent it up for an audience of one.

We arrived in midspring, so school wasn't an option. With time on our hands, Erich and I hung out together, roaming the beach, watching people act "be-zarre." The town was thick with bodies, but we moved in the still center of our own fascination. We spent hours at the ocean, fully clothed, staring out, as if someone had just given us a pair of Saint Bernards in a ribboned box, a startling present we didn't know what to do with.

Our conversations drifted. Some threads we'd follow for days, others we'd let go after minutes. We ran by Erich's clock, floating through the hours. It was Huck-and-Jim-on-the-raft time, puff of smoke, cloud. We drank Mexican coffee out of paper cups.

He'd tell me about things he was reading; he had one book about solar energy and an underground magazine he carried rolled up that described bomb factories kids were building in tenement basements. Or he'd make stuff up to delight me, spinning tales about aliens with fake breasts and platinum wigs living in Venice. I'd listen to his still-changing voice crack midword and follow the blue network of veins showing through his temples. When he sweated he smelled like copper.

He'd make offhanded comments designed to pique my curiosity. Like this: "What makes Astaire so great, and I consider him the single American genius in any field, is that he does one thing better than anyone else alive does any other one thing."

"What do you mean?" I asked. "A lot of people are great at one thing. They're just great at different things." I wanted to argue with him, to test out my brain against his, but he always parried me away.

"Mull it over," he said. "Mull it over, and you'll see." And then he'd shut up.

One night, at the end of a pier that seemed to be holding us an arm's length into space, he said, "You know, don't you, that the moon landing will be the end of everything. They'll walk on the moon, sure, they've planned for that. What they haven't planned on is looking back and seeing Earth. They'll freak. Just at the moment these guys feel most important, they'll glance up at this speck of shit we live on and realize how totally insignificant everything is. You think they'll come back and tell us what a great experience they had, bouncing around on the moon. No way. They'll get in front of the TV cameras and all the eager millions, and they'll stare these blank fucking stares and they'll say something like, 'We all live on this giant turd floating out in the middle of nowhere, and nothing we do means anything. That's how small we are.' And everyone will start crying and screaming and shit. Everybody will go crazy, killing the astronauts, looting stores, killing themselves. You think people can live with that? No way. It's all over." I looked into the sheer dark around us and couldn't argue.

With money left from what Oomie Doris had wired to us in Mexico, Mom rented a two-bedroom apartment near the board-walk. Erich called it a "sledgehammer special," since it looked like it had been smashed together overnight. Everything meant to meet in a corner didn't. Doorjambs, window sashes, Sheetrock — all had been pounded into place (you could see the brandings of hammer-heads) leaving gaping holes and jagged edges. Floorboards shunned the walls. Blond wainscoting had been nailed up by someone with an attention deficit. Whole pieces of paneling were missing; some hung by single nails, others by eight or ten of them, banged randomly in. A fresh coat of paint had been slathered on, but no one had bothered to patch the stucco first. "It's whimsical," Mom said.

There was a room for Erich and me and one for Deborah with a double bed. "A teenage girl needs her own space," Mom explained, when she announced the sleeping arrangements. Mom had a foldaway bed in the living room and first rights to the bathroom mirror. More often than not, though, she bunked in with Deborah. They'd sleep late and then, long after my brother and I had wandered away, get up and dress for the sixties. They were discovering the New World.

In Mexico, Mom had traded in the stirrup pants and white blouses of suburban life for the color-burst swathing of a gypsy-artist. At sunset in San Miguel de Allende, we'd watch her poised in the bell tower of a small church at sunset, wrapped in an orange shawl, adorned by a mosaic of large, bright beads. Taper-lit by candelabra, she'd sing arias in an Italian I couldn't translate, her clear soprano settling out over the town. Once in Venice, however, she pared down to the essentials. She'd dressed for carnival life in depressed Mexico, but she approached the Venice circus as a seat of authenticity — the place to reveal her naked self. Her skin was dark by now and her chestnut hair waist long. She wore it down with a plaited ring crowning her head and two long braids hanging in back. The loose hair fell straight and her ears peeked out. She'd put on simple things: a sun dress with a single-strand coral necklace or a man's white shirt belted over a denim skirt, a flower in the belt. Estée Lauder cologne was replaced by sandalwood soap and patchouli oil.

She and Deborah would finish cigarettes in the kitchen and stroll down to the Rialto coffee shop for toast and Pepsi. Gradually, their growing clique of friends would straggle into adjoining booths. They'd argue about the war and the tactics of civil disobedience, reaching over the backs of their seats for ketchup or cream. They staked out the leading edge of a youth revolution, whose coming would make gatherings like these as historic as Bolshevik planning sessions in Finland. Surely, the hippies noticed that Lorna was over thirty and, therefore, as the saying went, not to be trusted. But she was different, acceptable, in the way an old radical like David Dellinger was. She was young in spirit, compelling, and (unlike Dellinger) beautiful.

Before long the whole crew would wander down to Ocean Park. There they'd debate some more, toke up, toss a Frisbee around. Phil Zimmerman would play his Martin acoustic, fingers sliding easily from bar chords to lead. Lorna would sing with him.

Her repertoire, like her clothing, had changed with the passage of time. When we still lived with our father, Mom would occasionally write us sick notes for school (without telling Dad) and take us into Manhattan for her voice lessons. Sitting in her teacher's living room, surrounded by hanging plants and pictures of bronzed young men on motorboats, we'd listen to her vocalize. She'd switch to Schubert and finally to standards we knew from her Judy Garland and Perry Como albums. The summer we left, 1967, she took us into the city one night, where we trailed her from club to club. At each "open mike," she sang "My Funny Valentine" and "Here, There, and Everywhere" on the heels of Steve and Edie impersonators and guys telling jokes about the different words for "bosom." In Mexico, she learned French airs by Debussy and Poulenc.

She discovered a different sound in California: dark, melancholy ballads — British Isles folk — going back centuries, reinvented by Fairport Convention, Pentangle, Steeleye Span, and Venice's own troubadour, Phil Zimmerman. These songs suited Mom's darker self. Erich and I would pass by and the plaintive sound of her voice would tug at my chest. "O bonnie babes, gin ye were mine, / I would dress you up in satin fine." She was a medieval princess doomed to eternity on a lonely island across the bay, where she would never grow old and never know true love. I was a boat, too small for the crossing.

Chuck Mitchell and Sheila Deese would sing harmony. Deborah would listen, smitten. Chuck was her first thrall. A black actor from the L.A. cast of *Hair*, he was kindness itself. He big-buddied Erich and me, taught us harmonies for "Flesh Failures" and "Black Boys/White Boys," and dazzled us with backstage intrigues among members of the "tribe." He brought us Afro picks with black fists for handles to comb our stick-straight hair. He and Mom grew tight. They'd shop and giggle together, until it occurred to me that they, not he and Deborah, were the lovers.

"Deborah's stuck on Chuck," I'd say. "Tough luck, Chuck."

"Chuck chuck bo buck," Erich would reply.

Chuck did, though, treat my sister with great respect. He listened intently to the things she said. He held her hand in the streets. He called this fifteen-year-old girl his "lovely lady."

Mom looked for ways to draw Erich into her circle. She bought him a cheap guitar, took him out for night strolls after Deborah and I had bumbled off to bed, and even, he told me, suggested that they drive to the desert and drop mescaline together, as a way of "getting inside each others' worlds."

She took me aside to talk about him. It was the only time I was alone with her before he left. Erich and Deborah had been ordered down to the store for breakfast foods. Mom had a theory that if you concentrated on one meal at a time when you shopped, you'd never need a list, nor would you forget anything. This necessitated several trips to the grocery each week, but it gave each outing a coherence of its own. While they were out stockpiling cereal and Bisquick, maple syrup and jarred prunes, she and I found ourselves face-to-face.

"C'mon, mister, I'll buy you a sundae," she said, heading for the door.

We walked side streets to the Rialto, instead of going down to the ocean and turning there. I felt an urge to reach for her hand, but, as she made no move in that direction, I contented myself with gently bumping against her as we walked, as a kid much younger than me might have done. There was something wonderful about our silence, and I remember looking around, noting how completely unlike home this new landscape was, from the palm trees to the shapes of the houses. The light was bluer here, and the air wrapped you up in a way I'd never known air could do.

She ordered a hot-fudge "dream boat" with extra maraschino cherries for me and a cup of coffee for herself. She got up and went across the restaurant to talk to some guy she knew and came back a minute later. "I'm worried about Erich," she said, slipping into the booth, and lighting up a cigarette she'd just bummed. "I don't think he likes it here."

"Sure, he likes it. Why don't you think he likes it? I mean who wouldn't like it? I like it here. I like it a lot. What's not to like?"

"He disapproves. I can feel it."

"What do you mean, disapproves? He's a kid."

"No, no, that's just what I mean. He's not a kid anymore. I don't think he ever was. There's something else about him, something he's always had. He brought it with him into this life. He sees things. You know that. He's special, somehow, extraordinary."

I can't pretend not to see how harsh this seems: a woman confiding to one son about the superiority of another. At the time, though, I thought it was great, sitting there with her talking to me as if to her best friend. She was asking my advice. Everyone could see how beautiful she was in her apricot tapestry dress and how she spoke to me without condescension. I was tempted to reach across the table, pick the Lucky Strike from her fingers, take a drag, and tip it back to her. I pretended we were on a date. Of course, from a distance I realize I was right. We were on the kind of date where the girl spends the whole evening jabbering about some guy in her chemistry class.

The food came. She spooned several heaps of my vanilla ice cream into her coffee and then floated a glob of my whipped cream on top. I picked a cherry up by the stem and waved it back and forth a little.

"Don't play with your food," she said. "You see, it's very important, now that we're here, that we all be here *together*. No negative energy, no bad vibes. Understand?"

"I love it here."

"But there's something going on with him that I can't quite figure. Has he said anything to you?"

"Just the usual stuff. He likes it, I'm sure. We both do. I mean, it's great, right Mom? 'S'beautiful, don't you think? He's just being Erich."

"You see I need him behind me. I'm finding my feet, and I depend on him. You may not understand this, but he's fuel, Erich is, we need him to run."

"I understand."

"So what has he said to you?"

"Nothing."

"He must have said something. What do you boys talk about?"

"Just stuff. We don't talk about anything. Just stuff."

"He doesn't like hippies, does he?"

"Sure. I don't know. He likes hippies. I mean, in theory."

"That's what I mean. That qualification. Something's definitely not right."

"I mean he loves hippies. So do I. I more than love them."

That was true. I wanted to be among these magical beings so badly that I stayed away. I wanted to be inside them, to be them. When Phil Zimmerman played, I wanted his hands to be mine, bony fingers, silver ring and all. I wanted the thin choker of Sheila's onyx beads around my throat. I wanted her black skin for my skin, her gooseflesh, her breath.

"I mean I love those guys," I said. "Erich, he does too. He's just different is all. He *is* a hippie. He just doesn't look like one."

This was also true. Erich was the ultimate hippie — but out of costume. He continued to wear his hair stupidly short. He dressed in navy trousers and short-sleeved button-down shirts and wore a twist-o-flex Timex watch (which he never wound or checked). In his own offbeat, ungroovy way, he embodied what the others strove for: he was present, nonconformist, outside of time. He listened lovingly with his whole being. Erich was simply and completely himself, connected and alone. He just was.

"Exactly. That's exactly what I mean. If he only understood that. He's one of us. Exactly. Talk to him. For me. Talk to him."

So I talked to him.

"Mom's worried about you," I said.

"What, me worry?" Erich replied.

"She thinks maybe you don't like it here."

"What's to like?"

"I didn't say that. I said you did. Like it."

"Rock Hudson it is."

"I know."

"Rock Hudson forever."

"She thinks you disapprove."

"I'm seventeen," he said. "I disapprove of everything."

"That's what I told her."

"What'd she say?"

"She thinks you don't like hippies."

"I like hippies. I mean in theory."

"That's what I said."

"She believe you?"

"I don't know. I think she tried to."

"I mean I L-U-V hippies. Hippies are my life, man."

"She loves hippies."

"Yum."

"Maybe you could show it more."

"Show I like hippies?"

"Yeah. And her?"

"Oh, Mommy, Mommy, I love you, Mommy."

"She says you're fuel."

He farted in the crook of his arm and drag-raced around in a figure eight.

Summer came, though you couldn't tell the difference from the weather. Erich got arrested for mocking a cop. They never actually charged him, though, just called Mom down to the precinct, where he sat on a bench, staring down the officer at the front desk. ("Their customer service representative," he later called him.)

Lorna hurried Deborah and me to the station. Once there, we lingered by the door, watching her berate the arresting officer. Apparently Erich had fixed on this beat cop and followed him everywhere, silently imitating his gestures with absolute earnestness. Eventually, the cop got sick of it and threatened to lock Erich up, which only spurred him on. He started doing *Dragnet* dialogue, even as he mirrored the live policeman. The cop grabbed Erich and Erich grabbed the cop in the same manner, still with Jack Webb words. When they arrived at the station, Erich announced: "I arrest this boy on six counts of unflattering imitation. Lock him up."

In steady tones — an even better, if unconscious, Jack Webb performance than Erich's — the officer in charge told Lorna he could keep the boy overnight, "Disturbing the peace, resisting arrest, disorderly conduct. . . ."

Lorna laughed in his face. "Typical. A cop can't take a joke, so they lock up a fourteen-year-old kid."

"Kid's seventeen, ma'am."

"And you'd put him away for teasing your buddy."

"Happens."

"You want an even bigger joke?" she asked. "Let me tell you something. It so *happens* that I'm a comedy writer myself. I work for Johnny Carson. You ever hear of him? Well, he just loves stuff like this for his opening monologue. They'll be laughing at your bacon-y butts all over America."

"Johnny will love this," I pitched in from the door. Deborah jabbed her elbow into my side.

"Your kid needs help, lady. And you could stand talking to someone yourself."

With that Lorna swept Erich to his feet and pulled him to the door, turning only to say, "He's practicing to be a mime, you dumb galoot." And then we were outside.

"Mom?" Erich said, in his don't-yell-at-me voice. "When I grow up, I want to be a galoot." We laughed all the way home.

Next, Chuck left town and Deborah went slightly nuts. She sobbed gulpy sobs and looked permanently startled, like someone hit by a shoe tossed off a tall building. She stopped going to the beach and started getting high, alone, early each day. She wouldn't go near Mom.

In the house nobody spoke. We walked as if someone were terminally ill in the next room. I took pains not to slam the refrigerator door and hesitated, even, before flushing the toilet. Anything resembling regular meals came to a halt. We were on hold for days. One night Deborah wrote "I Hate You" in lipstick on the mirror and took off for the beach. Lorna sent Erich out to find her. I stayed in the living room behind my copy of *The Outsiders* and watched Mom prowl the kitchen. She poured juice glasses full of red wine, which she drank slowly while smoking cigarettes. She appeared to be searching the floor. When she found what she was looking for she'd take a sharp pull on her cigarette, prop it on the edge of the sink, and crouch down. She'd attack the linoleum with small disposal pads and begin obliterating scuffmarks. I tried to shut out the image of her in our rooms in Corpus Christi, smacking the floor with both my shoes, scattering a frenzy of roaches.

Hours later, Erich shuffled in and said, "Yeah, she's all right." Mom threw her arms around his unimpressed body, dousing the back of his shirt with Chianti.

Deborah would only let Erich talk to her. He had a way of being gradual, abstract. He wormed around your defenses by singing songs from *Mad* magazine or talking about the sex lives of barnacles. Deborah came back that night. She left a note on the kitchen table written in curvy letters on flower-power stationery. I saw it the next morning. "I'm sorry, Mommy," it said. "I just feel so-o-o let down."

I never found out why Chuck left or why Deborah blamed Mom for his flight. He did, however, send a couple of postcards, once he reached San Francisco. One exuberant note told us he had found true love — a young man from Minnesota named Jeb Stuart. Another whimpery one explained that Jeb had ditched him. These were both addressed to Lorna.

Deborah stayed away from the Rialto, and started hanging instead with a group of sullen, listless teenagers she'd never let us

meet, the kind who drop quaaludes for breakfast as routinely as kids
down chewable Flintstones. She was polite to Mom and helpful, but
that was all.

It had happened this way before. We would land in a place full of
hope and promise, then everything would sour. These were the
times I most missed Dad. None of us had spoken to him since
Mazatlán, when he'd refused to send more money.

This refusal proved to be the turning point of our trip. We were
staying in a hotel — one of the few times we'd done so. There was
a terrace there, attached to our room. We had a clear view of the
water with its rocky beach and fishing boats. The three of us were
leaning out, watching the tops of peoples' heads, waiting for Mom
to come back from calling him.

She entered the room and said, casually, "That's all folks. We're
going home."

The three of us looked at her and at each other and burst into a
spasmodic chorale of tears. Erich put an arm around Lorna, as if she,
too, needed comfort. We were crying from relief, though she must
have thought we hated to leave Mexico. I wanted to whoop with joy
and jump around the room, but want was certain sabotage with her,
and I knew better. Then she said, "You father has deserted us. Cut
us off without a nickel." And we knew the home she'd said we were
going to wouldn't be his.

We had Lorna, though. She'd get us through. We had Mom.

4

THE BALLAD OF ERICH

For all the times my mother's voice provided the soundtrack for our lives, there were others when we were driven, more than anything, by her silence. Sometimes, when we were still at home, Dad would shoo us away from the bedroom in which she'd holed up, explaining simply, "Your mother isn't feeling herself." In Mexico, we endured long afternoons of her despondency. She'd sit on a bench or step, in a gravel lot or in the dirt, cross-legged, curved over herself, inspecting her fingernails as if she'd only just discovered them. Her hair, matted and unwashed, would gather flies, which she'd do nothing to rid herself of. We'd hover nearby, turning in grand revolves so she couldn't see us on the horizon, tiny planets, microscopic to the eye, bound to her (and repelled) by a fierce and invisible magnetic field. In time she would reinhabit herself. Meanwhile, it was Erich who kept us in song.

Erich had always been a gatherer. At our school in Maplewood, he'd corral me and my little chums in the yard at lunchtime and lead us through songs or impromptu game shows. In Mexico, too, when we entered a new town, he'd round up a handful of Mexican street kids (and me) and start an a cappella singing group. We went by variations on the same name: The Erich Hofmann Eight, or Five, or Three, as we dwindled. We belted English-language pop tunes in wildly disparate dialects and keys. Erich took pains to teach us the lyrics of such favorites as "This Diamond Ring" and "Young Girl, Get Outta My Mind." With Job's patience, he'd try in pidgin Spanish to evoke life in "The House of the Rising Sun" or to describe a board-walk to a pack of eight-year-old orphans who'd never seen the ocean.

"Now remember," he said of "Sergeant Pepper's Lonely Hearts Club Band," "this song is part of a larger *oeuvre*." (That was the word he used. I thought it meant egg, that the song was one of their eggs.) "It's all about love and celebration and spectacle. Free your minds when you sing it. Go wild. Imagine wonderful sights — the sky full of diamonds. It's like a big playground with music coming out of all the school windows. We can only achieve the right sound if we understand this." The Erich Hofmann Singers of Querétaro (by then he'd given up on the flux of numbers) listened profoundly. Then we went back to our caterwauling.

California was different. Mother only disappeared once. Early in June, she left without warning for Tijuana (we learned later), where she spent more than a week throwing over a suitor from our Mexican days. She took the car but, as if by accident, left a wad of ten-dollar bills in a backup purse.

We'd grown used to fending for ourselves in Mexico. Deborah had tried to keep us fed when Mom was gone or out of commission. A bossy sort of Wendy, she was a Wendy nevertheless, making sure we had matching socks and rice, beans, or something cornmealy a couple times a day. She worked hard to nip our imminent vagrancy in the bud, and our mother's artiste friends thought nothing of letting this adolescent girl feed them or scrounge for their food. They would look up from their guitars, their brown paintings, or unfinishable great novels and tell "Debbie" not to forget oranges, beer, or chicken.

California, however, seemed to thwart our ability to close ranks. Abandonment in Venice Beach lacked the frightening edge it had in Mexico; we weren't scared enough to get organized. Deborah, still pining for Chuck, cooked a meal or two, with nothing, though, like the determined regularity with which she'd sought to keep order during Mom's Mexican vanishings. Erich watched over me, as he'd done then, but something in him, too, had begun to shift, and, so, his watch was distracted at best.

Familiarity breeds a kind of blindness, I think. The more familiar, the more inside you are, the harder it is to see outline or dimension in ways that even strangers can. I can't say, for instance, whether my own voice is nasal or resonant, because I hear the sound of it only within the wadded interior of my head; yours, though, I can describe after a first hearing. Likewise, I couldn't have told you then anything exact about my mother's age or character or beauty, especially as compared to other mothers. She was the house I lived in and that house only gets configured with distance. All these years later, as I think back, I realize, yes, of course, there was a dark, small room in which I felt confined or a window on the left from which I gazed hopefully out. Occasionally, someone would say, "Your mother has the most intense eyes," or "She's away a lot, isn't she?" and edges would appear, contour, where there'd been only shadow. It took years to distinguish my mother in this way.

Distinction came sooner with Erich. We had gone to school together in New Jersey, so I heard things, other people's perceptions, which forced me to consider that his character bore some readily perceivable stamp. For example, Erich never palled around with kids his own age. He hung out, instead, with whomever I did. That he was in sixth grade and we in first, or he in eighth and we in third, never mattered. He was our constant collie, nosing the flock of us from the dangerous edges of the playing field.

I knew from the testimony of the older kids that he was odd, and, so, I was able to view his behavior in that light. His classmates spared no torment, but he hardly seemed to notice. He'd smile his appreciation for their attentions, and then go his quirky way alone. He'd always been self-contained, with his own private jokes and twists of language. He'd pore over how-to books, but he'd never try to do any of the projects they illustrated. He'd spend hours working and reworking physical shticks drawn from cartoons and knockabout, Saturday-morning comedy (the Three Stooges, Abbott and Costello) or from his own bizarre imagination. I loved these Erich-isms, and liked to believe that they were performed for my benefit. I also knew that my parents had gotten advice from teachers and administrators to encourage Erich "to try and fit in," but such pressure made my mother rabid. It was part of what she called the mediocrity conspiracy, a plot to "make him more like their own little snot-faced, pea-brained bed wetters."

You didn't question her about Erich. You just didn't. Even Dad didn't. Once, when Dad had failed to challenge the principal of Erich's school over a negative report card, she'd taken a can of silver paint from the hobby closet and sprayed WORDS WORDS WORDS on the wall by his desk.

When something troubled me, I'd only go to him.

"Dad, what's a prevert?"

"There is no such thing as a prevert," he told me. "Pervert, do you mean?"

"What's that?"

"That's a strange question. Why? Why do you ask?"

"Is it like a bad thing?"

"Is it *like* a bad thing or is it a bad thing?" he asked, correctively.

"Is it a bad thing. Is Erich one of them?"

"He most certainly is not. Why? Did someone tell you that? Did someone say something?"

"Just some guys at school. They call him prev-o and that if I don't watch it, I'll be a little prev-o too."

"Why would they say that? What did he do?"

"He didn't do nothing . . ."

". . . Anything . . ."

". . . didn't do anything. He just thinks they're jerks, so they call him stuff. Since when do you have to do anything?"

"Clearly," he said, "it's nothing to worry about, then." And before I gave it up, he added, "It's not the kind of thing to talk to Mom about, do you think?"

"Maybe not," I said, though I already knew.

As our first summer in California began, I started to lose track of Erich. He gave up on the idea of a singing group. "We've missed the two most important years in rock-and-roll history," he explained. "Who would take direction from me? I mean in Mexico we were special, we had the music and the language. We're in California now. I couldn't presume." Erich turned inward, focusing instead on composing, not songs, but a single, continuous creation he called "The Ballad of Erich." "Life-as-song, song-as-life," he told me, adding, "Everything that happens to me goes in it. You'll be in it, of course. And it won't be complete until the day I die. One lifetime, one song — the absolute work of art. Not quite absolute. For that I would have had to start it the day I was born."

"Play me some," I asked him.

"Not until it's finished," he said.

"But I thought you can't finish it until you die."

"This is what it is," he said.

"What is?"

"This."

"The Ballad of Erich?"

"Yes. That's right."

I didn't understand, but I wanted him to think I did.

"I've got to work now," he said, dismissing me.

He kept extensive notebooks and charts in colored pencil, all to do with the "Ballad." When I'd nose through his stuff, I couldn't decipher it. There were symbols and arrows, repeated phrases — "ballad of ballad of ballad of" and "gone to the fair, gone gone gone to the fair" — and obsessive little doodles, including a whole page covered with crabbed pencil marks, slashes piling one upon the other creating what looked like a hailstorm but had, as far as I could tell, no meaning beyond itself. Years later I happened on the antic scribblings of Alfred Jarry and thought I'd met Erich's great influence.

It never occurred to me that Erich was a bad songwriter or that he was going crazy. I took it for granted that the "Ballad" would be a work of genius. But as Erich grew more intent on the radical purpose of his life's work, I found myself alone. I tagged along with him as much as he'd let me, and, while he rarely sent me away, it became obvious that something more compelling than me was taking him over, that he preferred for me to stand clear.

So, I took to spying on him. I didn't think of it as spying at the time. In fact, I played a game in my mind that I was making a candid documentary on "The Making of the Ballad of Erich." But, of course it was spying.

I'd trail him in the street, peer into our room when he thought he was alone, poke through his notebooks, and eavesdrop from the other side of doors on his writerly grunts of disapproval and bursts of delight. Sometimes it seemed as if he were creating performances for the sole purpose of including them in the "Ballad." One day he only clucked. He walked through town, greeting people as usual but only tocking his tongue when words were called for. Soon after, he began to speak sounds as if they were words: *"Tee hee.* I laugh," he'd say to a waitress who'd cracked wise. *"Aah-choo* sneeze," he'd echo when he sneezed.

The day before Mom returned from her unannounced trip to Tijuana, something happened that I've never been able to explain. Because I doubted my eyes, I never told anyone about it.

My memory is of an overcast morning. Erich left the house early, before I was up. I don't know where Deborah was or how she spent the day. Erich spent it gathering stones, large boulders from a lot in a more sparsely populated part of Venice. A small park with a yellow and red playground sat kitty-corner from the lot. Whether the lot was being fashioned into another park or a common garden, I've never been sure, but I do know the rocks were piled there for a reason.

It must have been a weekday, because the neighborhood was deserted enough that Erich could, without interference, transfer these boulders one at a time to an uncrowded stretch of beach about six blocks away. Erich dedicated himself to this boring, heavy work with mulish determination. One rock then another, he'd lift and haul through the streets, moving in a steady waddle. He'd walk back slowly, as if adding complex numbers in his head all the while. I tried to maintain a distance of at least a half block, but he never looked around. I was filming him in my mind, gathering footage for an experimental documentary that would unfold in actual time.

He finished late in the afternoon and headed home. I ran down to the place on the beach where he'd been laboring. He'd created a large circle of stones, perhaps ten feet in diameter, with each stone spaced an even half foot or so from the next. The interior sand was smoothed flat, all footsteps obliterated. The sky, water, stones, and sand all gradations of gray. It was, I remember thinking, one of the most beautiful things I'd ever seen. It evoked something ancient and unsettling, as if, by placing it there, Erich was calling up people from a lost tribe to take their places within the circle.

I found him at home polishing off a sandwich and a can of vegetable soup. He apologized for not leaving any in the pan. Then, while I piled bologna on bread for dinner, he took a shower. He dressed and sat down to watch TV, until just before dusk, when he left again. I followed after.

He walked toward the highway, the opposite direction from his stone sculpture. At the Union 76 station he bought two red cans of gasoline, which he lugged back through town and down to the beach. He spoke to no one and no one spoke to him. In fact, no one seemed to notice anything out of the ordinary about a teenager carrying spouted gas cans down the sidewalk in the early evening. When he reached the circle of stones in the sand, he set the cans down. With the heel of his shoe, he dug a rut along the inside of the circle, up against the rocks. Then he smoothed out the rest of the interior sand and, by reaching over the rocks from outside, covered his tracks.

He finished, surveyed his work, and then, after twisting the cap off one of the cans, walked the periphery of the circle, pouring gas into the canal he'd dug. He put the can down, closed it, picked up the other one and repeated the process. Then he took three giant steps into the center of the circle.

In an instant, he'd pulled out a pack of matches and lit, not just one match, but the entire book. Everything after that happened so quickly that it seemed to happen all at once. I heard sirens blaring and saw people running toward the fire, though this might have begun even while he poured the gasoline. The ring of fire that leapt up seemed to engulf Erich. I could see his face through the flames, and, I thought, he looked at me as I ran forward.

People started kicking sand onto the fire and a truck full of firemen jumped onto the beach with shovels. There was a lot of noise all at once — party noise — and a lot of excitement. But the strange thing, the part I've never been able to reconcile, was that Erich was gone. I couldn't have looked away for long, but by the time I'd turned back, everyone was asking around after the kid who'd started it.

The hoopla ended almost as quickly as it had begun. The fire engine started off and a few cops wandered around asking people what they'd seen. One of them kept inspecting the gasoline cans, as if they might tell him something. Then he slipped a garbage bag over each and carried them to the trunk of his squad car. Some boys jumped back and forth over the charred rocks making up rhymes about Harry Houdini and his miniature weenie until one of their mothers yelled at them to stop.

I moved away slowly to avoid attention and then tore back to the apartment. Deborah was gone. Still no sign of Mom. Erich was sound asleep. I smelled gasoline everywhere, but Erich's clothes, hung neatly over a chair, were clean. I didn't know what he had done or how he'd done it.

I went back outside. It was just after ten o'clock, but the night was spookily still. I walked down to the ocean and stood on the beach, making grooves in the sand with my feet. It was a little cold, so I perched myself on a bench with my knees up, wishing I had my sweatshirt. The stars were brilliant over the water.

One year, on my birthday, Dad had given me a book about the stars. It had photos of the constellations, which it named, opposite connect-the-dot illustrations of the things they described. My father and I had set up a small white telescope on the back patio to zero in on them. We used to challenge each other. Who could name all eighty-eight constellations? How many animals appear in the night sky? Recite all the star groups that begin with the letter *C*.

I ran to the avenue and found the first phone booth I could. I took a breath. Stick to description, I told myself — Mom's plans, Deborah's moods, California, Erich's ballad. Erich's magic. Erich. If I get emotional, he'll think it's momentary panic, just today.

I lifted the phone. I'd hardly spoken to him over the past two years. Mom would always do the talking. She'd park us in a café or hotel and go off to badger him, long-distance, for money. I dialed the operator and asked her to place a collect call. It was almost two in the morning his time. He'd be home, I knew. He never went anywhere at night.

It rang. "Pick it up," I said aloud, my face pressing against the glass booth. It rang and rang. Cygnus. Cetus. Cancer. Crater. Crux.

"Your party doesn't seem to be answering," noted the operator. "Would you care to place your call again later?"

Erich had explained that since the universe was expanding, the stars were in fact moving away from each other. Fleeing, he'd said. A man standing on Corvus might see the light from Erich's signal fire in ten million million years.

"Later," I echoed.

5

HELLO, I MUST BE GOING

My mother returned to Venice the day after Erich's fiery spectacle. She was in the living room recounting to Deborah the romantic twists and turns of her trip when I walked in. They fell silent and fixed me with looks that said, "You are a male and therefore evil." Mom said, "Fish sticks," and jerked her head kitchenward. She always cooked as soon as she returned to us. Usually, this meant she threw something frozen into the oven. As I stood by the sink, breaking off pieces of the breaded fish, I listened to the lilt of my mother's voice in the other room. I couldn't make out all the words, but the rise and fall had the music of "Can you believe he said that?" They punctuated her monologue with laughter, laughter, no doubt, at some poor Romeo's expense. When Erich came home, she leapt to the door, where she kissed his cheeks and made as if to dance him around the room. I'd come back into the doorway. He threw me a "Gimme a break" look and told her, "You better call Oomie."

"What's for dinner?" he asked me on the way to the kitchen, casting an ironic glance at his watch, which showed how much too early it was for an evening meal.

She didn't need to call Oomie, because Oomie called first. Then all hell broke loose. Mom threw open the bathroom door and, as toothpaste ran over my chin, demanded, "What did you say to her? What did you tell her? She says you wrote to her. What did you say?"

"Nothing, nothing," I said, not thinking to spit out. "Just stuff. The usual stuff. Nothing."

"Nothing, huh? Nothing? If you wrote nothing then why is she taking him? Explain that." She grabbed the toothbrush out of my hand and flung it against the wall.

I had no idea what she was talking about. "What did I do?"

"You lying little shit. You know full well what you did. You always know." Deborah was in the hall behind her, shrinking from both of us.

"What?"

"I knew I should have left you in New Jersey."

I looked around for Erich. He was in the bedroom but he didn't come out. In retrospect, I take his staying away as a sign of the changes that were happening in him. Before, he would have come to my rescue, defused Mom, something.

I'm thinking about a day in Mexico City. She was on one of her teaching binges, which she went on periodically, as if to prove we weren't missing anything by missing school. This time we stood in an open market. "A tomato, if it's good, has to smell like . . . what?" she queried. "A tomato, right? Deborah, here. What's that smell like? It most definitely does not smell like a tomato! It smells like the tip of your nose. Q.E.D. It's not a tomato. Throw it back.

"Question. If you were an Aztec in this very same market — (and if you were, you probably would have seen these same old ladies lurking around here; that's how ancient they are) — right here in Tenochtitlan — isn't that so much more lyrical than Mexico City? — So, you're at market in Ten-och-tit-lan. You have no money. Why?"

Erich waved his arm in the air like a schoolboy who needs permission to pee.

"Mr. Erich!" Mom cried, pointing at him.

"You spent it on tanning lotion."

"Very funny, sonny. You — stay after class." And she bumped him with her hip.

"Who else?"

Deborah and I just blinked stupidly.

"Hopeless, hopeless," Mom said. "There isn't any money. You haven't invented it yet!"

"I knew that," Erich said.

"Bull pizzle you did," said Deborah.

Mom went on with the lesson: "So then. No money. How do you pay for that tomato that's not a tomato?"

"Trade?" I ventured.

I couldn't tell if she'd heard me. She said, "That's easy, right? You barter. Now here's the kicker. How do Aztecs make change on the barter system? (If you'd read the guidebook you'd know this.) Any guesses?"

"Flowers?" offered Deborah.

"No. Erich?"

"I dunno. Turkey gizzards."

"You're a regular laugh riot today, buster. Give up?"

"Cigarettes?" I said, sure I was right.

"Cocoa beans," Mom said.

"Full of beans!" Erich howled, and she proceeded to tickle him. Right in the middle of the market, she attacked him, calling him "Mr. Full O'Beans" and tickling him until he was crying from laughing. He couldn't contain himself, even though he kept trying to look mock-serious, saying, "You stop that now." He dropped to the street, wriggling, and she practically fell on top of him, yelling "Full O'Beans. Mr. Full O'Beans."

I grabbed the tomato she'd thrown back on the cart and stuffed it under my shirt. An old lady pointed at me and shouted. Someone else came over and shook me by the shoulders. Mom got to her feet and started screaming back. It happened quickly. She grabbed my wrist and pulled me through the crowd. She bucked and reared and, with building fury, plowed through the crowds of dull, monolithic loiterers. I was her purse, banging posts, smacking her side. Erich and Deborah flew behind us like an animated cape. Other ragtag street kids, sensing excitement, tagged along.

"Places to go, people to see," she called, this manic pied piper.

Some little kid repeated: "Platsis to go!" as she tore around a corner and down a long alley. Our conga line followed. She cut across a park, past gaping men smoking on benches, and strode up the steps of a church. Then she turned and, not looking at me, addressed the teeming scrawnies trailing her. "The year he was born an earthquake leveled Mexico City!"

Erich reached an arm around my shoulder.

"Nineteen fifty-seven. Remember the year."

"Lebbeled Mehico Tsity!" shouted the kid triumphantly.

Erich patted my stiff shoulder. I stared over their heads, refusing to cry.

"The year of the earthquake. The year this sorry excuse for a child was born."

Erich began signing: "Blame It on the Bossa Nova" quietly in my ear.

The tomato that was not a tomato had, in our flight, gotten squashed against my stomach. It bled through my T-shirt and ran down my leg.

My mother took off in one direction, and Erich took us home in the other. He held our hands and led us into the hall bathroom of our ratty Mexican *pensione*. While Deborah watched from the rim of the tub, Erich peeled my shirt over my head and used it to wash the tomato off my chest and belly. He wetted his hand and forked his fingers through my hair, as though getting me ready for a school dance.

"Wait here," he said, ducking out and closing the door behind him. He reappeared holding a towel, a fresh shirt — one of his — and Mom's cosmetic bag. I dried myself and donned his voluminous shirt as he positioned Deborah on the toilet seat and knelt before her on the floor. He brushed shadow on her eyelids, rouged her cheeks, and daubed her lips with strawberry red. "You are the beautiful dancing princess," he told her, before turning to me. "And you are Hans, the dragonslayer, and of course, the singing bone."

And, with that, we acted out everything we could remember from MGM's *The Wonderful World of the Brothers Grimm* straight to the end, where Erich, as Wilhelm Grimm, lay in the bathtub, feverish and dying, while all his fairytale creations — Red Riding Hood, Rumplestiltskin, the Giant at the window (also played by Erich) — crowded around him. The room grew dusky, and people knocked to come in, but we played on, enchanted.

I wanted that Erich beside me again as I stood at the bathroom sink, crying and drooling toothpaste. "I didn't do anything, Mom. I didn't do anything."

What I had done was what she told me to do: "Write your

grandmother. She's making all this possible. She wants to hear from you." It was a litany we'd heard often in Mexico, after Mom had hung up with Oomie. And so, regularly, we'd jot off little "South of the Border" postcards to her in Skokie, Illinois. We'd cram all the good cheer we could fit into the little square opposite the address and decorate the cards with suns and flowers, *x*'s and *o*'s. But this time, when Mom was gone and Erich was otherwise occupied with his ballad, I'd sat down and written a solid letter to Oomie Doris and Papa Val. And in it, I'd said all the wrong things.

I told my grandparents that Erich was writing a song, that he'd given up on singing groups, and, in the process, I described how great he had been with the children in Mexico and how musically talented he was. Apparently, this was all it took. Within seventy-two hours my grandmother had signed Erich up to be counselor-in-training at a summer camp in Wisconsin, a musical-theater camp. Erich knew about it, but didn't say anything until Mom came home and he said, "You better call Oomie."

With less than ten days before the first session, Mom groped about for a way out, anything short of saying no to her mother, which, for reasons I don't understand, was impossible.

"Call your grandmother," she begged Erich. "Tell her you don't want to go."

"Her hearing aid's broken. She won't even know it's me," he replied.

"She'll know. She'll know. C'mon. Call her."

"You call her. She's your mother."

"You don't understand. It's like Siberia with her. She won't hear me."

"So send her a new hearing aid."

"Deborah," she pleaded, "call Oomie, will you? Tell her Erich's got to stay here."

"Why would I do that?" Deborah asked, half out the door.

"Tell her you need him to help you study for your high school placement exams."

"Like she'd believe it."

"You could try."

"I gotta go."

"Please?"

"She's *your* mother."

"And I'm yours. I order you to call her."

Deborah rolled her eyes.

"Do it for me?" Mom cooed.

Deborah snorted. Her hand was already prying a joint from the pocket of her jeans when the screen door banged behind her.

I was in deep freeze this whole time, but in her desperation Mom finally turned to me.

"I want you to dial Oomie and tell her you've been very sick. That you need Erich here. Doctor's orders. You have German measles. Erich's never had them, and the doctor doesn't want him to be around other children. They have a very long incubation period. He could start an epidemic."

"Here, I'll dial," she said. She handed me the phone.

"Hi, Oomie. It's me."

"Hello? Hello?"

"Oomie," I yelled, "It's me."

"Erich? Is that you? How are you dear?"

"No, Oomie, it's not Erich. It's —"

"— Let me talk to your mother, dear. I'm glad you called."

"Tell her," my mother mouthed.

"I have to talk to you about Erich." I said into the phone. "He's got the German measles."

"Thank you dear. Give everyone a kiss for me. Is your mother there?"

I handed the phone to Mom, who said, "Oh, yes, Mom, he's very excited about camp. Can't wait. We've been writing his name in all his clothes. Yes, Mom, we have the list. They sent . . . No, I wouldn't let him go without calamine . . . Yes, I know about the woods . . . What do you think? Do you think I don't think about my own children? I said, do you think I don't think. Mother, turn on your hearing aid. Your hearing aid!" Erich passed by, echoing every word she said just a fraction of a second after she said it.

Two days before he was to leave, Lorna took Erich to the doctor, armed with a list of symptoms that might preclude his going to camp, but the doctor gave him a clean bill of health and told him to stand up straight. "You see those old men hobbling around all cramped up and hunched?" he asked Erich. "They slouched when they were teenagers."

The night before he left, Erich and I went to our room after dinner. In the kitchen, Mom was calling Dad. Maybe he would call Oomie and refuse to let Erich attend camp, if she offered to let him come out for a weekend visit. "Desperate times, desperate measures," she had said. "Don't start packing just yet."

Erich started to pack. I sat on my bed and watched him. "Sing around the campfire. Join the Campfire Girls," he sang. I tried to climb into his duffel bag. He kept stuffing socks in under my arms. "Oh, no! You have to get out. I don't have room for my collapsible cup!"

Mom came to the door. "Your dad doesn't care if you go to that camp or not."

"Who does?" Erich asked.

"I do! I do!" I cried, imitating the kids in the gum commercial.

"Take your brother outside," she told him. "I'll pack." As we were leaving she turned to me. "Your father says 'Happy birthday.' He sent something, but it's late. Obviously."

It was my twelfth birthday.

Erich and I walked down to the ocean and stood on the beach. Everyone else had vanished. I missed Dad. Erich must have seen me shiver, because he took off his windbreaker and held it out to me. "Happy birthday," he said. Then he made as if to pluck an arrow from a quiver, load it in a bow, and fire it at a point in the sky. "*Thhheeewww,*" he sounded with his tongue and teeth. He sat down, looked back up, and said, "Missed again."

"Every fucking time," I said.

I pulled the jacket hood over my head and pulled the strings so that it sealed off all but my eyes. "Noony noony," I sounded through my nose. "Wimohweh, saheeb," he replied.

Then, as if he had intuited my thoughts, Erich said, "Dad is a very smart man. Probably in the hundredth percentile in intelligence."

"Do you think we inherited his brains?" I asked, trying not to show my eagerness to join that topmost possible percentile.

"I don't know," he said, giving the question full weight. "I think of myself as a highly rational being. I live largely in my mind, calculate the costs of life, try to make connections where they don't already exist. We both obsess over things like he does. That I think we get from him. We are more erratically brilliant than he is. He's a plodder, really, a hedgehog, though he does his best to disguise the fact. He's not erratic, but he's undeniably brilliant. Very twentieth century, very philosophical, all logic and ambivalence. We both got his logic."

"He's very logical," I added, not certain I remembered. "It's a good thing, too."

"Yeah. I'd say we're both a good deal like him."

"We've got a lot of her in us, too," I said, being careful not to exclude Mom from our thoughts for long.

"She's definitely got a brilliance about her," Erich admitted. "I'm not sure who inherited that particular quality. You have more of her intuition," he said, "while I have her . . ."

He broke off and stared over at the area where, by day, men hoisted huge barbells. Then he looked at me and mused. "I wonder if body builders really have stronger sexual appetites or if they diminish 'em by beating off all the time." We debated this for a couple of minutes, trying to figure out if muscle and desire were connected at the source, and then we wandered back toward the house. "Testosterone," he said, as if that answered everything.

"Rhinovision," I said, thinking he was playing a game of fusing nature names with those of household objects.

"It's the male hormone," he explained. "Testosterone. Puts hair on your teeth. But who wants hairy teeth?" Then he stopped walking and looked back the way we'd come. "Sadness. I have her sadness," he said.

I looked down at my feet, nodding like I knew.

6

Erich's Hands

He was reading them. Or they were talking to him. I couldn't tell which. It started as washing, then I shut the water off, the suds drained away, and his hands kept roiling around themselves. Fingers were tongues flapping. He executed the semaphore of possession — more exactly, of dispossession. The hands, I knew, were including me. The hurried hush of his signing was trying to tell me things.

I should go back, though, to how I got there, and where we were.

Those presummer weeks had the weighted, rolling feel of the inevitable. Mom had disappeared. Erich had started a conflagration on the beach from the middle of which he too disappeared. Then she returned and he departed over her proverbial dead body.

I expected the mechanism of the family to somehow shut down when Erich left, but it didn't. If he was the fuel that made things run, you wouldn't have known that the tank had gone empty. Mom was, in fact, quite productive. She actively engaged, for the first time in my memory, in preparations for the future. She found a singing coach, cleaned the house, and began clipping ads for part-time work in everything from retail to secretarial. "I almost finished a master's in English; I'm eminently employable," I heard her tell Deborah while circling Sunday want ads with a green felt-tip Flair. The turn from spring was marked by a flood in town of what my mother dubbed "the lemmings of summer break," so she and her friends resorted to the air-conditioned insides of restaurants and apartments in place of the beach. They still spent a part of every day there, but they did it with a grudge, surveying the frat-house scene with disdain.

Mom met Del, an intense older man with gray bushy eyebrows and jeans whose bottoms belled out like dervish skirts. He was going to help her, whatever that meant. With his guidance she'd begin her singing career. With his financial expertise she'd open a store of her own, filled with the knickknack treasures she'd brought back from Mexico, and which, in time, she intended to collect from the world over: painted dogs, bright scarves, handcrafted baskets, and ash trays. She'd decided to call the envisioned store "The World's Room," followed by the logo: "Great Stuff from Just About Everywhere." Erich had suggested the name, and now she and Del used it in their planning sessions, as if they were talking about something real. The whole thing gave me the creeps, but I was happy to see her happy.

Deborah got involved, too, as if Erich's absence had created space for her in the house. She pored over the classifieds with Mom, reading job descriptions aloud, and brainstormed wallpaper and fixture ideas for "The World's Room." Deborah even big-sistered me a little, asking me what I was up to when she saw me around the house, telling me about movies I should see, and occasionally offering to fix me a sandwich or scramble me some eggs. Mom pretty much ignored me, but she did it politely. She hated me for getting Erich sent away, but she didn't show it. She made sure I had shoes and shampoo. She'd introduce me to her friends and remind me to make my bed. I didn't have much to do, now that my documentary of the making of Erich's Ballad was without its subject, so I just hugged the walls.

I wrote Erich almost daily, but I never heard back from him. His "life-as-song" had begun to grow strange, as I would soon see close up. At the time, though, I imagined that he was in a kind of paradise of children and music, and, indeed, though he doubtless couldn't see it as such, I still believe he was.

My letter to Oomie had convinced her that Erich's talents were artistic, musical, and that the best place for him was a theater camp. The one she found specialized in musical comedy without sacrificing traditional summer activities. It divided the day between sport and theater. The arcadian setting, likewise, alternated horseback riding rings with rehearsal halls, baseball fields with stages. The volleyball net was strung across a court made up of a dozen years of children's handprints set in cement, Grauman's Theatre-style.

My brother left most of his books and notebooks at home when he departed for the summer. These he sealed in two boxes. The first was marked "Do not open! Violators will be subject to intense disapprobation and, probably, DEATH!" On the second he'd written, "Time Release Capsule. Not to be released *under any circumstances* until New Year's Eve, 1990!" He did, however, keep a journal during his weeks at camp, and, while most of it is incomprehensible, the more lucid entries detail, or at least allude to, his activities.

As a teenager, he was expected to put in time as both a counselor-in-training and a performer. He'd been assigned to *Paint Your Wagon*, the cabin with the youngest boys, ages five and six, many of whom were children of the camp's staff. By day he'd troop alongside these little buckaroos (in his journal he refers to them as the "space cowboys") and by night he'd take bit parts in plays at a red barn theater, named for a then-famous librettist who'd visited the camp once while vacationing nearby. The week Erich went crazy he was playing Officer Krupke in *West Side Story*. Earlier that summer he'd been the kindly mute king in *Once Upon a Mattress*. Clearly, he was perceived as the sidekick type, sometimes sweet, always abstracted. He seems to have seen it that way, too. On July 18 he made a fragmentary note in his journal about "My life as Wimpy, gladly paying tomorrow for a hamburger today." I'm not clear whether or not he took part in athletics. His only reference to sports is a weird little couplet he wrote a few days into the season: "Tennis, I'm the furry ball / Swimming, I'm the pier."

Nor am I certain what happened at the instant he disappeared behind his eyes. I've stood at the very spot where he stood, looked up at the same trees and the same sky. I know he was marching around with his campers, wearing a coonskin cap. They were searching the field for gopher holes and golf balls. They must have laughed when he babbled, conforming as he did so perfectly to a five-year-old's daffy vision of the world. A counselor from the oldest girls' cabin — I've always imagined her carrying a mesh sack filled with soccer balls — noticed him tilting his head up toward the sun. The little boys were following his example. She called hello several times and, when he failed to respond, began to round up the little boys. She herded them away from Erich, leaving him standing to the side of a bank of evergreens, cocking his head to look at who knew what. At least this is the story we were told.

The slippage of Erich's sense of the real into whatever it became may have been progressive, but it's hard to tell from his writing, which from the beginning of summer to the end seems maniacally abstruse, parenthetical, turned in on itself. Witness this passage from June 30, 1969:

> Boathouse perched upon decrepit (ancient perhaps) (even antediluvian) (how's that for a word, posterity?) piles of leaves, overgrown undergrowth, all rotting in the name of fun in the sun. Exactly the place my sweaty peers (piers, pears, pares, pee-ers, that's the best) would choose for their tongues and pores to find a way of huh-a-huh-a-huh-a-huh (hubba hubba, bubba Fred) — all in the name of love's sweet song, la la la la la la la la la. Boy flower girl flower. Me, can't stomach the heap of nature with its bubble gum trees and sand bonfires and mellow, man, marshes. Marshes of mellow. Punsch punsch punsch. Try to find Davy Crockett in that. I'm a great indoorsman. Krup you.

> Remember bug juice.

> Ceremonies everywhere. Use them in Ballad, book IV, verse something.

> Girl who is a mix of rabbit and playboy bunny said HI. I said HI back. Told her hair best thing about her, without it she'd be bald. Slightly offended. Prettily so.

So much to say (is it "saying" when you write it down?
Ponder ponder. Mull mull.), but space cowboys
breathing away here in the big room. Join the club.
("I'm tempted to join a club and beat you over the
head with it.")

Join the club. Yeah. That's a joke. Guy walks into a
doctor's office with a chicken on his head. That's a
joke, too. Or at least a yoke, what with the chicken.

The Ballad of Erich. No joke. (Radio.)

What this says about Erich's sexual repulsion and jokey decline is
one for the shrinks. To me it reads pure Erich, not to mention pure
smart-ass teenager. It's how I always imagined Erich's mind worked,
tripping all over itself with puns and homonyms — portrait of a dog-
gerel artist as a young man — and inside jokes for an audience of
one. What I don't understand, what I've never understood, is where
the kindness in him went. Erich was, as I've said, double, and this
doubleness — the ability to see through his own eyes and another's
— was predicated on empathy, a kind of sweetness that tempered the
cynical pose. None of that comes through in his journal. Nor did it
come through in person. By the time I saw him his eyes were shut-
tered shut and he'd disappeared somewhere behind.

I saw him because my mother sent me. She got a call from Oomie
in the middle of the night and by 8:00 A.M. I was flying to O'Hare.

Mom was all business. She called the airlines without waking
Deborah and me. She phoned Dad at school and left word with the
English department secretary for him to contact the camp directors.
She got me up and packed my things carefully, as if I, too, were
going off to camp. We sped to LAX.

"He's sick is all I know," she said. "Something, I don't know what,
happened, but I'm sure everything will be fine. I couldn't get anything out of your grandmother, of course. She wakes me up in the
middle of my first good sleep in weeks with 'How could you do this
to me? I send him to a nice camp, with the smartest, most talented

children in the country — singing and dancing. Why didn't you tell me he was sick?' Like I planned the whole thing. The poor boy is probably homesick as hell. I'm certainly sick for missing him.

"Well, I got her on that one," Mom continued, dodging in and out of lanes. "I said 'Who is this?' Can you imagine? She practically had a heart attack right on the phone: 'This is your mother who do you think and what did you expect me to say when they call me at 7:30 in the morning and start saying sick this and problem that and nothing *physically* wrong, blah, blah, blah.'"

We left the car illegally parked and ran to the gate. She took a breath and looked right at me. "I have to stay here," she said. "Things are starting to happen for us here. It's a good time, time to strike. And since we're only talking about a few days, it's better. I'm meeting Del over at the room tomorrow. He thinks we can work something out — maybe an extended run. Wouldn't that be something? Your mom with her own nightclub act? Besides, Dad will be with you when you get there. Then you and Erich will come home. You'll see. Mom will star for you guys."

There was a look my mother's eyes could have, a high-beam, you-are-there kind of look. It was the look a performer gives to transform a crowd into a room of yearning individuals, all dying to buy her a drink between sets. My mother's eyes had that look when she took the stage — in her Mexican impromptu concerts, in the California bars she later played, preparing for her "break." The heat from her eyes was so pervasive that you couldn't tell whether the blazing came from inside or out. It was a look to make a boy bold; it was a look for men. It said: "All this is for you."

"I need you to be the man of the family now," she was saying. "You have to take care of Erich, watch over him until your father comes. Oomie will need your help, too. God knows, she's terrible at things like this, really terrible. So it's up to you. But I have total faith in you. I know you can do whatever has to be done. You're a shining knight, off to rescue your brother. You're my champion."

I had seen her eyes like this before, but I'd never experienced them so close up, trained on me. My chest swung open like steel gates before the grounds of a palace. I was emboldened. It was the happiest, proudest moment of my life.

She started me up the ramp, encouraging me with those fierce eyes. At the door I turned and waved. She was gone.

There was wisdom in Mom's decision to send me in her stead. Behind the B-movie alibis, she made admission of her own unfitness. She wanted to avoid Oomie Doris and Dad, to be sure, but she must have also known that she required too much for herself, that she couldn't give Erich what he needed to get well. Her twelve-year-old son was better suited.

Oomie met me at the gate in Chicago. She fussed over how skinny I looked, remarked on my tan, and kissed me too many times on the neck. Then she drove to a nearby Poochies stand and plied me with foot-long hot dogs, fries, and a milk shake, before driving the two-plus hours to camp to retrieve my brother.

The grounds of his camp were lush and green. Trees overhung a paved road that encircled everything: a tennis court backed by camouflage netting, a large white main building trimmed in forest green with two floors of porches that seemed to be smiling, stables, ballfields, and pastures. A village of wooden cottages, also green and white, beckoned. There were children everywhere. They pivoted on the tennis courts, sashayed in dance studios, and swung from porch railings like laundry blowing dry. The instant I saw it, I thought: Wisconsin is the Neverland.

When we arrived, Erich was tucked away upstairs in the cavernous main building. I first encountered him there, in an off-white room, one of three that made up this camp infirmary-cum-sanitarium. He'd been locked in. The camp directors said they were afraid he would get out and hurt himself, though they didn't think to remove the drinking glass, mirror, metal-frame bed, sheets, his belt, or any other accidents waiting to happen. Nor had they thought of leaving someone to care for him.

Oomie sent me to fetch him, choosing to remain with the camp director and the doctor. The doctor's wife, the nominal "nurse" of the place, led me to Erich's room. All the way there I fought to keep from staring at the magical life all around. A teenage girl played the baby grand in the lobby. A rack of costumes, all glittered and furry, was wheeled through a screen door, which slapped shut with a bang. We climbed a high flight of extrawide carpeted stairs. The walls were skyed with black and white stills of children in costume and at play. Everything smelled of summer and mildew.

We walked past maybe a dozen doors, all with sequined stars and the names of staff written on them, with titles underneath. Beyond these was an empty shower room, door half open, and a corridor leading to the infirmary. Here was another row of doors, without the stars. At the last one on the left, the nurse fumbled with a ring of keys and unlocked the lock. She pushed the door open, and stepped back.

Erich didn't look up. He sat on the edge of the bed like a George Segal statue, back straight, head hangdog, eyes fixed on the tips of his nails — the statue of a boy sent to the corner for acting up, waiting stoically for his punishment, not realizing he's already received it. I walked past him to the window, which looked over a wooden balcony with chipping paint. Beyond the rail, I could see the back right corner of a nucomb game in progress.

"It's not bad here," I ventured.

Erich sat.

"Erich. Erich," I whispered to him when the woman had gone, locking the door behind her. "Erich, it's me. What are you doing? What happened? You can tell me. It's me. I'm here."

Erich rose, walked to the lavatory, and began washing his hands. He washed them and washed them and washed them. I moved from the window to the sink. "Erich. Erich."

I poked his arm. Nothing. I shook his shoulder. Nothing. I lifted Erich's soapy hand and put it to my own face. Erich just watched the hand.

He looked like my brother, this boy at the basin. He was his old nondescript self, down to the pink veins on his eyelids where a few blond lashes sprouted. His front tooth was still chipped. His cheeks were smushy-soft as always. Still no sign of beard, no acne, no lines. His pupils, floating on pools of dim gray-blue, were small and dead.

His thin hair, the color of wet sand, stuck out from his coonskin cap, looking greasy and confused. Erich's skin hadn't tanned this summer, which wasn't surprising. He'd remained pale even in Mexico, burning beet red and peeling snowy white but never browning.

I turned off the water and wiped his hands with a towel. When I hung the towel up, his hands began moving again, saying something to him. I grabbed his fingers and walked him over to the bed.

The first song that came to my mind was "Last Train to Clarksville," so I sang it quietly, still squeezing the tips of his fingers: "Take the last train to Clarksville and I'll meet you at the station. / Be there by four-thirty 'cause I've made your reservation. / Don't be slow. Oh, no no, no!" He didn't join in.

I sat next to him. The way our hands were joined, you'd have thought I was proposing. After a while, I couldn't take the quiet. I dropped his hands and began bouncing the bed under us. Then I took off his cap and smoothed his hair. Still nothing. I tossed the hat in the air. Tossed it again. I stood on the bed, flung up the former critter by the tail, and jumped for it. I trampolined to the other bed and kept flinging and jumping, bouncing the hat off the ceiling, looking down at my sunken brother, leaping back and forth between beds, brushing closer to him every time I landed or leapt. I sang "Mony Mony," bouncing from the head of one bed to the foot of the other. I swatted at the ceiling with the hat. Then I stopped bounding and started yodeling, for no reason clear to me, calling the cows home.

Erich looked up toward my face, broke into a great smile and said something convoluted. I thought he said, "Pops lives at the Y. I take him for walks."

Children were shrieking and running on the volleyball court outside. The room was oppressively quiet. Erich smiled his dopey smile and I stood wobbly-kneed and sweaty on the lumpy bed.

Before I could utter a simple "Who's Pops?" footsteps scraped our way, the doorknob rattled, and a doctor dressed for tennis brought Oomie into the room. He didn't seem to notice me, this doctor–slash–tennis pro, or, if he did, he must have seen nothing odd about a tear-streaked, raccoon-dangling twelve-year-old, shaking in his sneakers on one bed while his brother went insane on a second.

Oomie simply said, "We're going," and took Erich's hand. I climbed off the bed and stumbled behind as she pulled him past the two-person medical staff, along the hall, across one lobby, down a set of stairs, through a slamming screen door, down patio steps, onto a large gravel driveway, into her grapefruit-yellow Impala.

One boy, a couple years younger than me, watched us pull out. This single soldier, just passing by, was Erich's final friend. He waved idly, squinting into the sun, as we drove past the tall wooden gate, Oomie, in the front seat, lighting a cigarette, an absent Erich and me in the back.

7

THE FATHER AT THE DOOR

When Oomie, having pushed eighty miles an hour all the way from Sheboygan to Skokie, dragged Erich and me up the elevator and into her tchotchke-cluttered condo, there had been no word from my father. At first Oomie refused to believe it, no matter how many times the housekeeper said, "No. Believe me, Mrs. Bonnaci, no one called." Oomie's pushy mistrust hardly phased the housekeeper, who placidly answered a barrage of questions concerning her comings and goings, whether the phone had remained sufficiently on the hook, and whether she had heated my grandfather's lunch or merely dropped the refrigerated portions down in front of him, stone-cold. The woman took the interrogation like a trooper. She was one of a long procession of maids, cleaning ladies, and helpers who'd worked for my hawklike grandmother.

"She steals," Oomie mouthed to me when the "girl" turned her back.

Finally convinced that Dad hadn't called — and confirmed by this fact in her low opinion of him — Oomie delivered Erich and me to the couch beside Papa's chair and started cooking with a vengeance. She believed, within her power to believe a black domestic, that the phone had not rung all day, but she'd never believe that anyone else could have given her husband a proper lunch.

I kissed Papa, who had taken his eyes off the Cubs game to watch our arrival. He greeted us with smiles and a characteristic "Doo doo doo." Since his stroke in the year of my birth — also the year of the Mexico City earthquake — these were the only words he could find. He searched for other ways of saying what he meant, but could

locate none. Though paralyzed on the right side, he seemed otherwise alert and healthy. His verbal repertoire, however, was submin-
imal. He looked questioningly and sadly at Erich, who, in turn,
stared slightly to the right of the TV screen. When I asked him how
he was doing, he answered, "Doo doo doo," as if to say, "Not bad,
not good."

I began to suspect that something had gone wrong. It wasn't like
Dad not to call. When I ventured into the kitchen to mention this
to Oomie, she was already talking. "I hate to leave him alone like
that. He doesn't eat right when I'm not around. He just sits in front
of the TV." Then, looking at me, she added, "His brain hasn't been
right since the stroke. They had to take out most of his brain."

"He seems OK to me, " I offered.

"My hearing aid's not working," she said, ignoring my comment.
"He just sits there like a lump, doesn't listen to me, doesn't say anything, doesn't eat, unless I'm here to feed him."

"I'm gonna call Dad," I said, overenunciating.

"It's just like your father not to phone. To leave this on my hands.
What kind of a man does that? Sends his wife and children away and
then leaves them stranded in Mexico without a dime? Doesn't let
them back. I don't like to say unkind things, but no real man does
that. And I told your mother from the start, not that she ever listens
to me. I'm just her mother."

I assumed my own brand of deafness, nodding a couple of times
before repeating, "I'm gonna call."

The bedroom was all yellow and gold, from the framed floral
paintings to the gilt thread of the spreads. The bedroom suite was
yellow with white bamboo-style handles. On the glass-protected
surfaces were golden knickknacks: mushroom paperweights, uni-
corns, gold boxes the shape of ladybugs. Pictures of Deborah, Erich,
and me hung everywhere, as did pictures of Mom, onstage in school
musicals and local talent shows. We were wallpaper.

Dad answered before the second ring. "Hi, Dad, it's me," I said.

"Where are you?" he asked, probably thinking we'd started traveling again.

"I'm at Oomie Doris's. Erich's all right, Dad, but he's sort of gone crazy, and we had to get him from camp."

"Where's your mother?"

"She had to stay back home. She had to," I added. "Didn't you get her message? She called school first thing."

"Your mother knows I'm not there this late in the summer," he snapped. "They just shove messages in a slot."

"You're supposed to come get us. You were supposed to be here already."

"How the devil . . . ?"

"I think Erich needs help. They wouldn't let him stay at camp. He won't even talk to me."

"Where is he now?" He asked.

"On the couch. Next to Papa."

"Did they give him anything at camp?"

"Just his clothes and stuff."

"Any drugs, I mean, any medication?"

"Oh. I don't know. I don't know."

Even as he questioned me, I know he was mentally calling his own doctor, estimating plane departures, calculating costs, and confronting Mom over the phone. Dad's mind worked that way.

"Stay there," he said. "I'll phone the airlines and call you back. I should be able to get there by midnight or so. You won't go anywhere?"

"Where would we go?" I asked.

"Of course not," he said.

"Dad, are you all right?"

"Oh, yes. Fine, fine." And he was off.

That night Oomie served a dinner that caricatured her typical odes to gluttony. A terrific Jewish cook with a Neapolitan husband, she made every meal a heaping celebration of both cultures. This one, for instance, consisted of brisket, lasagna, a serving bowl of Italian sausage with peppers and tomatoes, noodle kugel, and cuts of boiled chicken. For dessert she scooped up ice cream, sundae-style to the maraschino cherry on top. Plates of Fannie May chocolate and lacey hard candy appeared magically. And then the baked goods.

Where this food came from was, to my mind, as mysterious as where it all went. The maid was gone, which meant all the conjuring was my grandmother's. Her freezer was a case study in emergency preparedness, the potential disaster consisting not of nuclear attack, but of a surprise grandchild visit. She expected us to take some of everything, seconds if we loved her, and thirds to prove we were hers forever. Papa shook his head, threw his nonparalyzed hand up in the air and said "Doo doo doo" with each new course. He ate what the chef put on his plate, all cut bite size by her. Oomie Doris ate nothing, except for bits of meat off our plates and some whipped cheese out of the cannoli. The rest of the time she was in motion: Nothing up my sleeve. Presto! Pesto.

Erich, who normally ate like a bear, said something like "Mmm-uh, mmm-uh" throughout the meal, but only took in what Oomie fed him in a spoon. I tried to make up the difference. We all wore napkin bibs, as was customary. By the end of dinner, Erich's looked like a Jackson Pollock.

There was no helping Oomie — no clearing dishes or folding napkins. She had her system. So we three "men" retired to the den and the TV, faces red, bellies distended, throats raw from swallowing. I helped Papa light a cigar, and we waited for Dad. Around eleven, Oomie put Erich to bed on the foldout couch, where he lay, eyes fixed on the ceiling.

Some people have a knack for taking the horrible in stride. In my grandmother this went hand in hand with a genius for making calamity of the ordinary. It was the unflappable Oomie who led Erich away, gabbing to him as if his vacancy were everyday stuff. She gave no sign of being cognizant of his pain or of the fault lines opening beneath our family. She just did her job: feed, tuck in bed, feed again.

When Oomie came back into the den, she offered us milk and cookies. I said yes.

It was after 2:00 A.M. when my father arrived, 12:00 my time, 3:00 his. I was pulsating with sugar, TV-hum, and dishwasher rumble. (At Oomie's, the dishwasher ran morning and night; she was always

cleaning up from some meal or other.) Papa Val, who'd been sleeping in his chair, beamed with relief when my father entered the
room. To Oomie, on the other hand, my father might have been a
stranger cleaning up after his dog and doing it badly. She ignored
him with an attitude. She directed no words his way and offered him
neither food nor drink. (A drink he didn't need. He smelled of the
several scotches I knew he must have downed to overcome his
intense fear of flying.)

Later, back in New Jersey, Dad compared my grandparents to
Beckett characters: he can't talk; she won't stop. She doesn't sit; he
can't stand. Stuck together in perpetuity. Always dying, never dead.

"How are you, Val?" he asked my grandfather, whose "Doo doo
doo" suggested, "How could I be, living in this hell?"

"You're looking good. Still young I see."

"Doo doo doo (I do my best under the circumstances)."

"Long day, today."

"Doo doo doo (You don't know the half of it). Doo doo doo (It's
always something)."

"I had a heck of a time getting a cab out here this time of night."

"Doo doo doo (Take your coat off. Have a bite to eat)."

Then Oomie to me: "Where is your father sleeping?"

I turned to my father, whose beard I had forgotten. His dead eye
looked alien to me.

Then he to her: "I hadn't thought about it. Just wanted to get
here."

"He should have thought," she said to me. "We haven't room
here. Our grandsons are staying with us."

"Doo doo doo (inarticulate burst of anger)."

Oomie wouldn't stop moving about the room. She still hadn't
looked at Dad. She addressed herself to me; then I turned my head
toward him and he answered.

My father had hugged me at the door, but, anxious to get inside
the apartment and take his inevitable lumps, he had barely said a
word. Now he put his arm around me. "I'll just call a cab and get a
motel for tonight," he said. "I'll be by for the kids early," he added

for his former mother-in-law. "We have to fly back to New York."

"What is he saying?" she asked me. "What New York?"

"Doo doo doo (Shut up for once)."

"Lorna and I agreed they'll come with me for a while. I have a doctor for Erich." My father could be a patient man, or at least a rational one, under duress.

"Erich is homesick for his mother," she explained to me. "He needs to eat right. Tell that man."

"Homesick . . ." I started to say to him.

"He'll be in good hands, Doris. I have the name of a fine doctor."

Oomie busied around, replacing coasters, emptying ashtrays, counting candies into a dish. She spoke under her breath for all of us to hear.

"What he's done. What he's done to her. Mexico, California, where is he all the time. All that time. Not a nickel. Ugly is as ugly does. Nobody listens to an old woman. But who drives a hundred and fifty miles when the camp calls? Who is humiliated? In front of strangers? Who finds the camp in the first place? My grandson . . ." She plumped a pillow. Boom! "Who loves me." Boom! "If I told her once . . ."

"Doo doo doo (Please be quiet). Doo doo doo (Don't listen to her)."

My grandmother's body started to erupt. Her false teeth clicked, her joints jerked, her hearing aid whistled. The skin of her neck and upper chest, once tight above her thick bosom, sagged in wrinkled folds like a shameful drapery. The blue blue of her eyelids, the red red of her painted cheeks and mouth, the stiff false lashes uprooting from their glue, the heavy brass elephant she wore on a chain across her breasts — all brought a circus gaiety to the meanness sizzling within. Fuss, snarl, spit, crack. This is the way the Jew suffers.

My father stood erect, polite, Aryan. This is the way the Austrian refrains.

My grandfather, Valerio Bonnaci, Italian to the end, was at war with himself. His blood boiled at my father's mistreatment, but his loyalty was with her. He exclaimed, good hand wagging open in the air, as if weighing a melon. He smoothed his shiny black hair; he held his forehead. This man of the nonsensical monosyllable knew what my father was up against. He, too, had gone blind in one eye. He, too, struggled for words to break him out of his half-dead state and came up with only gurgles, bleeps, baby talk. His good eye never left my father's face.

"Doo Doo Doo! Doo Doo Doo!" He rose on his cane and, steadying himself, began to lift the cane, waving it in the air.

"Doo doo doo!" The cane just missed a gilt-flecked sconce. My father reached a hand toward his shoulder.

Oomie's false teeth snapped in her mouth. My father's hand patted Papa. Papa's cane just hung up there. "Doo doo doo!" Once up, the stick had nowhere else to go. This strong-bodied patriarch, once so able, was reduced to the bluster of stage business. Gradually, the impotence of his threat came to seem humiliating.

Oomie slammed coasters onto a gold coaster rack. My father blushed. I looked away. Papa shook the cane a little at its apex, as if its rattle might stir a magnificent bolt of lighting. He grunted with the effort.

"That's all right," my father said. "That's all right." And gently he lowered Papa's cane, absolving it.

The steam seeped out of the room, and we were all moving to Erich's bedside. Oomie walked ahead, then Dad, holding my grandfather's dead arm while the living one prodded forward on the black metal prop. I took up the rear, a mortician.

We all stood along the side and foot of Erich's bed. Erich, on his back, tilted his head from side to side as if comparing shadows on the ceiling. We looked down at him, archaeologists, surgeons, mourners. In spite of himself, my father gasped. He put a hand on Erich's brow and started to say something. Then, apparently, he thought better of it.

8

Boys of Summer

It was late July. We stayed together, the three Hofmann men, in Dad's little lunchbox house in Maplewood, the house that used to be ours. Returning to it, and discovering the way our father occupied only a small corner of the whole, it felt cavernous. He had moved into the bedroom that once belonged to Erich and me, after, I suppose, it grew too painful to live alone in the room he'd shared with Mom. Erich and I camped in the living room, sleeping on the twin sofas, sheets tucked around the vinyl upholstery. We slept head-to-head. Rather, Erich slept and I lay awake, wondering what he was thinking.

Erich's state changed along with his medication. He went from drained and confused to almost lucid (in moments) to gone again. Sometimes it seemed to me that he was crying, though there was no evidence of tears. More often than not he was limp and dull. Each day felt like several days. We waited for some shift in his mood, and so the tedium of too-long waiting was compounded by the intensity of too much feeling. I was raw with my brother's mad life. Still, Dad and I never spoke of him.

Nor did we speak in any detail of the time since we'd seen each other last. There remained, however, on my father's dining room wall, a huge map of southern North America, which he'd mounted with electrician's tape. He'd marked the map with yellow thumbtacks, plucked from the bulletin board in Deborah's room: San Antonio, San Luis Potosi, San Miguel de Allende, Cuernavaca, Guadalajara, Chihuahua, El Paso, Tucson, Corpus Christi, Sonora, Tijuana, San Diego, San Juan Capistrano, and a dozen other yellow dots along the way. Apparently, he'd followed our course as best he could from the scraps of information he'd gotten out of long-distance operators and Western Union addresses. Our journey, as he'd mapped it out, finally read like a monitor that charts the heart rates of patients in a stress test: up, down, across, up, up, down, across, down, down.

The night we arrived at his house, I stared at the routing of pins, the slopes of Mom's excitable graph, and experienced again the way we'd traversed them, keeping our own expectations reined in, until they were background hum, barely audible rumbles, light wind in the trees. I ran my finger over the heads of the tacks. It cut a beautiful path, this trail of yellow dots along the map's network of red and green. It traced a colorful misery.

"I missed you children a great deal," Dad said, coming up behind me. "I never wanted you to go. That was your crazy mother's idea — mother's crazy *idea*. I didn't mean to suggest that your mother is . . . that."

"I know."

"It's what she always thought I thought," he added.

"It's ok."

"I should have protected you kids. I would have . . . When I tried, though . . . disastrous . . . botched . . ." His sentences were falling apart. I didn't know what he was talking about.

"You shouldn't worry about it," I assured him without noticeable impact. And we both studied the wall, our hands at our sides. "The Museum of Modern Art. moma." I said, remembering that such a place existed.

"Yes, but whose work would it be?" he queried.

I thought, "Andy Warthog," which was Erich's name for the pop artist.

"Doesn't matter," Dad said, moving toward the living room.

Dad tended to us in the manner of a children's director on a cruise ship. He cooked our meals, oversaw our hygiene, and tried to provide activities. In the years since he'd seen us, his life had been simplified. Over summer intersession, for instance, he had only two goals: to tune into every televised Mets game and to "stroll through" *The Magic Mountain* in German for the seventh time. The combination of his newly adopted baseball fanaticism and the Mets' "amazin'" 1969 season made his thirteen-inch black-and-white television even more compelling than Thomas Mann in the original. This solitary life had, I believe, given him order, a way of muting the pain the loss of his family caused. With us there, he did his best to maintain his saving routine. When there was baseball we watched. When there was not, we read. When these options turned oppressive, we went bowling.

Dad was no bowler, no athlete of any kind. Still we bowled, game after game after game. Over one three-day period, during a hiatus between the doctor visits and Mets appearances, we rolled twenty-four lines, two for every year of my life. Erich sat in the scorekeeper's seat, and Dad and I leaned over him to tally the points.

We were fairly evenly matched. We rarely broke 120 or fell below 95. Dad bowled like an astrophysicist, factoring arc, speed, and spin, plotting distant objects perceived through his single lens, setting into motion actions that would trip numerous reactions over the course of time and space. I just threw. I tried not to care how I did. I tried not to excel. Neither his method nor mine led to any significant improvement. Still, we'd congratulate ourselves on our prowess, brandishing our blistered thumbs and babying our achy shoulders with barely concealed pride.

Sundays were divorced fathers' days at the lanes. Almost every alley mirrored our configuration: forty-something dads with a boy or two or several children of different sexes, one flinging herself onto the lane, another rejecting all advances to join in, a third weighing the momentousness of each shot as if a strike on a red pin would reunite Mommy and Dad. We Hofmann boys, though, were above such fantasies. We took our bowling straight, with a certain academic interest.

Meanwhile, I spied on Erich as if he were practicing magic tricks in a corner. How does he turn that scarf into a cane? Where'd the rabbit go? What finale is he planning for this dime-store legerdemain? I wanted to believe it was all a ruse, a series of disguises he cast on and off when Dad and I weren't looking. And so I'd sneak peaks, trying to catch him at it.

I had spied on Erich before, when he was working on the "Ballad," but now I was less concerned with his behavior than his state of mind. I tried to imagine myself into his head. I washed my hands and let them speak (he had by this time stopped doing it, though he'd acquired other ticlike gestures). I filled my mind with turbulence one minute, still blue water the next. I paged through a book on van Gogh when no one was around and searched for clues in the swirl of colors and the glare of the sun. I pretended that my father mooned over me as he did over my brother; made believe my mother reached for my hand on long night strolls along the ocean. I acted at Erich in the mirror. I dreamed into him at night. I mumbled his name under my breath like a guilty mantra. I'd brush against his arm or touch his shoulder to let him rush through me, vibrate in my veins, osmose. In the end I couldn't tell whether Erich was experiencing excitement, serenity, or driving pain.

I must have believed that his illness would kill him, because I prayed to take his place. During the day, when Dad took Erich to the doctor, I'd crawl under the desk in the living room, out of sight from my father's books and paintings. I'd whisper, hands pressed together like those of little praying boys in pictures. "Let me come to you God. Leave Erich here. Kill me instead. Take me instead."

Each night at seven Mom called collect. Dad let me answer the phone and eavesdropped from his chair while I recounted the day's bowling scores and tried to answer her questions about Erich. The intimacy of the phone was intense for me, my mother speaking into my ear, directly into my head. I'm not sure I'd ever spoken to her on the phone before; I'd never been anywhere away. She was, for a few minutes every night, mine. She'd fill my head with details from her days and I'd listen carefully. "Great," I'd say. And "Oh, Mom, that sounds perfect."

She had begun singing nights in a hotel lounge, and she listed her numbers for me. She'd recite her patter on the phone and even ask my opinion, describing the effect she was going for. She recounted lunch meetings with people who'd offered help to start her shop. Everything would happen as planned, she told me. I was never less than positive. Then Dad would retreat to the bedroom, close the door, pick up the phone, and talk facts, prognoses. Meanwhile, I'd replay my conversation with her, her voice still buzzing through me. When Dad came out into the living room, his eyes and nostrils would be red.

We stopped bowling and started waiting in earnest. Erich turned from passive to unpredictable. One midnight I went into the kitchen and found him curled up like a cat in front of the oven. The door was open and the gas on, though it had only been a few minutes since I'd heard him climb off the couch. I can't say why I did what I did, except that I wanted so badly to be near him again. Instead of turning off the gas, I lay down behind him, tucked up like a fetal twin. The gas had a sweet, appealing smell. The moonlight came in the window next to the refrigerator and fell across Erich's face and arm. I could see a glinting in his hair.

Dad, awake as always, came out a moment later to investigate. He flicked the light on, switched the gas off, closed the oven, and slid the window up. He shut off the gas at the source. He walked us back to the living room and covered us up. He opened more windows and sat in his desk chair, wearing a quilted robe, even though it was summer, drinking something he poured from a bottle, guarding us through the night.

After that he dogged us. He never left Erich alone. He slept on the floor next to us, pouring his Dewars over rocks in the dark, a scoutmaster on a perverse overnight. He couldn't control everything, though. When Erich suddenly slammed his head against the side of the bathtub, Dad, kneeling beside him, could only hug his wet body until it went slack. Afterward, he cleaned up the blood. When, on our way to a doctor in the city, Erich stepped into traffic on upper Broadway, Dad did all he could to block the cars braking around him. Erich ranted from the middle of the street, "Wannamerdafolla! BeepBeep!" and Dad pursued him in a twitchy dance: one hand out stop, one up to his forehead, other hand out, other up. "Stop!" Dad cried. "Stop! Stop! Stop!"

Safe on the other side, it was Dad who vomited into the gutter. I thought I saw Erich's consoling hand touch the small of Dad's heaving back.

I started to cry. "He's *doing* this! He's *doing* this! Stop *doing* this!" I shouted. But Erich just stood there, blank and mute. Dad straightened up, wiping his face with a handkerchief. He put a hand on each of our upper arms and steered us into a nearby lobby.

That night was the last.

Dad spoke to Erich and I together. He split his focus between us, as if we were both equally present. He measured his words. All very formal. We would be traveling down to Washington by train. (My father still didn't drive.) Erich would be going into the hospital for observation. He would have to stay there a little while for tests. Dad and I'd be in D.C. the whole time. We'd be staying with his friend Mac, and so be close by if Erich needed us. The doctors there were the best. Erich's doctor, Dr. Rosenberg, had gone to school with several of them and had spoken to his colleagues about Erich.

"They are looking forward to meeting you," he said. "There are closer hospitals, sure, but none so good. And St. E's is federal," he added, as if that clinched it.

He went on: "Some very important people have stayed at St. Elizabeths. That's where Ezra Pound lived after the war, and everybody came to visit him: e. e. cummings, Eliot, Auden, Archibald MacLeish, Robert Lowell. William Carlos Williams came down from Patterson. Robert Frost." Dad failed to mention that one of Frost's sons had, like Erich, gone schizophrenic and, later, killed himself.

"Very important people. Scholars, poets, journalists. I even visited him, would you believe it. Yes, a friend of mine who knew him took me — a classicist. I met the great man, the great, mad, hateful genius. Didn't say much. You know how damned shy I get around strangers. I do remember noticing how beautiful the lawns were.

You can see the Capitol. I seem to recall they have tennis courts, too. Maybe we'll learn to play."

Our father continued, singsong, until St. E's seemed a cross of fairy-tale kingdom, college campus, and literary salon. Then, he said, "If it looks like we have to stay for more than a short time, Mommy and Deborah will fly in to join us and we'll all be together."

My brother looked so droopy then, so dishrag. My father's loving, living eye rested gently on him. And he just sat. Nothing could reach him. Nothing could hurt him. He hoarded up his quiet secret, the sadness he shared with my mother. Wherever we're going, I thought, he's already gone.

9

ERICH'S BODY

On the train to D.C., Dad tried to joke with Erich (at Erich) that a good, short stay at St. E's would be like starting college. I didn't want him to feel bad, so I laughed along. Soon he shut up altogether.

Erich was already shut up. Dad had been dosing him with the "big drugs" since he'd started getting wilder. Dad periodically threw various capsules into the back of Erich's throat and tipped glasses of water to his lips as a wash-down. Erich swallowed automatically, letting liquid overflow from the corners of his mouth. I watched, trying to adopt my most blasé, seen-it-all-before attitude.

Dad cracked a book, but didn't turn its pages. I looked out the window. I made note of the crumbled and abandoned warehouses all along the rail line from Newark to D.C. From a train, America looks like a ruin, the promise of twentieth-century industrialization gone to rubble. Tourists traveling this way must think we all live like rats or junkies, that both sides of the tracks are the wrong side, that we send messages not in bottles but through spray-paint scrawl on rusted viaducts: Razz 69. Massive colorful names spread out across the sides of buildings, giving the impression of living large, no matter how specklike the life really is. I wrote a name on the window with breath and my index finger: Erich Erich Erich.

St. Elizabeths was nothing like a college. No tweed-suited literati smoked on the lawns. There was, from the front of the building, no evidence of the lounge chairs Pound had found so comfortable. "One has to go nuts before you have the sense to buy proper chairs," he'd quipped. There were just big ugly buildings, shaded by trees.

The central administration building could have housed any bureau-cracy, though its single tower gave it an ominous look. All in all, the asylum looked liked one, but for a single touch of whimsy. Attached to the tower were three tiers of iron balconies, fronting bay win-dows, the kind French political leaders wave from. These were the only niceties, though, unless you count that the road up to the hos-pital curved or that there were pleasant little benches scattered along that road.

The benches were as far as I got. I was too young to visit, or at least that's what Dad told me. So, from the first day, while Erich was checked in and over, I waited outside, moving from bench to gate to curb in the swamp heat of Washington in summer, squinting over toward the top of the Capitol. We were staying with my father's best friend, Mac, who every morning packed me provisions and then walked us to the bus. I always had a book, but no patience for it, and a sandwich, but no stomach. When we returned to Mac's, I'd hand them back, sweatier but otherwise inviolate.

Each day, for almost two weeks, Dad and I would be back in our places: an hour over on the bus from Northwest, two visitor hours with Dad inside Cedar Hall and me out in front of the central admin-istration building, lying on a bench, then an hour ride back to Mac's.

As we rode, I would try to keep conversation alive, to draw Dad's attention from the blur beyond the window. "What did you do in the war?" I asked.

"Which war?" he asked back without looking.

"The world war. You know, the Hitler one."

"The Hitler one." Dad seemed to notice me for the first time. "World War II. I was a student at Columbia, then I finished being a student and worked on my dissertation. The book I gave you about the Confederacy. Remember?"

"About the Van Dorn guy?"

"No, not about him — Van Doren — he was my advisor, Mark Van Doren. I dedicated the book to him. Did you read past the dedication?"

"Oh, yeah, yeah. It was about a Civil War guy."

"Right. A southern senator."

"So why do you call Mac your army buddy?"

"It's just a private joke," he explained. "Since neither of us went."

"Why didn't you go?"

"Well, for one reason, my eye."

"Oh, yeah. Why didn't Mac go?" I asked, determined to keep the ball in the air.

"You know, I don't remember. Something about his feet maybe?"

"'Cause he's so tall?"

"I really don't know."

"He is tall."

"Long drink of water."

"Except when he hunches over to talk to everybody. Like he's walking through a door. A real low one."

"Alice." Dad offered.

"Yeah, in the rabbit hole. And how his paintings and sculptures and stuff are so tiny."

"Or maybe," Dad said, "he was too intelligent."

"You mean they keep you out of the army if you're smart?"

"Not really." Dad took advantage of my confusion to look away.

"Was he working on his dissertation when you met him?" I asked.

"No. He was painting. He was sitting on the steps of the library, painting girls, making them look like Picasso paintings."

"How weird. You know I never understand anything you guys say to each other."

Dad chuckled, pleased.

"Dad? Why do you always write about wars you weren't in?"

His smile melted. He couldn't locate an answer.

"I'm gonna write about Vietnam," I announced.

"You do that," he said. "You do that."

On the twelfth day, we waited for what seemed like forever for our bus. We traveled back to Mac's without talking. When Dad and I finally got across town, Mac was waiting for us at the bus stop. He flicked his head from side to side as if working out kinks. We headed toward the apartment, no one saying anything. When we passed a neighborhood convenience store, Mac pulled out a five-dollar bill. "Hey pal," he said. "We need milk for dinner. Be a sport?" He tucked the money into my palm and gave me a wise-guy little kick in the butt with his lanky leg. "Oh, and potato chips for dessert," he called to my back.

I could see Dad and Mac through the store door. They were both looking down, Dad at the ground and Mac at the top of Dad's head. Mac kept tugging his ear. I could see his lips moving. He and my father had this way of murmuring together, intense and coded. I could never make out what they were saying even when I could hear them. My father's mouth was obscured by a sign across the glass of the door. I remember it was a Kent cigarette sign, because I had two Clark Bars in my hand. I took the sign as an omen, a reason to stick the candy into my pocket, thinking, "Clark Kent." My brother had just died and no one was going to punish me for swiping a couple of nickel Clark Bars. If they accused me, I'd just run. If they shot me in the back, so what? "Clark Kent," I said to myself, "Man of Steal."

I knew Erich was dead. Nobody needed to tell me. I just lingered in the store, walking up and down the aisles clutching a big bag of Ruffles and a *Life* magazine with pictures of earth taken from the moon. I paid and crammed the change into the pocket without the candy bars and joined them on the sidewalk. Dad looked away from me, as if checking out the cloud cover. Mac played a two-finger drum roll on the crown of my head, saying, "We're off." Neither of them noticed, nor mentioned if they did, that I'd forgotten the milk. Mac blushed when I handed him the change. In the apartment lobby, he asked me if I wanted to go for a walk. Dad went upstairs with the magazine and the chips.

Mac loped along beside me. He reached his arm around my shoulder, curving his long spine to do so. "There's a famous story about your father," he said in a tone that let me know it was OK to laugh. "One day, back in school, we'd been walking across campus — he was off to class — and your dad stumbled and fell. He banged himself up pretty good, pants knee ripped a little, palms and forehead scraped. Some blood. He got up all distracted, real serious. He said he was all right and went on his way. I think it was Trilling's seminar."

I blinked in nonrecognition.

"That doesn't matter. He was a teacher. Anyway, that afternoon I saw Willy again. He was in a state. He hadn't been able to focus in class, he said. He was too distressed, couldn't think of anything but his fall. He remembered falling and standing up. It didn't hurt so bad. But he couldn't remember the angle at which he'd fallen. He had to know the angle. 'Forty-five degrees,' I told him. I thought it was forty-five degrees. And he looked at me — your dad looked at me with such relief and nodded his head, repeating, 'Forty-five degrees. Yes, I think that's it.' And then he was fine."

We ate dinner that night with the ballgame soundless on TV, and Dad tucked me in early. I could still see the faint blue sky out the window at the foot of Mac's couch. Dad reeked of scotch and ciga-rette smoke. He told me he loved me and my brother both. We were the greatest kids he ever knew, could ever have hoped for. "You are sweet, intelligent boys and I hope nothing sad ever happens to you. Ever ever. And I'm sorry if it does. So-o-o sorry, because it's all my fault and you can blame me. You can always blame me, don't ever ever forget that." And he bent down to kiss me, even as he wiped his eyes and nose with a folded handkerchief.

I could hear their voices from the kitchen, throughout the night. I knew they were standing, since there was no place to sit. Dad's voice, usually so lulling, was wild as water slopping over the sides of a pail. "Fugging doc say dish never happened to ush before like I'm guh blieve that, like it hammoned to *them!* No, no, I'm flattered my son's the only one special enough you let him walk into the shower stall carrying a fuggin' sheet! Whu? They gi'm a fuggin' hall pass? Juz got away, fuggin' quack sez."

". . . art kid . . ." was all I could make of Mac's reply.

"Damn fuggin' right, smart kid. Wun'ful kid. Never happened to ush before! Never happened to him either! Beautiful kid. Wily and in'resting. You han't seen him lately but even crazy was sharper'n

those dil'tantes I teach. Oh — and I shouln't worry — din't do dam-
age to the fuggin' shower! I'm worried I'm worried!"

". . . go tomorrow . . ."

"After bloody autopsy after bloody mortician. Sez's best to let
pro-fess-ion-alls clean'm up a little like he's a fuggin' oil spill."

". . . easy . . ."

"Cunt! Zer fault. Did zish do him —"

". . . love her . . ."

"Fugno, z'my fault, z'all my godammm fall . . ."

"Shhh," it sounded like Mac said, "ache the boy."

Mom and Deborah arrived at Dulles Airport the next afternoon.
We picked them up in Mac's car. Everyone was polite. Mom was
sedate and adult. She kissed me in a public way, as if my being away
had been the only thing on her mind. She said, "Hello, Willy," and
kissed Mac, saying, "Peter MacKinsey, my old flame."

Something awkward passed between Dad and Deborah, maybe a
kiss, but I caught only the end of their clunky two-step. The adults
headed for the parking lot, and Deborah towed me behind. Even
though she'd missed everything that had happened to Erich, suddenly
she was in charge, my protector. I let her get away with it. Ahead, Dad
rehashed for Mom the details of the past day in a low rumble.

We stopped by the apartment long enough to drop off Mom and
Deborah's bags. Mom commented on some of Mac's paintings, a
lineup of Modernist masterworks redone in miniature: Braques,
Mondrians, Delauneys, and recent Rothkos six inches square, all in
oils, colors dead on. "Why you old copycat, you," she said.

Then we went to view the body, the pale serene pillow that was
my dead brother. Mom wouldn't go in. "I think not," she said, sitting upright in the car with her purse in her lap.

Erich was laid out in a small funeral-parlor chapel that resembled
a hotel conference room. He was wearing a light green, short-
sleeved shirt, so his white elbows and forearms seemed to float by
themselves. I had never seen a dead body, never felt how cold it
could be. Now he will open his eyes and sit up, I kept thinking. Mac
blinked and blinked and dabbed at his eyes. The three of us just sort

of stared around, trying to look at Erich, then trying not to. I was clutching a tape of *Abbey Road* I'd brought along in case they had an eight-track deck.

When everyone headed for the door, I tried to linger behind. Dad blocked my way, not forbiddingly, but as if he were the usher who would guide me out and then pull fast the door after. "I just want to say good-bye again," I said.

He watched me from the door while I crossed back to the narrow end of the room where Erich was arranged for his final levitation. I peered down over him.

"Adios, amigo," I whispered, as if I did this everyday. "R.I.P." I said, adding, "van Winkle," before turning for the door.

The night of the wake we held a nearly silent dinner at a steak and seafood restaurant. Then we went back to Mac's so they could plan the funeral. Deborah and I, meanwhile, took turns calling Chicago, Wisconsin, California, New Jersey, Mexico, and Florida, in accordance with separate lists our parents made up. "I'm just calling to let you know that my brother Erich died," one of us would say, as if reading off a cue card to stunned second cousins, teachers, or family friends on the wire. "No, she (he) can't come to the phone right now," was our second scripted line.

We were still on the bedroom phone when we heard Mom and Dad boil over. They'd been drinking all evening and were by now in a fierce stew. They were talking about Erich's body.

Mom wanted him buried in California, or, at least, for his ashes to be scattered in the Pacific. Dad wanted him "home" in Jersey. Mac, who'd known our mother for a long time, and whom she'd always respected, did his best to stay neutral.

For only the second time I remember — the first being his refusal to keep money coming to us in Mexico — Dad dug in. "I'm never going to go to California," he was saying when Deborah and I came out of the bedroom to see why they were shouting. "You know that. And I want a place where I can go, where I can be with him."

"We've settled there," Mom said. "He loves it by the ocean."

Dad took his glass to the porta-bar on the opposite wall. He dropped in a pair of ice cubes and poured it half full of whiskey. Then, setting the lid on the silver ice bowl, he spun it slowly, watching the embossed penguins dance in a circle. "Look," he said softly, as if to the spinning penguins, "You can use *my* ashes for compost if you want — spread them on your frigging Cheerios if it makes you happy — but I'm not going to let you fling that boy's remains off a pier somewhere."

"You're so pathetic, Willy. You still think this is about you and me."

"No," Dad kept on. "Erich goes home with me. For the last time. Where he should have been all along."

Only then did they notice Deborah and me.

"Please kids," Dad said. "Go back into the bedroom."

We hesitated in the hallway for a second. Deborah, in a rather stagy show of defiance, crossed the room and rested her hand on Mom's shoulder. I hung back, present but barely visible to them, a third-world country.

"What about Chicago?" Mac asked, leaning against a bookcase, twitching slightly. "There's family there. It's a midway point of sorts."

In retrospect I realize that Mac's day job, teaching writing and literacy to convicts in Lorton prison, must have prepared him for this encounter by honing his diplomatic skills. He had an unusual capacity for mediating between the dangers of individuals in rebellion and the world's need for civility. This time, though, Dad would have none of it. "Butt out," he snapped, raising his glass as if to heave it. The willowy Mac ducked, but Dad just drained his drink. "Duck duck goose," he said, flashing a dark smile at his chum.

He poured himself another drink. Everyone listened to the rush of liquid.

"Sure," Mom said to Mac. "Why not Chicago?"

"Right. With Doris and Val and how long?" Dad grumbled. "They already spend half of every year in Florida. It's just a matter of time before they move there for good, or die themselves."

"Daddy!" Deborah exclaimed, a shocked little girl in spite of herself.

But he went on: "I don't want that woman guarding my son's

grave. I don't want to run into her at the cemetery or anywhere else. She wouldn't even admit he was sick."

"You don't know anything about it . . ." Mom said without explaining what "it" was.

"And why isn't she here, I ask you? What's her excuse?"

"Oh, shut up, Willy . . ."

"Why? Just give me a simple answer."

Deborah cut in: "Papa can't travel just now."

"Now who could have told you that, Deborah?" Dad asked turning to her. "Did your mother tell you that, dear? How strange that he can fly back and forth to Florida twice a year, but they can't make it to our nation's capital for a really bad time."

"Shut up, Willy," Mom warned.

"Maybe," he continued, addressing Deborah, "you should ask your Mom if she's even told the Oomie bird what happened . . ."

"Willy . . ."

"You see, I doubt very much if your mother has even made that particular call just yet. Have you, Lorna?"

Mom looked scared, trapped.

"When are you planning to tell her, Mom?" Dad sneered.

There was a huge, evil silence.

Mac passed dangerously close to Dad, plucked a wine bottle out of a cooler and freshened Mom's drink. She stared at it.

"My mother didn't kill him . . ." she finally murmured, leaving her thought unfinished.

"I won't bury him in goddamned Chicago," Dad said. "I hate the Midwest."

"Oh, fuck you, Willy!" Mom screamed. "You'll never move, you'll never fucking move. He won't move, Mac, he never has. We should all just give up, isn't that right. Willy. Nobody should *want* anything, nobody should *feel* anything. Just tamp it all down, nothing changes. Well, I change, and I want things. And I won't go back in the bottle!"

Dad seethed. "I'm not talking about you. I'm talking about my son's body."

"You can't have him. You'll never have him!"

"I never did have him!"

"That's right, you never did."

"If I so much as talked to him alone, you went hysterical! She burned holes in my shirts, Mac! I took him out for a walk one night and when I came back, she was sticking cigarettes through my shirts. . . ."

"He was mine — he felt what I felt . . ."

"And now you're off playing Jackie fucking Kennedy —"

"He *felt* things, Willy. And with half a chance you lock us up and throw away the key —"

"— sitting out in the car in a new goddamn hat while your children cry over their dead brother's body!"

Deborah was weeping convulsively without sound. Mac's fidgety hand was jumping from ear to nose to pant leg. Someone upstairs banged on the floor with a chair.

"Shut yourselves the fuck up!" Dad shouted at the ceiling, straining his throat, the dead eye wild.

More banging. Soon Dad, Mom, and Deborah were all craning toward the ceiling, screaming back at the tops of their lungs. Mac reached over to the stereo and popped it on, twisting the volume dial up. *Pictures at an Exhibition* blasted out. Everyone startled to silence. Dad covered his ears. The banging ceased. Mac bumped the sound off.

The silence felt as shrieking as the music had. Mac surveyed the room, peering over his glasses, but no one would meet his eyes. He made little calisthenic circles in the air with one thumb. Then he said a strange thing: "Why not share the ashes?"

They all looked at him.

"Yes," he continued, "why not have Erich cremated and placed in a beautiful urn, something really beautiful — I'll make one myself, if you want. And take turns. A year or half-year with one of you, then the other?

Mom and Dad eyed each other. They both knew what Mac was doing. We all knew that his beautiful urn would be one more treasure they couldn't share. He might as well have said to a room of Palestinians and Jews, "Jerusalem? Just take turns."

"We'll split them," Mom said. "Two urns. Two sets of ashes."

The pause that followed said this had gone too far. Tearing Erich's body to pieces? Already been done.

Mac's suggestion that Erich be buried in the place he'd died was met with the slightest of nods from both my parents. All that was left, then, was to find a plot and set the time. They'd give him up to D.C. the noncity where neither of them lived, lay him in a grave they'd never visit.

They settled down to details. I retreated farther into the hall. I laid down on my back, closed my eyes, and folded my arms across my chest. I felt the low tones of their planning in the living room, but heard nothing else. All sound seemed to come from without me, nothing from within. I was hollow, a bowl, a shell, the cove of an ear. I pictured Erich carrying rocks across Venice Beach, up streets and down.

There was a knock on the door, the super come to investigate a complaint. On his way to answer it, Mac nearly stumbled over me. He squatted down, put his large palm over my forehead. "Hey, pal. How you doing?" he whispered.

I didn't respond. "Hey." I kept my eyes closed. He smoothed my hair back. "Mr. Possum," he said quietly.

I lay there, not speaking or moving as he stood and stepped over me toward the door. I was trying to leave my body.

It rained throughout the next day. We passed it numbly, taking care of business. Mac took Mom and Deborah to pick out a coffin. He took Dad and me to scout gravesites. Mom and Deborah bought clothes and went to church. Dad kept me by him all day. He studied me without appearing to. The night before, he had suggested that we check into a hotel, but Mom said, "No, that won't be necessary." And Mac said, "That's right. You should all be together, hard as it is."

Late the following morning, our final one in D.C., we all stood around a grave in the northeast part of the District, wedged between Rock Creek Park and what Dad said was a ghetto. We watched a cherrywood box get lowered into the earth. We were joined by cemetery workers, the Lorton Penitentiary chaplain, and one of my mother's suitors, Larry, whom we'd called in Miami that first night. He met us at the gravesite, with a calla lily for Mom and one for Deborah. He shook hands with the men and mumbled, "Sorry." When he reached me, he patted my shoulder and, inexplicably, passed me a plastic bag containing a new shirt — Yves Saint Laurent — dress white. "Just a little something . . ." he said. During the service, he stood apart, behind Lorna, close by a tree.

The day was gray and humid. Everything was muddy from the rain. It caked our shoes and the cuffs of our pants. The ground squooshed and farted as we walked over it. Our dress clothes stuck to our skin. My tie (which Mom had bought the day before) felt too tight around my neck. The cemetery director carried umbrellas we never used. I passed my new shirt back to Larry to hold, its plastic wrapping by then smeared brown from my having dropped it.

In my head, I arranged shots for a movie I was both making and in. He would have wanted this on film: "The Ballad of Erich," closing scene. Roll credits. Or he might have said, "No way a funeral. Too obvious. Cut away to the Indy 500 or Jacques Cousteau or something. You've got to avoid cliché."

The chaplain talked about unfulfilled promise. My mother sang "Love Walked In," which she said was the last song George Gershwin wrote before his own early death. Dad had written something out to read, but when it came his turn, he just stood there. The cemetery director reached down for a handful of earth and sprinkled it onto the coffin. We followed his lead, all stepping forward, dropping little mud balls on Erich's box. Mom tossed her flower in. Deborah did the same. One of the cemetery staff handed us towels to wipe up the dirt, but it already covered our hands and wrists and ran in lines on our cheeks, where we'd swiped at tears.

The whole proceeding felt like a vague afterthought. When our ceremonial grieving was done, we walked away, pulling our feet up, out of the sucky ground.

Deborah and I kissed Dad and Mac and climbed into the back seat of Larry's rented car. Mother walked over to both men, offering each her cheek. Mac and Larry loaded our bags into the trunk while my parents exchanged a few words.

When Mom got in on the passenger side, next to Larry, she removed her hatpin and her pretty black hat, and turned her slightly puffy face toward the grave. We pulled slowly away, leaving two figures, one tall and stooping, one small and erect, standing by an old Volvo, watching us go.

Songs are like tattoos . . .
— Joni Mitchell

10

How We Knew

Whether my grandmother ever knew what happened to Erich, I can't say for certain. I'd guess she was never told. Being uninformed is, of course, different from being unknowing. She'd seen his mad implosion on the day we retrieved him from camp. She'd watched Dad pack Erich and me into a taxi to remove us east. We were with her for two weeks after the funeral; Erich was not. She saw that, too. "Don't trouble trouble," my mother had once said of her. "Just rake everyone else over the coals and close your ears, so you can't hear 'em scream." Oomie could call me Erich without flinching.

Papa, I suspect, was told. Everybody told Papa everything. He always seemed to understand, and he couldn't contradict, which made him the perfect repository for confidences. He had to know. He was visibly shaken. His good hand rubbed his beardless mouth as his head shook a slow no no no. He brooded on the wrongness of it. His eyes maintained a dark, puzzled look. His same words — "Doo doo doo" — spiraled down in meaning: "How did this happen?" "He was so young." "What have we done?" "What kind of God allows this?" "What kind of universe am I condemned to?" "Doo doo doo. Doo doo doo." He knew.

Papa watched me and I watched him watch me. His were the eyes in the picture that seem to follow you across the room. "Erich, not-Erich. Erich, not-Erich." At least it was an acknowledgment, his watchfulness.

Everyone else just blabbed. It's the native tongue of Skokie, Blab, words emptied of meaning, pronounced through a cinched-up smile. Deborah was fluent. She wouldn't stop talking to breathe. "Oh, Papa, there's Mr. Roiter getting into his new car. I don't think the mail's come yet; maybe we can get it when we come back from our walk. I see they've been fixing up the pavement here — very nice. Do you want to stop by the field and watch ball practice? It's not raining yet. They'll probably be out there, don't you think?"

And a chorus of neighbors would chime in: "Hey, Val, old boy, who's that young gal on your arm? You better watch it or I'll call Doris on you!" Everybody had words for us. Nobody had anything to say.

Papa didn't need words. He walked with a clop, slide, and chank. One leg — one-half of his body — was in fine shape. When he stepped with the good leg his polished wing tip would make a clop against the ground, as if planting itself for balance. Then he'd slide the paralyzed leg forward, set his cane (whose rubber tip kept it nearly silent), and place the other foot, the heel of which made a wooden sound at the very moment his leg brace (metal supports with leather and Velcro straps) chanked like a retarded sleigh bell. Ordinarily, he push-pulled his half-dead body in this manner with great enthusiasm and pride, especially when he was accompanied by us kids. Now, though, the step dragged, the slide scraped, and the chank sounded doleful. His walk lost its unity and threatened to break down into its constituent parts, to lose its forward momentum, its lift.

He was fighting with the earth, and he, this once vigorous Italian with permanently jet black hair, wanted to give up the fight. I could hear it in his walk.

When we weren't walking, we were eating. For two weeks Oomie served what was, in essence, one continuous meal, with intervals. We ate family-style — minus one son and one father — at the dining room table under a yellow wicker-webbed lamp shade and the shifty eyes and swinging tail of a black, rhinestone-studded cat clock. We took turns cutting my grandfather's food. We reached for seconds and thirds. My mother called me Erich. My grandmother called me Erich. Deborah blabbed, avoiding names altogether. Papa watched.

In the privacy of my head, I spoke to my dead brother. I stuck to the quotidian: "I wish Oomie'd sit down. She makes me nuts. I'm going to cut Papa's lasagna for him. Sure he can cut it with one hand, but you know how fastidious he is. He likes bite-sized pieces and hates to get anything on his bib. I'm wearing my napkin like a bib too. I look like a mental patient." "No offense," I added, inwardly. I listened for the reply that never came: "Bibbity bobbity boo." I kept up this thought-speech stream to Erich, who was now me and not me.

Denial is said to be an early stage of mourning. For my grandmother, this was surely the case. She wouldn't admit that anything had changed, a nonadmission that manifested itself as not noticing. She refused to count — there were three of us now instead of four — refused to acknowledge events or to register the vibration his name made in space when she spoke it. My mother, on the other hand, seemed eerily accepting of our loss, as if she had known it would happen before it did. As if — I came to think — she truly believed that Erich had not died and that I was him.

Maybe "denial of death" is really denial of grief. We'd cried quietly over Erich's grave. But once we'd buried him, there were no torrents of grief, that body wracking you see onstage or on the nightly news: the lurching processionals, mothers wailing over dead children in the street, Electra's relentless keening, the tearing of hair. If that is grief, we denied it entry into our house. If that is only one form of grief, if silence and drift are another, we were pros.

No one said anything about our family dividing, though clearly this was the beginning of the end of us as a numerical whole. First, we'd been seven together (five plus two). The five became four when we left Dad, then three when Erich died. The two would age and die, first Papa, then Oomie. Mom would also die, even before her mother, and Deborah and I would be left as two. I'm calculating ahead, though.

At the moment, I was concentrating on inner division. I was one boy in body and another in name. Who might be whom and which of these constituted the "I"? Feeling my way through this split occupied my energies. I knew that physically I remained unaltered. Age twelve; weight ninety-eight; eyes and hair brown. In my mother's eyes, however, I'd been transformed, from a blot on her fair life to an object of some fascination. She stared at me now with a kind of burning "Yes!" that made my chest rise. Simultaneously, I shrank a little, the shrinking that attends any whopping, fantastic lie. I am a prince! dreams the frog, choking back the taste of bug on his tongue.

I wanted to hollow myself out, so Erich's spirit could fill me. I was a willing vessel, but my mind was still mine. I could script Erich's responses to any situation. I could picture his gestures and routines, but I couldn't suddenly change my behavior to ape his. Ultimately, I had to accept this division, the way an actor does. People would see the boy they always saw, unless, like my mother, they entered the scene with me. In that case, we would, by means of mutual imagination, suspend our disbelief. Otherwise, I would move through life in the same old ways, knowing that a different essential something moved inside me — his essential something, which was now mine. "Erich," my name, named that thing, not the outward illusion of my body.

"People see what they want to see, anyway," I told myself.

"I see the real you," said my mother's eyes. "Erich."

11

LIFE IN VENICE

The transition back was strangely easy. My mother stayed home. Her departures and visitations would come later, after Deborah, too, was gone. We set up household routines, made plans for the future, as if we believed in it, and acclimated ourselves to being citizens of the place we now lived and where we now prepared to dig in for the long haul. We moved from our month-to-month apartment near the boardwalk to a small three-bedroom bungalow about seven blocks from the water. We each decorated our own quarters and filled the common space with Mom's collectibles from Mexico. Dad shipped us some of our old things from Maplewood, as he was also planning a move, from the house in the suburbs to an apartment near Columbia.

Our new home mixed early sixties suburban, Mexican crafts, and Woodstock chic. Lorna pasted red bamboo wallpaper everywhere. Doorless arches were hung with green glass-bead portieres. Large primary-colored throw pillows littered the floor. Our old coffee table (shaped like a painter's palette) was crowded with knickknacks from the rec room in Jersey, the kitsch my mother used to load up on to aggravate Dad: golf coasters, cocktail napkins with sex jokes, turquoise ashtrays, crocheted-poodle Kleenex holders, a wooden hula dancer with a grass skirt and Christmas lights for breasts. This postwar paraphernalia mingled moronically with maracas, grotesque animal masks, spectacular baskets, and other whatnots from south of the border.

My room — the first one I didn't share with Erich — stayed nearly bare, until, gradually, I unrolled and hung my brother's

posters of Kubrick's *2001*, the Royal Shakespeare Company's pro-
ductions of *Two Gentlemen of Verona* and *Richard II*, and the movie
version of *20,000 Leagues Under the Sea*. The theme was twos, and
Erich elaborated on it by including an eleven-by-seventeen picture
of NASA's Gemini 4 spacecraft. He had one other wall hanging that
didn't conform with the rest: a large profile of Bobby Kennedy, now
also dead, dreaming of things that never were and asking why not.
Beyond those, my "pad" consisted of a Wild West–style bureau and
a pair of single beds with Indian print spreads. I possessed a hundred
or so albums, many predating our years in Mexico, and a three-
in-one turntable, receiver, and eight-track player, walled in by stacks
of tapes: The Doors (our local celebs), The Byrds, The Fifth
Dimension, Jefferson Airplane, Buffalo Springfield, Frank Zappa
and the Mothers of Invention, and, most coveted, Joni Mitchell.

Before I went to sleep at night I slid shut the closet doors. Even
so, I pictured my brother hanging in there by his neck among my
clothes.

I enrolled for eighth grade at the Venice Free School, the only
school in town unbothered by my two years on the road, away from
formal education. I tested at high-school levels in language skills and
math, so they let me slide, even without sixth- and seventh-grade
transcripts. Besides, VFS had long disposed of a grading system, in
favor of written comments and "talk-backs" with teachers. I was
prime material.

Deborah opted for public high school, which meant she'd had to
submit to a more extensive battery of placement exams. She would
be turning sixteen in December and was let in, on schedule, as a
sophomore, with the condition that she make up required classes
during summers. These requirements would be left incomplete by
Deborah's virtual withdrawal from school in spring and her complete withdrawal that summer.

Mom went to work, singing nights in the lounges of hotels, rack-
ing up promises for capital toward her own store by day. The space
she'd discovered in Santa Monica hadn't panned out, just as a half-
dozen other locations wouldn't. She practiced her music, taking les-

sons, rehearsing with a pianist, writing her own patter. Her repertoire was going through a shaky change. To her usual selection of
standards and show tunes she was adding folk ballads, written or
popularized by the likes of Judy Collins, Mary Travers, and Joan
Baez. The switch wasn't very successful, however. Her voice handled
the new material, but, as a performer, she was a little too "out there"
to get into the soulful, introspective "groove." She had, I sensed,
missed her moment.

So, for a time we were normal-ish. We ate meals together, did
schoolwork, had a mother with a job, lived in rooms with doors to
slam, and cashed regular checks from Dad to pay the bills. Deborah
and I would get up at the same time each morning, bicker over the
bathroom, snipe across the breakfast table, and then make sure (as if
by silent pact) that one of us headed off for school earlier or lingered
longer, so that we wouldn't have to walk together.

I took to wearing, as a badge of my individuality, an old fedora
Papa Val had given me. Everyone at school had some such badge
over the standard issue of patched jeans, work shirt or embossed T-
shirt, army jacket, Adidases or sandals. Some distinguished themselves with bandannas around their heads or thighs, or keys hanging
off their belts. Others brandished campaignlike buttons with no
writing on them, medallions, military bars, or Mexican beads.
People called me Erich and Erich I was, except at bedtime when I'd
hold whispered conversations with the brother in the closet.

I quickly fell into friendships that would last through high
school. One kid, Soapy (whose real name was Larry), had originally
gone by "Soupy," after his television idol. He modified his name, as
he explained upon introducing himself to me, when he heard the
shaggy-dog story whose punch line is "No soap, radio." Soapy
loved everything pointless and obnoxious and was the self-anointed
leader of the "Ob Squad" — obscene, obnoxious, and obviously
obstreperous.

"What's the Ob Squad do?" I asked him when he offered to let
me join.

"Mock waitresses, mostly."

Soapy never asked me about my brother. He took it upon himself, though, to point out the "worthwhile types" at school, including a girl named Holly, who I'd spend much of tenth grade trying to talk out of killing herself.

"She's a lesbian," he explained, "for now. Last year she used to drop Quaaludes and sleep with basketball players from the real school. I told her to stop it, but she's obsessive, whatever."

When Holly noticed us looking her way, Soapy yelled out: "We're all xenophobic lesbians!"

"Fuck you, Dobrow," she mouthed and retreated to the back of the resource center with a black girl named Theresa.

"Soapy's and my relationship is in transition," she said to me when we first talked. "He's withholding a lot. Besides, he's *become* the Ob Squad."

Venice Free had classes like no other school. Where "real" students took English, we had "Language and Society." History went by the name "Ethnocentrism & Other Social Contracts." Natural science — which we called "Splendor in the Grass" — carried the official label, "Ecosystems, Large and Small." (Instead of dissecting frogs and fish, we studied the mistreatment of animals. The Sierra Club magazine was our official textbook.) And so on, right down to gym class or, as VFS's collective administration would have it, "The Body in Space." We were free to take our lunches in restaurants, to skip classes in favor of "meditation and self-reflection," and to create environmental art happenings in lieu of writing papers. I could be the new boy, dead brother and all, and aside from a few questions about how he died, nobody seemed to find me any more "irreg" than anyone else.

Deborah made a concerted effort to blend in at the normal kids' school. She wore gauzy blouses and peasant skirts, carried her books across her chest and volunteered as office manager for the yearbook. At home, she talked about her friends and what this teacher did or that one said. After dinner, Mom would leave for the evening and Deborah would back into her room saying, "Gotta call Karen (or Wayne or Cheri)." I'd eavesdrop through the door or peek in from the hall. She didn't talk on the phone. She listened to the radio and doodled over homework until some suitable period of time passed. Then she'd wander into the kitchen for ice cream and cookies, which she'd eat in front of the television. When she'd eaten enough, she'd go into the bathroom, make herself throw up — an unmistakable sound — brush her teeth, and put on one of Mom's long men's shirts as a nightgown.

Around January, she took to hanging out with a lanky experimental psychologist named Andy. Andy tested the effects of Methedrine on lab rats and "dug" Salvador Dali. De*bor*ah — at some point that winter she decided the accent should go on the second syllable of her name — gave up the yearbook. Before long, she gave up on school as well, attending classes or ditching them as the spirit moved her. She came home for dinner less than frequently and was nowhere to be found on weekends. One morning I tailed her to Andy's, where she hovered outside his building for several minutes. When I left she was still standing there, peering in through the lobby door.

With Deborah out more and my mother working nights, I tended to my own meals and occupied myself in the evenings. Music kept me company. I picked away at my no-brand-name steel-string guitar without much improvement. I listened to the same recordings over and over, the very music that my mother was trying to incorporate into her act: the aching songs of women. Joni Mitchell, Laura Nyro, Roberta Flack, and Sandy Denny were among my sweet, anguished company.

With a house to myself for the first time, I discovered sex. I took long, ritual baths with soap and shave cream. I pilfered my mother's massage oils and explored her and Deborah's underwear drawers. I fantasized about women folk singers and girls at school. I tried to prolong my pleasures for a side of a record or to synchronize my peaks with a specific line of song. I made love with the sound of women's voices.

Erich paid silent witness to my ecstasies. The music nearly edged him out of my consciousness. When the music stopped, however, I would feel his mournful eyes staring at me, as if he were watching me die. "I have already died," I thought to him. "I'm just picking up where you left off." He would retreat to some dark corner of the house, gray and mum, while I dried myself and dressed.

He was always there. None of us would talk about him, but when my mother called me Erich or when Deborah, despite her determination not to, did the same, I knew they also knew he was there. With time the word came more simply out of their mouths. It was becoming my name.

Still, I could hear the other current, the sublanguage of fear and confusion. Secondary meanings were added to our simplest words: our most rudimentary namings grew ambiguous. I was him and not-him. He was dead and alive. We were family and not-family. Our words were losing touch with their referents.

I wasn't the only dissonant one. Erich himself, by dying, became not-Erich. Deborah had altered the pronunciation of her name, as if by altering the label she could change the girl so called. Lorna was still Hofmann by name but was, in legal terms, no longer Hofmann by marriage. Willy, too, as father was no longer active or present, father and not-father simultaneously.

I didn't choose Willy's retreat from us. In fact, for one moment, just after Erich died, I tried to choose otherwise, and if I'd succeeded, everything might have been different. At least this time-lapsed disintegration of names and family might have slowed or stalled.

I'd asked my father to take me home with him. I'd all but begged and he'd refused, not bluntly but sadly, with shamefaced acceptance of Lorna's rights of possession over their kids.

We had been walking cemeteries, in search of the right setting for Erich's grave. Mac waited for us in the car.

"I guess this'll do," Dad said, barely glancing up from the grass at our feet, just as he'd barely glanced up at the last two graveyards.

"Yeah," I agreed. "It'll do, I guess."

I started to turn back but he hesitated. "You know, we send condolences to other people when someone dies. Somebody might think about making cards you send to yourself . . . or to the people around — " He stopped.

"Like self-congratulatory, right?"

"Yes. Like that, only condolences, sympathy."

"That'd be good," I nodded.

He just stood there.

Then he said, "I'm sorry this happened, Teddy. I'm sorry for you. You're too young to have to . . . It shouldn't."

"It's ok Dad. I'm not so young."

He raised his hand to my shoulder. "You're a fine boy," he said.

I swallowed.

"Dad?" I swallowed again.

"Yes, of course," he said, in reply to I don't know what.

"Dad. I want to go home with you."

"All right," he said. "I think we can go now. Let's just sign whatever papers."

"No, I mean New Jersey. When this is over. I want to go home, there, with you."

The earth, all at once, stopped. Somewhere old barns creaked in high winds and shifting plates set off tremors under cities. Somewhere oceans plowed up the seafloor and smashed it against the coast. But here all the motion of the world was concentrated behind my father's right eye. It was wildness and churning.

"Your mother needs you," was all he said.

I didn't say, "She needed Erich." I didn't say, "Look what happened to him." Nor did he explain that he couldn't take another son from her now, couldn't punish her that way, blame her like that.

And because he didn't say, "I owe her another chance," I couldn't fire back, "You owe her me?"

I only said, "Please."

And he said, "I can't."

And then he wept. His body shook and bobbed.

I put my arms around him. "It's ok," I told my father, blessing our separate fates.

Of all of us, Dad was probably most sensitive to this discord between name and thing named, a situation further confused by his remarriage the following summer. Maybe that's why he never grew casual with my name change the way Mom did. He italicized the name. On the phone, he would make a special point of saying, "How are you, *Erich*" and "Goodnight, *Erich.*" His delivery had the odd formality of a man who refers to his son as "Son." He addressed me in the same way he bowled: figuring the angles, analyzing the hit. Probably, he was waiting for me to say, "You needn't call me that anymore."

Dad couldn't filter awareness the way Mom could. He couldn't deny his denial. Language, naming, was too potent for him. Too much had changed. Lorna had gone from "Mom" to "your mother"; Deborah, who mostly refused to speak to him, had become "your sister."

Deborah had turned problematic as well, in nonlinguistic ways. She and Mom fought continuously. She defied any rules Mom tried to set: curfews, household duties, homework. She grew disdainful of me. Her alienation at school evolved into paranoia. The teachers had singled her out from the start, she said. They'd scapegoated her.

"It's as if someone sent a telegram ahead: NEW GIRL STOP FROM NEW JERSEY STOP GET HER!"

"Now honey, don't you think you're being a little oversensitive?" Mom asked, trying to calm her.

"No. I don't think that at all. And since when am *I* the oversensitive one in this family? I think in fact that I'm just about the least oversensitive one in the whole history of this family."

"What's that supposed to mean?"

"Figure it out for yourself, *Mother.*"

Mom took a breath. "Maybe it feels worse than it is. Maybe your teacher didn't mean it the way you took it."

"Oh, right. When Mr. Devries has me do the whole recitation and then, when I sit down, doesn't say anything for five minutes. Finally he says, 'Well, Deborah has just demonstrated exactly the way *not* to speak the French language.' No. Then I don't think I'm being paranoid."

"Nobody said anything about paranoid."

"We sure thought it, though. Boy, did we ever," Erich said, through me.

They both swung around to look at me, as if they'd just heard a ghost. And they had.

Mom turned back to Deborah. "You'll go in and talk to him."

"I will not," Deborah nearly shouted. "He's a pig. Andy says they use the same methods to train American teachers that they used to train Gestapo officers."

"I think Andy's exaggerating."

"You always do that! Why do you always have to put him down? As soon as I have something of my own, you either take it away or run it down. Well, I love Andy, and nothing you can say will change that."

Mom was silent.

"I'm not going back there, whatever you say," Deborah said. "I mean I can't. I ran out of class in tears and everybody laughed."

"It sounds pretty funny to me," I contributed.

"Sit on it, you little shit," Deborah said.

"Deborah! That's enough."

"Why don't you ever tell him to shut up, Mom? You let him say anything, no matter how obnoxious, but as soon as I get upset, you try to beat me down."

"Now that's just not true," Mom said.

"Yes, it is, and you know it. You've become so establishment, you don't even know it. You can't possibly hear what I'm saying."

"You tell me and I'll listen. What are you saying?"

"I'm saying I'm not going back. Period. Fuck French. Fuck phys ed. Fuck all those repressed little Nazis they call teachers! This happened to *me* today. It happened to me and not to you, so I think I'm the one who knows what really happened and how bad it really is!"

The screen door slammed behind her. Mom and I avoided looking at each other. I made faces at the reflection in my soda glass.

"You shouldn't talk to your sister like that, Erich. You know how she gets."

"I thought it was funny."

"You were being smart."

"Smart is as smart does."

"Just don't."

"Sure thing," I said, as if Deborah's problems were my fault. I found it hard to deal with my mother when she was being sane.

My sister had an easier time with Andy.

"I don't have to take it," she told him over the phone. "I didn't choose to be in high school. I didn't decide to live in Venice."

When she said, "I should. I will." I knew he'd advised, "Just leave."

Around her boyfriend, Deborah went docile. She was his flock, which was fine with him. Andy enjoyed being a guru unto himself. He was that model of sixties man: a mellow, fascist intellectual. All wire-rim glasses and hushed tones, Andy encouraged Deborah's revolt because he reaped its fruits. Her sexual freedom meant his service, her individuation from us increased her dependence on him, her rejection of other teachings primed her for his.

"He's a genius," she told me, "way superior to anything that ever crawled out of this family." And so she attended him — cleaning the filterless Camel butts out of his coffee mug, cooking his red-hot chili, sterilizing syringes and other lab materials, washing his stringy hair. When he called her "dumpy," she fasted to lose weight. And when Andy went north in late spring, she followed him.

"It's just for the summer," she told Mom.

"It's what I have to do," she informed Dad.

Even packing she was defiant, bustling about her room, gossiping about Jerry Garcia as if she knew him, peppering her conversation with the scientific names of street drugs. She shoved into an army duffel bag only the newest of her clothes and books, only those things that had been acquired by De*bor*ah to Andy's tastes. The refab Deborah talked Mao and dressed "bows and flows of angel hair." She carried *Gravity's Rainbow* and *Soul On Ice*. By all signs, she'd never lived in New Jersey, never had a daddy, never washed milk off her depressed mother's face. She'd forged a new self and stuffed it into a rucksack.

"It's a communal house," she told me, as I loitered in her doorway. "But they only let really brilliant people in. All these guys Andy did grad school with and their girlfriends. One guy turned down a fellowship in nuclear physics to build sitars. Andy's best friend, Davis, has his studio in the barn. He's gone beyond anything Warhol might have imagined. You'll come visit me sometime. You'll see." She paused, then, kindly, added, "Erich."

It was Saturday morning. Deborah fixed a pancake breakfast for Mom and me. She sat on a high step stool by the sink while we ate. When we were finished, she took the plates away. She and Lorna lit up cigarettes and smoked them down.

"Well, I guess I should boogie," Deborah said. "I'll see you guys in the fall."

She and Mom kissed each other, and they both cried.

"You can play my records," Deborah told me. "I don't care."

"Thanks," I said, and watched while she half dragged her belongings across the kitchen, out the door, and down the sidewalk on her way to Andy's and the great Northwest.

12

Eyes, Face, Hands

She never came back. None of us expected her
to. We felt it in that Saturday morning air as we sat over breakfast
together, Deborah perched on the high stool. We heard it in the
burble of the percolator, read it in the way the butter smeared our
pancakes. This was another of those moments I experienced so often
then — moments when you notice (because you can do no more
than notice) that what must happen will happen. Life, it becomes
clear at such times, has its own roll. You can't stop or slow the roll.
You can only feel the tumble as it takes you, only hope to come out
in one piece.

Deborah had to leave, and if Andy hadn't come along, she would
have found some other ticket to ride. Once gone, she had to stay
away, because to come home would have announced defeat. Mom
and I had to stand by, dumb as cows, because it was our season to do
so. If I believed in destiny, I would say it was our family's destiny to
lose one another, in the drifty sense of losing track or misplacing,
rather than in the dramatic way that you blow twenty thousand dollars at craps or lose your leg in the war. Nowhere does such destiny
seem more palpable than at the kitchen table.

After watching Deborah drag off down the street, we moved
back to our places at the yellow Formica table. Have I said that my
mother was a beautiful woman? She was, and never more beautiful
than in her sadness. She gathered her hair and twisted it into a rubber band. The sweep of brown accentuated the angularity of her
unmade-up face. The ponytail made her young. She wore some
man's button-down pinstripe shirt. Her hands looked like carved

things, nestling her coffee mug, balancing a freshly lit Tarreyton. Except for the spider-web lines forming around her green eyes, I could have believed my mother was still a graduate student, after an all-nighter, preoccupied with Yeats and Jung.

Except for the crow's-feet and another feature, one I'd never seen until the morning Deborah moved away. My mother had changed the way she smoked. She no longer pulled from the front of her lips, the sensual drag shared by novice, closet smokers and unabashed veterans. This morning I noticed for the first time that she sucked the cigarette from the corner of her mouth. In the process her lips thinned out, and her eyes, shifting to the left, squinched up. She looked mean as she inhaled, bitter and pissed.

The morning was in no other way momentous. I finished every scrap of pancake, and Mom drank the coffee down to the grounds. She smoked. We made idle talk, trading prophecies like, "It won't last with Andy. She'll be home by August." We had to say things like that, though we didn't believe them.

"Andy's an asshole," I said. I said it all the time in those days.

"Andy's an asshole" had become a refrain for me, so much so that all I had to do was mention Deborah's name to Soapy and he'd shake his head and say, "Andy. What an asshole," while his eyes lit up with glee.

It was a saying. It fused with his name: "Andy Asshole." And it was a phrase that might have fallen from my brother's lips any day. My diction, syntax, attitude, were naturally aping his more and more. My voice was picking up his color. Clearly, my mother approved.

"Just you and me," she said. I watched her hand float above the table and settle itself on mine. My breath held itself. Carefully, I lifted my other hand and with the nail of one finger began to etch the latticework of lines crossing her knuckles. I skated the hills of the back of her hand, down California, across Mexico, up the eastern seaboard and into the heart of myself as a small boy. My heart, my mother's hand.

And I said, "Randy dandy asshole Andy."

Andy was an asshole because he took Deborah instead of me.

Unlike my older sister, I was smart, my mind nimble. I would have been a natural in that house of hippie geniuses. I was made to live in the Northwest, I thought, to listen to New Riders of the Purple Sage and perform experiments on lab rats named Mike. I "got" all that stuff in a way that desperate Deborah never would, but the "asshole" picked easy sex over intellectual sympathy. He failed to see my potential, referred to me in my presence by the simultaneously intimate and demeaning moniker "Kid Bro." He only took me half seriously, while he wasn't serious about Deborah at all, but he took her anyway.

Which was another reason he was an asshole: I knew he would hurt her. I wanted to save her from him. I tried. I told her he was an asshole. I told her: "He only wants one thing. You shouldn't trust the guy. I mean he shoots vermin up with speed. What's he gonna do with you?"

She only said, "Who's the asshole? Let's take a poll."

Not wanting to prove her right, I shut up.

It was summer again. It was always summer when our family numbers dwindled. Summer didn't pronounce itself as clearly in Venice as it had in New Jersey, but it made its wobbly presence felt. My time had even less structure than at the Free School (known to the Ob Squad as "Venice Free Fall"). The beaches were busier. The whole town was, as tourists came to dip into our waters. Some days it felt too hot to live. I hung out with Soapy or Holly or both, in addition to other kids from school and visiting cousins they brought with them. I spent whole afternoons hunched over my guitar or spaced out over the same four pages of a book. I had a crush on a girl named Irma, who had blond bowl-cut hair and amber eyes. She stayed for three weeks and then went back to Cincinnati or Akron or wherever she was from, leaving me with a broken heart and sticky memories of us mushing around together against the outside wall of a large clapboard house.

My mother stayed home. Suddenly, she was around all the time, and while she was there, she was the "Mom." She set times for lunch and, sure enough, when I'd wander home at 1:15 there'd be a

Dagwood sandwich and chips or cold chicken on a plate with cottage cheese, bread-and-butter pickles, and a glass of lemonade. She insisted I bring friends home with me for lunch, dinner, overnight. When they came she'd make up all sorts of stories about me.

"Erich knew his way around Manhattan before he was five," she bragged to Irma. "He always wanted to hang out at the used bookstores uptown by Columbia, reading about stuff like necromancy and alchemy. He was older by then, of course. Ten or eleven. Just before we moved to Paris."

"I didn't know you lived in Paris," Irma said.

"Just for a couple years," I lied, digging around in my dessert.

"More pie?" Mom asked.

Soapy spent a lot of nights at our house, though his parents — his father was a veterinarian and his mother an administrator for Head Start — thought my mother was a flake. Mom urged me to have parties, too, and she let me hold them any night of the week. Then she stayed out of the way or left the house altogether. "You don't need my watchful eyes cramping your style," she explained.

This was the beginning of a stretch of several years during which my mother didn't work regularly or full-time. Her singing engagements dwindled over the summer and then stopped altogether. Occasionally, she'd help out a friend decorating store windows or showing rental apartments, or she'd sell face creams as part of a pyramid-structured, self-employment scheme, but nothing steady.

"I don't want to invest myself in anything that would take my energy away from the store," she said. "Piecemeal work is part of the plan. It's practice. When my time comes I'll have the most beautiful, most innovative little treasure-trove business this side of the Grand Canyon: a one-room journey around the world." And she'd make notes on yellow legal pads of spaces for rent, design concepts, marketing plans, and budgets for "The World's Room." Ashes from her ever-present Tarreyton would fall to the paper and she'd backhand them off without missing a beat.

She befriended my friends, insisted they call her by her first name. She was the "cool" mom. It was unnerving to stumble into the

kitchen and find her with Holly and other girls from school, and to
have them all stop talking when I entered, as if my male presence
had tainted the room. They were, I knew, sharing the most intimate
secrets of their private lives, and Mom was hungry to hear. Other
times, I'd walk in and there she'd be with Soapy, sitting at the table
over twin iced teas, Mom smoking and Soapy talking about this girl
or that. She fed off the most trivial details of our teenage dramas. I
don't know what she got out of it.

Once, I came in while Soapy was describing a scene between his
dad and a woman who'd accused him of killing her Corgi. "I told him
he'd been too nice," Soapy was saying. "Calm down, nothing. I would
have just said, 'Obviously your dog died to get away from you.'"

Mom flinched, as though he'd chucked his tea in her face.

"Speaking of dead dogs," Soapy went on, looking toward me,
"you look like something they serve on a bun in the cafeteria."

"Shut up, Soapy," I said.

"Touchy, touchy," he said. "I meant it as a compliment, of
course."

"What makes you say that, Soapy?" Mom asked, ignoring our
banter. "Was the woman so terrible?"

"You want me to freshen your tea, Mom? Soap, we've gotta go."

"Was she that bad? You think? That he'd want to die?"

"Freak from hell," Soapy explained. "'Course, I never met her.
Like who yells at a vet?" He paused to fill me in. "I was telling Lorna
about my dad killing that lady's Corgi."

"I picked that up. Can we go now, Soap? You want anything,
Mom?"

"You don't really think a dog would feel that way? They love
their owners, don't they? No matter what. What does your dad say?"

"You ask me, Corgis aren't dogs. I mean dogs are supposed to
have tails," he was saying, as I pulled him out of the room. "If they
don't, they don't qualify. Just little walking butts. One more or less,
who gives? Thanks for the tea, Lorna. The sympathy was good, too."

She called after us. "Dinner's 7:15, Erich. Bring the gang."

My mother's eyes betrayed little of the attentive sadness they'd shown in the months immediately following Erich's suicide. A determination had taken hold of her, a kind of like-it-or-lump-it, woman-in-the-world spirit. For the next year, she presided over a table littered with coffee cups, glasses of red wine, half-eaten sandwiches, and dirty Mexican ashtrays in a kitchen peopled by teenagers, workmen, delivery boys, street buskers, other divorced women, and me. She talked back to clerks in stores, laughed over private jokes with supermarket managers, knew surfers by name. Through it all, she fixed me two meals a day, made me clean my room, and gave no indication that I was any other than the Erich we'd buried.

"Remember those strolls we used to take after the others were asleep?" she asked one morning, as she washed the previous night's dishes while I dried. "We should start that little ritual up again."

"Sure," I agreed. "That'd be great."

She also threw parties of her own, small, motley affairs. The "girls" would be there, members of a circle of divorced or unhappily married women my mother's age. They'd whisper in corners over lipstick-stained rocks glasses of booze and dance a bit too sloppily with younger men, recruited from the remnant ranks of her hippie coffee-shop klatsch. "Business associates" showed up, people she'd met singing or drumming up money for her dream store. And then came the strays, acquaintances from anywhere in town. Our home, however bereft, was hardly ever empty.

Despite the desperate hedonism in the air, the goosey party games and array of dipso- and nymphomaniacal behavior, Mom kept a level head at these shindigs. She remained mysteriously sober. She was a hostess. She flirted, danced, told stories, held weepers' hands, and carried hors d'oeuvres. She played matchmaker, gossiped, and engaged in earnest, wee-hour debates with the same easy intensity. I would come and go, marveling at my mother's grace, even as I mocked the foibles of her chums.

I liked to help her clean up after these revels. There was satisfaction in making order out of the anarchy, dumping glutted ashtrays, stacking plastic party cups, flipping paper plates into garbage bags. I liked, too, to hear her explicate the events of the night: who went home with whom, who tried and failed. Sometimes she'd take a break from the tidying and pass out in a chair. When I'd finished straightening, I'd wake her up and help her to her room, where she'd lay down fully clothed. It was my job to slip her shoes off, throw a cover over her, and turn out the light.

One night I found her on the bathroom floor, asleep. Her head was resting on the bathtub rim and she was holding a double-edged razor blade between two fingers. This was the only time I carried my mother to bed. It was a year to the day after Erich had died.

I watched her sacked out on the bed, but I couldn't leave the room. I knew I'd taken the razor, but for some reason I felt I had to keep checking her hands to make sure. I'd peel her fingers back, checking the palms and the sleeves of her blouse to be certain there was nothing. Then I'd circle to the other side of the bed and repeat the inspection. Again, nothing. Her breathing remained heavy except once when it quieted altogether. I held my own wrist to her mouth, thinking that it was the most sensitive spot on my body, that it would feel any breath there might be. And it did register an indelible warmth. I'd turn to leave and then go back to check again, or to lift her eyelids to make sure she hadn't passed into some kind of coma. She was only asleep. There was no blade. I think I stood there for an hour or more: Erich, someone to watch over her.

In the bathroom I wrapped the razor blade in several layers of toilet paper. I pulled a Dixie cup out of the trash and, tearing it along the seam, folded it around the enwrapped blade. I wound this, too, in toilet paper and then shoved it back into the garbage can, which I carried to the kitchen, emptied into a larger bag, tied up, and hauled outside to the alley cans. This done, I went back into her room to make sure I hadn't missed anything, then back into the bathroom to look for a second razor, one that might have fallen. I wanted to — but knew I shouldn't — remove every razor blade, exacto knife, and cutting edge from the house in the same manner. That night, during rare moments of sleep, I dreamt about slashed fingers and necks, spurting blood.

There were other kinds of nights, too, nonparty nights. I'd come home and there she'd be, sitting at the same table, a glass of wine, half drunk, before her, her eyes baggy and dark. A pile of broken plates and glasses — some food too — would be heaped by the sink, half on a dustpan, the broom leaning stiff and confused against the counter. And each time was the only time; each time we behaved as though it had never happened before:

"How was your evening, Erich?" she asks dully, not looking up.

"Nothing special. Same shit, different day."

"There's ice cream."

I get it.

"You want some?"

"No thanks, Erich."

"You sure?"

"Sure."

"Positive?"

"I've got wine." She keeps her eyes vaguely on the rim of her goblet. She seems so windless at times like these.

"Yeah, mint chocolate chip and burgundy — never mix, never worry."

"No, thanks."

"Linda Swenson might be moving," I inform her. "Butte or Des Moines or somewhere like that. Her father might have a job."

"That's nice."

"No, it sucks. I mean, who wants to spend three years at a high school in Idaho? Fate worse than death. Or Wyoming or wherever."

"I guess not."

"You want more wine?"

"That would be nice."

I open the refrigerator.

"It's on the counter."

I close the refrigerator. "Right. Red wine, room temperature. I forgot."

I pour her wine. "Pretty blouse," I say.

"Pardon?"

"I said that blouse . . . it looks pretty on you. 'S'it new?"

"Do you think so?"

"Yeah. Very nice. Good color."

"It's new."

"That's what I thought."

"I wasn't sure . . ."

"No, looks good. Knockout. Where'd you get it?"

"That little place off Windward — Impressions."

"With the potpourri?"

"Why? Does it stink? I never noticed."

"All over the place. I start wheezing a block away."

By now she's looked up at me.

"So you like it?" she asks, bashful.

"It's great. You look like a movie star — Ali McGraw or something."

"It was cheap, too."

"Great. Thrifty as well as decorative."

"You think?"

"You bet."

"You don't really like it."

"No, I do, really. Looks fab-o."

After a while, I'd scoop some ice cream into a bowl and she'd start to dab at it with a spoon.

Still other nights: Before I'd even reached the house I'd hear *Turandot* blasting down the street from our living-room turntable. I'd know my mother was in there, ranting and pacing, Chianti spilling from her goblet to the shag rug — the drunk's genuflection. "You hear that?" she would be saying, shouting really, as the singers on the stereo unleashed their own operatic fury in response. I was never sure what she wanted heard — other than the Puccini — or who she intended to hear it. Clearly, whatever it was, wasn't pretty, and whoever it was, was better off staying out of range.

If I ventured inside, she'd come shrieking after me: "What are you doing here? Wipe your shoes. Get out of this house! Who let you loose in here? Don't talk back to me, I'm your mother." Then like a giant soused hawk, she'd wheel back into the living room and join the singing. She'd cry operatic tears as she sang full voiced, shooting basilisk glares at the door to make sure I'd gone.

Later, when I'd crept off to my room under her maenadic attack and gone to bed (never to sleep), she'd come in without knocking and stand by my pillow. Sometimes she'd just hang there for what seemed like hours as I kept my eyes shut and breath regular like a person asleep. Other times she'd clamber into bed beside me, drunk and sorry, watering my neck, shoulders, hair, and pillow with her steamy tears.

13

Here / Not Here

And then she was gone. I headed into sophomore year at the Free School, and my mother hurtled into the world again. Raoul, a painter who sold drugs, but, as far as I could tell, no paintings, continued to pine for her from San Miguel de Allende; he occasionally scraped together air fare to fly her back. Larry ("A good buddy, that's all," she insisted) zipped back and forth from Miami to California for her. An Asian guy we called Nocky (short for Nokamura) took her to Sicily, and an old fart named Harve flew her to New York City for long, platonic weekends full of high-priced meals and Broadway shows. I once read an article about the fear of flying that claimed that the odds of dying in a commercial plane crash were longer than those of having all the air sucked out of your living room. At the time I thought the comparison absurd; people often die in plane wrecks, whereas I'd never heard of anyone getting the air sucked out of their living room. Now, I think, yes, our living room had the air sucked out of it every time she left.

For all her unpredictability, my mother kept things hopping. Even when she was gone, what little excitement hit the house emanated from her. I'd come home after dinner at the coffee shop and find one of her girlfriends sitting in the kitchen, waiting for her.

"She's in the Yucatan," I'd say.

"Oh, I thought she was still in town," the girlfriend would say.

"No, the Yucatan."

The girlfriend would not budge from the chair. They never budged, these girlfriends.

"You want some coffee?" I'd ask, moving toward the cupboard.

"No. I made myself a rum and tonic." Sure enough, a freshly opened bottle of rum stood attendance on the table.

I'd open a Coke and pull out a chair opposite.

"Joey didn't come home again last night," she'd say. I picked up the narrative effortlessly. Months of serving as Mom's surrogate ear allowed me to distinguish the girlfriends with the cheating husbands from the ones with the drunk lovers. I learned to mix their favorite drinks. I got to know their physical complaints. Joey's wife was a henna redhead, whose limp, girlish bangs clashed with the sun-dried lines of her skin. The muscles in her feet were always cramping up, so she carried furry slippers in her bag. These she changed into, removing her stockings and pumps, immediately after sitting down. A few drinks later, she'd pry the slippers off and stick her knobby feet in my lap, saying, "Oh, my aching dogs. Give 'em a squeeze or two, will you? My masseuse moved to Tahoe and I haven't been the same since."

"Why don't you leave him, if he's such a prick?" I'd inquire.

"I love him," came the inevitable answer: Blah blah blah.

Still, blah blah blah was better than empty-house hum. So I held their proverbial hands and doled out advice, no charge. My wisdom was confident and sound, as cocktail-hour wisdom goes, though none of it ever got heeded. Without fail, after a week or two passed, the same lady would be back, drinking Puerto Rican rum and narrating her own continuing adventures.

"I found his credit-card bill. The bastard. Two hundred dollars from a jewelry store on Rodeo Drive I've never even heard of." She'd swill her drink down to the lime and add, "He hates Rodeo Drive."

"Mind if I crash on your couch?" she'd ask, in the midst of doing just that. I'd bring a blanket. It was fun, in its way.

More than once I woke up at 3:00 A.M. to the sound of pounding on the front door. It was always Brad, the wallpaper guy, drunk as a coot, banging away and calling "Lornaaaah!" like some cheap Brando imitator in black glasses and a button-down shirt. We, too, always had the same conversation:

"Where *is* she?" he'd ask, when I told him he was making a lot of noise for nothing.

"She's not here. Not even in town."

"When's she back? Let me in."

"She was supposed to be back last night, but she's not. Your guess is as good as mine."

He'd quiet down and I'd open the door wider and watch him through the screen. "Where out of town?"

"Ask her."

"When's she get back?"

"I don't know. Go home, Brad."

"I should go home?"

"Yeah, go home. Lorna's not here."

"She's out of town."

"Bingo. Go home."

"Have her call me, all right? When she gets back."

"Sure, Brad."

And he'd veer off, meek and repentant as a naughty Disney doe, stopping on the walk to double-check, "When d'you say she's home?"

"Soon, Brad. She'll be home before you know it."

Sometimes, she wouldn't come home when she was supposed to. I'd imagine her plane or taxi crashing or her being raped or beaten in some foreign place. I couldn't call the airport, in case she was trying to reach me. Instead, I'd prowl from room to room, pounding my fists into wood paneling, wanting to scream and tear the phone from the wall but not letting myself. I'd picture her the way she'd been in Mexico when she got depressed — bowed over herself, head too heavy to raise up, waiting for harm to come to her. I'd map out hiding places, in case someone broke in to kill me.

Inevitably, she'd call the next morning before I left for school to say she'd missed her plane. She'd only stay a few more days. How could anybody be angry with her? My mother was finally happy, finally free. She was a making herself a new woman in a world where the new woman was in vogue. She's been through so much, I thought. She deserves a life.

"Where is she this time?" Deborah asked as part of her biweekly phone ritual.

"Hawaii. She's meeting someone named Jim in Oahu. She's been bringing home great stuff. Who knows what she'll find around the volcanoes?"

"Who's Jim?"

"Some guy, Deborah. I can't keep them straight. I think he surfs."

"Great. My forty-two-year-old mother's trucking around Hawaii with a surfer. What are you eating? Are you getting enough to eat? Who's cooking for you?"

"I eat all the time, Oomie."

"Real funny. I just want to make sure you're taking care of yourself."

"Who else would I be taking care of?"

"Yeah, yeah."

"Soapy and I are going to the Joni Mitchell concert in San Francisco."

"I would have thought your tastes in music would have evolved a little bit by now."

"What's wrong with Joni?"

"No one listens to Joni Mitchell anymore, Erich. They just don't."

"What do *they* listen to? And who are *they* anyway?"

"They are people with taste and good sense, baby bro."

"They are assholes."

"*They* are wonderful and doing just fine, since you ask, so keep your smart-ass remarks to your pip-squeak self."

"I'm taller than you are."

"Yack yack yack. I gotta go. Tell Mom I called."

"Tell Andy I think he's cute."

"Funny. Real."

"And tell him that Blue Oyster Cult sucks and King Crimson is a homo."

"Consider yourself ignored. When'd you say she's getting back?"

"Sometime next week. Wednesday, 10:00 P.M. She said."

"Well, as long as she's happy."

"Oh, she's happy," I confirmed.

"It's been real," she said.

"And tell him even Lou Reed doesn't listen to Velvet Underground anymore." Click.

Dad inquired after Mom more obliquely, and I met his inquiries with indirection. "How's your mother?" he asked in the middle of one memorable conversation.

"Fine, she's good."

"Is she there?"

"No, not right now."

"When's a good time to reach her? I need to talk something over with her."

"She's out of town for a couple days right now."

"Oh, can you have her call me when she gets back, Erich?"

"Well, it'll be about ten days."

"Oh, where'd she go?"

"She's in New York, mostly."

"Then maybe she could call me from here."

"Except that now she's on her way to Europe."

"I see."

"Yes, Europe."

"Well," he said, pausing to think. "I wanted to talk to her before I told you, but I might as well tell you now. You can let her know."

"Sure, ok," I said, without a clue. "Should I get a pencil? I mean is it something I need to write it down?"

"Oh, no no, nothing like that. I'm sure you can remember."

"I have a pretty good memory."

"I'm sure you do."

"Shoot."

Again, there was a thinking pause.

"Erich," he said finally.

A moment of panic, disorientation more like. Something happened to Erich, I thought, and I almost asked what. Then I realized he was addressing me. "Dad?"

"Well, Son, I've met someone, a woman. I'm getting married."

My father always called me "Son" when he was confused.

"That's great, Dad. Married, wow."

"I want you to meet her."

"That'd be great."

"I want you to," he repeated, apparently for emphasis.

"What's her name?"

"Hilda."

"That's a funny name."

"Portuguese. Yes, it is a funny sort of name."

"What do I call her?"

"Hildy, I always call her Hildy."

"No, I mean what should *I* call her."

"Oh, well, Hildy too, I guess."

"Hildy 2. Willy and Hildy. Wow."

"How about that?" he allowed.

"That's great."

"Thank you. You'll have to come to our wedding. We want you to."

"I saw a wedding in Mexico. Puebla."

"Yes. Well now you'll get to see another. Hildy very much wants you to."

This time I paused. I remembered the wedding I'd seen. The couple seemed very young, even to me. As the priest intoned, the teenage bride rose on the balls of her feet, unaware. Her left hand held her right behind her back. The fingers of the held hand wagged quickly up and down, as if urging the aging father to hurry hurry hurry and pronounce her married before she burned and died. Far from cute, the gesture seemed panicky, greedy, ambitious.

I'd looked up at my mother. She smelled of fresh lipstick. She was rapt, as though she were seeing herself on some ideal altar, young and beautiful before God. I made myself look away, back at the bride's hand, beating swift time. It was my mother's hand, the gesture of her restlessness, her hunger.

"That girl can't wait to get laid," Erich had said in a stage whisper. Deborah snorted at him. Mom broke out of her trance, smiled, and tousled his hair.

"So, how are you, Erich?" my Dad asked, audibly relieved.

"I'm fine, great. Soapy and I are going to San Francisco to the Joni Mitchell concert."

"That's fine. You'll tell your mother, won't you? What we talked about."

"Sure, soon's she gets home."

In family photos my father nearly always has his hand resting on one of our shoulders or backs. It's a placating hand, and I could remember its gentle, reticent pressure. It sits with the negative force of desire stanched, the need to grasp or clutch quelled, as if my father, battling to overcome the coldness his parents bred in him, got only as far as touch.

"Good. Well, I'll sign off now," he sighed. "Are you eating all right? Is someone looking after you?"

"I'm fine, Dad."

"All right, then." He added, more to himself, "That being done."

"'Bye, Dad."

"Yes, yes. Good-bye, Son."

My whole absent family asserted a presence in the house, powerful and impalpable. Even Erich was there, invisible but there, like carbon monoxide or pheromones, and the more Mom was gone, the more he began to spook me. I lived in a state of almost-seeing, as when you spot something out of the corner of your eye and spin around to find it gone. I almost-saw him in the closet, I almost-saw him peering through the door, I almost-saw him sitting at the foot of the bed. He was as real as I was, and he was as insubstantial as the color gray. I was growing up like Pollux, marked for eternity by Castor's absence, by being where his brother wasn't.

I would lie awake at night, the house's quiet pressing in on me, small sounds startling like gunfire, and I would listen for Erich. One night and only once, he spoke.

I lay unsleeping on my side, back to the closet. I heard, quite distinctly, the sliding of the closet doors and footsteps. Erich leaned over me. I could feel his breath on my ear. He was solidly there, a body in space. He whispered to me: "I'm never more than three feet away."

I couldn't make myself roll over. I didn't want to lose him and I didn't want to see him. When I finally looked he was gone. I experienced all the clichés of fear: trembling, sweating, heart pounding. My dead brother had whispered in my ear and, in doing so, confirmed that he was living — existing? occupying nonspace? — parallel to me, never more than three feet away. I turned the lights on — in my room, the hall, the bathroom, the kitchen, the living room — not to find him but to blot out any trace of his dark parallel world. Then, because I was frightened of anything I couldn't see, I turned on all the lights in my mother's and Deborah's rooms. I switched on the TV. I wrapped myself in a blanket and balled up on the couch, trying to get lost in Johnny Carson.

One morning Soapy had sauntered into Owen Hammer's psychology class — which we called "I'm OK, you're OK, so why is Owen Hammer so fucked up?" — with an even-more-irritating-than-usual grin plastered across his face. I asked him what was happening, but he just pressed his lips together and giggled to himself. I retreated to another part of the room. We had been reading Fritz Perls and doing exercises about creating personal space, so I felt justified in going off by myself. Soapy kept up the silent act until astronomy, during which he launched me a note in the shape of an airplane with triple wing folds: "Dead Meat Café at noon. Joni is God."

"Dead Meat" was our name for a luncheonette across the street from an old people's apartment complex. It had old employees and old clients and even the food tasted like it had been sitting around for a couple of centuries. It was a place we went when we didn't want to run into anybody.

We walked the six blocks to the café in silence. Once in the Dead Meat, where we were at least fifty years younger than anyone in sight, he immersed himself in the menu. The waitress came by — huge liver spots on her gnarled hands — and took our orders. I still couldn't tell whether Soapy really had a surprise up his sleeve or this was some tedious Ob Squad practical joke.

The lady came with our Cokes. Soapy reached into his front jeans' pocket, where he kept his wallet. ("It's safer there," he claimed when anyone called attention to it. "And it makes me look better hung.") He pried it out. From the wallet he produced a small white envelope, which he slid across the table. It had an ad for Jack-In-The-Box tacos on it and, inside, two pale blue Ticketron tickets to Joni Mitchell's next California concert. We'd been reading Carlos Castaneda in "Language and Society" and were both taken with the idea of behaving "impeccably." To us this meant finding the perfect gesture. I pulled off my fedora, which for two and a half years I'd worn everywhere except to bed, and I presented it to him. He put it on.

Walking back to school, everything seemed new and happy. I tied my hair back with a red bandanna and placed my hand over the heart pocket of my workshirt, where I kept my ticket. Soapy looked taller in my fedora.

We had agreed not to tell anybody about the concert until we had figured out how to get the three hundred–plus miles from L.A. to San Francisco (to third row center). Holly came up to me before I sat down for class. "What's with the headpiece, Hofmann?" I kissed the palm of her hand. She rolled her eyes, said "Fuckin' men," and went over to whisper in Linda Swenson's ear. I went up to Mark Greenburg, our creative writing teacher, and thanked him for a magnificent learning experience. "You're a beautiful person," I told him. He laughed and pretended to throw an eraser at me. It was the best day I remember.

My mother was in Mexico with Raoul at the time, so Soapy and I set up a planning center in the house. The problems at hand were how to get money, transportation, several days off school, a place to stay, and a way back. We had *Ladies of the Canyon* up loud, maps spread out, phone books standing by. We made notecards to put on ride boards around town and fantasized about a couple of college girls driving us up Route 1 in a convertible. ("Or *three*," Soapy said. "Three would be even better.") Soapy wouldn't agree to hitch upstate. "On purely aesthetic grounds," he said. "It's too Woodstock."

When we'd laid out several alternate plans, Soapy went home. I called Holly and told her, even though I'd promised not to. "It's late," she said, with an I-don't-give-a-shit edge to her voice. "I haven't finished my reading for Owen's class."

I asked her what was wrong, and she started to cry. Her uncle, the one who was always trying to have sex with her, was moving in with them. I wasn't sure I believed her. I wasn't ever sure I believed her.

"I just took six Valium," she said, adding, "I'm in love with Owen."

"Don't do this to yourself," I begged her. "I love you. We all love you. Get out of there. Why don't you come live here? Do you want me to come over? Will you be all right? Look at all the good, wonderful things in your life. Why do you want to hurt yourself? Stop it, goddamn it, you're too good for that. Life is too precious, too short, too important." I said all this and more of the same, trying, as I did almost every night, to inspire her to care more for herself, to esteem life. She grew tired, while I grew agitated and wakeful.

"Promise me you won't take anymore pills tonight."

"ok," she said. "Goodnight, Hofmann."

"Goodnight, Hol."

Blue had clicked off early in the conversation, and I was afraid to put any music on again, afraid I wouldn't hear the phone if I did, wouldn't hear someone trying to break into the empty house. I made my nightly rounds, checking windows and doors, flicking on and off lights, so that potential intruders would know that people were home. It was natural to be vigilant, I believed. Babysitters got murdered all the time; kids went crazy and shot up whole families. Even when I brushed my teeth, I kept the water off and listened.

I switched on the tv, keeping the sound off. I filled a bowl with cereal and milk, and, as I did every night, ate. I looked over the lists and maps Soapy and I had drawn up. I knew they were worthless. I started singing, "I could drink a case of you darling / Still be on my feet. . . ." As I sang, I danced slowly across the shag carpet, still clinging to my cereal spoon and to the image of her beautiful blond head emerging from the royal blue cover of the *Blue* album.

I turned off all the lights, made sure the shades were down in the living room. I dropped my clothes in a neat pile on the floor. Then, by the light of the television, I ran my hands over my nipples, belly, down between my thighs. I thought, "Why are you so blue? I love you blue. 'I could drink a case of you. . . .'"

My mother bailed us out. She called from Mexico. When I told her how Soapy and I were agonizing over how to get to our dream concert, she hit on a workable solution. "Why don't I drive you two up there. We'll make it a mini-vacation, stay overnight, ride the trolley, and motor back along the coast? I'll just make sure I'm home that weekend. I don't think I'll be traveling anymore after this anyway. I miss my Erich too much."

We were ecstatic. Now Soapy's dad couldn't refuse. Now we'd get permission to skip out on school. We had the wheels, and we had Lorna to foot the bill.

I prepared a great dinner for my mother on the occasion of her homecoming: lasagna from Oomie's recipe, green salad with three colors of peppers, wine, and a peach cobbler from the *Better Homes* cookbook. We laughed and laughed, as she pilloried all her Mexican cronies.

"Their lives have become so small," she said. "They are stuck, stuck, stuck. Haven't got the merest inkling what's happening in the world around them."

Raoul had, in a manner, proposed to her.

"He's met this twenty-two-year-old local girl who doesn't have a thought in her head but lives for him," she explained. "He told me that if I wouldn't come back and marry him, he'd marry her. Of course, I told him I'd never marry him, but I promised to fly down every now and again to make his life miserable — to show him what he settled for. No, I'd never marry Raoul, of all people. He's a terrible artist. He's not really an artist at all!"

And we howled together at the kitchen table as we ripped Raoul's talent to shreds. She even brought some of his paintings and photos to the table, where we heaped scorn on them. I told her about the time I'd stood beside him in the belfry of that old church in San Miguel, his arm around my shoulder, wet and limp like a dead eel. "My leetle boy," he had said. His breath smelled

like a cross between tequila, rancid coffee, and the cheap-shit
cigars he mouthed all the time. "My leetle boy," he said, and with
his free arm he made the sweeping gesture conquerors make in
the movies when they survey the land spread out in front of them.
"Here is my Paris."

"Stop," she said, laughing out of control. "I'll pee . . ."

Later, after we'd nearly killed a second bottle of red wine, I outlined our plans for San Francisco, and showed her my ticket, next to
a seating plan of the auditorium.

"Third row, smack-dab center," I boasted.

My mom cried that night. She said she was tired of traveling. She
couldn't take being so far away from me. It was time to settle in and
start a life. It was time to stop talking and open up her store. She
called Deborah and they cried together. I half crawled to the bathroom, where I threw up the dinner and wine.

Mom stayed put until January. Raoul — whom she now referred
to as "the leetle sheet" — was getting married about ten days before
our concert trip.

"I'll have a half week breathing room. Not to worry," she
affirmed. "I'll be back with time to spare."

After two delays, she arranged to fly home on the night before
we were to leave. It was a Thursday, and Soapy was sleeping over so
we could get up early and go. I called the airport three or four times,
and each time was told that the plane was on schedule. I called again
and learned that it had landed.

When my mother didn't show, Soapy and I just stared at the TV
and tried to avoid reaching conclusions. "A lot of times she stops off
for a drink with a friend," I told him. Finally, the phone rang.
"That'll be her," I said, relieved. It was.

"Erich, dear, you'll never guess who I ran into down here at the
wedding. I should have known Larry couldn't stay away. He's got a
house in the mountains through the end of the month. It's a once-
in-a-lifetime chance. Don't be mad at me, baby. We'll go to San
Francisco for a whole week when I get back. You understand, don't
you?" she asked.

"Sure," I said.

I ditched school the next day. I couldn't face it, the tail-between-the-legs shame of admitting that no matter how footloose I was, how "free man in Paris," living in my bungalow all-but-alone, I was still a kid in need of a ride. Soapy and I went from crowing too loudly for too long to eating crow. I couldn't do it. My anger made me inert.

I said that Erich spoke to me only once, and in the literal voice-from-the-hereafter sense that's true. But he sent me one other message.

My brother had stowed two sealed boxes when he left for camp that last summer, one warning probable death to violators and the other dated to be opened at the turn of the year 1990. No one knew about these boxes but me. While several hundred miles north Joni Mitchell got ready to go onstage, I pulled out Erich's first box and cut into it.

Slicing the scissors along the seams, I felt like a surgeon, knifing through my brother's chest to reach his heart. Erich had packed away a variety of memorabilia. In addition to a couple of notebooks, the box contained a stack of cartoons from Bazooka gum from the early sixties, back issues of *The Beachhead*, our local alternative newspaper, and a photo of the house in Santa Monica where Stan Laurel had died. The books he chose to preserve ran from inexplicable — a guide to submersible marine vessels — to sweet — a carbon-copy manuscript of my father's dissertation and an autographed volume of his critical biography of Hawthorne: "To my son," signed "Wilhelm Reinohl Hofmann (Dad)."

Another book, *English and Scottish Popular Ballads*, attracted me because of its bookmark. It was a lock of my mother's hair. I don't know how he'd gotten it or when, but there it was, curling softly toward the seam between pages 24 and 25. He might have been using the book to preserve the hair, but the hair was sticking up out of the book, rather than nestling inside, pressed between the leaves.

I began to read the ballad printed there, which appeared in several versions, changed over time by people in different parts of the

British Isles. It was a grisly little number called "Edward." In it a
young man, carrying a sword that drips with blood, passes his own
mother. She stops him, asking why the blood? Killed my hawk, he
answers, heavily. She's suspicious, though, and presses on. Blood's
too red for your hawk, she says. Then it's my horse's blood, he tells
her. "Mither" challenges his lie. You've got other horses, she says.
No, you suffer some other grief, some other *dule*, than the death of
an old horse. Her intuition nails him, and he erupts in a howl: Killed
my father! Woe is me!

I turned the page and saw, marked in yellow, a section that sent
a literal shiver through me. Having confessed to killing his father,
Edward's mother asks him what penance he'll do. He will exile himself, he tells her, set out in his boat and "fare over the sea, O." What
about your children, the mother asks; what will you leave them?
Erich had run a highlighter across his response:

> The warldes room late them beg thrae life,
>> Mither, Mither,
> The warldes room late them beg thrae life,
>> For thame never mair wul I see, O.

This was the name Erich had given Mom for her store: The
World's Room. But it wasn't, as she thought, a phrase of expanse and
possibility. It was a curse: the empty space of the universe, the tomb
of the living, everything that is nothing. Let them beg through life.
Could Erich have misread the line's intent? The next stanza, also
highlighted, dispelled that idea:

> And what wul ye leave to your ain mither dear,
>> Edward, Edward?
> And what wul ye leave to your ain mither dear,
>> My dear son, now tell me, O?
> The curse of hell frae me sal ye bear,
>> Mither, Mither,
> The curse of hell frae me sal ye bear,
>> Sic counseils ye gave to me, O.

When I'd overcome the chill of finding these passages, I began to sink into a deeper, even more terrifying realization. He had hated her. Erich, my mother's fondest and, I thought, requited love, was cursing her from the grave.

I had the impulse, or maybe it should be called a fantasy, strong enough to recall after all these years, to fling open the closet doors and confront my brother's ghost: "Is this true?" I would demand of him. "Are you telling me that this is true!?!"

Instead, I began rifling his notebooks for an answer. I found one in a "Ballad of Erich" journal — an entry that, by referring to this poem, confirmed my realization:

A Will

I, upon being of soundless mind and body, bequeath
unto my solo survivors:

My records
A string of nonworking phone numbers
memories of:
    rampaging through Mexico
    (yawn) New Jersey
    two sons and a daughter
no visible means of support
my posters
love, sadness, and the American way
good counsel never heeded
Spike Jones and Sam Beckett
songs that make it easy to forget and songs that
    make it impossible
Tommy James and the Shondells (what is a
    Shondell?)
the curse of hell

For all our meandering, continuous conversation, Erich and I had never talked about Mexico. We'd never gone over the history of our flight, the events leading up to her spiriting us away. We'd never analyzed our feelings or traded war stories. Dad was there one minute, left in our dust the next; Mom was everywhere and then gone, moment by startling moment. And it had never, until I saw the bright yellow window left by Erich's pen, occurred to me that Erich thought about any of it at all. Or that he had feelings about it, let alone passions, traumas, curses. He'd gone crazy, I knew, but I'd never drawn a line between the two things — his life, and his illness and death. Everything that had happened had happened gradually. The shifting, the division, had been interior. What I'm trying to say is: you get used to things. Or we had. I thought he had.

14

THE WORLD'S ROOM

The curse of hell. This was, for me, a strange place to have come to. I immediately recognized the truth and irony of Erich's fury: he had hated the very person whose love his death let me win. I didn't choose my response. My own fury — my disgust — was unleashed. The problem: it was my job to protect her, even from myself.

There she was again, making plans to open a store called The World's Room: Great Stuff from Just About Everywhere. The house was overrun. She was unpacking every box and bag she had. I'd lived with the cartons in the cellar, I'd kept up with the storage locker bills when she was gone, I'd signed for the Air Mail packages from places I didn't know she'd been. But still, I couldn't conceive where it had all come from. Flying painted things, masks with teeth, silky and woven fabrics for hanging on walls, kitschy this and tchotchke that — it was like roach infestation, only the roaches were stuff. She called it "inventory."

She kept packing supplies on the coffee table and little piles of receipts, tallied in every imaginable currency, like stacks of poker chips on the kitchen table. When we ate the only place to rest our plates was in our laps. She made lists in ledgers: name or description of object, place of origin, her cost, sale price. This last was a tricky one — what to charge for oddities, what value to assign. She spent days worrying over an ivory Ganesh or a box of beads.

"It's small, I know, insignificant," she said about a carved turtle. "And if I told you how little it cost me you wouldn't believe me. But I can't bear to part with it, certainly not for less than thirty-five, forty dollars. Am I being greedy? Money has never been the point. But I'm attached to the little fellow. You know you can't get this color jade just everywhere, even on the island. There's a right price for everything. You just have to alight on it. Maybe thirty dollars. Or thirty ninety-five, around there. What do you think, Erich? Or am I in the wrong ballpark? I certainly couldn't sell it for less, but maybe I'm thinking too small. This isn't the time for thinking small. Maybe I should display it singly. I could set it on that little octagonal table, you know, with the mother-of-pearl inlay. Where did I put that? Would you check the walk-in? I could set it there by itself, call it an *objet d'art* and price it ostentatiously high. Two hundred twenty dollars, say. And just let it be *that*. Just let it be its starkly beautiful self. Would anybody *see*? Would they see what I see in it? Or is that outrageous? The point has never been money. I'm not trying to con anyone. Though looked at alone, it's pretty exquisite. Can you find me that table? If not in the closet, you might check the bottom of the stairs under the stairs? Probably twenty-two, twenty-three dollars would be right. . . ."

This went on, and she came back to it again and again, until I wanted to fling the little sucker into the Pacific. It was the same with every item. One night, middle of the night, she barged into my room, into my sleep, flicked on the overhead light and plopped down on the edge of my bed. She was holding a string of five paper cranes — a silly little origami mobile from Hawaii — and was trying to decide whether to display it overhead or on top of a shelf or glass case. "It would be like they're swimming, you know. Still pond. Birds of gratitude. Six bucks."

"It's a mobile," I croaked. "Just hang it in the air."

"You think? I do have a couple dozen of them. I could hang some in the air and leave some out." She got up to leave. "'Night again." She switched the light off and I smashed my face into the pillow. I heard the light switch flip. "Six bucks is right, right?"

"Perfect, Mom. Not too much, not too little."

"I knew that," she said, walking out without turning off the light.

I crawled out of bed, squeezing my eyes shut as a way of clinging to that corner of sleep still in reach, and I stubbed my toe on a box of teacups she'd shipped from Taiwan. It hurt like hell, but I swatted the light switch before hopping back to bed to wait for the throbbing to stop. Two seconds later she was there again, in full light, which, now that I'd landed on my back, blared into my eyes. "What was that?" she asked. When I told her, she insisted on inspecting every cup in the box. "You probably didn't chip any, but we should double-check for hairline cracks, just in case." One little blue cup came out at a time and one little blue cup got rewrapped and replaced. When they were all packed up again she said, "I thought they'd be all right, but it's still a relief. Sleep tight."

The light from outside was just beginning to gray up the room. I could make out clothing racks on wheels, towers of small boxes on my bureau and the shapes of large ones on the floor. I was living in her playhouse and these were her blocks. And so nature's abhorrence of a vacuum proved itself again. Those rooms, whose air had been sucked out by her absence, were suddenly filled, glutted with her gewgaws.

Finally, in the spring of my junior year, she signed a lease on a space. She twittered with excitement, and I, anticipating the reclamation of my living quarters, was almost equally thrilled.

Day after day, she went down to Hurricane Street, walked past the trompe l'oeil of a street corner painted on one side of her building, stuck her key proudly in the lock, swept, dusted, scraped, and painted. Day after day, she came home with ideas and plans. Months passed this way, three or four, I can't say for sure. "When's the move?" I'd ask. "Have you rented the van? Can we start shifting boxes toward the back door?"

And she'd say, "Soon, real soon. I just have a few finishing touches." I'd pop around after school and find her at the store, figuring where to hang pictures, or holding swatches of curtain fabrics up to the new paint.

As part of the Free School's mission, students were expected to perform community service. I chose my obligatory good deed the way I chose so many things then, by asking what Erich would have

done. (That's how I'd come to devise research projects on the letter
Q, famous bearded ladies, and "Buddhists and Self-Immolation: a
Response to Responses to Vietnam.") I decided to become a Big
Brother.

I was spending two afternoons a week with my "little brother"
from the YMCA's afterschool program. We were left pretty much on
our own, free to roam or play as we saw fit, as long as we met at, and
returned to, the Y at the appointed times. I'd never before been
older than anybody close to me and, so, was enjoying my responsibility. My charge was a towheaded ten-year-old named Charles,
whom I always called Chaz in my best hipster dialect, an affectation
he loved. He was a great kid, goofy and loving, but one who suffered
from roller-coaster mood swings, the highs of which had him running maniacally wild, and the depths, shutting himself up in a
brooding I couldn't penetrate. His father (whose existence I
doubted) was, he told me, a high-paid fashion photographer who
traveled the world. His mother, I learned firsthand, was some kind
of crazy. A sweet lady with, maybe, an eighth-grade education, she
saw a psychiatric supervisor every day, spent several months a year
in hospitals, and took medicine that made her teeth and gums green.
Chaz lived with his grandmother and, when she was competent, his
mother, in the rooming house the grandmother ran.

Mostly, we avoided talking about such things and just kicked
around town, making fun. We cooked up mystery stories while
walking the canals (we were detectives, Dick and Shamus), ate pizza
when I had money, and noodled around with guitars (I played
Erich's and Chaz played mine). Sometimes, Chaz helped my mom
and me with her store-to-be. One day toward the end of June, he
and I swung by the shop with screwdrivers and wrenches we'd
brought from the house; we were going to assemble a wall of metal
shelves in the stockroom. We found Mom tearing posters off the
walls. She had a piece of paper — a letter of eviction — rolled up in
her fist. We entered into the middle of a rant:

"He knew I was good for it. He knew I was getting the place
together. I never lied to him. I told him from the beginning what we

stood to make from this place. But all of a sudden he decides he can't wait. All of a sudden I owe him two months' rent and that's it, time's up. Did he give me fair warning? No! Did he ask me if I'm good for it? No! He didn't even come by himself, the fucking geek. Sends by his henchman, his goomba son. 'I'm sorry, Lady, but Nikos says you gotta get your stuff out.' He wants my stuff out?" She ripped down a pair of curtains. "He can fucking have my stuff out!"

And as she flew around the rooms she kicked furniture over, knocked pictures down, unscrewed lightbulbs and smashed them against the walls. She kept saying, "I made this place beautiful. I made his slummy little hole beautiful!" She strode into the bathroom and turned the water on, after shoving rags into the drains. I ran after her, turning off the faucet and unstopping the sink. By the time I noticed Charles, he was crouched in a corner by the windows, scowling and silent like some mud-stained grunt gone mad, scouting enemies in the jungle.

"Mom," I called, moving to the boy, "Stop it! Charles is here!"

But she kept shouting, pounding her fists against the walls, "I made this hole beautiful!"

I ignored her and tried to soothe Charles, who seemed to be growing darker before my eyes, as if someone were slowly pulling down a shade nearby. I put my arm around his shoulder and talked quietly. "It's ok, man, it's ok. She's just upset. It's got nothing to do with us. Shut up, Mom! You're upsetting him. It's ok, Chaz, it's nothing, man."

"He should be upset!" she shouted back. "It's a terrible thing, a terrible world!"

I hustled him into the street, practically pushing him. Outside, he set his little body, clenching his fists and hunching his back — assuming a position to stalk. He strode away from me, down toward the beach. I followed him, trying to talk comfort. I don't know what she did after we left. I didn't care.

In time Chaz uncoiled slightly, and we were able to walk back to the Y. It took more than an hour, though, and we got back late. I got chewed out.

One of the senior counselors took him home. I stayed away most of the night, traipsing the streets, watching the oil derricks bobbing on the outskirts of town. As I moved through town I narrated my wanderings to myself and occasionally stopped to make notes in the "Ballad" journal I'd started carrying.

Over time I filled these notebooks with phrases, messages to myself, most of which I can no longer decipher. But I scribbled away in them constantly. Sometimes I would follow people, usually a group of girls my own age, and mark down everything they did and what time they did it. I had no reason for doing this, except that sometimes I would develop a crush on one of the girls and just prowl around hoping to see her. Beyond that, I was only following the mandate of Erich's "Ballad": life as art, art as life, every little thing a part.

I conceived of a senior project that would contain parts of the "Ballad" without giving away the lifelong intention of the whole. I would make a documentary, beginning this summer and ending whenever I had to show it in class: "My Life As Erich." The film would encompass my travels through Venice over the course of a year, tour guiding, talking to myself, watching people on the streets, interviewing strangers, whatever came my way. All I lacked was a camera.

I wrote to Oomie, telling her about my idea in a way that skewed the truth. It was an assignment, I said, to spend the last year of high school making a movie, but I wouldn't be able to fulfill it since I didn't have the right equipment. As expected, her next letter came with a check. They usually did. A postcard to her was usually good for ten dollars; a letter, twenty. This indirectly direct plea for funds reaped thirty-five dollars. I cashed the check and took the money, along with a gold pocket watch Mom had brought me from Geneva, to a pawnshop.

"Nice watch," the man said. "Looks new."

"Swiss," I told him. "It is new. So's the chain."

"Fob," he corrected.

"Right, fob. What'll you give me for it?"

He stalled, studying the watch through a loupe, winding the stem, checking a couple of books. He came back to the counter and squinted at me over a pair of half-glasses. "How do I know this is yours to sell, young man?"

I plucked the timepiece from his hand and, taking his jeweler's screwdriver from the counter, popped the back cover. I held it out to him. "See. That's me."

"'Missing my Erich. Switzerland 1972,'" he read.

When he looked up I was holding my student I.D. card before his eyes the way a TV cop displays his badge to a peephole. "C'est moi."

He nodded subtly and looked back at the watch. "You selling or pawning?"

"Final sale," I said. "Closeout. All inventory must go."

He nodded again, running his eyes over my face. "What you need the money for?"

I pointed to a shelf over his head. "That," I said.

He shoved a small stepladder with his foot and climbed it. "This, huh?"

"That."

He turned back toward me holding a Super-8 movie camera with a tag hanging from it. He cupped the tag in his hand and peered down at it. "Told me she'd only used it once. Tried. Couldn't figure it out." He slipped the price off and dropped it in a little drawer. The camera did look new. He inspected the camera and the watch side by side. "Nice watch," he said again, "but not nice enough. I was asking eighty dollars for the camera."

"How much for the watch? It's real gold."

"Not quite that much."

"I've got money," I told him.

"How much?" he asked.

I knew I'd need cash for film and developing. I lied. "Fifteen bucks."

"You got twenty, you got a deal."

I turned my obvious back to him and peeled two tens off my roll of bills. I put them on the counter. "Deal." I reached for the camera.

"You want a spotlight for that?" he asked, taking out another box with an attachment. "For night movies?"

He had me. "Naagh," I said.

"It goes with the camera. I can't do anything with it, you take the movie camera."

"I need money for film and stuff."

"Acchh," he said. "There's always money for that later."

I hesitated.

"Look," he said. "It's a good camera and a good price. The light cost half again as much. I throw it in for a sawbuck. Who knows? Maybe you're the next Alfred Hitchcock. Ten bucks it's yours. Even got batteries. Even in California the sun don't last forever."

I left with the camera and light and five bucks in my pocket. That night, armed with a roll of Super-8 film, I came back to the store and began my movie. I zoomed in from the building's facade to the PAWN SHOP FAST CASH sign. I panned to the side window and tried to film through it, scanning the items displayed in the window case. Mostly, though I picked up light bounce and what I thought of as arty — my own reflection, filming my own reflection. Since I didn't have simultaneous sound, I sat on the curb, writing narration to go under these opening shots. It was mostly drivel:

> A pawnshop in Venice, California. They call it a pawnshop because, once inside, you become a pawn in the seedy underworld of American capitalism. Desperate people enter this world to borrow money against their prized possessions: musical instruments, wedding rings, coin collections passed down across the generations. They trade beauty for bucks, and, more often than not, they never scrape together enough to buy that beauty back. I walked into this store today with the opposite intention. I was after beauty, in search of art, and I'd pay whatever it took. I walked out with everything I needed to begin making this film. Welcome to my first movie. Welcome to "My Life As Erich: Senior Year."

This inauspicious beginning kicked off a year of similarly horrible, self-referential filmmaking, in the process of which I thought about little else. I stopped hanging out with kids from school, including Soapy, and I drifted away from my responsibilities with Charles. I hung out in my room or walked the streets, camera and notebook in hand. I thought up voice-overs while panning the murals of Venice. When I didn't have film, I carried the camera anyway and shot away, empty canister. Late that summer, Holly called me.

"We're worried about you," she said. "Nobody ever sees you anymore."

"I'm working on something" I told her. "There's nothing to worry about."

"When do we get to see it? Is this that 'ballad' you were talking about?"

"I can't really say anything more. I don't want to think too much about it. I'm just trying to let it take me."

"Well, you need to let yourself be obsessed, I guess," she said. "But don't stay away long."

"I'll be back," I said.

Soapy was more roundabout. He dropped little notes in our mailbox. They had jokes on them and pictures, to which he added captions that either made no sense or referred directly to my disappearance. He drew a thick mustache and long beard on the Mona Lisa and wrote "Rip van Winkle, Erich Hofmann, or the Missing Link?" Once, when he called, I picked up the phone (usually I didn't answer it).

"Long lost Poobah," he greeted me.

I told him I was expecting an important call. I couldn't stay on the phone.

"Whoa. Mister important," he said, obviously hurt. "What's the matter, your friends don't count?"

"I don't have time for friends now," I said, hanging up.

One day I was out filming along the boardwalk when I saw him, through the lens, walking toward me. I kept filming, zooming in on just his face. He stood in front of the camera and sang the whole of the Beatles' "I'm Looking Through You." When he was done he flipped me the finger and sort of goose-stepped out of frame.

I saw him again when school began, but we avoided each other. Ordinarily, this would have been hard to do in such a small school, but all the seniors had to find internships or jobs to fulfill our requirements. Soapy and I found ones that took us away on alternate days. He went to the phone company as an observer/journeyman on the mainframe computers in data entry. "Typical corporate bullshit," I wrote in my journal the day I heard about it. "Soap on the slippery slope." The placement lady at VFS, when I told her I was doing a documentary for my senior project, lined up an apprenticeship in a film-processing lab in Santa Monica. Between these work hours, my time on "My Life," and preparations for college applications, it was easy enough to stay out of everyone's way.

Including my mother's. Over the course of the year, she'd found and, one way or another, forfeited, three more spaces for her store. One of them she started to fix up and then walked out on, complaining that there were "strings attached," which I took to mean a man wanting something from her. Another turned out to be a scam. She paid a deposit, waited the weeks required before her lease took effect, and then discovered that the key she had didn't fit any of the locks and the guy who'd rented it to her didn't exist. In the spring, she signed on another space, the one she'd been waiting for all along, she said. This contract, like the first, ended in a late-summer eviction when she failed to open the store in time to generate rent money.

I did my best to stay away from her. She was obsessed with her store and I with my own plans: to continue my movie and to find a college far away. The first part wasn't as easy as I thought it might be. I was able to develop my film for free after hours at the lab, but, except for the couple of times I stole a reel or two of film from there, I never had enough money for what I needed. Even being selective, I could easily go through a roll a day. The extra twenty or twenty-five dollars a week was more than I had, since the stray cash I got out of my mother had to go for food and clothes and college application fees.

I started pilfering Mom's "Stuff from Just About Everywhere," one item at a time, and selling it where I could. Mostly, I'd walk the beach trying to hawk a Mexican ashtray or Balinese rod puppet for an even five bucks. I did pretty consistent business. Originally, I'd film the transactions, but my customers got antsy in front of the lens. One guy, a bodybuilder who fancied a celluloid art deco electric clock, threatened (on film) to punch me out and break the camera if I didn't turn it off. From then on I kept business and art separate.

I'm pretty sure everybody who bought from me thought I was a junkie who'd stolen this stuff and was selling it to buy dope. I looked like a junkie: stringy hair hanging greasy out of my fedora, patches of adolescent beard, thin hayseed body. People were more generous with junkies in those days; besides, I didn't care what they thought as long as I could buy film.

Whether or not she ever noticed stuff missing from her stagnant collection of international bric-a-brac, I don't know. I did my best to circulate among the cartons, to cover my tracks, and not to sell more than one of anything. There was a lot to choose from, and, though I probably made off with a couple hundred items over the course of the year, I doubt she was onto me. Sometimes I'd trash some of the stuff, doing my best to make it look like it had happened in the shipping or moving. I lopped the tails off half a box of Guatemalan lizard statues and took one box out of a dark corner of the cellar and rolled it down the stairs before putting it back. When she asked about something that was missing, I just said, "Don't you remember, that was in the box of stuff that got broken in the move? You threw that out." The realities of her dream shop had become so chaotic and unbearable by then that she swallowed every gaslight excuse as just another defeat.

Erich's spirit had inhabited my body. I hated her.

My father offered me a way to prove it. He reached out across the five years since he'd seen me, since he'd stared down at the ground we would bury Erich in and given me up to her. "I can't," he had confessed.

This time he said, "Why don't you think about Columbia?"

"You mean for?"

"For next year. For college. You could get to know your little sister . . ." (He had a baby daughter, Amanda, by now.) ". . . And then there's me. And Hildy. It's not a bad school. Not what it *was* maybe, but look who've they've got teaching."

"Dad," I said.

"We could get a 'rate.' When they tenure you and make you a full professor, you get a rate."

There was the sweetest plaintive strain to his self-mockery, a grace note of entreaty. He was offering me a chance to do what I was champing at the bit to do — go home, be near him, and sell my mother out at the same time. It would be the blow to end all blows. I could smash her stockpile of collectibles from here to Tucson and it wouldn't have the killing impact of choosing Dad.

I drank air. I filled up, balloonlike, with the expectation of flight. And then I said, "I can't, Dad, do that to Mom."

"No. Of course not," he echoed, as though suddenly remembering something.

So I did what Mac had tried to do with Erich's ashes: I found a middle ground. I had the vaguest reasons for picking Madison. I remembered thinking, on my trip to Wisconsin to retrieve Erich from camp, that the land was kind. I pictured the University of Wisconsin as one large Venice Free School without the squalor of a beach town. Deborah, meanwhile, had resettled a state away in Minneapolis, where she'd hooked up with a man named Richard, after more than three rainy years in Seattle with Andy and his genius friends.

I filmed my mother's response, when I told her. Her eyes flamed open then glazed over. She put on her best camera smile and said: "My days are full enough. I have a million things to do. Dozens of people are already angry with me for neglecting them. Besides, Erich, you need to go. It's the best thing: get out and grow up. Deborah will be nearby, and Oomie and Papa, at least for half the year. It's perfect, really. For both of us. I'll visit you all together. I really should be getting on with things, anyway. Besides, we still have one summer to kick up our heels before you become a college man." I could see what she was really saying, even on the bad Super-8: "I have no one! You're killing me! Stay!"

Lorna had suffered a string of losses in the year or more since

she'd stopped traveling. The World's Room fiascoes multiplied.
Several of her admirers — including Dad, Raoul, and the old guy
Harve — had gotten married, all to younger women. Deborah
accentuated the trend by moving in with Richard, a fifty-year-old
man. Also, inexplicably, my mother had begun to grow fat.

She threw herself into a dazzling regimen of positive thinking
and self-mastery studies. The house was festooned with little notes
to herself, which she'd scribble off and tape up on the fridge, the
mirror, a door — anywhere: "So many people love you." "You're a
woman with vision." "Your vibrancy makes the air shiver as you pass."
She bought books with such titles as *The Loved Self, Conquering Self-
Defeat Through Self-Hypnosis*, and *Mind Over Other Matters*. These,
along with others on astral projection, reincarnation, and EST, were
a far cry from her previous stacks of poetry by Blake and Yeats, novels by D. H. Lawrence, Henry Miller, and Thomas Hardy.

By my last summer at home, I could barely look at her. I didn't
want to hurt her, but I couldn't help myself. She used me the way you
use a mirror after a long sleep — to prove to yourself you still exist.
I kept dark. I attacked her with the full weight of my indifference.

I showed some clips of my documentary for finals. The teachers tripped over themselves to support my "intentions" with it and
to find details they liked. My classmates were befuddled. I had my
own critical response, which I repeated, mantralike, during the
several hours it took me to unravel and trash a couple hundred
rolls of film: "You suck. You suck. You suck." I disemboweled the
movie camera, taped a note to it, marking the time and date of its
destruction, and tossed it into the alley behind our house, con-
signing it to cat hell.

I skipped graduation. Shortly after announcing to my mother my
decision to attend school just miles from where Erich had cracked
up, I went out and got a job stocking produce at the supermarket. I
booked every hour I could, overtime, double overtime. I'd steal off
to work before she woke up and rarely see daylight. I watched
Nixon's resignation speech on a portable black-and-white TV while
leaning against the door of a meat freezer.

Coming into the house at night, I'd say, "Hi. I'm beat. Going to bed." I'd ignore the plate of food beckoning me from the table, avoid her red eyes. She'd say, "I love you," all wheedly. "Me too," I'd mumble back, without feeling a thing. It was duty, not love, and I made that clear.

She took her revenge.

She was just coming in to do a little shopping, she said. All I saw were heads turning in the checkout lines as a crowd encircled some lady on the ground in front. A little kid, one of the baggers who'd been outside gathering carts, came flying back to find me. They wanted Erich Hofmann outside. We waited for the ambulance in the middle of the street, like some scene from the nightly news, where the mother kneels over the sprawled corpse of her son, traffic stopped all around. Only this was the opposite: the mother lay sprawling and crying, while the son knelt over her, frozen with embarrassment as the crowd stared. Eighty-year-old women fall so, not strong, selfish forty-five-year-olds. I got into the ambulance with her, dutiful and close.

I spent my first week of college at my mother's bedside. My freshman orientation consisted of fetching and carrying for this woman with casts on her right ankle and right wrist. My foot locker and duffel bag sat packed in my room. My books and records waited in boxes, ready to be shipped (they never were). And I sat, wearing the same jeans and Heineken T-shirt, for nine days. I fashioned a shoe box into the kind of card holder my grandfather, with movement in only one hand, used, and we played gin rummy. While she slept I watched TV, until she rang the bell I'd put beside her bed in case she needed me. I cooked and served her meals. In the first shaky days, I forked the food into her mouth. But when she sang along with the radio, I left the room. She would sing more loudly, more prettily, as if, by creating the perfect tone, she could woo me back. I wouldn't come back, though. I'd had enough of my mother's siren songs.

She couldn't use a crutch or cane, because she carried her broken wrist in a sling. The doctor waited a week to undo the sling and put a walking cast on her ankle. The whole effect physicalized the split in her: one side of her was solid and strong, ringing for service. The other half was crippled and pathetic, hobbling on a wobbly foot, weeping from one eye, wounded wrist cradled like a small bird.

Everyone else had gone away: Soapy to the University of Las Vegas (a whim, he'd announced to the class) and Holly to Taos, New Mexico. When she could walk with some confidence, my mother allowed that I, too, might leave. And I did.

I took a cab to the airport and left her where I'd last seen her: sitting, ankle extended, in a kitchen chair propped against the back screen door, smoking a cigarette and waving to me casually — with her good arm — as if I were going down the block for a quart of milk.

15

Vow of Silence

I didn't see my mother for two and a half years. The reasons were partly economic; neither of us had money to travel. Nor, we each complained, did we have time to spare. The real reasons were, of course, other and implied. So, we stayed put, me in Madison, she in sunny California.

I wrote lengthy, upbeat letters that revealed as little as possible. I conscientiously kept her unapprised of my increasingly odd life on campus, the monk's robes I'd started wearing, my solitary experiments with speed and psilocybin, or even the months I went without attending class before I officially took a leave of absence junior year. Instead, I issued a bright, periodic gazette filled with sketches of teachers, impromptu essays on prison recidivism and medieval religious iconography, and anecdotes about tending the counter at a Lebanese delicatessen, where no one else spoke more than a few words of English. I wrote to emphasize the distance between us. I wrote to emphasize my silence.

She never wrote. She called erratically, sometimes less than once a month and sometimes several times a day. She either reproved me for not calling or chatted manically about such and such a friend, whom, nine times out of ten, I'd never met. The store was still and forever a pie in the sky. Until she could "actualize" it, she picked up work where she could. She supervised rentals at one of the myriad new apartment complexes that had sprung up since the renewal of Venice had begun a few years before. She filled in at a girlfriend's lingerie store, Honey Bare.

Mom saw Deborah, who visited a few times a year with Richard

in tow. I saw my sister, too, when she'd send me Greyhound tickets
to Minneapolis for holidays. Likewise, Mom flew to see Oomie and
Papa wintering in Florida, and I took the bus to see them in Skokie
in summer. I even saw my father a couple of times. He flew me out
to New York, where I sat through long weekends with his new family like some atavistic lump. But Mom, no.

Occasionally, I'd take a bus up to Elkhart Lake, to Erich's summer camp. It was deserted there off-season, and the grounds had
numerous inlets for prowlers like me. I spent many nights there over
the years, curled up in my coat on a stripped bunk bed in one of the
cabins. I would photograph the empty buildings, eat alone in the
vast dining hall, and sit cross-legged at the center of the stage on
which Erich had debuted. I got high in the dance studio, staring at
myself in the mirrors that covered two walls. I dropped peyote buttons and floated through the infirmary halls where my brother had
been locked away. The grounds were so vacant, so silent, that the
only sounds were the ones I made, my shoes on the grass and gravel,
the chafing of my pant legs, the clucking of my camera's shutter, the
hiss of my mouth dragging on a joint or cigarette. I was a ghost in
the camp, haunting the grounds like one of the phantoms in camp
legends: the purple lady, the handless butcher, the boy who cries in
the woods.

Once at college, I all but abandoned the "Ballad." I had too much
work, and, on top of that, I'd come to distrust words. I blamed them
for the failure of my documentary. I had, in narrating the film for my
classmates, felt so heatedly embarrassed by my pretentious tone —
alternately smart-ass ironic, abstruse, and humiliatingly earnest —
that I'd, finally, only minutes from the end, stopped speaking altogether. I was sick of lying, and words, the instruments of my lies,
became the enemy.

Even two thousand miles from home, though, I couldn't get
away. If I'd hoped to start fresh, my first expository writing assignment squelched that hope: "Write 500 to 750 words about your
name." The teacher directed us to "dig into the meaning of your
name, both personal and historical. How do you feel about your

name? Does it describe the real you? How do others respond to it? Are there any stories you can tell that relate directly to your name? Our whole lives attach themselves to our names. We grow into them; they contain us. Write about it. Whatever comes to mind. There is no right or wrong." He meant this to inspire us and we — dutiful, scared freshmen — did our best to be inspired.

Here's what I wrote:

The Rest Is Silence
By Erich Hofmann

As a kid, I told people I'd been named after the goatherd boy in *Heidi*, but that was a lie. I told this lie because I wanted to feel that my name was more interesting than it was. Instead of being just another pointy Aryan boy, I wanted people to see me as a fictional character, a fairy-tale lad, free of spirit and almost wild in my connection to nature, animals, and earth. It wouldn't be such a bad thing to have Heidi as a girlfriend either, I thought.

Oddly, I'd never read the book *Heidi* and still haven't. I'd read a lot of books but, as this wasn't one of them, I based this concocted history of my name on what I'd heard about the story, thus compounding lie upon lie. Since you only get one name, though, and since your self keeps changing within that name, it seemed to me only fair to make up whatever I wanted. I couldn't have articulated this then, of course, but I knew in my child's mind that my name was my privilege, to do with, dispense with, alter, or provide meaning for as I saw fit.

I was about to write that I was born with the name "Eric" but added the "h" to add color and mystery. I'm aware that I could lie again here and no one would be the wiser. Because this is an expository writing class, however, and not a fiction class, I've decided to stick to the strict truth: the story of my name.

There's not much story, which is, perhaps, why I felt compelled to bring Heidi into it in the first place. (Seven hundred and fifty is, after all, a lot of words to write about two.) My name is only half reflective of my heritage. I have one Russian-Jewish grandmother, one Italian (Roman Catholic) grandfather and (had) two Austrian (Lutheran) grandparents on my father's side. Hofmann, then, comes from these latter ancestors, while Eric, which was a name my mother preferred, suggests neither the Jewish nor Italian influences.

"I just liked the name," my mother told me when I asked her about it once. "And I thought Eric Blore was the funniest man in the movies."

You might not remember Eric Blore, but, if you turn on any old Fred Astaire and Ginger Rogers movie, you'll find him. He's always the butler or solicitor or someone who lives by propriety while being continually rattled by events. My favorite line of his is "Scone, sir?" I'd never heard of a scone (which is a kind of English biscuit) until I saw *The Gay Divorcée* or whichever movie this was in.

So my mother, who'd been a featured dancer in films herself before she went back to school for an advanced degree in social work (she is now senior faculty at Berkeley, in addition to maintaining a small private practice), chose the name "Eric." My father, being a linguist and a fairly fastidious man, had two thoughts about it. First, although he generally liked the name, he found it just a little ordinary. Second, his idea to add the silent *h* to the end would, he believed, enhance its Germanic quality and, so, make it fit better with "Hofmann" (which still retains the German

spelling). The added letter might also make it stand
ever so slightly apart among American names and
spellings. They were agreed, then. All that remained
was for me to be born.

My strongest feelings about the name center
around this silent *h*. What does it mean that the most
unique — special — qualities of my name (and by
extension of *me*) are created by a letter that goes
unspoken, keeps quiet, silent? There might be mystery there, some secret hoarded joy, or some sordid
secret. Let this mystery stand. Let silence reign.

My poor teacher, an adjunct A.B.D. who had no idea what kind of
weird psychological terrain he was walking, was as pleased as Punch.
He copied the paper and read it out loud, thus turning me into a
mini class star until the next assignment, with which I got even more
clever and coy, *too* clever and coy. He moved on to adulate other
budding writers. I slacked off, until, by midterm, I was doing the
bony minimum.

I couldn't overcome my disgust with words. I turned to images
instead. I began taking pictures with Rob Takke, my first college
friend. Rob turned me on to hallucinogens and loaned me a camera.
We roamed the campus and town, shooting everything in strange black
and white. I gravitated toward empty classrooms, bathrooms, and
dorm rooms. I did a series of shoots of Erich's camp, abandoned and
waiting. Rob was more into nature, harsh — bare trees, road kill — and
lyrical — rime on branches, whitecaps on the lake, the northern lights.
We both sneaked candids of young townie women, alone and in
groups; these we collected in an album entitled "Wisconsin Girls."

A word about my monk's habit. Late freshman year, I met a man
who had lived in a Benedictine abbey. Oliver had dropped out of
Yale School of Drama to answer what he felt was a direct call from
God. After five years in the monastery, on the eve of his ordination
vows, he answered another call: the cry of the flesh. He became a
Broadway gypsy, dancing and singing in a range of cheesy musicals.

When I met him, he'd come back to academia, where he was trying to blend his love of ancient Greek and Latin religious ceremony with his passion for Gower Champion and Michael Bennett. He was resident advisor for my dormitory, and I think he singled me out as someone who needed attention.

One day, midafternoon, Oliver came to my room, holding a brown-paper grocery bag with my name written in blue ink across it, like a large packed lunch. He said something about skins and how they change. Then he sang a campy version of that number from *Mame* about needing a little Christmas and he handed me the bag.

"I want you to have this," he said finally. "Don't worry, I have others."

And so I began to wear monk's robes. I wore them to class, into town, in my room. People recognized me on campus, pointed me out, made the sign of the cross when passing. They didn't talk to me, these strangers on the quad, except perhaps to raise a hand and call, "Good day to you, Brother Madison."

Rob thought the "monk's getup" was a trip. "Wish I'd thought of it, man," he said, clicking my picture. "I look really fucked up in brown, though."

Oliver had stumbled on to a truth about me, continuous with a past I'd almost forgotten. In Mexico, I'd practically lived in churches, sneaking off to them wherever we went, especially during my mother's depressions. The reasons were hardly mysterious: I wanted my parents with me in ways I couldn't have them. Since I couldn't talk with them in the flesh, I'd talk to them in spirit. I'd sit in the damp cool of the quietest spots in Mexico and carry on conversations not with any God, but with my mom and dad. I'd tell my mother how beautiful she was. "You have so much to live for," I'd say. I'd tell her not to be sad, not to worry, everything will work out. "When we get home, I'll do more stuff around the house. I'll get a job and earn some extra money, so you can be a singer." To Dad I'd describe whole towns and narrate the events of our adventure (leaving out the parts about Mom not speaking for days on end). I went over the story of Erich's chipped tooth a dozen times, how he'd fallen into a cement fountain playing statue tag, how wacky his smile looked, how Jerry Lewis.

"So don't worry about us," I told my father. "We can look after ourselves. Of course, we miss you like the devil."

When these talks were over, I'd kneel down, as the dark-swathed Mexican women around me did, and, leaning forward over folded hands, I'd ask God to look after us. I wanted to believe that my thoughts were heard somewhere, that they rose up through cloud and star systems, making their whispery way to some guardian ear. Erich and Deborah watched me come and go. They started calling me "church boy," "baby Jesus" (pronounced *hey-Zeus*), and "little monkey-monk." Then, seven or eight years later, my R.A. sprang a set of robes on me. "This is who I am," I thought.

In the two years I wore this habit, only one person asked me about it. It was December of my third year at Madison. I was heading into the terrace when a girl walked up to me and asked, "What's it like, being a monk?"

"I wouldn't know," I said.

"I didn't think so," she said. "I'm Anne," she continued, extending her hand. "I always wanted to ask you that."

"Always?"

"Well, since September. I'm a freshman. This is my last day, though; I'm transferring to Delaware. Home. My parents are finally getting a divorce, and my little brother and sister need me around."

"Oh," I said.

"You should throw me a farewell dinner," said Anne.

"Sure," I agreed.

So we walked into town until we came to a Holiday Inn. "Here," she said. "I want my farewell dinner here."

I was used to being an oddity on campus, but this middle-American decor threw my outfit into uneasy relief. Anne seemed to think nothing of it. She led me to a table in the center of the dining room, dropped her book bag, and sat down.

She launched into the story of her family: "Everybody's trying to pretend like nothing's happening. You know, 'This won't change anything. We both love you all just the same as always.' Typical middle-class bullshit. Of course, Dad's been screwing this really vulgar woman from the school board for a couple hundred years, my little sister's gained fifteen pounds in two months, my brother's all of a sudden discovered Led Zeppelin, and my mother doesn't think there's anything to talk about. Nobody thinks I should move back, but somebody needs to be there for Leslie and Dale. My mom says, 'They're still young enough. Kids heal fast.' They're fifteen and thirteen, for God's sake; they'll be circus freaks the rest of their lives. I was always this really wild child, you know. All of a sudden I'm the only adult."

I looked at her across the table from me, half lit by a small candle floating in one of those holders with the jagged, diamondlike surfaces. She wasn't beautiful at all; in fact, she was plain as day, and that's what was great about her face. Everything she felt spoke plainly through her features. As with the instant intimacy of her ready-or-not-here-I-come life story, nothing was hidden. Her hair was too short — almost butch — to hide anything. Her nose was straightforward. She had a watermark scar under one of her salt-of-the-earth brown eyes. It was as though everything she did or said confirmed her character, made apparent more of the same self. I felt, by contrast, distorted.

She was staring back, gathering herself it seemed. "What about you?"

"What about me what?" I asked.

"What about, like, your family? Your parents still together? You mind if I ask?"

"Ask away," I said, trying to make my face look as open as hers.

"I mean who are you? Where are you from? Who are your friends? What'll you do when you're done with school? What's it like knowing people are looking at you, at your clothes?"

I took a breath. "That's a lot of questions."

"Pick one. Whichever."

There's a kind of stage fright reserved for revelations in restaurants, those moments when you can actually feel your blood coursing. You become aware of yourself as a mechanism and, at the same instant, as a person with fears and desires. I was suddenly afraid that she would get up and go.

I studied her for a long time. I saw that she had three earrings in one ear, thin silver circles that ascended the tanned cartilage in small steps. I noticed the bleached hair above her lip. And then I told her everything. I *blurted* everything. This strange girl I'd known for less than an hour, who in a day would leave Madison forever, asked me a couple of questions, and, for the first time, I spewed up my life: brother, mother, Mexico, name and not name.

She said little in reply, but she encouraged my revelations wordlessly: "Uh-huh." "Oh." "Yaagh." When I wound down, she squinted at me, nodding, and said, "You must feel so cut off."

How could I convey what I felt to this watermarked girl? I could tell her stories. I could describe Erich or Lorna feature by feature. But I could never express to her the shape of the space in a room from which they'd been removed. I could never tell her whether we augment the world, having passed through it, or the opposite, that we deplete it, as if the world were fuller before our passage.

"Cut off from what?" I asked.

The room grew intensely cold. I began to shiver. More than a quaver or tremble, this was a full-body shimmy, as if an Arctic front had blasted through the room and taken my clothes with it. Anne watched calmly as I knocked over and tried to right my water glass, as I retracted my hands up into the sleeves of my robe, as I wrapped my arms around my arms and clenched my jaw to keep it from rattling. I didn't know what was happening. I wanted to call out to her, but all I could do was try to stop shaking. Bumps rose on my skin. The ice water rolled into my lap.

Anne reached across the table with her napkin. She folded the corners of the tablecloth and dabbed at the pool spreading over the linen. She kept her eyes on me.

I stood up, wiping the water off my thigh, vibrating until I thought my legs would buckle.

"Breathe," she said.

I tried.

"Deeply," she said.

The waitress came by to see if we were all right, if we wanted dessert. When I'd subsided and sat back down, I glanced over at Anne. She scrutinized my face, but whether she found me pathetic, disgusting, or compelling, I couldn't tell. Finally, she said, "I've been thinking a lot lately about how in the movies, just when things reach an impasse, a new force enters in. You know, like when a couple is fighting and their fight has peaked, reached a stalemate, the phone has to ring or someone has to burst into the room. Help has to come from the outside."

"Yeah, but it doesn't," I said.

We paid our bill and left.

"This was nice," she said, when we stood at the perimeter of campus ready to part. "It meant a lot to me. Don't let's lose touch." Then she added, "Erich."

"Let's don't," I said, looking away from her.

The next morning, I began a three-day sitting fast at Picnic Point on Lake Mendota. Attired in only my robes and sandals with socks, and protected at night by a sleeping bag, I spent more than seventy hours in the woods on the shore of the lake. It didn't rain or snow while I was out, but the ground was cold and hard and the water had started its deep freeze.

I knew about this place, a peninsula nestled off to one side of the campus, from the year before, when Joni Mitchell had shot her "black crow" cover for *Hejira* there. On the front of the album, Joni, dressed in a beret and black furs, stands, apparently on the frozen lake, with a bank of trees over her left shoulder and a road seeming to appear where her torso should be. Inside, the same furs are spread to reveal large black wings. Joni skate-flies across the ice. On the back, a male figure skater bends with curved arms before a woman standing at some distance in a bridal gown. The peninsula is a smoky line behind them.

The peace of Picnic Point — you have to walk a half mile through the woods to reach it — intrigued me. The image of the crow flying across the frozen water and the skater's arms curved like Atlas with the globe, framing the angelic bride, seemed as mysterious as a Zen koan, a riddle for me alone, if only I could solve it.

I'd gone out to the Point the year before, after Joni had left. I did my own photo shoot at the time — empty ice, empty woods, empty space. When the beautiful *Hejira* was released, she revisited Madison for a concert. Now, the morning after I'd met Anne, I went back to the Point with a half dozen tabs of white cross speed and no food. I planned to stay for three days and nights or until I could penetrate the mystery of the crow on ice.

I experienced body rushes but no visions. I grew sick and sad. I didn't sleep. After returning to the attic apartment I rented in town, I couldn't keep food down. On my second day back, I called Oliver, who brought me chicken soup and a carton of rice. Later, he drove me to the hospital, where I was diagnosed with pneumonia and fed intravenously for a time, before being sent home to bed.

I burned my monk's costume in a rusted oil drum down by the train tracks.

16

Words for Papa

Somewhat recovered, I met Deborah at O'Hare and we flew together to Florida in time to see Papa Val die. Papa had lived through a series of strokes. He'd survived for years like a city that, having suffered a severe quake, was sure to be shook with more. The only question was whether they'd come as tremors or major hits along the fault line. In the end, there was hardly movement at all, certainly no cataclysm, just a gradual stilling and settling and out.

The next day, we drove back to the airport to pick up Mom. I counted the months since I'd seen her — twenty-eight — and braced myself. She spotted me as soon as she reached the gate and, dropping her carryons, stretched her hands toward my face. Her grip was iron on my cheeks and her eyes, dewy with cinematic sentiment, were willing me to meet her gaze. "She's rehearsed," I thought. She pulled my face down to hers, to kiss or threaten I couldn't tell. Then she flung her arms around mine and clutched on. Deborah stood by, shifting on her feet.

We had both been transformed. I was aware of my insufficient beard and mustache, my bad skin, long hair, and raggedy body. I'd lost weight fasting and more in the hospital. I could have been poster boy for "anorexics of the avant-garde." She was no longer young; she was nearly fifty and looked it. She'd ballooned out, plumped up. Even her once strong hands looked porky. Her beauty was buried in the folds of her skin.

Later, looking at her thinning hair from the back seat of the rental car, glimpsing, when she turned, her darting, distrustful eyes and puffy face, I thought, for the first time in my life: "My mother is crazy." Then I thought, "She's not me." By crazy, I guess I meant a kind of general, lifelong crazy, not anything acute or limited to that moment in the car. By "not me," I'm not sure what I meant. That night, though, on the sofa of my grandparents' Miami apartment, I woke from a frightening dream in which my stomach was torn out of my body by a rope that held me over a dark pit. I fell and fell and fell, terrified but free. Free, I thought, from Lorna.

When we returned to the apartment, Oomie was pacing, trying to cook, trying to clean. Deborah had offered to take her to the airport with us, but she'd declined, so we left her in the care of a neighbor named Sadie, who seemed impervious to my grandmother's maniacal mourning dance. Sadie washed dishes.

Mom went right over to hug Oomie, but Oomie broke away. "I have to do this," she said, and started whisking eggs in a steel bowl.

"Mother," Lorna said, "sit down just for a minute. Let's talk."

"Can't sit," said Oomie. "I'm not a sitter. Gotta do this."

Soon they were shouting at each other — screams of sympathy and concern, no doubt — as my mother wrestled her mother away from the sink. Deborah and I tried to pry them apart and calm the scene. When Richard arrived, Deborah moved into a hotel with him, and I shared the guest room with Mom.

The funeral was a sweet thing, held in the chapel of the condominium complex — no coffin — and attended by a bevy of pert old people who'd known Papa from his daily treks around the pool and his nightly pinochle games. The men wore knee-length shorts and guayabera shirts, some with ties, and the women wore pale, floral housedresses. Canes and walkers could be seen in abundance, parked alongside the bare, brown knees and crusty ankles of the mourners. All were respectful but not grim, as if the loss of their friend were offset by the chipper prospect of an afternoon with something to do. Oomie refused to come downstairs for the service, in spite of our strongest urgings and those of a delegation of lady neighbors.

Lorna, Deborah, and I were the service, sharing some reminiscences, alongside a minister my mother rustled up from some New

Age church she'd found out about through her friend Larry. Larry, having adopted the role of our family's designated mourner, stood by, as he had in D.C. eight years prior. The minister's hair was blond and longer than mine, even before I'd had it trimmed at the insistence of my sister. Nevertheless, the congregation insisted on calling him "Rebbe." They seemed to have forgotten that my grandfather, an Italian, was, in fact, a kind of interloper in their little Israel. Or maybe they felt that the dead man, after thirty years of "Doo doo doo," deserved an honorary place in the league of suffering to which they all belonged.

Slower than the parade of years, we all made our way out to the lobby and up the elevators to Oomie's. The women took her by the hands and clucked and shook their heads, even as she snapped at them, "I don't want to talk about it; I don't want to talk about anything."

The men, as if by magnetic pull, immediately arranged themselves on the sectional couch and folding chairs, a mini-amphitheater facing, on the circular glass coffee table, a spectacle of noshes. The women shuttled from the dining room to the kitchen, until it was clear how the Jewish tradition of separate seating by sex had evolved. They surrounded and stroked my mother, while she cried and called up her father's memory.

"Yes, dear," they said.

"It's always hardest on the living," they agreed.

And "We know, dear," as, indeed, they probably did.

It felt good, despite the circumstances, to get away from Madison, into the society of others and the warm Florida air. Even before Papa went into the hospital, I'd arranged a leave of absence from school, using my own health as an excuse for chronic nonattendance. Between the embrace of the ocean air and the plentitude of Oomie's table, I started to return to what I thought of as myself. I tried to stay above the fray, especially the ongoing battles between my mother and hers. I fought to hold on to the relief and release I'd found in my free-fall dream.

It took fight. Deborah and Richard spent long hours at their hotel, and I was saddled with Mom. Her harping on Oomie found its perfect counterpoint in Oomie's running critique of her:

"What did you put on your eyes? That color's all wrong on you. You're not young anymore. You look fat. Give me that. What are you doing? Haven't you ever squeezed an orange before — one teaspoon of pulp. God, what a pampered girl. Your father always said we'd spoiled you."

Lorna would fire back, "How dare you talk about Daddy that way. He never said that. You're the one to talk, pushing and pushing him . . ."

"He used to warn me, 'Doris, if you don't stop giving in to that girl, she'll never learn the value of a good day's work.' . . ."

"He couldn't stand it. He would have walked away a hundred times —"

When Mom broke off, I filled in under my breath, "If he could have walked." Then I told myself, "Stay out of it, stay out."

"'You're spoiling her, you're spoiling her,' was like a song with him. . . ."

"He always hated the carping and criticism. . . ."

"And now I see he was right. We've spoiled you rotten. You can't even squeeze a piece of fruit!"

"He hated it! It killed him! *You* killed him!"

"Mom, stop!" I shouted, appalled out of my detachment. I grabbed Lorna's wrist and dragged her to the living room couch. "Shut up with that," I commanded. "Don't say that to her. He's dead, all right? Don't say that."

"He told me," she whispered, "how she drove him . . ."

"He didn't tell you anything. He couldn't fucking talk."

"He talked to *me*," she insisted. And then she cried and cried.

Bile has a taste. Sitting next to my blubbering mother, I tasted it.

"She's not me, she's not me, she's not me," I thought to quiet myself. But she kept crying and in a minute I was wiping her nose and holding her shoulders and whispering, "I know. I know. It's all right."

At the end of our week there, Mom and I went out to lunch with Deborah and Richard before dropping them at the airport. I'd spent

some time with Richard in the past, on my visits to Minnesota. He
was nice enough. He ran his own business, distributing lawn and
patio furniture to department stores, and he had some knowledge of,
and pretensions about, the world of opera — as a connoisseur, not
as a performer. He genuinely seemed to care about my sister, and he
showed interest in me. On this trip, however, we hadn't spoken
much, hadn't wound up on the same side of the room too often.
Now, he asked me if I was feeling better, a question that kicked my
sister's head around, an "I told you not to say anything" scowl pos-
sessing her features.

"Pretty much better," I said.

Mom looked at Deborah, then stared me down. "I didn't know
you were sick."

"Erich had pneumonia," Deborah said deliberately. "He was in
the hospital. I told him he should call you."

"I didn't want to worry you," I told my mother, as I loaded my
mouth with shrimp in Cantonese lobster sauce.

When we'd finished lunch and dropped Deborah and Richard in
Fort Lauderdale, I drove back to Oomie's with my mother. We were
silent most of the way, except for perfunctory chitchat about how
happy my sister seemed. We parked the rental car in line with all the
oversized sedans. As Mom undid her safety belt and stepped out of
the passenger seat, she grumbled in my direction, "You're coming
home with me."

17

THE LANGUAGE OF LUNGS

There was a catch. With my mother there was always a catch. She failed to tell me the most essential thing: she was commandeering me back to Venice not for my health, but for hers. She had lung cancer, and she was going to die. And I was going to sit in attendance on her one last time.

The truth became known to me piecemeal. Too many days she'd leave midafternoon and wouldn't tell me where she was going. Too many calls came in from friends that sent her into her bedroom, where she spoke in whispers. Too many bills from doctors, labs, and hospitals came in with the mail. Then one day, she simply said, "There's somebody I'd like you to meet." That somebody was a friend of hers, a faith healer or, as she seemed to me at the time, a faux gypsy.

The meeting took place at her apartment, near the beach. My mother walked me there, escorted me to the door, introduced me to the friend she had said was "psychic," and left. The moment had the feel of an initiation, a twist on the old rite of the father taking his virgin son to the brothel. Eureka Collins was her name (I do not lie), but whether it was a chosen name or a given one, I can't say. A middle-aged Jewess whose favorite holiday was Halloween and whose favorite dress-up role was fortune teller, she came festooned in skirts and scarves and bracelets, all as colorful as the makeup on her eyes and cheeks. Oomie goes to Mardi Gras. The sorceress took my right hand in both of hers, looked deep into my eyes, and, after sufficient inspection, said, "I'm so happy to meet you at last, *Erich.*" She put a world of emphasis on my name, intimating some knowledge of my history, or so I thought.

She led me to an old wicker chair, strewn with paisley shawls and Indian silks, and sat me down. She deposited herself in a chair facing. I kept hoping that she'd ring a bell and a beautiful young girl would enter and lead me off to a plush red bedroom to service my desires, but it didn't happen. Eureka just stared at me.

After a while she rose, no-nonsense, and came around behind me. Her coarse fingers probed my neck for glands. "Your mother tells me you've been sick with pneumonia," she said. "It's not good to let that kind of energy stay in your body. It'll scar you up inside in ways you can't even imagine." She laid her beringed hands on my chest, still from behind (was she planning to unbutton and kiss me?) and told me to breathe into her hands.

"No, really breathe!" she commanded. "You're holding on to it. The disease won't leave your body until you want it to. It's up to you to let go of it. You know that, don't you? These things come in with our blessings and only flee when we banish them."

"So now," she said, seating herself across from me again and boring into me with her eyes, "Why pneumonia?"

I mumbled something about being outside in Wisconsin in the winter.

She took it in, bobbed her head, as if in agreement, and said, "Yes, all that's fine, but why pneumonia?"

"Well," I ventured, "it started with a cold."

"Erich," she said with pity in her voice, "you're a smart young man, I know that. Deeply intelligent. I can tell just by looking in your eyes. Now, you may not buy this, but I can see your aura. And, frankly, it's not a pretty sight. So, whatever's going on with you, it isn't about 'I had a head cold and it got into my lungs.' You invited it in, how I don't know and why I don't know. But you know. And you can choose to tell me or not."

I didn't want to offend her, certainly didn't have the energy to challenge her, so I made something up: "I wanted to stop breathing."

"OK, go on," she said, interested. (I half expected her to shout, "Eureka!")

"I'm afraid of the air — it's polluted. I wanted to keep pure, to purify myself."

"Interesting," she said, seeming to mean it. "What do you think that's about?"

"Guilt, probably."

"Guilt for?" she asked.

"I don't know, just about everything."

She grew quiet. "OK, now listen to me. Guilt is noxious. It's useless, worthless, and noxious. It's a waste of emotion. It doesn't do anybody any good. It's a kind of disease in and of itself, and like all diseases, it needs to be treated. But, also like all diseases, the only one who can really treat it is the one who's got it. You have to do the work. You have to Let. It. Go."

She told me to take off my T-shirt, which I did, and close my eyes, which I half did. She came over to me, took a pillow from a pile near her desk and knelt on it in front of me. She rubbed her hands together as one would do to charm a pair of dice before rolling them. She inhaled deeply several times and put her hands to my chest. They were hot, her hands, and I took her cue and tried to breathe into them. I wondered if she would touch my nipples, but she steered clear. She began chanting, which became humming, then moaning. My mother's psychic surrogate pressed her closed mouth to my sternum and moaned what sounded like an Arabic desert prayer. After a while, she stood up and ordered me to lie on my back on the massage table across the room.

"What I'm going to do is tape small magnets to your chest. Your body is an energy field — magnetic, like all energy — and these are going to help get that energy flowing. The bandages are homeopathic ones. You'll smell like cayenne pepper for a while, but you could do worse. Girls like the smell, believe me.

"The most important thing, however, is mind-set. You may not fully understand this, but we choose these things. They don't just *happen*. To us. And we can choose to get rid of them.

"Take your mother, for example. Why cancer? Why her lungs? Because she smokes? Why does she smoke? Because she's a singer, who won't let herself sing? Why won't she let herself sing? What kind of poisonous attitudes about herself has she been breathing in? Why does she want the poison? You see? Every answer leads to another question. BUT! Ultimately you always come back to *the* question: What do I *get* from this disease? Why am I letting it take me over? If you can answer that one, if you can get to the *source*, then maybe you can encounter those needs in a different way, instead of making yourself sick. Then you can let the disease go. *Let. It. Go.*

"Now in your mom's case — she's a very, very strong woman, and she knows that she has chosen this for herself. She also knows that she must choose not to succumb. She must change and she must fight, however long it takes. Take your lead from her: *Choose* health. Choose *purity*, if you want to call it that.

"And don't think I haven't noticed the connection. It's hard to miss. Pneumonia in your lungs, cancer in hers? That's a very strong bond you've got there, sonny boy, and a noble one. Maybe you were trying to take the pain for her. Maybe you want to save her, carry her disease. But I'm telling you something, and I'm telling you straight. It can't be done. As much as you love the woman, as much as you want to make her pain yours, you can't do it."

I didn't tell her that my mother's ailment was news to me, or that I'd been a thousand miles away for nearly three years. Could her pain travel that far to possess me? Should the feeling that had kept me away be called love? I doubted it.

"Yeah," I said. "Probably not."

"Now, one more thing," she cut in. "This won't be an easy year for you — it's time for what we call the Saturn return. But you can get through it and come out strong. Next year looks good for your love life, so you'd better get ready. Now. Go out and have some fun. Polish up that aura of yours. Get out of here."

I did.

It was never clear to me whether my mother had pressed Eureka Collins into service for the sole purpose of informing me that she was sick, or whether that part of our encounter was fluke luck. In any case, it freed Mom from ever having to say outright what ailed her. Whether from Eureka's magnets and oils or from her words, my body felt both numb and tingly, like your cheek when Novocain wears off. My head, though, was wild with all the things I hadn't asked, hadn't made sense of. I half ran home, wobbly as I was, not to confront my mother, but to see what I could see, if the signs had somehow been on her all along and I'd missed them, or if, as Eureka believed, I could look at the space surrounding her head and see sickness and imminent death.

Mom was watching for me out the front window. She turned full view when I came in.

There was a loopy expectancy in her eyes, the hope of a little girl as she waits for Daddy to come home, toss his briefcase aside, and fling his arms wide, a love trap for her to run to. Daddy's little princess, under a sentence of death, dreaming that a man arrives with good news.

I was all she got.

There's always a chance, at moments like this, to do the right thing, the generous thing. Even the crooked young man can find the grace required to sweep his dying mother into a kind embrace. What small thawing would it take to kiss her tears and allow her to be the princess again, while I became the comforting father? I could swear to make things right, to ease her suffering. These were small promises under the circumstances. She was my mother. She was dying. It was my chance to do it right.

"Well, how did it go?" she asked.

"Fine, great, nifty," I said. "She said I should go dancing more."

"What else did she say?" Such a good little girl, so perky, so prim.

"She said my lungs weren't bad, a little scarred up maybe, but that my aura was dented. She stuck girl magnets on me and slathered me with Tabasco."

"That stuff just might work, you know."

"That's what she said. But she said I have to want it to work; I have to choose to *Let. It. Go.*"

"Yes, I believe that," my mother said.

"She said we get the diseases we want — that we make ourselves sick, pick our poisons, that it's all our fault, but that we can make ourselves well too, if we so desire. She said she'd been talking to God, and he agreed that I should '*Let. It. Go.*' I think they'd been talking right before I came in, you know, her and God. Can you believe it, they use the same massage oil! Isn't that a coincidence? I mean, wow! God shops in Venice!" My mother tried to laugh, enjoying her clever son, appreciating his caustic wit.

"You should get his address, Mom, maybe he'll decorate his apartment with stuff from your store — when you open it. Wouldn't that be a trip!"

She started to speak, but I couldn't stop myself. "Oh, yeah, I almost forgot. Eureka said that God said that Papa's floating around in the ether right over Venice. And guess who's with him? Erich! How about that? Remember him? My brother, you know, the one who died? They're playing canasta! At least that's what God told her. But you won't go there, she said, because she has magnets! And jalapeños! And because if we really really really want everything to be all right and if we clap our hands really really hard, Tinker Bell will live and everyone will love each other forever and ever."

She was quiet.

"You want something to eat?" she asked when I started to leave.

"Naagh. Food fucks up your karma."

I could hear my mother crying behind me. I kicked shut the screen door and went down to the water. Everybody there reminded me of Eureka Collins — a beach crammed with members of the same crystal-sucking, pepper-rubbing, spirit-raising meditation circle. I doubled back. Before long, I found myself outside of Soapy's father's veterinary clinic. When I went in, Dr. Dobrow was standing just off the waiting room, leaning over the appointment book with his office manager. He hurried out and greeted me enthusiastically, pumping my hand like an old army buddy.

"Erich! How are you? How's Madison treating you? You've gotten taller, haven't you? You know, Helen and I were just talking about you the other day, wondering how you were."

"Fine," I said. "School's pretty good, you know, same old stuff."

"Sure, sure," he said.

"How's the vet business?"

"Oh, you know. It's raining cats and dogs. A lot of fur balls and eye cysts. We've got a number of ferrets in town now — big thing, ferrets — even see some pigs and a raccoon or two. Keepin' busy, can't complain."

"Soapy's not around, huh? Still in Las Vegas?"

"No, no. He's — he's Larry again, you know, decided Soapy was a tad on the sophomoric side. Have to say I agree. He's in Hawaii now, taking a little time off school. Don't ask. Some farm commune or something out there. I'm convinced it's a religious cult of some kind, but he assures me, no, no."

"Hawaii. Wow. Bet he just loves those things — what do you call 'em — you wear around your neck?"

"Leis," he said, "lays." And we laughed.

"Yeah, I'll bet he loves those Hawaiian lays." And the office manager chuckled along with us, looking up from her paperwork.

"Gee, say," Dr. Dobrow said, "I was sorry to hear about your mom. How's she doing?"

"Oh, you know, fine, not fine. She'll be all right."

"You think so? That's good. That's the attitude you have to have. Positive. They can do a lot with that sort of thing now, an awful lot. Chemo, radiation — all solid stuff. You've got to have the right attitude, though. I'm sure she'll be just fine."

"Sure."

"You tell her we're thinking of her. Wish her well for Helen and me."

"Sure. Will do. And if you talk to Soap — Larry —"

"You bet. I'll tell him to give you a call, same number right?"

"Oh, yeah. Same number."

"If you're going to be around for a while," Dr. Dobrow offered, "stop by, come say hello. Helen would love to see you."

"Thanks, I will."

"And give our best to your mom."

"Sure."

My mind made a list of reasons to be pissed, starting with: everyone in Venice knows more than I do.

I was being too hard on my mother. She had her father's death and now, in all likelihood, her own, staring her down. Meanwhile, she was locked in with a warped and hateful son whose capacity for empathy fell just below that of a wood chip. At my worst, I'd shown more compassion for strangers and spiders. I couldn't summon a soft word or Hallmark condolence, couldn't dredge up a love tap or "Poor, pretty Mommy" from the boy I'd been. My anger was all I had. I clung to it as a drowning man to a splintered board.

Why all the anger, I wondered? I flashed back to Eureka Collins. And, like Eureka, I had to answer: Because I know she brought it on herself.

I wasn't thinking rationally. I knew that no one wills herself to have cancer, that we're not, in reality, responsible for every illness we suffer. Eureka had shoveled up a heap of mystical crap, and I'd recognized it as such. Nevertheless, the explanation my mind rejected was the very one I instinctively pinned on Lorna. She would go to any length to make me take care of her, even to the final length. She would die to keep me tied to her.

18

My Mother's Body

It worked. I stayed home. The world shrank and my mother grew, until, like Gulliver, she filled the whole of my native Lilliput. She was my vista, morning, noon, and night. We took meals together, watched television, played cards. I kept house, turning down a job offer from the lab where I'd done my high school internship. During the healing groups Eureka Collins led in our living room I served coffee and said nothing. I indulged the faith circles, the ten-day kelp diets, the self-hypnosis tapes and walking meditations up and down the hall. I chauffeured Mom to and from doctors. When the time came for chemotherapy (which I still believe failed because she had preempted it so long with snake oil, spiritual cure-alls), I cleaned up her hair and vomit, read to her, held her hand, and stayed small.

We never, during the months that followed, spoke directly of her disease. As a result, I didn't find out how long she'd been sick or how she'd come to be diagnosed. I did speak to my father, to tell him what I knew. He was stunned, naturally, and short of words. He grilled me for details — medical terms, prognoses, a chronology of symptoms. I couldn't tell him much. My father refrained from asking the "How long?" question. He kept saying, "But she's so young," and I knew he was thinking of her as a graduate student or young mother, and not as the gigantic forty-nine-year-old hag lying under an afghan on the couch.

He asked to speak to her.

"She doesn't know I'm calling," I explained.

He inhaled audibly, and then held his breath before saying, "It must be hard." Another inhalation, another hold. "Should I send flowers or something?"

"Wait till the funeral," I told him.

He ignored my icy realism and asked, "What will you do?" He sounded sad.

Whether he wanted to know about my plans for the present or for after she died, I couldn't tell. I gave him my standard reply: "I still intend to finish school."

"Yes," he said, as if he'd just met me on a bus, "One must do that." After a pause, he added, "Well, Son, keep me posted."

Deborah flew out several times over the seven months I was home. She was working as bookkeeper for Richard's lawn-furniture business and, so, had some freedom. The business was thriving, but their relationship had turned rocky. She wanted to get married. He had been married once and, although he led her to believe that sometime he might want to give it another go, now was never the time.

"His friends are my only friends," she told Mom and me. "And they're old, old friends, army buddies, high school buddies. Buddies. I don't have friends of my own. And when I have — you know, a couple of times I met somebody my own age, but they don't fit in with him. And, as much as I try, I just can't get excited about Puccini, you know? He collects all the books and records. He sees opera everywhere he goes. Just once I'd like to go see Gladys Knight and the Pips. This just doesn't feel like *my* life."

"So why would you want to get married?" I asked.

"Then it would be my life," she replied, inexplicably.

I was too grateful for my sister's presence to pick at her faulty logic. When Deborah came, Deborah took charge, and I was reprieved. Unlike me, she took interest in the merest details of my mother's symptoms. She was a good daughter, thoughtful sister, and a much better cook than I was. She stood in long conference with each and every doctor and accompanied Mom to any and all healing-cult activities.

She enjoyed them. And she adored Eureka. The three of them would lunch together every time my sister came to town. When she came home, she repeated everything the sorceress had said: "Remember, Mom, what Eureka told you about breath as life. Keep working it up from the abdomen." Or "It's body memory, Mom, just like Eureka said. Our bodies are so much smarter than we are. Don't you think, Erich?" She raised her eyebrows at me, egging me on to provide backup bucking up.

"Sure," I agreed. "It's body memory all over. Total physical wisdom."

Deborah flashed me a "Thank you, now shut up" smile. I was happy to oblige.

It dawned on me that my sister was suddenly becoming a Christian or, more precisely, some kind of neopagan, proto–New Age Christian. She read Mom lovingly to sleep with passages from the Bible, which she continued reading to herself long after the patient had fallen off. She brought home from the bookstore stacks of paperbacks on healing prayer. She copied life-affirming quotations in longhand and taped them to the fridge. She and Mom even practiced deep breathing together in the living room, cross-legged on the floor in sweat suits.

"We've got to stay positive," Deborah exhorted me.

"I've been positive, only positive, nothing but positive," I grumbled. "While you're here, you be positive."

But I wasn't angry at her. I'd never been happier to see anyone in my life. And, although I was too cynical to admit it aloud, her influence appeared to help Mom. The right reverend Deborah (she had long since returned to the original pronunciation of her name) lifted Lorna's spirits. I, therefore, heeled to her mandate of mutual positivism and steered away from any talk of "What if?" or "What will we do when?" Deborah believed that Mom would get better, so there was nothing to think about other than the now.

"Call Dad, will you?" she urged me. "And see if he'll extend her alimony payments until she gets better. They're up in January."

I didn't say what I thought, which was, "But that's eight months away! There won't be anybody here to receive alimony in eight months!" I just accepted her assignments and did her bidding. I wouldn't be the naysayer. I'd keep my negativity to myself. When Mom died, there would be plenty of time to take care of business. Moreover, it was clear to me that if there were a God, Deborah — not I — was the kind of angel he'd send to help. So I shut up and did what I was told.

Then, having fed us, aired out the mattresses, blown through the house like a gale of spunk and optimism, my sister returned to her gray little life, and we were alone again with our inadequacies. I'd hit the ground with a bit more energy, and my mother would regurgitate every bit of wisdom Deborah had fed her. Before too long, though, we'd sag back into the dull duties of a halfhearted belief in the future.

The worst episodes, as might be expected, were the hospital stays. She'd go in for tests, or when the effect of the chemo overwhelmed her, or just because. Even when she was obviously suffering, her belief system didn't allow her to talk about the pain — only the healing — so I never knew whether the cancer or the treatment hurt more.

The spiritual community she flew with had a broad wingspan. Someone from some group went wherever she went. I drove. They held prayer meetings around her hospital bed, sat vigils in waiting rooms during examinations, and traipsed in and out of our house like it was theirs. They brought cassette tapes, amulets, books, pamphlets, and special foods. At times, however, even these carriers of sweetness and light stooped to factionalism. Her friends from Christian Science stopped coming when she submitted to chemo. The couple from Wellspring shunned the "energy masseuse," whose hands never actually touched my mother's body. Mostly, though, they were a good-natured (dare I say "positive") bunch with kind words for almost everyone. I took their entrances as cues for my exits.

My mother wanted more from me. She wanted my vibes. Once, returning from a weekend in the hospital, she grasped my hands in hers. "Pray with me, Erich," she said. The next thing I knew, I was on my knees beside her ashen self. My eyes were squeezed shut. She began chanting at my ear: "Nam Myoho Renge Kyo," over and over, convulsively rising and falling in intensity. I was tiny and clenched, a speck. Suddenly I felt her hands grip my face and smelled her disease breath. "You're the only one I love, Erich. You're the only one I love. Help me. Help me. Pray with me. My Erich, my Erich." I began moaning, "Nam Myoho Renge Kyo," loudly, as if in a trance. Get off me, off me, off, I dreamed, slithering down into the shaggy fibers of the rug.

What was my problem? Aesthetic aversion, to begin with. Her ugliness appalled me. Her head grew bald in patches, she blew up and then withered alternately, she made up her hairless eyes with an excess of color. Eaten away as much by internal furies as by cancer, she would sit up in bed, chewing purple cabbage in quarters, and I would see two images at once: the figure before me and a Dorian Gray portrait of another — a young singer, chestnut hippie hair hanging down to her waist, descanting from the steeple of a Mexican church. That woman floated so far above me, I couldn't even touch her in a dream. She hated me with all her beauty. This woman, though, rotting from the inside, wanted me to want her, to find her lovely again, sufficient, home. Each image now carried the photographic burn of its opposite twin.

Everything my brother and I hated in her had begun to manifest physically. Erich and I were, finally, one in our disgust.

I redoubled my efforts to be sweet and dutiful. I brought her special treats — magazines, flowering plants, and, when she wasn't on some kind of seaweed-and-fig regimen, half gallons of Heavenly Hash ice cream. I doused my hands with musk cologne and let them linger near my nose when I sat beside her. I studied her like an object, subject of a photo essay I might shoot on the aging and ailing. I tried to remain a detached but committed observer.

Then, late summer, she began to vocalize her pain. She groaned and cried. She called my name as soon as I left the room, "Erich Erich Erich," as if it were some dark incantation of suffering. I stayed with her so I didn't have to hear it. She screamed, and the doctors prescribed stronger medication for the pain. I read Kübler-Ross in

secret and wished my mother back into the "denial" phase of her
dying. Instead she entered high anxiety. For three weeks she didn't
sleep at night — neither of us slept. She was, I figured, afraid she'd
never wake up. She paced the kitchen and hall, banging and clatter-
ing everything in her way. She lived in an almost constant state of
panic. This panic was transferred onto the smallest detail of daily life:
the electric coil under the kettle, the dust mites floating in the air, the
thing she forgot to tell someone. She worried at fever pitch. Did she
have too much makeup on? Too little? Why hadn't her mother
called? Why was Deborah calling so often? Were her storage lockers
safe enough to protect her stuff? She trained her anxiety on me. Was
I paying the bills? Cleaning? Checking the ingredients on everything
I fed her? In her panic, she came more and more to resemble Oomie,
hawkish and sizzling. She bossed and badgered me. "Why are you
looking at me like that?"

"Like what? I'm not looking at you any way. I'm not even looking at you."

"That's it. You won't look at me. You hate me. You want my
things. You want to take over my store. That's the only reason you're
hanging around here. Vulture!"

"All right, you want me to go, I'll go."

"How nice for you. So mobile. So whole-life-before-you. I detest
you. Get out of here." I shrugged and turned to go. "Erich Erich
Erich," she keened. I came back, her source of pain and dream of
comfort.

I was a small boat, and I rode the tides as best I could, but I
resented like hell the ocean. I wanted her to die and she must have
sensed it. One hot August afternoon, she started shouting at me for
failing to put a clean case on her third pillow. I stormed out of her
room and into my own. "Erich Erich Erich" groaned through the
house. "Erich Erich Erich."

I intended to pull out Erich's ballad, not the one he was writing
but the one he'd highlighted in a book. I was going to stick it in her
face — his curse, shoved right up under her nose. I pulled the desk
chair over to the closet and reached up to corner of the high shelf.
Boxes and stuff filled the space, the chaos I used to hide my private

writings. I started pulling it down, my junk, his junk. I grabbed his last box, the one unopened one, his time capsule, dated New Year's Eve, 1990, almost a dozen years in the future. I left everything else midwreck. I clawed the packing tape. I pried the flaps apart.

She was still crooning my name when I walked back into her room. I dumped the contents of the box onto her bed, where they slid across her lap and down the hills of thigh and knee, sheet and quilt. "Comic books. A little kid's fucking D.C. comic books. Fucking Archie and Jughead for godsakes. He had a crush on Betty, Mom."

For the first time since the week he died, I was talking to her as me, the one who'd caused all this by living. She stared at me and said, "You're crazy. I don't know what the hell you're talking about."

I left the house and, at the first phone I came to, called Deborah collect. "I'm going back. To school. My leave is up and I wrote and told them I would. She's all yours."

Deborah swallowed. "I just can't. Erich, you know, I'd do anything I could to help out, but she can't fly out here and I just can't abandon everything. Won't they hold out another semester? Maybe by January . . ."

I didn't ask her to complete the sentence. I simply said, "Maybe they can hold out, but I'm getting eaten alive. Sure, she's great when you're around, but then there's the rest of the time. I'm no martyr."

"You've been a good boy, Erich, the best son she could ever hope to ask for. Don't you think we all know that? Don't you think she does? You've been so good."

"Yeah. So?"

"So just be patient. There are forces at work you don't even know about — you've just got to hold on and everything's gonna be fine, you'll see. Everything. I don't doubt it for a minute."

"Oh, fuck you, Pollyanna. And fuck Lorna, too." And against my will, I started blubbering like a brat, right there at the senior center pay phone.

"Shh, shh, baby bro. It's OK. Just . . . be . . . patient." People always want you to be patient when you're taking the heat for them. I hung up on her.

And then I hung up on Mom. I walked back to the house, past the metal trash can with Erich's comic collection spilling over its rim. She was sitting up in bed, flipping through a copy of *Cosmopolitan* as if nothing had happened. I gave her two days' notice. "I'm going back to school, I have to leave on Saturday. You'll be all right."

She looked at me as she might have if I'd ripped her oxygen tube out of the tank. And then she went back to her magazine, reading and turning pages — all alone in the room.

I was shocked by my own abrupt cruelty. So I sat down in the chair I kept at the side of the bed. I tried to explain. "I have to finish school. We both know that's best. I have to remember my own life. Besides, you're going to get well and then you'll come out to stay with me. We'll be together at Thanksgiving and Christmas. What's the difference? You're going to be better soon and then it won't matter where I am." Whatever stupid shit I said, she wouldn't look at me, wouldn't let me meet her eyes. She lay down, rolled over, and turned her face to the wall.

This time I left as scheduled. Lorna didn't speak to me when I came into her bedroom. She didn't glance my way. The food I brought her during those two days sat on the tray until I removed it. She talked to her friends and even left the house for a short walk with one of them. I was banished. I said good-bye without seeing her eyes.

I called three or four times a week from Madison and there was always someone there to answer the phone. Mom wouldn't speak to me. As the fall wore on, the person answering was Deborah. She had, for all intents and purposes, broken off with Richard, though they described it as a "trial separation."

Deborah called me a couple of days before Mom died. "She's been asking for you," Deborah told me. "She wants you here."

"How do you know she's been asking for me?"

"Don't be silly, Erich.'"

"How do you know she meant me?"

She was silent. Then, "Please won't you come?"

I said no.

She died on Thanksgiving. Richard, kindly, flew to Venice to help Deborah out. They hired a boat and strewed Mom's ashes in the Pacific. They cleared the house and put its contents in a storage room, near the one Mom already rented, rooms it would take my sister and I three years to enter and another year to empty. Every Kenyan dish, every painted giraffe, every Mexican bride-and-groom statuette waited in the dark for the day they'd be sold off in a lot.

Something happened in him while he slept. It was not the sleep of refreshment or restoration. He had no dreams. Afterward his lids clicked open like a marionette's and he *saw:* what he saw, before he had formulated even a word of it, was his finished work. He saw it as a kind of vessel, curved, polished, hollowed out. In its cup lay an alabaster egg with a single glittering spot; no, not an egg; a globe, marvelously round. An eye. A human eye: his own; and then not his own. His father's murdered eye.

— Cynthia Ozick,
The Messiah of Stockholm

19

GOD'S MOUTH, OOMIE'S EARS

Florida again. Deborah and I stood outside the airport, one bag each, sad little stoics on the threshold of who knew what, straggling hand in hand into the taxi line. We must have seemed such darkling, ill-bred creatures. I was the waif, taller and bony like my mother had been in her earlier incarnation, a scarecrow. Deborah was the solid sister. She'd inherited the female version of my father's stocky body and firmed it up with years of hiking and rowing, first on Puget Sound and then on Minnesota lakes. Grief had given her that direct, suffering strength you find in Victorian heroines. Sadness had wormed its way under her considerable armor and revealed her maturity, the doleful maturity of the almost-whupped. It made her beautiful.

Together we were suddenly twelve and ten years old again, suddenly at a loss. We were suddenly homeless, too. Deborah had left Richard, though her nursing duties with Mom had somewhat masked the fact. I'd given notice on my old attic apartment in Madison a couple of weeks before in order to find cheaper quarters. I could barely afford part-time tuition working at a copy shop. If I was grieving or in shock, I couldn't have said. But the world appeared to have been emptied of adversity, even of movement, except for the natural — the sun's glare, the ocean breeze, the murmur of Earth turning. It was a kind of peace, the peace just before or after aerial bombing.

Mom had left almost nothing behind financially. She'd died with debts. Alimony and child support stopped with her death, since she and her ten-year-old divorce settlement expired within weeks of each other. There'd been no funeral or shivah, only a few condolence cards, a short stack of sympathy, so we were alone with her absence, too.

"Richard will help me out for a while," Deborah said, as the cab jerked from light to light. "I'd rather not take anything, but God knows I've given enough to him and the business. I mean, I'd saved up a little, but these trips back and forth to Mom's ate that. Anyhow, I don't have much choice, do I? Besides, we were, for all intents and purposes, common-law married — as-if married. Consider it alimony."

"Dad cried," I said. Deborah didn't respond. "More like sobbed. The phone, I thought it would shake." Still nothing. "How did he sound to you? You did talk to him, didn't you?"

"He called."

"And? How'd he sound?"

"He asked a lot of questions," she said.

"About?" When the subject of Dad came up, Deborah clamped down.

"About the end. About what now. About you."

"Not about you?" I pressed.

"I guess."

"That all?"

Deborah let out a scornful breath through her nose. "He acted like it had happened to him, like it was his loss."

"It was. He loved her."

"Right."

"I was there, too. I know he did."

"You were young. You don't know. You don't know."

"What, Deborah? What don't I know?"

She closed her eyes. Her chest rose and fell with purposeful breathing. She looked back at me with half a smile, "Not now, ok?"

I sensed that I would never move my sister off the position she'd staked, the place where every reason to blame was a reason to blame Dad. Dad had made Mom miserable. Dad had broken up our home by letting us go. Dad had cut us off in Mexico. Dad had locked Erich up. Dad had stayed away. Now he had the audacity to mourn Mom's death and ask a bunch of nosy questions about us. And I sensed the source of her implacability, the sad dream under it all: she wanted Dad to save her, to swoop down like a movie-studio superhero and take his darling girl up in his strong arms.

"Oomie's going to freak," I suggested. "I don't think she even knew Mom was sick."

"She didn't hear it here," Deborah admitted.

We sat looking out our separate windows, breathing. "Maybe we shouldn't tell her."

"Oh, Erich, we have to tell her."

"Why?"

She hesitated. "She *deserves* to know, to have her own grief."

"But she won't. She'll pretend not to hear."

"At least," Deborah said, "at least we will have told her."

"Tolded," I said to myself.

"What?"

"There should be a word — *tolded* — 'at least we will have tolded her.' I understand why there isn't, though. It's ugly." Deborah put her hand over mine and patted it.

"She has to know," Deborah explained, looking right at me. "What if she tried to call Mom, didn't hear from her for years? She'd be distraught. We'd have to tell her sooner or later."

"There might not be a later with her."

"Erich —"

"Besides, she already complains that Mom never calls her."

"It would be *wrong*," she said, adding emphasis to morality.

The meter clicked on. I looked at the back of the cabbie's head. My grandmother hates Cubans, I remembered.

Oomie met us aflutter. Lunch was on the table. Bowls of candy everywhere. She only ate M&M's now. "The doctor says I should take medicine. I tell him these are my medicine."

Deborah listened patiently. Then she carefully explained her situation with Richard, assuming that Oomie could understand and care. "I just want you to be happy," Oomie said, adding without transition, "Everyone's waiting to see you two." With that she led us on a ritual dog-and-pony tour of her building, exhibiting us to the doorman, people in the halls, the old couple across the hall (the man came to the door wearing a bib that read, "Because I'm the Dad, that's why"), and her most hated neighbor, Lily. "My grandchildren are here again," she told Lily, frowning. "Can't keep them away. Come on kids, I made cake."

After dessert, Deborah pushed back her plate and took Oomie's hand, just as she was standing to clear the table. "Please, Oomie, sit down. There's something I want to tell you."

"I don't like to sit," Oomie said. "I have to *do* things."

"Just for a minute," my sister urged.

I shielded my eyes with a hand and poked around at the German chocolate icing.

"All those years taking care of your grandfather I had to do everything. You get used to being busy. Even when I play bingo, I have to get up and walk around."

"I know, dear," Deborah said, as though she were the grandmother and Oomie a six-year-old. "But it's a good thing and I want to share it with you."

I snapped my head up to look at her. Mom croaking a good thing? This I had to hear.

"I wanted you to know, Oomie, something very important has happened to me, something very *positive*. I wanted to share it with you."

"That's nice, dear. I'm happy for all you kids." She tried to rise, stacking plates as she did.

"Just for a minute," Deborah said again. And Oomie reluctantly, painfully it seemed to me, sat. Deborah took a breath. "I've become a Christian, Oomie. That's what I wanted to tell you. I've found God — Jesus — and since I know you were raised Jewish, well, I wanted to let you know and to answer any questions you might have. I've thought about this long and hard, even though, in the end, it isn't something you have to think about. You just *know*, do you know what I mean? But I wouldn't want you to think that I was in anyway being untrue to you or your heritage. This is just something right for me."

"I never really had time for God and all that," Oomie said. "But if it makes you happy, that's all I care about. I just want my children and grandchildren to be happy."

"I am, Oomie. God has made me so happy."

"That's nice, dear. I better clear these dishes away." With that, my unfazed grandmother made the remnants of dessert disappear.

Deborah turned toward me and looked troubled by what she saw. "I assumed you knew," she said.

"Sure," I said. "I guess I did."

"I could never have gotten through all this otherwise. It's been a . . ."

"Godsend?" I offered as she groped for the word.

"Pillar, I was going to say. Support, foundation, something structural. For me. And I thought if Oomie knew, the rest wouldn't be so hard."

"She's gonna freak, God or no God."

That night, after dinner, we played pinochle. At one point, on Deborah's deal, she put the deck down and rested her hands on top of it. "Oomie," she said with a small explosion of earnestness.

Oomie stopped her. "I'm an old lady, dear. I just want to hear good things. I want my children and grandchildren to be happy. If that God makes you happy I'm happy. I just want to hear good things." She glared at me, a way of stressing her point.

Deborah looked stricken. She turned her face to me, and I, involuntarily, shook my head. She looked down at her hands and mumbled something to herself, a prayer, I suspected. She dealt the cards.

When we left two days later, Oomie was no wiser, no dumber. At the door of the cab that would take us to the airport and our separate flights, she pushed a yellow envelope into my hands and another into Deborah's. "Just a little something for making an old lady happy. Don't thank me. Just write me a letter once in a while."

Deborah's plane took off before mine, so we said good-bye at her gate. She continued a conversation begun in the taxi when she'd revealed her plan to move to the sticks to study Scripture: "I'm not becoming a Moonie or anything. It's a Bible study center, a fellowship."

"Yeah, but the South is the South. They find out your grand-mother's a Jew and they'll string up your white butt."

"You're worse than Oomie. I hardly think Fairfax, Virginia, counts as Deep South. We'll probably just sit around on the lawn and talk about the Gospels. I heard the head of the program speak in Saint Paul — the minister. He's great, so benevolent. Sharid Alfijay — how's that for a Christian name. It's all about God and personal transformation, nothing old-time religion about it. I'm so happy, Erich. Please be happy for me."

"Sure," I said. "I am. I want you to be."

"Mom would have been, too. You know, I really feel like her being sick helped me with it, helped me accept — not just what was happening with Richard — but what was happening inside me. Faith. It's almost like her death gave me faith. I really believe she's here with us, that we'll see her again."

I felt a folding in my stomach, a kind of fright. I fixed my attention on Deborah's sandaled feet. Her toes were short, round little buttons, nails filed in low half circles and painted a deep red. They looked so beautiful to me. I understood the impulse people have to throw themselves at the feet of others, to kiss those feet. My upper body was a curve, a willow drawn down by the heaviness of its own yearning for the ground.

"You were so lucky to go to college. I always wanted to." She put her hand on my shoulder. "I need you to be happy for me, Erich. You're all I got left. We're all we've got left."

"And Dad," I added, not looking up.

"Dad wasn't here when he was here," she replied from the hardest place she could find.

"I am. Happy for you," I muttered. "I'll just miss you — being so far away."

Deborah leaned forward and kissed the side of my head. She put her arms around me and rocked a little. My chest was melting. My hands sort of flipped up to the sides of her waist. "We'll see each other before you know," she said. Deborah placed one sad hand on my cheek and, when I met her eyes, quickly glanced over to the line forming at the door. "I should board," she said. "I'll call either from Minneapolis or when I get to Virginia. Let you know my address. It's something something Maid Marian Lane. How about that for godly?"

With that she pivoted into line, looking back only when she'd reached the runway stairs. I hadn't imagined being so sorry to see her go, but I'd never been sorrier. I was standing at the men's room sink before I realized I'd left my bag at her gate.

By the time I was set to leave, a few hours later, the Midwest was snowed in. I don't know what happened to Deborah's flight, but mine was, first, held on the ground for several hours, and then, routed through Atlanta, where it remained all the following morning and most of the next day, before being canceled. My trip, meant to last under three hours, took two full days, during which I slept on airport chairs and floors and fed off the bag of sandwiches and tin of cookies that I'd tried, unsuccessfully, to keep my grandmother from making me carry. I was grateful to have them. I also carried in a yellow envelope in my pocket, a check from her for twelve hundred dollars, but had, besides, only about nine bucks in cash, intended to get me home from the airport.

It was a period of singular freedom for me. No one knew where I was or expected me anywhere else. In all probability, no one anywhere in the world was thinking of me. I could have fallen off the face of the planet and it would have been months before anyone would even think to try and find me.

I was on leave from the world — between lives.

And I was flush. It occurred to me that I could go anywhere with this money. I could start over. I could, if I wanted, become myself again.

20

Dream of Jeannie

Deborah has said that we don't choose our paths so much as get chosen by them. I can't see how a course of events can be reduced to either statement. I don't think in terms of paths and have never seen a "way," even in retrospect. I think, instead, of currents, always moving, usually at counterpull. Sometimes you drift, sometimes rush; sometimes the currents smash you between them, and sometimes your own movement gives you the feeling, accurate or not, that you are directing your travels. Sometimes the current isn't strong enough to carry you beyond yourself.

On holdover at the Atlanta airport, I bought a disposable razor and a pair of travel scissors. In a men's room crowded with stranded businessmen, I shaved my face clean and, opening the scissors, cut my hair as closely as I could. I washed my body with paper towels — a jet-set whore's bath — and put on a clean shirt. Then, as soon as air traffic would allow, I returned to Madison and to my life as Erich.

I didn't know where else to go. I'd never had a traveler's dreams, never fantasized a life in Bali or Maine. Internally, too, I was without a map. With my mother dead, the audience was dead. There was no one to be Erich for, nothing to gain by being him. Going forward — to another city, name, or self — demanded a leap of invention for which I lacked both energy and wit. Who would I be if not Erich? Where would I make home now that I had no place or person to call home? What would I call myself?

Going back was no option, either. After nearly ten years, I couldn't touch the boy — the name — I'd been. He seemed as distant to me as Polaris or a figure from the mythology of a former civilization. In post-Lorna America, circa 1979, we had been severed more certainly than Erich and I.

Who now? Wait and see, I told myself. One step at a step. Go back to Madison and make a life. Make a free, clear life. So, I returned as I was, but physically altered, shaven and sheared.

What few connections I had were gone. Oliver had left to teach theater at a college in Iowa. Rob had, in the time I'd known him, grown obsessed with the business of drugs. The year before, when state police cracked down on a network servicing several Wisconsin campuses, he'd gotten busted. My job at the copy shop was waiting, though, and before too long I ascended to the post of assistant manager (in charge of nights) for the additional sum of $2.25 an hour. I celebrated by buying white cotton shirts. I was determined to make myself approachable, clean-seeming. I enrolled in two classes and found a small fixer-upper apartment in a house in Middleton about twenty minutes from town. I sold the old Pentax camera Rob had given me and bought a cheap, overused vw. Then, just as these necessary engines of my life were starting to hum, I met a girl.

In fact, I remet her. We'd taken some classes together over the semesters and had been in a study group sophomore year. She'd struck me by her serious focus, as well as by her ease in dealing with me, this ghoulishly robed guy, who made everyone else more than a little itchy. I'd responded in kind — easily. More, I'd been taken by her speaking voice. She spoke in a warm alto that seemed to have been heated by deep feeling and which, even as it moved toward you, retreated ever so slightly. Her voice was a stepping horse held gently in rein.

"I almost didn't recognize you," Jeannie said across the counter, about to hand me a stack of papers to xerox. "You're so changed."

"To protect the innocent," I replied. Miraculously, she laughed, an exuberant little boy's giggle. Then I added, "Yeah, I look in the mirror sometimes and don't remember it's me."

"I know, I know," she said.

I had no trouble recognizing her. She had the same short auburn

hair, sparkling dark eyes, thin curveless body — bright tomboy
looks, like a girl version of young Paul McCartney. And small white
teeth that angled ever so slightly backward into the pink of her
mouth, little pearls you might have mistaken for baby teeth. The
papers were grad school applications: essays and recommendations,
forms begging entry into an array of philosophy and women's studies
programs. I tilted my head at them as I glanced, inadvertently reading while trying not to read. "I know," she said. "Can't make up her
mind. Nietzsche and his whip or feminists who would have flayed
him alive. Poor, poor, ambivalent me."

"My family used to celebrate Nietzsche's birthday. Our counter-
Christmas," I said.

"You're kidding."

"No. It was my dad's favorite holiday. And my mother hadn't
read Betty Friedan yet. Or whoever."

"Does she now?" she asked.

"She died," I shrugged. "Just."

"I'm so sorry. Was it sudden?"

"I don't know," I lied. "I wasn't there."

"I'm really sorry," she said.

I turned to her papers. "Do you want to come back for these?"

"No, I'll hang out here."

She put her head down on the counter like a second-grader at
nap time.

"Sleep tight," I said.

"Not bloody likely," she responded. "I don't think I've had a
good night's sleep since sophomore year. Have you?"

"That was a bad year. Now I work nights. Best cure for insomnia."

She laughed to herself — horses rearing slightly.

I finished her copies in minutes, but she stayed and talked. She
was especially interested in the events surrounding my mother's
death. I told her about Oomie and how we'd left Florida without
enlightening her.

"You can't make people see what they don't want to see," she said.

It was a harmless statement, but one that hit the world loaded with so many contrary intentions that I've often replayed it in the years since. On the most mundane level it was a palliative, a superficial attempt to respond to the story I was telling her — folk wisdom doled out across a store counter. In a slightly deeper sense, she was trying to comfort me, to reach out to someone she thought might be suffering remorse over an important task left unfulfilled. This motive was reinforced by her hand, which rose gently to my chest — a small, kind, comforting touch. (Under whose pressure, it felt to me, a cluster of flowers bloomed all at once.) The angle of the hand, though — the perpendicular we usually read as "stop" — signaled another intention, a distancing, keeping at bay, even as she touched me. Although I couldn't have said so at the time, I took this in, read it as a warning: "You can't make people see. Don't try. Stay back." And the warning was more than casual. It came infused with specified anger, a bitterness whose depth I could never have guessed from this snapshot of a moment.

"No way I'm going to sleep tonight," she said, well past three. "You want to get breakfast when you're done? I'll just drop this stuff home, do a few things and come back."

"Great," I said. "Copying makes me ravenous." She giggled again and I swelled. Somewhere, apparently, I had a reservoir of charm to dip into.

We went to breakfast off campus, beginning a two-week pattern of late-night talks followed by mornings together. On the third day, we went to her apartment. I was surprised to see how girlish her room was: apricot bedspread, colored bottles arrayed on a small art deco vanity with a circular mirror, framed sheet music from the twenties on the wall, alongside tinted Maxfield Parrish prints and a photo of Jean Arthur and Gary Cooper in *Meet John Doe*.

She started kissing me and, gingerly, as if afraid I might scare, unbuttoning my shirt. I was scared. I didn't know what to do with my arms. I had stale coffee on my breath. When she slipped her hand into my pants, I came immediately. She made a slight moaning sound and said, "We'll have to work on that." She helped me out of my clothes and undressed herself. She sat on the pouffy ottoman she used as a

vanity stool and inserted her diaphragm, while I waited on the edge of
the bed. We got under her covers and kissed and touched until I was
ready. She guided me into her and, as I entered, I came. "Don't worry
about anything," she said, nestling close to me. I knew I had ruined
my chance, though, to be with this incredible woman again.

But I hadn't. "*I* won't die," she said. "We have all the time we
need."

For the next ten days she made good her claim. Time, it seemed,
was exactly what we had. She hung by me at work. We shared pancakes and sampled all the IHOP syrups. We set out in my VW for long
reckless drives in the Wisconsin snow. We drove to Erich's camp. As
we huddled in an empty cabin in the steamy orange cocoon of
Jeannie's sleeping bag, I told her lies, tales of summer camp from the
years I'd never spent there.

We had sex every day and she was patient and helpful. I was the
young boy, and she was the woman of experience. I came to see that
I could never please her the way I thought a man should, so I began
to rely on the more persuasive and sustainable powers of my fingers
and tongue. My own quick orgasm, a source of almost emasculat-
ing shame for me, I allowed to become a minor by-product of our
lovemaking, something that happened parenthetically against the
sheets while I was working my determined mouth against her. She
would climax too; then she'd show me her large pool eyes and say
again, "I won't die. We have all the time in the world. I won't die
on you, baby."

On the fourteenth day she didn't come to the shop. It was all I
could stand to keep the store open through my shift, to restrain
myself from flying out the door, locking it behind me, and racing to
her apartment to prove to myself she was where she said she would
be. I didn't, of course. And, of course, she wasn't.

"I had to see for myself," she said later, explaining why she'd spent
the night with her old boyfriend, the prosaically named Jim. "We
have this really strong connection, but we fight like dogs. We can't
be together. Both of us know it. But the sex is electric and there's
nothing either of us can do to change that. That's all, though. It's

nothing to do with you. I really care about you and I want to be with you. Jim's just Jim, though, and I had to see what he meant for me."

"What does he mean?" I asked, almost ducking, as if the world was raining down in huge chunks around my head.

"Don't press me, Erich. I have to do this my own way." I put my arms around her, but she shook me off. "I better go home now," she said, too coldly for me.

"You'll be by tonight?"

"I'll be where I am," she said and left.

I called throughout the day — I don't know how many times — but there was never any answer. I wanted to tell her how sorry I was, that I understood, that I'd never pressure her again. I didn't sleep or eat. I drove by her place in the middle of the day in the middle of a snowstorm. I couldn't see anything from the street. Later, on my way to work, I circled the block several more times. Until I heard from her, nothing else existed.

That night, several hours into my shift, she called. "I'm pretty wiped out. Don't think I want to walk out in this. You want to come over after work? I'll make an omelet or something."

"Sure," I said. "That would be great."

"Then, then," she said.

"Then." Wherever she'd been all day, whatever had happened last night to make her tired today — all that was history. Outside the snow kept falling, pinked up by the neon sign in the window. It was as simple and beautiful as a kiss in a dream.

Jeannie knew nothing about my brother, and I planned to keep it that way. I wanted to tell her, naturally, wanted to unload the whole sad story, but I couldn't. "Yeah, I had a brother. He killed himself ten years ago. I'm him now. Sort of." Unleashing Erich would amount to pushing her out the door.

Jeannie found a "cultural studies" program at Tufts that married her disparate interests. We'd been together for nearly five months, five months longer than I'd been with anyone else. I was adding up the days, each one a dollar in the bank, a marker in my wallet. Every month another man from her past faded out of the picture. Every month was another month she didn't leave. Now we were planning to live together.

We sold our stuff in late July. In reality, we sold my stuff, while most of Jeannie's was deemed too vintage or valuable. My books and record collection — everything—went at our yard sale, except some clothes and two boxes of photos and notebooks (Erich's), which I kept hidden. We also kept my electric typewriter for Jeannie to use at school.

Jeannie was hyped up during the sale, schmoozing and hawking, bills clutched in one hand, apron pockets gravid with coins. Afterward, she was quiet. She recounted the day's take, whispering numbers to herself. She ambled among half-boxes of unsold paperbacks, high-intensity lamps, and spatulas, silently taking stock, I thought, not of what was left, but of what was gone.

"I think I should go by myself," she said.

All the blood squeezed out of my heart. I knew what she meant, but pretended I didn't. "You don't want me to meet your parents. That's OK."

"No," she said. "Maybe I should go to Boston alone. You don't need to follow me halfway across the country to watch me study. You should finish school."

"There are nine million colleges in Boston," I argued.

"Your life is here."

"You'll be *there*," I said, in my simple anguish.

"But I won't. I'll be gone all the time. It's not good for you."

She was trying to be gentle. She was trying to convince me that the end of the world was, seen in a certain light, good medicine.

"We just sold all my stuff," I said.

"That's no reason for leaving."

"You are." I was begging.

"I don't know," she said.

We had planned dinner out to celebrate our last night in Madison. We went but didn't celebrate. The evening wound on in slow motion like something turning on a spit, over a low flame. I tried not to call attention to the heat.

When we got back to her apartment, she sounded certain. "I need time. To decide what's best. I think I should go home by myself tomorrow. Then we'll see. You can stay here. It's paid through the end of the month. I'll call when I get there. Then we'll see."

"Please, Jeannie," I said, clenching my lips and teeth against the flow of anything more.

"You want too much from me," she said, switching off the overhead light and lowering herself onto the sleeping bag we'd spread out. I stepped out of my pants and crouched down beside her. She slept, or seemed to, and I sat through the night, half breathing, memorizing her.

In the morning she showered and dressed while I fixed breakfast from what was left in the refrigerator. I suggested that she take the car; that way, I figured, no matter what she decided once she was away, I'd see her at least once more. She agreed.

At the door, she said, "I'll call" and allowed me to kiss her.

Back inside, her apartment looked like something stripped, a tireless car up on blocks under a city viaduct. I walked through the three rooms — living room, bedroom, kitchen — all bare, except for a couple of cheap pots and pans and a low, Salvation Army coffee table that had been in the apartment when she'd moved there. I had a clock radio, a suitcase, a couple of boxes, and a tiny tower of leftover books. The bathroom still smelled of her perfume.

I called the phone company to postpone our service shutoff until the first of August. I needed food and knew I wouldn't want to leave the apartment again until I'd heard from her. I ran to the store, bought cigarettes and supplies and hurried back in case she called. I tested the phone to make sure it was still hooked up.

I couldn't concentrate on reading or on anything. I just traipsed, sat, traipsed, sat, lighting one cigarette on the end of the last. I configured shots for a camera I didn't have: Special Export beer bottles lined up on the rim of the tub; a square of dust like a great trapdoor where the box spring had rested on the floor; a note she'd thumbtacked to the front door beside the deadbolt: "Keys, bimbo!"

Time eked by in this way. The numbers on the clock radio

flipped down. I smoked my throat raw. The first day passed. I tried
to sleep, but spent most of the night watching the patterns of light
on the ceiling. "I'm never more than three feet away," I thought to
Jeannie across the Midwest.

At about four that afternoon the phone rang. I stubbed out my
cigarette. It was Deborah.

"I couldn't remember when you were leaving," she said. "I tried
your number and got a disconnected message."

"Yeah. I'm closing up Jeannie's."

"How exciting," she chirped. "My little brother in love. Off into
the great unknown. I'm so happy for you." Tweet tweet.

I carried the phone into the bedroom, where I could see the
clock. Every minute that passed was a minute Jeannie wouldn't be
able to get through. "Yeah," I said. "Love's wings."

Left to her own devices, Deborah could jabber on for all time.
We only spoke every couple of months, but conversations lasted an
hour or more. She'd gone off to Virginia and gotten HAPPY. At six-
or eight-week intervals she insisted on sharing this happiness with
me. "God has given me so much, Erich. I've never felt this way,
never felt so close to so many people." On and on. Sharid this,
Sharid that. Jesus Jesus Jesus. Inner peace tweet tweet. Little bird in
a Christian cage.

"I just had to tell you," she was saying. And she paused for a
response.

"Great. Sure. No problem," I answered.

"Erich, did you hear what I just told you?"

"What?" I asked, pretty angry by now.

"I said I'm getting married. Married. Isn't that amazing!?"

"Deborah, I can't really talk now. I've gotta go," I said in a burst.

It was only after I'd hung up that I heard what she said, as if in
an echo or time delay. She was marrying somebody in her church.
Her guru Sharid was performing the ceremony. She was dreaming
flower girls and ring bearers. I was supposed to give a shit.

I was sure that Jeannie had tried to call while I was on with
Deborah. This surety didn't, however, give me permission to call her

at her parents'. "Goddamn it, Deborah! Why couldn't you wait?" I hollered. My stupid, brainwashed, nubile sister.

I thrashed the night away before falling off just as the sky was lightening. I woke up a few hours later, sticky and rank. I pictured Deborah, on Maid Marian Lane, bowing over her breakfast to give thanks before skipping off to morning service. I imagined my pudgy-fingered father bouncing his new baby boy in his arms. Jeannie would still be sleeping.

I opened a Coke and walked around naked while I drank. I held the cool bottle against my groin until I felt myself stir. The sensation of pleasure frightened me, as though by giving in to it, I would release Jeannie's presence from the room, lose her forever. I pulled on my jeans and ran cold water over my face.

Shortly after 10:00 A.M. she called. "Hi, baby," she said. "I miss you."

"Me too," I said. I looked around the room again. Light filled up the walls. The sky's blue pressed right up to the windows.

"Meet me in Boston, day after tomorrow. Can you?"

21

LIVING IN PARALLEL

I'll spare the redundant details.

Three years passed. The high/low points were as follows: I met Jeannie, as scheduled, in Medford, Massachusetts, on the twenty-sixth of July, 1979. We rendezvoused at the Tufts housing office. I was nervous and excited. She got there first. When she saw me, she looked stricken, panicked. She stared at me as if I were a stranger. She couldn't cover her response, and I couldn't blame her.

Her instinctive recoiling was, I believe, a response to truth glimpsed instinctively. I was a stranger and not in some existential, Albert Camus sense. In concrete terms, she didn't know the first thing about me, that first thing being who I was. I might as well have been the Belgian ambassador's son with beautifully inflected English, who, as his longtime girlfriend discovers through a series of movielike coincidences, really grew up on a farm in Kearney, Nebraska, surrounded by pigs. No, I couldn't blame her for finding me foreign and ugly. I was that way to myself.

We looked for a place, snooping under sinks for signs of mice and roaches, calculating the space necessary for joint living and Jeannie's studies. Then, after a couple of nights at a bed-and-breakfast in Medford, Jeannie made a decision. "I know what's wrong, Erich. I've figured it out. I'm beginning something new, something so new that I have to create space for it to fill in its own way. I can't bring so much to it that it has no chance to happen however it wants to happen. What I mean is, I think my trouble with this arrangement all along isn't our being together. It's our living together. I want to live alone. There, I said it. I want you there, near. But I need my own

— God, I don't want to sound like one of those support groups —
but it's space. Plain, simple, and figurative space. Imaginative space.
Say you understand."

"I do."

"I did want you here. I do. But I want you to be the boy next door
or the boy from the next town. You know, I want to go on dates with
you at the end of the day. Do you believe how conventional I
sound?"

I would have done anything she asked in order to stay in her life.
I did this. Jeannie found an apartment just off campus, a half floor of
a subdivided Victorian. I rented a smaller place — a room with an
electric burner and a shared, hall bathroom — over a pizza joint in
Union Square, a bus ride away in Somerville. Jobs were easy to come
by in early August. People were quitting before summer had ended,
and students hadn't yet returned to town. I wanted to work within a
walk from Jeannie's, so I took the first, nearest opportunity: man-
ning the counter at a Chinese take-out place near the university.
That the work was dull and my presence there odd hardly mattered
to me. My days were ruled by the expectation of seeing her, or, when
I couldn't, by the need to kill time until I could.

I tried to keep up with Jeannie's studies, copying down the titles
on her syllabi or buying textbooks off the store shelves designated
for her seminars. It was difficult going. Her coursework took her
places I'd never been: structural linguistics, Derridean philosophy,
feminist theory. She read French geniuses known by last names —
Foucault, Lévi-Strauss, Lacan, Saussure, Barthes, Cixous — whose
convoluted prose made ordinary philosophical writing look like *Hop
on Pop*. Love, though, was a fierce headmaster.

Jeannie displayed the fanaticism of the convert. Suddenly, everything was a "construct": "So finally, I got what he was saying in class,
what he was saying to me: You, me, man, woman, tragedy, comedy,
sex — especially that — it's all performance, Erich. Choices of
power, creations of history, economics — this vast manufactured
archive of human convention. Consensual archive — I mean, who
consented? Did you? Did I? Well, you did more directly than I did,

simply by being born white, by being born male, whatever that
means — whatever it's been *made*, constructed to mean. But no, I
didn't consent. Sure, I'm created too, a performance of this historical power, but just wait. Get me a beer, will you? I mean, you find
the language, you — what? — disencumber it, free yourself from its
construction, from the performance that history has given you and
watch out! You know? Incredible freedom in the disempowerment
of these linguistic constructs."

"What about self," I asked tentatively. "What about the coherence of self?"

"Oh, Erich," she clucked, shaking her head. "I thought we'd
checked that at the Wisconsin border."

She was right. What did I know about the coherence of self?
Maybe that had been the problem all along — trying to reconcile
myself to this shift of identity I'd undergone. Erich, not-Erich, who,
what I was — all such questions blew apart in this new light. Each
was performance. Each performance was shaped by the material and
historical relations that gave it context. Each was a construct of language; call me what you will and I'll respond, mutate, reconfigure
under that label. I was no more coherent or intrinsically myself
before Erich died than he was or than I was at that first moment
Jeannie leaned across the copy-shop counter, feigning sleepiness. I
began as a "construct"; as a "construct" I remained.

"So," I hypothesized. "I'm not innately me, anymore than I'm,
say, American by nature. I'm a product, a constellation of all those
things — those fictions or mutually agreed upon conventions —
male, twenty-two, North American, college dropout — that my
existence implies?"

"Something like that. I mean, that sounds a little reductive, but
essentially, yes."

"You're saying I'm not precisely me, because there is no me outside of all that convention and contract. I'm me but in quotes, right?
I'm 'Erich.'" And I made little quotation mark signs in the air with
my fingers.

"Right. 'Erich.'" And she made quotation marks back.

This became our salute. Quotation marks in the air. I became "Erich." She was "Jeannie." She "loved" me. I "needed" her.

For all our quotations and deconstructions, all the dismantling of our fictions, there was for me only one true thing: Jeannie was real. Maybe only Jeannie.

I knew about Jeannie's first "affair" before she did; that is, before it happened. It was latent in the way she said his name, Avery, squeezing the interest out of her voice as she spoke, as if resonance were something that could be hidden, even to herself. He was a postdoc who'd come back to Tufts to spearhead a conference on the history of consciousness. Jeannie was working on the conference as part of her graduate fellowship. When she stopped mentioning Avery, I knew she'd wind up sleeping with him, even though he was married, even though the idea hadn't yet, I think, occurred to her.

I lived in the land of quotation marks, while, for her, other men were flesh-and-blood, intense coherences. Avery was just the first such. I would wait and forgive. Forgiveness seemed the thing she wanted most from me. I would writhe away in my room or tramp along the streets of Somerville, Cambridge, Medford, Watertown, night after night — sometimes a week or two at a stretch, until she would call me again. I'd go to her. She'd cry and tell me all about it.

"There's this other woman in me, Erich, and she needs to get out."

"I want you to let her out. With me."

"I can't. That's not who you are."

"I can be whatever you want me to be."

She laughed a little self-loathing laugh and made the sign of quotations in the air.

Finally, in May, a week before we were to go to Deborah's wedding, she said, "I'm not good for you, Erich. You shouldn't see me anymore."

"Why would I do that?" I asked. "I love you."

"You 'love' me," she said, making our sign.

"I know what I feel. I know what you mean to me."

"It's not good for you. And I feel guilty all the time. I took you away from Madison, from school, from your life, from everything."

"I was nothing until I met you."

"Nobody is nothing."

"You don't know."

"I can't do this anymore. You want too much from me. You have to go away."

"I can't. I don't want to."

"I can't deal with this now. I'm trying to finish finals, these papers. You don't understand."

"You're wiped out. Don't worry about me. Just do your work. Call me after finals. I'll be here."

"I don't want you here!" she screamed.

"Just concentrate on your work. You'll feel different when it's over," I said.

"No! I won't feel differently! Go away! Please!"

I left her house, but I couldn't leave the block. I waited near the corner, out of sight of her windows. I wanted to see if she left the house. I wanted to be close to her. I couldn't leave the block.

I don't know exactly how long I was there, several hours probably. It was very dark when I noticed a campus police car passing me on the street and then, after circling the block, passing me again.

I went to Deborah's wedding alone, hoping to give Jeannie the space and time she needed. When I got back, finals would have ended and things would have settled down. She'd be seeing clearly.

Deborah had arranged her wedding for Memorial Day weekend. She'd asked me to walk her up the aisle. "It's not like you're giving me away or anything," she said. "I'm giving myself. In the presence of God and everybody. But I want you to walk partway with me, be the brother of honor sort of."

"Doesn't the dad usually?" I asked.

"The dad is paying; the brother, I hope, is walking," she replied.

"Won't it seem strange, leaving him out?"

"He won't be left out, unless he leaves himself out," Deborah explained, adding, "which has been known to happen."

In the performance of my fraternal duties, I was expected to dress formally, in a baby blue tux with black collar — the sort of thing kids wear for senior prom. My sister didn't want to leave anything to chance, so she had taken my detailed measurements over the phone and ordered the outfit. She'd also bought me a sports jacket for the rehearsal dinner, at which I was supposed to give a toast.

I had never met Deborah's fiancé Dan before, but I felt as if I'd known him all my life, not because we instantaneously connected, but because he was such a type. When he shook my hand and said, "Hey Erich, I can't tell you how nice it is to finally meet you," I looked at the joyous expectation on my sister's face and thought, "He's her teen dream." His type, I guess you could say, was Wonder-Bread-as-Boy-Wonder, that gentile middle-American class of mothers' favorite sons, so innocuously nice looking as to appear, to anyone operating outside of their system of values, almost menacing. When, years later, I caught my first glimpse of a vice-presidential candidate named Dan Quayle, I thought for an instant that Deborah's Dan had changed his family name.

He was, of course, athletic in the tennis, golf, and weekend-scrimmage-football-with-the-guys sense. And he possessed exactly the kind of intelligence neccssary for a successful life in business or local politics. He'd gone away to college at Georgetown — his family lived in Norfolk — and in his junior year he found God. As a result, he switched from pre-law to a major in occupational therapy. After school he settled in Falls Church, where he rehabilitated people with job-related illnesses and attended services and classes at the Church of Grace Fellowship Center. "I love your sister," he said, as if to reassure me, the first time we were alone. "She's a great girl with a profoundly deep sense of service." Then, in a shift of direction he didn't blink at, he added, "A very exotic girl."

The day before the wedding was spent picking up things: clothes, food, Dad and Hildy. They'd taken the train down, no doubt to accomodate the children, as well as my father's fear of car trips. Mac met them at Union Station, and I met them at Mac's.

Hildy answered the door. She took my hand and gave me a brief upright hug, in that muscular, forthright way she had. "Erich," she said, as if I were a hearty soup, "Good to see you. Willy, Erich's here." My dad looked up from his comically stooped position of spotting Willy Jr. as he toddled among the various hazards of Mac's apartment. Mac was across the room, lifting seven-year-old Amanda up to the ceiling. "Hello, Son," Dad said. "Hey pal," said Mac. The kids seemed, as on previous occasions, sort of congenitally wary of me, as, no doubt, their birthright gave them every reason to be.

Hildy went off to get her family unpacked, and I joined the chaos of men and children in the living room. "Where's your girl?" Mac asked, simultaneously rubbing noses with pudgy Amanda and saying, "Here's my girl. Here's my girl."

"She had too much work to do," I said. "Finals. Papers. Grading. We decided it would be better . . ." I trickled off halfway through my prepared response.

"We were looking forward to meeting Jeannie," my father said, reaching up to pull Willy Jr.'s hand away from a small sculpture it was about to topple.

"She's looking forward, too." I said. "Next time, I guess."

"Next time Deborah gets married?" Dad asked with an edge of either sarcasm or stress, I couldn't tell.

Hildy appeared in the doorway, frowning slightly. "It just occurred to me," she said with an air of disapproval. "Jean. She's not here."

"Finals," I said. "We thought . . ."

"It's better this way," Mac said. "Otherwise she'd spend all weekend worrying."

"Of course." Hildy said, adding, "We're certainly disappointed, though."

"She'll come to Deborah's next wedding," my father repeated.

"Willy," she called, ignoring his last statement, "I thought you were keeping an eye on him." My father turned to see his namesake standing one shelf up on the stereo cart.

The day followed this herky-jerky course, until the time came to dress and find the restaurant for the rehearsal dinner. I drove separately but reconvened with Dad and the others in the parking lot before going into the restaurant. Dan's family was already there. They were what you'd call pleasant people. His mother had stiff frosted hair and a kindly smile; his father was a proud spitting image of Dan, only with a paunch. There were a couple of Waspy-looking brothers with manicured wives and a thin sister with an uneventful husband whose tie seemed always to be choking him. He worked for Dan's dad. Dan's youngest brother was obviously the black sheep, a restless, slouching teenager with whom I never spoke but for whom I felt a vague affinity. Ron, the best friend–best man, was there too.

Deborah moved among us in a kind of hectic ecstasy, kissing everyone — including me — squeezing her half sister and brother, hooking Dad and Hildy's arms to introduce them around, touching the elbow of anyone who said something funny. We were served Greek food and Saint Helena wine by a flight of gray-haired waiters who were always there when we needed them and who referred to each of us as "My friend." Dad, Mac, and Hildy took turns chasing Willy Jr., while Dan's sister-in-law, Sheila, kept Amanda under her wing all evening, initiating her into the secrets of folding linen napkins, squeezing lemons, and the ladylike art of French-braiding hair.

Everything went smoothly enough. The waiters danced for us. Mac danced with Deborah, Dan with his mom, and I sat around, trying not to imagine Jeannie sleeping with someone else. At one point, Deborah leaned over me and whispered, "Tell Dad not to drink so much. It's humiliating." Then she said, "Why don't you ask Dan's mother to dance?" Before I could explain why, she was gone.

"Deborah thinks Dad's drinking too much," I told Mac, when he sat back down next to me.

"Girls always think their fathers drink too much at their wedding parties," he said.

When the time came for toasts, Ron clinked his glass and made some witty remarks, essentially a "Dan the Man is dead to us" speech, about trading the bachelor's freedom for the sleepy bliss of conjugal life. Then Dan's father rose and welcomed Deborah into his family, saying, "When Dan told me he was getting married, I said, 'Well, one more or less doesn't matter.' But, having met Debbie and gotten to know her, I can attest to the fact that she's definitely one *more*."

"Oh, Steve," his wife said, affectionately swatting his arm.

"Glad to have you, Deb," Mr. Monroe said. And everyone drank.

The possibility of a spontaneous salute by my father was ruined by a tantrum from his baby son. I shambled to my feet, taking a piece of crumbled paper out of my jacket pocket. People were still chattering. Willy Jr. was sobbing spasmodically.

"I have a poem I want to read for Deborah and Dan," I said. "It says how I feel better than I can. It's about love, of course, being a poem. It's by Theodore Roethke." I sort of mumbled his name, then added, "I don't really know how to say his name." My father did, though, and he said it loudly enough that people turned their heads. He abstractly waved his hand in front of his face.

"It's called 'The Dream.' For Deborah and Dan:" I cleared my throat and read.

> I met her as a blossom on a stem
> Before she ever breathed, and in that dream
> The mind remembers from a deeper sleep:
> Eye learned from eye, cold lip from sensual lip.
> My dream divided on a point of fire;
> Light hardened on the water where we were;
> A bird sang low; the moonlight sifted in;
> The water rippled, and she rippled on.

Glasses rattled, chairs scraped, throats were cleared. I read on in a husky voice.

> She came toward me in the flowing air,
> A shape of change, encircled by its fire,
> I watched her there, between me and the moon . . .

Willy Jr. cried and cried. Dan's sister leaned over to her husband and said, "I don't get it," loudly enough for everyone to hear. Deborah and Dan stared at me with frozen, "Thank-you-so-much-for-that-lovely-poem" smiles. I droned on.

I saw Hildy snatch Willy Jr. from my father's arms with a flash of disgust. It seemed to me as if everyone was watching them. I skipped to the end of the poem.

> Like a wet log, I sang within a flame.
> In that last while, eternity's confine,
> I came to love, I came into my own.

When I'd finished I said, "In love we come into our own. I hope so for you two, too." Deborah came over and hugged me and everyone sipped wine and sort of applauded. Dan stood up and thanked everyone, most especially Willy, in advance, for footing the wedding bill. Dad nodded assent. Dan went on to say that he wished Deborah's mom could have been here for these happy days. Everybody bobbed their heads and sadly cast their eyes down. Then he toasted his bride-to-be.

The waiters brought baklava and Greek coffee with twists of lemon, and everyone went back to their fussing and murmuring. Mac curved forward above his plate, delicately peeling the layers of filo pastry with the tines of his fork. "I knew Roethke, you know," he told me. "Didn't really know him. Met him. We played doubles a couple times at Michigan. Friend of a friend. He was a bit older, of course. Scary guy, very regular, very intense. Good tennis player. 'The edge is what I have.' That's what I always think of. Very intense. Read a lot of him in the fifties."

I nodded and waited for Mac's roundabout ways to land him somewhere. They always did. "That girl of yours must really be something," he finally said.

"The one true thing," I said. "Look around." He did.

"Know what you mean," he agreed. Then he took air in through his teeth, sipped on the coffee, and offhandedly said, "Steady as she goes." I assumed he was talking to me. "Love's dream and all that. I always found it very slippery. As in slope." He glanced my way.

"One true thing," I said.

The next day, we rehearsed in the morning and performed in the afternoon. The rehearsal wasn't much more than who stands where when, and how to walk slowly down the aisle. I immediately pegged Sharid as a huckster, born in Florida probably, under the name of Pete Davis or some such, who, when he decided the New Age needed more Elmer Gantrys, changed his name to the vaguely Eastern, unidentifiably ethnic, swami-esque-sounding moniker Sharid Alfijay. I also suspected that he was punning on the name of the movie star Omar Shariff, to whom he'd no doubt been compared. He did look vaguely like Dr. Zhivago, had Zhivago come from Jacksonville and fancied his own bright smile a bit too well.

When I ran this by Mac at the wedding reception, he added, "High school tennis team, mother a beautician, father traveled." I nodded. Then Mac said, "Your sister is very happy. In place and so on. That's not an altogether bad thing."

The wedding was held in the fellowship center's small chapel, which, in place of pews, had folding chairs. At the top of the aisle, before we began walking, Deborah squeezed my arm several times in very quick succession. "I can't believe Mom's not here," she whispered, making it sound as if Mom had simply missed her train or failed to RSVP. Then she began rolling her lips together, forward and back, to smooth her lipstick. It gave her the appearance of a semiretarded bag lady popping dentures in and out. She was so eager to get down the aisle, I felt I was being pulled. Dad was leaning into the aisle, holding one elbow with a crossed arm. His fisted hand was under his chin, thinker-style. His eyes were wet and I think Deborah saw them, because I felt her lose step.

Standing by the altar, I crossed my own hands over the general vicinity of my crotch and watched Sharid lead the congregation in a prayer to the Father, before marrying Deborah and Dan. The couple took the usual vows, then facing each other, hand in hand, sang "Devoted to You." A frizzy-haired girl accompanied them on the flute. Sharid blessed the bride and groom again, reading a passage about the miracle at Cana, and, finally, pronounced them, whom he called "my son and daughter," man and wife. They kissed, and, when she turned her hysterical smile to the crowd, I thought Deborah would explode out of her skin.

We moved outside to the lawn, where a permanent wooden structure sheltered the buffet and picnic tables, a dance floor, and a Christian bluegrass pop quartet. The reception area was crisp with midday sun. The head table was set with an extra place, which no one noticed or bothered to remove, for Jeannie. As Deborah and Dan danced and laughed and flitted from table to table, I stayed rooted to my spot between Deborah's empty chair and Jeannie's. At some point my father came over and sat down where Jeannie would have been.

"I'm sorry we haven't had more time to talk, this visit," he said. "You know how it is with small children."

"How's it going?" I asked.

"Oh, fine, fine. I feel a lot older than I did with you kids, but then I am."

There was a silence between us, as we both scanned the chipper crowd.

"Deborah seems happy," I said.

"Yes, yes," he said, adding half aloud, "everybody always seems happy."

"God helps, I suppose."

"One would suppose," he agreed. "What about you?" he asked, his sighted eye focusing on my left eye.

"No, he doesn't help me much."

"I meant school. Do you think you'll be finishing soon? It wouldn't hurt, especially your being so close."

"When Jeannie's done," I said "and there's more time. Or more money. I'm virtually in school now. I read everything she's assigned."

"That's fine, but it won't graduate you. You've always been a bright young man."

"That sounds so nineteenth century. Assessing my prospects and property."

"I suppose it does," he said, looking away. He put two twenty-dollar bills in my hand. "Hildy and I want you to have this. It might defray —"

"Deborah paid my way down."

"Then use it for whatever. Take Jeannie to, what's that place? Café Budapest."

I noticed again the wine glass, where her lipstick would be.

"Well, I suppose I should say something to your sister."

"Yeah," I said. The band kicked up a bluegrass version of Paul Stookey's "The Wedding Song," a signal to cut the cake.

I watched him walk over to Deborah, startling her as she crossed behind Dan's folks on the way to the cake stand. He reached one hand to her arm and half leaned toward her, to whisper or kiss I couldn't tell. She glanced down and just to one side of him, gripping her upper lip with her bottom teeth and holding a dangling arm with a crossed one. She looked sheepish, a little girl in Halloween bridal dress on the verge of tears. When he was finished speaking, she ticked her head slightly to one side, as if to say, "Me too, Daddy." He pulled her closer awkwardly and kissed her cheek. Her tired eyes swiveled up and met mine, over Dad's shoulder. Dad reached into the breast pocket of his Harris tweed and withdrew an envelope, which he held out to her. She took it and pecked his cheek.

Cake followed, a vast yellow sheet cake with chocolate fudge frosting and myriad edible icing flowers. In the middle rose a white plastic pedestal, on which kneeled two figurines, a bride and groom, heads bowed in prayer or thanks or, just possibly, despair. Pink swirly letters read, GOD BLESS THE UNION OF DEBORAH & DAN.

Deborah and Dan fed each other and began rounds of good-byes. Everyone stood around in ambling discourse while the newlyweds went inside to change. Hildy made her way to me and stood by, eyes aimed at the door from which the couple would emerge. "It was good seeing you, Erich. You and Jean will have to come down to the city to see us. Anytime. Amanda and Willy will enjoy having a big brother."

"I think he's scared of me," I said, also watching the apartment-building door.

She snorted a little laugh. "He's a toddler. They're scared of all sorts of things."

"No. Dad, I mean. He's scared of both of us."

Her head bucked slightly. "Oh. No, no. Just worried. He's just worried about you. And stiff. You know how rigid he can seem. Trouble expressing himself, I guess."

I glanced over at her. She looked like what she was, a linguist, thin and scholarly — terse. I would have thought her fifty-five, if I didn't know she was ten years younger. She'll be a department chairwoman someday, I thought. "He gave me money," I said. "Thanks."

"He wants to help however he can." She was watching her kids, scooting across the lawn with Mac, folded almost in thirds to reach their level, scuttling in pursuit. Then she said, "I'm sorry your brother couldn't be here today."

"Here they come," someone shouted.

"I doubt he's sorry," I said, not meaning to be snippy.

The door opened. Deborah and Dan came strolling down the walk, carrying overnight bags. People threw rice and confetti at them.

"What? Oh. No, no — your mother. I was talking about your mother. Not being here. I think I said mother. I'm sorry."

And she thinks Dad's stiff, I thought. "Yeah," I said. "She would have liked it. The spectacle."

"I'm certain she would have," Hildy said. "Oh, well." Then she added, "Congratulations on Deborah." She put her lips to my jaw-line and took them away.

"You too," I said.

Deborah and Dan got into the streamered, coffee-canned car, and her fingers flapped tiny good-byes out the window. Everyone applauded and called out "Bon voyage" and "Have fun!"

I drove straight to Boston, stopping only for gas and coffee. I was outside Newark, Delaware, before I realized I hadn't returned the rented tux. The pale blue jacket lay across the passenger seat. I still wore the ruffled shirt, the bow tie dangling from my neck like a pair of binoculars. I touched the satin stripe on the side of the trousers and became aware of the hard leather shoes against the accelerator. I did not turn around.

I called Jeannie from my apartment as soon as I got in. She answered. "Don't call me again, Erich," she said. "I don't want you calling me. I'll call you when I'm ready. If I'm ready." And she hung up.

Everyday felt like a year as I waited for her to call. I literally counted minutes, sometimes seconds, but I couldn't have said how many weeks or months passed. There was about it all an ongoing sense of the eternal, eternally painful, present. Jeannie changed her phone number. She moved to another apartment. I'd see her crossing campus or running at the track. Once a man I'd never seen came to the take-out and asked me if my name was Erich.

"'Erich,'" I said, two fingers in the air, either side of my head.

"Stay away from Jeannie," he said grimly. "She doesn't want to see you anymore."

I smiled at him and nodded. "OK," I agreed.

The Chinese spoken around me had begun to penetrate. I found myself dreaming in broken phrases of Cantonese. I hated it. This other language diluted the purity of mind I was trying to maintain, the purity of the single thought, the one true thing.

She haunted me, and I wouldn't have had it any other way. I wanted access to the world outside of myself; Jeannie was the only port of entry. I would wait, and I would hope. I would hold her in mind: string of pearl teeth, laughing shoulders, quotation marks in the air. I would read alongside of her, even at a distance. I quit the Chinese takeout and found a job at the order desk in a Harvard Square bookstore. I read every graduate-level book listed in Jeannie's department. I singled out those I knew she would be most taken with. I wanted to be ready for her.

At the end of twenty-two months, I was arrested. I didn't worry too much, initially. I assumed that the Tufts campus police thought I was selling drugs on school grounds or something. When I got to the station, though, I realized I was being held by the Medford police. They made me sit for a long time in a detention room. Then two cops came in, accompanied by a woman in secretarial-type clothes who took notes but never spoke.

They asked me my name, where I lived and worked, if I went to school. They asked me lots of questions about myself, including where I'd been on certain days. Then the younger of the two cops, who'd barely spoken, asked me if I knew a woman named Jeannie Munson.

"She's my girlfriend," I told him.

"Your girlfriend?" he repeated, nailing me with his eyes.

"Old girlfriend," I said.

"Old girlfriend?"

"We're going through a kind of trial separation, you could say," I explained.

He looked at the other officer. Then he turned back to me and said in a quiet, but threatening way, "Listen, Mr. Hofmann. I could arrest you for several different things, including trespassing, harassment, disorderly conduct, invasion of privacy — any number of things. If I told a judge that you've been hanging around, stalking college girls, he'd lock you up and bury the key somewhere. But you're a young guy with your life ahead of you. I don't want to ruin your chances in life. I know what it's like. You like a girl. She slams the door in your face. You tell yourself you love her, you need her. I don't have to tell you.

"But I want you to hear what I'm telling you. I see your face this side of the Charles River and I'll not only put you away, I'll hurt you, personally. You catch my drift, son. You are out of here. And I'd suggest that you get out of this whole state. Go back to New York or Washington, where your family is. I mean what I say. I don't want to ruin your life, but I won't see anybody else's life ruined either. I'm going to keep close hold on this just in case." He walked over to his partner and picked up the forms they'd been writing my answers down on.

"You can go now," the other one said.

"Go far," said the young cop.

I looked over at the woman taking notes. I wanted to make sure she didn't believe what they were saying about me. But her face was a blank. I held less interest for her than a lab specimen.

"She still has my typewriter," I told her. Nobody said anything.

I was halfway through the door when I heard the young cop mutter, "Sick fuck."

22

Reason to Believe

I crossed the Charles River, the East River, the Hudson, the Delaware Water Gap, and the Potomac, my car filled with little more than I'd brought to Boston three years earlier. I drove through hail in Massachusetts and rain all down the New Jersey Turnpike, until, somewhere just north of Baltimore, the water stopped and only the gray day remained. My crying, however, didn't stop, proof to me that the loss of Jeannie — the loss of a future with her — was a greater loss than anything I'd previously faced. I could stand to lose a brother, grandfather, or mother. These deaths were merely bitter childhood pills compared to the death of Jeannie's faith in me. She thought I meant to hurt her. She called in the police to keep me from her. She didn't know the first thing about me, that she was the first thing, the only thing.

I began to compose a letter in my head. Everything sounded melodramatic or sensational. "You'll never have to see me again!" "Now you'll know how much I loved you — enough to leave your side forever!" I thought to send a postcard to let her know she was safe and free from me and, in place of a signature hang a pair of empty " "s. "I *am* a sick fuck," I said out loud, "a lousy fuck, and a stupid one." I kept driving, wishing for an accident, for the car to lose control and spin me into a bloody ditch. I turned the tinny radio up until my ears shrieked with songs I hated by bands whose names only reminded me of the wreckage of my life: The Police, The Cars, The Attractions.

I drove to Deborah. I didn't know where else to go. I hadn't seen her since the wedding, had barely talked to her.

Dan came to the door of their apartment, an excessively clean

two-bedroom in a two-story townhouse at the Fellowship Center.
He hesitated before greeting me, as though he was having trouble
placing my face. I had no trouble placing him; he was eminently the
same. Suddenly I dawned on him. He gave me a hail-fellow-well-
met sort of greeting and, before I could even put my bag down, disappeared and reappeared, thrusting an open Coors in my direction.
"Just throw that stuff anywhere," he said. "Deb's out at the store. I
was supposed to be doing the dinner dishes, but I got sidetracked."
He threw a glance toward the TV. "One day Washington will have
its own team again. Until then, it's the Orioles all the way." He thrust
a fist in the air and exclaimed, "Spring fever! Yes!"

"That makes sense," I said, not knowing what the hell he was
talking about or even, really, where I was, what planet. They had
orange shag carpet running wall-to-wall, a green sectional sofa, and
a small oval dining table on a piece of gold-flecked beige linoleum,
around which the carpet had been cut. The table had the kind of
wooden veneer you sometimes see on elevator walls, with little
brown swirls that look like faces screaming. There were some paintings on the walls, those country-scapes and reproduced Renoirs you
buy at Holiday Inn fine-art sales. There was a small mounted cross
by the table and a photo of Sharid on a bookshelf containing James
Michener novels and biographies of pro-sports figures. The coffee
table boasted a *TV Guide*, several back issues of *Guideposts*, and a well-
thumbed Bible with pieces of notepaper sticking out.

"Sometimes I wish I'd gone into sports medicine," Dan was saying. "Now that's a line of work where things happen." I must have
looked at him oddly, because he appeared to notice my uninvited
presence in his otherwise immaculate home for the first time. "Deb
didn't tell me you were coming," he said, cheerfully. "Of course,
you're always welcome. It's great to see you."

"I didn't know I was coming."

"Sure. Sometimes you just have to light out. Man, if I wasn't an
old married geezer with responsibilities, I'd do that, too. Just take
off every now and again. Oh, shoot!" he exclaimed after somebody
struck out on TV. "Hey. How's Janie?"

"Jeannie," I said.

"No. I could have sworn Deb said it was Janie."

"No," I said. "Jean. E."

"You mean all this time I've had the wrong darn name in my head. Man, what a dufus. Well, how is she anyway — Jean-Janie?"

"Fine," I told him. "Can I use —? Where's?"

"Right down the hall. Sure."

Their bathroom had two bowls of those little pastel soaps in the shapes of sea shells. I picked up a blue conch and broke down again. I don't know how long I was in there. Long enough for Dan to knock on the door. "You OK, Er?"

I mumbled a "Yeah."

When Deborah got home, I was still there, sitting on an aqua bathroom scale, my back against the wall beside the toilet. She knocked several times and, when I didn't answer, came in. I don't know what she saw, but whatever it was seemed to terrify her. Before she even said hello, she said, "You'll be OK. You'll be OK. You need some Valium. I have some around here somewhere."

She began feverishly opening and closing drawers and cabinet doors, flipping through jars and tubes. Dan stood in the doorway, blinking at me. I covered my face with my arms. I think he asked, "Where's it hurt, big buddy?"

"Here," Deborah said. She gave me several pills and held a Dixie cup of water to my lips. "Now I want you to lie down in the guest room. I'll pull out the couch and make up the bed." She led me into a room with a desk and convertible sofa. Dan's diplomas were on the wall, alongside plaques, and, on the shelves, childhood sports trophies. Deborah turned on the guest TV. Judy Garland was singing. "It's *Easter Parade*," my sister said. "That'll cheer you up." I heard Dan yell at the umpire down the hall. "Here's an extra pillow," Deborah said. "We'll see you in the morning. Everything looks better in the morning." She closed the door behind her, careful not to let it slam.

A few moments later — I hadn't moved from the chair she'd left me in — Deborah returned. She was carrying a Bible, which she laid

on the arm of the sofabed. "Something to read," she said, offhandedly. "Who knows? It might help." Again, she went out.

I don't think I slept. I lay on the bed all night, my body water-
logged, a dead thing. Only my eyes and mind were working, making
their way over the little sparkles in the stucco ceiling, making their
way back to Jeannie. I could remember so little about her: a puppy-
dog look she sometimes gave me, the slope of her shoulders, the
bone of her hips. I could recall almost nothing of the last two years
but one endless moment of waiting.

When Deborah came in the next morning, I didn't sit up or
speak. I just watched her, as she spoke to me. "I don't know what
happened, Erich, but I do know it can't be any worse than what
we've already been through, several times over. So I know you'll be
all right. And I want you to know that, too. The worst thing is living without knowing that, living without faith. That's the worst
thing, I'm telling you. You can't go on like this. Let me help you." I
said nothing. "Faith is everything, Erich."

All day like that, in and out. Dan had, apparently, gone to work.
Deborah tended to me, bringing plates of food and cups of coffee,
none of which I touched. Later, she came back and picked up the
Bible she'd left the night before. She thumbed it, searching for something. She began to read: "In thee, O Lord, do I put my trust; let me
never be ashamed; deliver me in thy righteousness. Bow down thine
ear to me; deliver me speedily; be thou my strong rock; for an house
of defenses to save me. For thou art my rock and my fortress; there
for thy name's sake lead me, and guide me. Pull me out of the net that
they have laid privily for me: for thou art my strength. Into thine hand
I commit my spirit: thou hast redeemed me, O Lord God of truth."

She persisted, since I didn't stop her: "Have mercy upon me, O
Lord, for I am in trouble: mine eye is consumed with grief, yea, my
soul and my belly. For my life is spent with grief, and my years with
sighing: my strength faileth because of mine iniquity, and my bones
are consumed."

Deborah wept silently at my side as she read — a woman bury-
ing the last of her kin. She recited through tears, wet proof of

David's way with a psalm. "I am forgotten as a dead man out of mind: I am like a broken vessel."

As she read, I began to feel the impact of these phrases, as well as their power over her. I had no comfort to offer, though, no words of my own. I couldn't tell her I'd be all right. I couldn't tell her anything. "Be of good courage, and he shall strengthen your heart, all ye that hope in the Lord."

She marked the page she'd been reading with a ribbon and closed the book, setting it down within my reach. "That's my favorite psalm," she said. "I've been reading it. We. We've been trying to get pregnant. Since the wedding. Dan thinks the reason we can't is my faith isn't strong enough. I don't know, Erich. I think he may be right. I keep hearing Dad's voice in my head, him laughing at people who believe. You remember. When he'd have a couple of drinks and do his little Nietzsche thing, his 'Doncha know? Haven't ya heard? God'll-do-you-too! Thus sprayed Zara the Rooster!' and we'd laugh at him crowing around and making faces. I don't know. I try so hard here. 'I'm like a broken vessel' — 'Broken vessels can't carry,' Dan says. I know he's right."

Later that night, Sharid came into my room, Dan and Deborah behind him. "That's OK," he said to them. They left the room — small children backing out. Sharid ran his eyes over me. He noticed the Bible on the bed and picked it up. He turned to the marked passage and said, "I see Deborah's been here." He closed the book and tossed it gently on the bed. "You know, when I met your father — I hope you don't mind my saying this — when I met your father at the wedding I thought of that passage, that line: 'Mine eye is consumed with grief.' It was an instinctive response to his eye, the blind one. I tend not to question my responses at moments like that, so I didn't think any more of it. Until just now, of course, or rather, until Deborah brought that same passage with her to our last tutorial. (I have weekly meetings, consultations with the good people here, with my flock, you might say.) Then I recalled seeing him and thinking that. Deborah's more concerned with the grief-consumed belly, as I'm sure she's told you.

"Of course, I have no idea what sort of grief may have consumed your father's vision or Deborah's *reproductive* faculties, any more than I know what brought you here. You are here. That's all I know. That's all we really have. That's the part your sister has so much trouble accepting: what *is*. She wants to know why, who's to blame, what she should do. She thinks she can control her destiny by being — who knows what? — a good girl, a righteous woman. That's *hubris*, plain and simple: thinking you can control God. You don't dictate to God. God deals. We play the hand. Or we don't. We fight it, wish we'd been dealt otherwise, throw over the deck, tip the table.

"Let me tell you what else I know. I'm going to save your life. It's that simple. I'm going to save your life by saving your soul. It doesn't do any good to tell you I want you here. You are here. I want to keep you here, and I'm going to do that because my will is that much stronger than yours. It's stronger because it's not merely my own. Do you understand what I'm saying to you?

"Listen, son. I look at you and I don't think, 'Let me never be ashamed.' I think another psalm: 'Their sorrows shall be multiplied that hasten after another god. . . .' Sound familiar? 'Hasten after another god?'

"And I think, '*I* shall not be moved.' I'm going to turn this life around — to help you turn from the worship of whoever or whatever brought you here, brought you to *this*." He spread his hands above my horizontal body, as though displaying a burnt casserole to a class of wannabe chefs. He might have added, "Nasty little mess, eh?"

"And I'm going to help you turn to the path of life. There's only so long you can go the other way, hanker after the kind of death you've obviously been pursuing." Abruptly, he looked at his watch and walked over to Dan's desk. He picked up the phone and punched a few buttons. "Hi," he said into it. "I'm running late. I'll be there in a few minutes." He signed off, "Right-o."

He came back to me. "Let me ask you something. If I'd told you two days ago that you'd be lying here tonight listening to me, would you have believed it?"

I couldn't not answer. He was too good. "No."

"Of course not. What about at the wedding? I come up to you at the wedding and I say, 'You are mine. Two years from now, more or less.'"

"No."

"You would have laughed, right? Sneered, more probably. Exactly what I've been telling you. You can't control these things. They are so far beyond our understanding that they often seem contrary to what we think of as truth. Absurd, you being here. Ridiculous. Unimaginable. Completely out of character. But you're here. With me. Ridiculously, unimaginably, uncharacteristically. And if I reach down and take your hand, you won't withdraw it." This he did, and I did not.

"It always hurts, Erich," he said, my hand still in his strong grip. "It is always heavy. Everyone has such a grief; everyone has such a burden. But you carry it. With help. You can't carry it alone. No one can." He let my hand go. "There is no further down to go. It stops here. We're going to lift you up." His fingers floated over to my forehead. "Rest now," he said.

I could feel my breathing release and deepen.

When he turned to go, I marshaled my last ounce of resistance and said, "Sharid. Is that your real name?"

A smile eddied across his mouth, before settling in one corner. "It's the name I was born with. If that makes it real."

When the door clicked shut, I closed my eyes and sank through everything I thought of as this life. I heard Deborah come in and felt her lean over me, but I kept sinking. I slept for three days.

23

Self-Storage

Deborah saved me from Sharid. He was right: his will was stronger than mine. If I'd stayed, I would have been his. He would have "flocked" me.

Unknown to either of us, however, Deborah had bought a plane ticket to California for later that week and, while I slumbered, she'd bought a second one. "I'm sick of paying rent for Mom's storage rooms," she told me when I came to. "I don't even know what all is in them, and I want to. Then, when you showed up, I figured we could make it a reunion. I didn't expect you to sleep so long or I would have changed the reservations." Her tickets were for that evening. "Do you have to be somewhere?" she asked.

I lacked the energy to laugh. "I guess I have to be somewhere," I said.

"Might as well be back home, huh?"

"Home," I echoed with much less certainty.

Deborah brought me a washcloth and towel. "You can use Dan's razor — it's in there — and anything else you need. I guess you don't need time to pack," she added, indicating my duffel bag, sitting where I'd left it several days before.

I shaved and bathed and sat down to a plate of dry toast and a bowl of soup from a can. "I didn't think you should overdo it at first," she said.

"Oomie would disinherit you if she saw this meal," I said.

Deborah managed a smile. She'd seemed anxious since morning. She kept looking around, opening cupboards, writing notes to herself. "Does Dan know we're doing this?" I asked her.

She took a huge breath. "He knows. But he thinks I'm coming back."

We flew all night, though the hours moved in reverse. Deborah had booked a room in one of the hotels across from the beach in Venice. I slept on the plane and for most of the next day in California. Deborah wandered the town. She said she was looking for apartments to rent, but I suspect she was getting reoriented. She spent several hours reading her Bible and mouthing prayers. She brought me rolls from a local bakery and scrambled eggs in a Styrofoam carton.

I felt so heavy. Just walking from the cab to the plane and plane to cab had sapped whatever reserves of energy I had. Jeannie was still there, though no longer as a beacon. She was the weight I couldn't get out from under, or, maybe, the loss of her was the weight, a black hole, something empty and massive at the same time, magnet and void. It wasn't her image I carried. I could barely picture her, could summon up none of the specifics that, recalled, produce the whole. Her name was the only thing left of her — "Jeannie" — the magnificent, deadening weight of name without body. Deborah never said the name. She waited for me to reveal what I was under. I waited for her to tell me where she was going, if not back to Dan.

On our second day in Venice, we took a slow walk along the boardwalk. Deborah put her arm through mine. I was Papa. Clop, slide, chank. She was my nurse, steadying me, moving by my side in quiet shoes. I got winded, but somehow having my sister there let me keep going. She talked and I listened. The familiar scenes of Venice ran on around us like blurry background action in the movies. We attended only to each other, the sounds of our feet and breath, Deborah's words, and the pressure of our bodies leaning one on the other.

"When I got to the Center, I had just left Richard. I guess I needed something in my life that I could believe in. Or maybe I already believed. Mom had died. There was nothing keeping me in any one place. The whole first year, I felt the most intense relief. Do you know what I mean? Not about Mom, but about me. I had found *my* life; I had found the thing I was good at. Belief. Faith. Whatever you call it. The confusion just vanished. Kaput. I felt such incredible peace, nothing I ever felt growing up.

"And Sharid acted so kind to me, so positive. I was a total idiot about anything to do with the Bible or Christianity itself. We had a running joke. He'd ask me what the Holy City was, and I'd say, in my best Valley voice, 'Like, Beverly Hills?' But he taught me. Patiently. No one had ever made me feel intelligent before. No one had ever make me feel *right* before, not right-wrong right, but all-the-pieces-in-the-right-slot right. Adjusted right.

"I knew Mom was with me. I knew she could see what I was doing. And I knew that she knew it was right, too.

"Then I met Danny. He was so sweet to me. I can't tell you. I thought I'd died and gone to heaven. It was unbelievable to me that anyone could treat me like that, that anyone would want to. We'd read out the Bible to each other and talk about what we were reading. All night sometimes. Staring into each other's eyes, like teenagers practicing Romeo and Juliet, like we were reading love sonnets to each other. And this incredible respect he had for my ideas. I thought, this man listens to me. I thought, I'm going to marry this man.

"And when he asked me, I felt like I was going to burst into a million pieces. That's how the wedding felt, too: my body, this mess that's me, can't contain so much happiness; I'm going to explode any minute. You know those paintings of angels — the Renaissance ones — where their halos look like sunbursts of gold, not bands of gold but rays raying out from around their heads and shoulders? That's what it felt like. Golden.

"I remember walking into a public bathroom once and seeing graffiti; someone had written 'God works in mysterious ways.' And I took out my lipstick — didn't have a pen — and crossed out the last three words.

"Then it changed. Then it wasn't like that anymore. Almost immediately. We went down to Kiawah Island off South Carolina for our honeymoon. Danny's parents bought us two weeks there. I was so excited. We'd just celebrated this amazing thing. God — I believed — God had touched us. I just wanted to talk, to remember every little detail of the wedding. Danny humored me. I could tell he wasn't into it. He began almost immediately talking about having children, how many, what sex, all that. We'd talked about it before, but now it was almost as if it obsessed him. I didn't think I was ready, and I told him. But he didn't see that as an issue. It's our responsibility, he said, our God-given responsibility.

"He was right. I knew that. We were married. We loved each other. We believed. And there was no greater service, no greater love than the creation of family. But I felt dead. Sexually, I mean. That had never happened to me, not with Andy or Richard. Not even with Danny before. But when we got married, it was almost as if a door locked, a vault, sealed me off from feeling sexual. And the deader I felt, the more he seemed to want. The more he wanted me to do.

"It was my fault. I had, for some reason I didn't really understand, broken faith with him, broken our contract. I've lied to him. I'm cheating him out of everything he deserves."

Deborah kept her head angled down, eyes on the ground before us as we walked. She didn't check for my reactions or pause for response. She didn't hurry either.

"Sharid tells me to forget blame. He's thinks I'm a control freak, trying to control God. Keep praying, he says. Stay with what's there. God will show me the way. But what if I don't believe enough? That's what Danny thinks. Sharid says, you provide the vessel, God gives you the spirit. In other words, keep doing what you do and, when he's ready, God will fill you. But Sharid doesn't know.

"For a while, I thought he was the problem. That I was in love with him. I had these fantasies — all the time. Me and Sharid. He would put his arms around me or just put his hand on mine and I felt electric. I told him I loved him. He just smiled and said, 'You just don't know where to put it all.'

"But he doesn't know. It isn't love I have too much of. It's hate.

I'm hateful. I — no one knows this, but I know you'll understand, Erich. I've been taking birth control pills. That's why we can't have children. Danny would kill me if he knew. I just can't. Now. Yet. So I take them. You see, I am hateful. I can't go back."

She stopped talking. The sounds of chatter and traffic and bicycle wheels on the walkway filtered in. Beyond were the sounds of voices on the beach, the whoosh of wind and surf.

The next day we rode a bus out to the self-storage. Deborah had the keys and all the paperwork with her. Mom's stuff occupied two midsize lockups, twelve-foot cubes. One room was mostly furniture. We had to move some of it out to the hall in order to get inside. Of course, I recognized the pieces, a small deco blue glass table, a wooden lamp with a black fringe shade from Mexico, a dining set of Hawaiian bamboo, the art-palette coffee table, the green rattan queen-size bed, the living-room chair with a built-in footrest — her favorite.

The second room was a mountain of boxes. These we began to open, taking out this or that and holding it up for each other's scrutiny. In less than an hour, we were both worn down, over-whelmed by the size of the load. "I'd forgotten how much stuff there was," Deborah said.

"I hadn't." This was true. I remembered every ivory dragon in my mother's possession. I'd shared my room with them, lived among them when no one else was home.

"These are cute. You think they're worth anything?" Deborah said, unearthing a shoebox of stone hippos from Kenya. She found a small velvet sack, which she cupped in her palm as if it were a robin's egg. Then she spread the thin ribbon knotting the top and pulled out a gaudy filigree brooch. She carried it out of the locker into the more brightly lit warehouse hallway. She held the trinket up to the overhead light and began to cry. She sat down, back against another storage-room door, and put her hands over her eyes. "This. This was her life," she said. "These things."

I sat down next to her. The concrete floor was smooth and cold. We both drew our knees up. She would stop crying and sigh. Then she'd cry again, stop, and sigh, trying to catch breath. She looked over at me. My head was back against the door and my face turned slightly toward her.

"There's something I have to tell you," she said. "I don't know how you'll take it, but I owe it to you. I've meant to tell you and I just never could, more because of what it says about me than anything else. I know it's long ago, but I still feel bad about it. I hope you'll forgive me, though I'd understand if you didn't."

My stomach fluttered. Whatever she had to say, I probably didn't want to hear.

She went on. "When Mom was dying, you know, after you were back in Madison, when she was dying and I was here?"

I nodded.

"She asked for you."

"You told me that," I said, somewhat relieved.

"No, no, that's not what I mean. What I said was, 'She asked for you, Erich.' And you said something about her meaning Erich and not you and that's what I let you think. And really to this day I don't know why. But she didn't. That's what I'm trying to tell you."

"It doesn't surprise me that she didn't ask for me. Why would she? She hated me at the end. She wouldn't even talk to me."

"That's what I'm saying, what I didn't tell you. She *didn't* ask for you — Erich. That wasn't the name she used. She wanted Teddy."

My mind went gummy. I couldn't make my way through her words to what they meant. I was holding my breath.

"And I let you think that it wasn't you she was asking for. That she only ever wanted Erich, the way she always did. I could have told you, but I didn't. Then you said you wouldn't come. You thought she didn't really want you there. And I don't know why I didn't tell you."

Deborah looked straight at me. She was sobbing with her eyes wide open, staring at me. "And now I see you, looking so sad, so beat. And you were always good to her, even when you didn't believe she had a chance. That's why she asked for you. Whatever you felt, you were always good to her."

"No I wasn't," I said, sternly. I didn't completely understand Deborah's confession. She was telling me that my mother wasn't confused when she called my name, that it had been unequivocally me she'd called. And my sister was telling me that out of some buried spite of her own, she had lied to me, to keep me away from Mom at her death.

"I probably wouldn't have come anyway," I told her.

"It was cruel," she insisted. "Erich was dead. You were there with her. You had been."

"I don't care who she thought I was. I wouldn't have come." I said it, but suddenly I wasn't sure. Would I have rushed west to be with Lorna before she died — back from the dead myself — or did I hope to punish her to the end with both Erich's hatred and my own? Deborah blames herself for the reconciliation that never happened. I don't know who to blame. We're all sorry. We all expect an apology.

"I can't sell her stuff," Deborah said finally. She began reassembling boxes and stacks, pushing pieces of the mountain back into place. I got up and helped her. When the furniture was reestablished in front, we swung the large wooden door shut and padlocked it. She went into the office and, as I watched her through a sliding window in the reception area, settled up the rent and explained that we'd be continuing the lease. She watched the man as if expecting him to say, "No, you can't." As she watched she pulled back a piece of hair that kept falling over her eyes. She had, it seemed to me, grown more tentative, more fragile, and, at the same time, more thickly herself over time.

That night, after going downstairs to call Dan, she came back up to our room to tell me that she was flying back to Virginia the next day. "I can't die like her," she said. "Like that." She gestured to the hotel room as if it were a wooden locker filled with packing boxes of bric-a-brac.

24

URBAN RENEWAL

Deborah left the next day, as announced, but, in spite of her pleas, I didn't go with her. I told her to sell my car and send me the money; I would stay in Venice until I got sick of it or found some better place to be. "I'm worried about you," she said.

"There are more credible things to worry about," I replied. She pushed four hundred dollars into my hand. I didn't resist. "I'll pay it back as soon as I can."

"Don't you dare," she insisted. "And cash the ticket. Or use it. Just don't let it go to waste."

"Do you have my number?" she asked.

"Somewhere," I told her.

She scribbled on a miniature notepad she kept in her purse, the kind with a minipen attached. She tore the paper off. On it she'd written her phone number under "Deborah. My sister *Deborah.*" She handed it to me. "Don't lose it, goose." I stuffed it in my wallet, in which I kept not much else.

When her cab came she hugged me. I put my arms around her and grew physically sad. "Let me know how to reach you," she said, stepping back.

"OK."

"Let me know." The taxi pulled away and she mouthed something through the back window. "Let me know," I think it was.

I hadn't realized precisely where in the world I was until that moment. I'd been "with Deborah" — "with Deborah" was the place. Suddenly, she was gone, and I was somewhere I'd been before, somewhere my brother had lived, somewhere my mother had died.

The streets, shops, water — everything was strange and familiar at the same time, strange by virtue of being familiar. There were new condos where crumbly old buildings had been, pretty restaurants where there'd been shanties. I was standing inches from the layered bark of a palm tree. A silver BMW parked in front of me; the driver was talking on the telephone. A little girl in a bright green bikini walked out of the hotel with an inflatable seahorse around her hips. I couldn't breathe.

I sat down in the middle of the sidewalk with my arms up over my head the way I'd seen people do when they were trying to catch breath. A lady stuck her head out of a boutique. "You can't sit there like that," she said. I suddenly felt what I would have said was impossible to feel in Venice: derelict.

I walked away, thinking, "When I find something I recognize, I'll feel better." But I did and I didn't. The building that had housed Venice Free School was now a therapy clinic with a daycare center in the basement. The photo lab I'd worked in during high school had closed. I forced myself past our old house. It was dingier than ever; it looked like death. The whole town had grown sour and dark, in spite of a decade of gentrification, in spite of being born again under the star of greater Los Angeles.

I searched out the strip of beach where Erich had staged his fiery disappearing act. Once there I grew so tired I couldn't continue. I lay down with my face turned sideways in the sand. The rush of ocean sound permeated me until it was inside and outside at once. We are liquid, I decided. Out of context, without family or someone to love, without name — identity or being is, not merely fluid, but absolutely liquid, changing, formless. "Erich" had always been the vessel; without that vessel there was nothing to contain me.

I fell asleep. When I woke up in the late afternoon, I could already feel the burn on my right cheek and ear, and on the rim of my neck above my collar. Over the next several days, my skin bubbled and flaked.

I rented month-to-month in a modular cement apartment building, overlooking a canal being filled in. I found a job washing dishes at night in the kitchen of a twenty-four-hour family restaurant. I lived in countertime to the rest of the world, sleeping days, working nights, and pacing Venice in the mornings, looking for something to *want*. I turned twenty-five without speaking to Deborah or Dad. There was nothing to report.

This was life after Jeannie, this subzero. It bore no resemblance to the time in Boston, waiting for her. Then there'd been hope. I'd had a purpose, deranged as it was: to hold her in mind, love her, and prepare for her, for the day she'd recall me to life.

In Venice, I believed that the gray pervading everything was fallout from the loss of her and her only.

The fallout was death. It was everywhere. Faces, bodies, buildings, daily events — every living thing and every object carried death, its implication, its colorless color.

I cut off contact with my sister and father, not explicitly — I didn't announce to them that they were out of my life — but in action. There was nothing tying me to them, I believed, except the worst things: the past, the shame of my failures, the absurdity of what or who I had become. Moreover, I pained them, held them back, and, so, they'd be happier without me.

I didn't live in total isolation, though. Nor, I suppose, did I appear as strange as I had earlier in my life, senior year in high school, for example, or at Madison in monastic robes. Over time, I made contact with people at work, as well as with people in my neighborhood. Around dawn one morning, I saw a man taping up fliers on telephone poles and lampposts along the canal. I recognized him as Mark Greenburg, my creative writing teacher from Venice Free School. He was an activist now, he explained, and at the moment he was publicizing a town-hall meeting to support a local referendum on building — amidst the Yuppie renewal of Venice — low-income housing.

"It won't fly," I argued with him. "We're all on Reagan time. Nobody gives a shit that some poor suckers can't afford higher rents. And why should they?" Mark had the same pop-bottle glasses, the same collar-length hair, now threaded with white, the same Kennedy youth button-down white shirt.

"Oh, man, Erich, you're yanking my chain! This is irony, right, just like I taught you? You're having at me. Ex-student's revenge." He gave me the same kidder's grin and a backhand across the shoulder, the way he used to pretend to throw erasers at us in class. Someone had shielded him. Someone had forgotten to inform him that the world is a terrible place.

"It's not my revenge," I said. "Look around."

"Man-oh-day, Erich. What are we going to do with you?" he asked, and he actually mussed my hair, as if I were still and always fifteen. Then he pulled out a pen and wrote an address on the back of a flier. "Here," he said, handing me the paper. "You need some sawdust on you. Any weekend day, eight to six. I'll flunk you if you don't come." He smiled the smile of an old hippie whose mother loved him.

"I work nights," I said.

"Come after work," he parried. "Bring breakfast."

I answered an ad for a paid reader. An old lady, a New York Jew in her bustling, meticulous dotage, hired me as soon as she heard that my father had studied with Lionel Trilling. Her tastes were thick 1920s American tastes: Theodore Dreiser, Frank Norris, Sinclair Lewis. In the late afternoon before work, twice a week, I'd drink iced rose-hip tea with her in a large apartment filled with cats and birds and heavy furniture sporting lacy antimacassars. She'd pull out a water-damaged first edition of *Death Comes for the Archbishop* or *Winesburg, Ohio* and conspire, "Look see what I found. I haven't read this in a hundred years. Let's give it a whirl, what do you say?" And she'd sit in an oversized white wicker chair, lift a cat onto her lap, and, as I began to narrate, stare over one shoulder toward the wall, where I imagined she saw projected scenes from her heyday in Greenwich Village, poring over *The Masses* in Washington Square with girlfriends in hats. On third Thursdays, she'd invite her aged friends over for afternoons of H. L. Mencken or Dorothy Parker and crustless sandwiches made with whitefish and chopped pimento.

I passed time like other people and, however they saw me, I

looked at them and saw only sadness, life's possibilities being eaten away by the everyday. I set deadlines for myself : "If I still feel this way on August third, September seventeenth, Thanksgiving, I'll . . ." And in my mind I toyed with fatal things I could do. There was nothing sweet about dying, as I imagined it, but then there was nothing sweet anywhere else.

I'd taped Mark's flier up on my wall and, after postponing for a month or more, I took him up on his invitation. One Saturday morning after work, I crossed town to a desolate neighborhood that was, literally, just on the other side of train tracks now used solely for hauling freight. The address he'd given me was a ravaged old Victorian house that looked like a tumbledown, gold rush brothel. A couple of Mexican kids — maybe eleven or twelve years old — were sitting on the porch steps smoking cigarettes and drinking coffee out of Styrofoam cups. As I walked up, they heckled me.

"Hey, what you doing here, man. Don'tchou know it's too early for white guys around here. You better go back where you came from, man, or somebody's gonna carve you a tattoo —"

"No, man, they ain't gonna tattoo him, they gonna give him an earring — in his butt."

"You grody, boy. Nobody round here getting anywhere near that butt —"

"Your mama already been there "

"Watch what you say about my mama —"

"Watch your mama —"

I looked down at the address Mark had written. "Do you guys know Mark Greenburg?"

They did spontaneous double takes. One of them, the littler, quicker one, said, "Oh, man. Ain't he that white guy got arrested last week? Yeah, I'm sure he's that guy. Man, they took him away in handcuffs."

"Shit," the other one exclaimed. "He that guy they say was messin' around with little boys?"

"Yeah, man. Greenburg, that white guy."

"Jesus, man. What you want with an old pervert like that?"

I went hot in the face. My heart was whipping around in my chest.

Mark appeared at the screen door. "Octavio, what kind of trash are you talking to my friend?"

"Nothing, man," the little one said. And he broke into a huge grin and a chicken laugh. He and his buddy hooted and performed a series of intricate hand slaps and shakes before he turned to me. "Psych, man," he said. And they cackled some more.

Mark put us all to work that morning, removing pieces of porch railing from the back of the house, pilasters that we'd later strip, sand, and paint. Before the morning was gone, a gaggle of other kids came by to work on various projects around the rambling building, a house that Mark had been refurbishing for a year and a half and would continue to tear apart and put back together for at least another year. He paid the kids pocket money for their efforts, fed them, and, in effect, provided a kind of community center on weekends until dark. "I didn't have to do much to attract help," he explained to me. "It was just Tom Sawyer stuff. I stood in front with a bucket of paint and a plate of sandwiches."

I came around to help almost every weekend. I got to know some of the kids. They called me "Weirdo," as both name and term of endearment. I watched them while they goofed on me, and sometimes I'd imagine they were the children of the children who, fifteen years before, Erich had gathered on street corners in Mexico to sing songs he knew from American radio.

There were no particular highs and lows during these months, just maintenance. I did dishes, read to old women, and provided free weekend labor with a bunch of Mexican boys renovating a former flophouse. I waited for the day I would feel better or bad enough to do something decisive.

Except for Mark, who viewed me as another one of his projects, like the street kids he gave constructive refuge, I avoided reminders of my previous years in Venice. At Mark's house-in-progress this became difficult for reasons of geography. Looming over it, just behind and across a street to the left, were the stolid walls, the color of nicotine stains, of the self-storage, where the leftovers of my mother's life sat in boxes behind padlocked doors. I couldn't move from one side of the house to another, approaching or retreating, without sensing this towering presence. It bore down on me until the prospect of crossing the tracks after work on a Saturday morning felt like anticipating a fist in the skull. By the time another summer cast its pall over the city, this prosaic fortress of Lorna's collectibles had grown as large in my imagination, as terrible, as she might have been if she'd risen from the dead.

Another third Thursday rolled around, and brought me into the familiar company of the town's dowager literati. I was in a corner by the buffet with a teacup and saucer in my hand when I heard an almost ecstatic voice call, "Erich!" Immediately, I was eyeball to eyeball with Eureka Collins, the shaman-atrix of my Mom's bitter end. She didn't speak again, but she seized my upper arms and visually ransacked my face for the answer to something essential. Mercifully, we were called to order by our hostess and the late afternoon theatricals began.

The day's feature was a play by Susan Glaspell, so, fortunately, I wasn't reading alone. I oversaw the stage directions and filled assorted male roles, but the women's parts were attacked with universal gusto by a septuagenarian ensemble. Eureka stared at me. When the revels ended, she confronted me again and said, eyes blazing, voice positively volcanic, "I miss her, too."

I lurched past the food, my palm flattening several deviled eggs as I stumbled, and I bolted from the room. This time I headed for the tracks, for the very building I'd been afraid of, the lockup holding my mother's remains, not her ashes but her artifacts. I only made one stop on the way, and that without premeditation. At the Sunoco, I bought a gallon of gasoline.

I sat up against the chain link fence surrounding the self-storage and my brain lit out in every direction at once. It inventoried the keepsakes tucked away behind me, it ticked off the names of just about everyone I'd known, it scrolled across this country and another, a personal travelogue, like some cheesy nineteenth-century stage backdrop, stopping at checkpoints along the path. I lifted the spout of the gasoline can to my mouth.

I was sweating and shivering. I was watching myself sweat and shiver. I couldn't drink. And I knew why: Erich. I could kill myself, but I couldn't kill my brother. I couldn't bring myself to erase the last vestiges of his life without anything to show for that life.

25

Hejira

In this mixed-up way, Erich fathered me. I was heir to his memory. To preserve that memory, I had to save myself, whoever that might be under all this Erich. But I had to find myself first — myself before.

The next day, I bought a $250 piece-of-shit car off a guy from the kitchen I worked in. I left Venice.

I made my way, northwest to southeast, into the horn of Mexico, looking for anything familiar — town names, buildings, landscapes — anything that would recall my life to me. I didn't literally expect to see Erich here, rounding up a ragamuffin singing group, or my mother, mumbling into her sleeve on a curb. I hoped, though, that some train of association might click in, awakening memory from the time before we came to California, before I came to be Erich. Moreover, I hoped that, together, these memories would establish a narrative thread for my earliest life — a thread that would lead me to me.

The first such association was dread. I had no sooner shown my I.D. at the border of Tijuana than I felt a queasy terror below my ribs. Something dangerous was imminent and I was unprotected. I recognized the feeling at once; it was Mexico. Nor was this terror entirely existential or atavistic. I was driving a Plymouth Duster with more than 110,000 miles on it and a way of shimmying when it exceeded forty miles an hour. I had a few hundred dollars in my pocket and no obvious way of getting more. I spoke about as much Spanish as a native two-year-old. Whatever happened might happen without anyone who knew me ever knowing.

San Ignacio was no different than Colima or Cuernevaca. There was nothing of me there. More than a dozen years had passed and everything I thought I remembered remained unconfirmed by what I saw. Where I'd pictured fishing boats there were high-rises; where I'd seen old men with dominoes there were droopy pottery shacks. There were churches everywhere, but they seemed to me dirty, unevocative little places. The boy who'd lurked around God's house for imaginary talks with his parents no longer dwelt in me. I found it increasingly hard to believe that he had ever existed.

I drove from town to town, sleeping where I could, sometimes in hostels or cheap rooms, sometimes in the Duster. When the car gave out a day's walk from Ixtlan, I tramped the rest of the way. I made my way to Mexico City. Without being conscious of it, I'd been heading there all along. The city was hard, but I tried to settle in. I found a room above a curtain shop with the woman who sewed there, Mrs. Avila. Her son had gone north, so she had his closet room to let — a bed and a prie-dieu with a statue of the Virgin.

I walked everywhere, scouring the city for anything I recognized: avenues, markets, cathedrals, empire buildings, and mountain vistas. I studied bus routes and checked plaques. I made note of the horizon at different hours of day. I put my hands on the skins of buildings. Nothing I saw, smelled, or touched resurrected anything I'd known before. I grew more systematic in my pursuits. I kept a book of maps on which I drew in black marker. I created grids within the city's grids, logged the names of streets. I walked sections of the city twice, facing one direction then another, in hope of reorienting myself toward the familiar. I hung out in parks and at street corners.

When I'd exhausted the city and its neighborhoods, I scanned library microfilm of Spanish- and English-language papers from late '67 through early '69 with the expectation of some event or headline that would jar me to recollection. One day I was flipping pages of an old sports magazine and something clicked. We had to have been here during the Olympics. You don't *not* notice the Olympics. They overtake a city. But I couldn't recall a single scene or poster image or inconvenience. I knew we'd been here all of 1968, and I couldn't remember a thing.

The realization that I had blacked out something so huge terrified me. I raced around outside, frantic, crossing neighborhoods without paying attention. In University City I asked some little kid about the Olympics, what he had heard. A boy who hadn't been born yet would know more about the Olympics than I did, I thought.

He recoiled. His urchin buddies mocked him for letting me close. I could understand their catcalls: "He's crazy, man. You crazy, too, you talk to him." He looked past me to them. He shouted at me to get away, calling me *loco*, calling me names.

He punched at me. I scissored my arms in the air to block and stop him. The sudden gesture startled him for a moment and there was a pause.

Whatever they saw in my eyes — I suspect it was fear — they all saw, because instantly, as if they were one animal, the horde of them reared back, bared their outsized teeth, and swarmed me. They beat me with sticks and fists, kicked me with bare feet and sandals, picked stuff off the street and hurled it at me. They knocked me to the ground and kept stomping.

The first time I saw Erich's camp I thought I'd found the Neverland, but I was wrong. This was it, lost boys with sticks and stones.

They grabbed the cash in my pocket and scattered. I'm blurry on what happened next, but somehow, with help, I got back to Mrs. Avila's, where she cared for me for a couple weeks. She brought in a doctor to stitch my mouth and reset my shoulder. Then she threw me out.

I hobbled and hitched to San Miguel de Allende. I was all but certain we'd lived there. My sturdiest images of Mexico were from there: a church tower rising above the square; the pale adobe house where my mother splattered corn chowder after a fight with the landlord; Erich's and my legs dangling from the high pink wall beside the bank. Once in town, though, I couldn't get my bearings.

The puzzle had been rearranged. Had I only heard about San Miguel? I vaguely recalled a picture of a young man — me? — carrying chairs through the streets. Had I only seen photographs?

I found a phone book and looked up my mother's boyfriend Raoul. There were three men with the same name. I went to their houses, or, rather, to two of them. One address wasn't a house at all, but a little one-room post office where nobody had heard of the guy. At the second place, I encountered a young man. He wouldn't tell me if this was his name or not. He wanted to know my name and why I was asking. He grilled me with questions, but I couldn't make sense of what he was asking. He spoke into the back of his hand, covering his mustache as, I suspected, his mustache covered some deformity, a harelip or tumor of the mouth.

I explained in slow English peppered with fake Spanish in a confusion of tenses. I was looking for a man who'd known my mother. I was looking for a man who'd known me when I was a little boy. I used to live in San Miguel de Allende. I used to live here. I wanted to find this man who knew us. His name was Raoul. He was a painter. He knew us when we lived here. We lived near a church. We lived near a town square. I can't find our house. It was here. Somewhere near here. Raoul was an artist. He'd married a younger woman. We knew him when we lived here. Nineteen sixty-eight or nine. Around the time of the Olympics.

The mention of the Olympics set him off. Again, I couldn't understand him, but to judge from the body language, I'd have guessed that the organizers of the Olympics had stolen his home and killed his family. He couldn't have been more than a small boy at the time, younger even than I was.

"Did you know Raoul?" I asked. "Did you know this man?"

No, he said, in English. "I Raoul. I nebber seed you." He closed the door and watched me from the small open window just to one side of it.

At the last address I met a small, pretty woman about Deborah's age. She treated me with the polite wariness reserved for stray dogs. Yes, she said, in elongated Spanish, with broad gestures for my ben-

efit, this was Raoul's house and she was his wife. He had died three
years ago of a heart attack. He was a businessman, not an artist. No,
he had never mentioned a woman named Lorna or Mrs. Hofmann.
He had never mentioned an American friend with three children.
No, she hadn't known him in the sixties, as she was young then herself; she had met him in 1972 and married him a year later.

"Do you have a picture of him?"

She looked at me for a long time. She hadn't let go of her door.
Maybe she thought I was a lost son, coming back for my inheritance
or revenge. Stray dog was closer. I was on best behavior, but feeling
wild. She was my last hope, I believed, for finding a piece of myself
in this place — even a memory of a memory. I kept my hands folded
in front of me, my head bowed. I didn't mean anybody any harm.

"A moment," she said, backing into the house. She closed the
door gently, as though any sudden sound might startle me into
attack. A few seconds later, she came out again. She tendered me a
filigreed silver antique frame. I took a breath and looked at her
instead. The whites of her eyes reddened, tears welling in the corners. She held my gaze. I noticed the house, curtains in the windows,
boxes of flowers on the two visible sills. It was one of the nicer
houses I'd seen in San Miguel, in one of the wealthier parts of town
— middle-class by American standards. She had kept it spruce, I
thought, without the means to do so; it was a kindly house, but sad,
like a widower, down at the mouth, trying to keep his spirits up by
smiling. She watched me.

I took another breath to calm the pounding in my chest and
glanced down. A wedding picture: a woman — this woman —
arrayed in full, billowy bridal drag; a man outfitted in black tuxedo,
ruffled shirt, and bow tie. Was it the man I thought I'd known? His
hair was short, his face shaven. Everything about him said businessman, middle manager; nothing suggested drug dealer or wannabe
Diego Rivera. Still, he might have been. He might have known my
mother and her sad little entourage of three. He might have sucked
on a cheap cigar, thrown a limp arm around my shoulder and, surveying the town of San Miguel, said, "My leetle boy, here is my

Paris." He might have, but I doubted it. The face in the photo was as strange to me as I was to myself.

I passed the next few days in a state of high panic. I was staying at a men's hotel, a blunt dormlike place with chipped-up walls the color and smell of urine. The men had to vacate between 9:00 A.M. and 9:00 P.M., except for two siesta hours midday. During the out-time I mostly clung to a bench in the square across the street. My mind was chasing itself.

The only explanation for my inability to remember events and places, I determined with a kind of whacked logic, was that none of it had happened, that I had never existed. Having never existed, it became evident to me that I could not be presently said to exist. No history, no body. Maybe I was a kind of Platonic entity — the mind in contemplation of itself, disembodied life hanging around ongoing life, unseen. Maybe I was shadow.

I have no right to the claim of craziness for these thoughts, except in the more mundane sense of "That was some crazy shit, man." A part of me, some click in my watchful brain never absolutely let go. I was in pain and I was suffering. I was feeling, even *acting* crazy, but I was merely, as I had been for so many years, approximating Erich. I was killing myself in my mind. This was the critical difference between my brother and me: He made his wish to die actual; I was bent on keeping mine a metaphor.

I had to hold on, I knew, until Deborah came. She would come, I told myself. Dad would see to it.

I'd called Deborah the day I saw the photograph of the man who may or may not have been Raoul. I'd turned away from the woman with the picture in time to see another woman, maybe twenty-five yards away, slap a small boy. As I drew closer, I could see the boy quake and cry, pee spreading down the front of his pants. His mother continued to scold him, gesturing toward his lower body.

I fished a piece of paper with Deborah's number out of my wallet, fumbling the wallet itself. I half ran to a bar with a phone. A scattering of old men stopped talking to look at me. I grabbed the

receiver and spoke to an operator in pidgin Spanish. The ringing
began. Dan answered.

"I have a collect call for Deborah Monroe," the operator
explained in careful English. "Will you accept the charge?"

"She's not here," Dan said, with a steel in his voice I didn't recognize. "She doesn't live here."

"Where is she?" I asked, over the operator.

"Fuck if I know," he growled. "Maryland somewhere." With that
he hung up.

"Wait," I urged the operator. "My father. Call my father." And I
gave her the number as I remembered it.

Three grueling days later, I saw Deborah get out of a taxi and stare
up at the hotel. I crossed the street to reach her.

"I thought I'd lost you," she said, taking me in her arms. She
pulled back and looked at me. I could see her pupils contract as they
registered my strangeness. Her reaction read as fear.

"Oh, God, I hate this town," she said. "I hate Mexico. I always
hated Mexico."

"Always."

"That's right. I hated it when we lived here, I hated it when I
landed today."

"When we lived here," I echoed, almost a question.

"Yes, then too."

I tried to bring all my thoughts into focus.

"Dad called me after you talked to him. He kept calling. He
wired money. He bought the tickets. Don't ask about money. I'll tell
you everything later, Erich. But please, let's go, get you away from
here. Do you have anything, stuff?" And she glanced up at the building whose address I'd practically shouted at Dad long-distance.

I kept watching her. I wanted her to prove she was real.

"You all right?" she asked.

"Do. I. Look?"

Deborah laughed a convulsive "Haagh." She took my hand and
guided it toward the front door.

—◆—

Deborah was my good-shepherd sister. She presented me with gifts to raise my spirits — the commonplace book of a popular poet, a polished stone engraved with the word "serenity," a bottle of musk cologne. She gave up her couch to me and, over the half year I roosted there, helped locate me in time. Life after Jeannie had obliterated chronology. As Deborah filled me in on the events that transpired during my absence, this period gained contour.

Almost nothing was as I'd left it. Deborah lived ostensibly alone in Gaithersburg, Maryland, no longer Christian, no longer married.

Her odyssey to this place sounded as absurd as mine. She'd returned to Virginia from Venice Beach ready to work things out with Dan. He was game too, he said, claiming to understand her flight to California. She could tell he was angry, though, not from any overt cruelty, but from a kind of pervasive scorn in his attitude. Apparently, he'd found her guilty of something unnamed, and he couldn't forgive.

"We set out to have a family," she explained on the plane home. "I set out to. Sharid blessed us. Danny and I made this kind of heartless love like clockwork. I kept house and read my Bible like crazy. Nothing happened. Nothing. And this time it wasn't my fault, unless I was popping pills in my sleep. I was visualizing this life growing inside me. I was picturing — as part of an ongoing meditation — my womb as a field of grass and flowers. I was talking to Sharid. I was praying. Still nothing. For the longest time."

As Deborah talked, I sipped a Coke and tried to concentrate on concrete things: the taste of the soda, the cold of the ice, Deborah's lips as they formed words. I tried to track the story she was telling.

"Danny was furious, of course, though he never came out and said it," she continued, enunciating strenuously, as if speaking to a slow or partially deaf child. "He just mocked me. Teased me. With an edge, you know. That furious male edge. He barely spoke to me. Except in bed. Except to tell me to move my arms or go faster or slower in bed. I did everything he asked me. I was his and I wasn't going to make any mistakes.

"I wanted to be *good*, you know. Everyone was talking about the homeless, so I volunteered at a soup kitchen. Dan felt I needed structure, so I took GED classes, bought a copy of *What Color Is Your Parachute?* and worked my way through all the exercises, on a strict schedule. He complained about being the only one working, so I signed up to temp.

"The strange thing was, Erich, I started to like my life on the outside. He could sense it, I'm sure. He got needier, tried a little harder, which was nice, but he also got angrier quicker. He smashed things in the house. Nothing big. Just a plate here and there. And then he'd do these please-please-please scenes with me, where we'd get down on our knees on the living room carpet and pray together, out loud. I wanted everything to work out. I did. But I was becoming detached, floating away."

I nodded. Yes, I knew something about detached and floating away. Even at that moment we were floating, in a big metal plane with blue patterned fabric everywhere and the steady sound of air washing through the cabin.

"Then Oomie died," I heard her say.

It didn't register, though. I heard the words. I knew what they signified, but they carried no weight.

"Did you hear me?" Deborah asked.

"Oomie died. Then."

"Yes. I'm sorry you had to find out this way."

"What. Way?"

"So much later."

A beverage cart bumped my elbow. I looked at it. A stewardess leaned down, reaching a hand toward my arm. Her fingers touched me lightly, just below the shoulder. "Excuse me," she said in English with a Spanish accent.

I turned back to look at Deborah. Her eyes were flicking from me to the stewardess. They settled on me.

"I'm sorry," she said again.

"Oomie," I reminded myself. "When? When was it?"

"Oh, it wasn't long after I left you in Venice — less than six months. You've been gone almost two years. Do you know that?"

"Two years. Yes." No, I had no idea.

She took huge sniffs of breath into her lungs. I had seen the look on her face before, a kind of fright of what comes next. We'd been sitting in the hallway of a warehouse building, but I couldn't recall when.

"She left us money, Erich. Oomie did when she died. No, that's not right. She left almost no money. She left the condo, paid for. I sold it, easily, for sixty-six thousand dollars, forty-something after fees and taxes. Add to that a few stocks, another ten thousand or so. Fifty-five, fifty-eight maybe all together."

"She left us money," I repeated. Listen to what she's saying, I told myself.

"She must have known. About Mom, you know. She must have known. There wasn't anything about Mom in the will."

"She must have known," I said.

"What I mean to say. What I have to tell you, Erich. She named me executor. I held the money, the checkbook. Half the money was yours."

"Mine."

"Was. Was to have been. There's no money now, Erich." Her eyes were red and wet. Her nostrils were winging like the flippers on a pinball machine. "No money now."

Her head pivoted toward the window of the plane. She'd already pulled the shade down to block the glare. Now she pushed the shade up. Her head swiveled back. She was squinting. At me. I hadn't noticed before, but sometimes Deborah's face quavered as if it was made up of crazy vibrating cells, fighting to leave the skin.

"It was wrong. I know now. It was guilt at not being what I was supposed to be. I held off as long as I could. I tried to find you again. After several weeks in Florida, settling the estate, I flew to Venice. I went looking for you. I called the police in. I called the Madison police. I called the Boston police. I filled out missing-person reports. I held off as long as I could. You were gone almost two years," she said again for emphasis.

"I was there," I said.

"Where?"

"In Venice. Then."

"I couldn't find you," she said again. "So I gave all the money over to the Center. All of it. Yours and mine."

I was working hard to make sense of her story. Danny had insisted the money was hers, that there was a statute of limitations in a case like this and a year was it. He didn't believe they'd find me. He'd argued that what was Deborah's belonged to the Center. That was the deal. Everything held in common. Everything for the benefit of the community.

"I gave our inheritance to them," Deborah said. "To Sharid. Do you understand what I'm telling you?"

"You gave it to them."

"And now it's gone. I had it. Your money and mine. I had it and I gave it away. To them. I still don't know why."

She stopped and looked away again. Something fierce had possessed her. I couldn't touch it, but I saw it on her face. Her skin was made of a million tiny jumping beans. She turned her head my way.

"I left three weeks later. Moved out for good. They wouldn't give me our money back."

Deborah worked several days a week as a "permanent temp" at the National Institutes of Health in Bethesda. Each day or two she attended what she called "my meeting." At home she pored over books with titles like *Codependent No More*, *Drama of the Gifted Child*, and *How to Break an Addiction to Another Person*, the way, once, she'd done with her Bible.

She had a new boyfriend, Dave, who came and went like bad weather. Initially, Dave tolerated me. He demonstrated a firm disinterest in Deborah's family skeletons, however, of which I was most pronouncedly one, and, before long, let it be known that I was cramping his style. He'd snap at my sister behind the flimsy closed door of her only bedroom and glower at me on his way out. Deborah had met him while temping for his business. I never got straight, though, whether he practiced patent law or if his job had something to do with electronics. At some point, however, I realized that he was "keeping" Deborah to augment an actual wife.

Dad called many times, and talked to me in low, careful tones. He attempted to tell me how happy and relieved he was that I'd come home, while I did my best to express gratitude for his concern. We were equally inept, hemming and hawing like a pair of stiff-backed old soldiers, trying to remember the feeling of love. He and Hildy had separated even before I'd vanished — years ago for him, minutes for me. He was, for the second time, reduced to the role of aging, solitary bachelor, biding time between the sanctioned visits of his children.

"Promise me, Son, you'll come soon, Son," he said, his private melancholy loosed by drink. "I want to see you with my own eyes."

"Sure Dad. I want to see you, too. With my own."

Hem haw.

"When's good?" I asked.

"For what, Son?"

"For me. To come there."

"Oh, sure, sure. Anytime."

"But should I wait. Till the end of the semester? You used to want me to wait . . ."

"Oh, no. Didn't you know? No, how could you. They bought me out, scrapped me. Early retirement. I've been teaching the *Ulysses* seminar one night a week. For fun. That's all. Slipping into my anecdotage. Anytime. Come anytime. That'd be, well, nice, of course."

He and Deborah spoke regularly. She'd beam when she hung up, and I knew that he'd thanked her, yet again, for rescuing me, for doing what he couldn't do: board a plane and fish his second lost son out of San Miguel. They arranged for me to see a psychiatrist in D.C., a guy who seemed to define his job as prescription adjustment. I'd sit on the couch and he'd ask me how I'd done on that week's dosage of antidepressants. I'd say, "OK, I guess" or "Couldn't sleep," and he'd scribble down something for the druggist and hand it to me.

"That oughta do it, I should think," he'd say with a head bob that indicated we needn't take up anymore of each other's time.

Once I asked him if he wanted me to talk about Jeannie or my family for a while. He let out a congenial little laugh and rested an avuncular hand on my shoulder. "Have to get you in the room first, now don't we," he said, ushering me to the door.

"I guess," I answered.

"Next week then," said he.

26

WILLY'S LIFE

My father's first heart attack began under his dining room table. New York City was in the middle of a severe thunderstorm — the reason my phobic father was under the table. The sweating and sudden pains must have, on some level, justified his irrational fear of thunder and lightning and, even, seemed to spring from them. It's a wonder, then, that he was able to distinguish panic from pain, that he didn't dismiss as psychosomatic the tearing in his chest. He was, though, and he didn't. He crawled to the desk and placed one life-saving phone call.

Willy's good fortune began when, instead of dialing 911, he phoned his upstairs neighbor, a colleague since the sixties, who kept a second set of apartment keys. The neighbor, Curt, found him on the floor, draped over the desk chair, and called the ambulance. While he waited with my unconscious father, he dialed Hildy. Hildy, in turn, called Deborah's. I answered the phone. I didn't know where Deborah had gone that morning or how to reach her. I wrote a sketchy note, fetched a handful of cash from her cookie jar and left for New York.

Because it was Thanksgiving morning, Dad lived, the city streets being mercifully free of traffic when EMS raced him uptown to the operating table. An eminent cardiologist — home prepping the turkey, no doubt — was summoned. For eleven hours, the doctors patched Dad's aneurysm-dissected aorta with Teflon and routed his intestine to a colostomy bag. Arteries in his right leg, wanting blood for too long, caved in on themselves, and one kidney failed.

He was still in surgery when I arrived. Curt, who had ridden in

the ambulance with him, was still waiting for news. I thanked him
and sent him off to holiday dinner. Hildy had come and gone alone,
not wanting to subject the kids to a deathwatch for their father. I left
serial messages on Deborah's machine, full of information but
devoid, as far as possible, of alarm. "Don't waste your energy on
hope," my father's dour internist came out to say — the pithy advice
of an efficiency expert who reads Dante before bed. He meant, of
course, that Willy would die. I called Hildy, Curt, and Mac to let
them know. I tried Deborah again, but hung up when the machine
clicked on.

At 1:00 A.M. another doctor, the chief surgeon, settled into a
chair next to me and said, "Your father's a lucky man. Give him the
night and tomorrow and — barring the unforeseen — you'll be able
to visit him in intensive care. It'll probably be a few days, though,
before he's able to visit back."

I gathered Dad's clothes and keys and took a cab back to his
apartment. There was no answering machine and, therefore, no
message from Deborah. I poked around a little, fixed a bowl of
cereal, thumbed through a metal box of postcards from Samuel
Beckett — short, handwritten answers to twenty years of scholarly
and increasingly friendly questions — and fell asleep.

The next day was a version of the same — waiting, calling, short
visits with Hildy, Curt, and another man from Dad's department,
and laconic conversations with doctors. They let me in to see Willy,
who had, in addition to a catheter, tubes in his nose, mouth, arms,
chest, thigh, and neck. He didn't open his eyes, though he breathed
steadily and sent heartbeat signals to a screen. He looked like himself but older and greener.

I sat near him, hour after hour, studying him: the thinning hair
combed back from his broad forehead, the cracking lips, the mottle
of age along his jowls. I felt as if my ears, stuffed from months of
infection and altitude had suddenly cleared. Into them came the regular hush of my father's breath.

I should tell him a story, I thought, the way he used to lull me to
sleep with the intricate escapades of the Spanish adventurer Dos Es

Ulalingua. I should tell him a story of everything will be all right, a story of remembering good times. I gave him the best I had: stories of loving Erich.

"You probably don't remember when Erich tried to teach me to play Risk. I was maybe nine. Eventually he must have realized I was too young for global strategy, because he changed the game. We started using those tiny colored Risk cubes to fashion the finest temple, somewhere in the west of Africa. We fortified our little creation with all the furniture in our bedroom, the beds, chairs, and bureaus, as well as pillows, boxes, and books, everything we had, all shielding our sacred structure. You and Mom would appear at the door, every so often, barely able to contain your horror, and then sort of shrug it off and leave. All our junk was heaped up around this itsy-bitsy block building. We brought our dinners into the room that night and took turns sleeping and keeping guard. Erich fell asleep on watch, though, and rolled onto the board, devastating the whole mess. He scattered all the cubes and thoroughly smushed the board. The next morning we couldn't stop laughing. He kept saying, 'Oh, no! I've just killed millions at prayer!'"

As I talked, I remembered. "Another time, one of the first nights we were alone in the apartment in Venice Beach, he lit a candle he'd pilfered from Deborah's room, one of those big strawberry sixties things, and turned up Laura Nyro's *Christmas and the Beads of Sweat*. You know Laura Nyro? Really soulful, really morbid. Very lush stuff. Anyway, he pressed auto repeat on the eight-track. We listened to her and watched *Duck Soup* from beginning to end, volume turned off. There were Groucho, Chico, and Harpo, doing what they do, with Laura Nyro wailing underneath. It was a moment, you know, Dad. We'd laugh, we'd cry. We'd make ourselves laugh, we'd pretend to cry."

As I recalled Erich, I missed him with the most precise sadness, crystal and direct. "Are you missing him, too?" I asked my unconscious father.

I knew I'd come to the end of something. I couldn't travel any farther than Mexico; I couldn't lose my way any more elaborately without giving up on life altogether, and, since I'd had every opportunity to do just that, I had to admit to the desire to remain here, lodged on this earth. I sat where my half-dead father lay in a web of wire and tubing and noted, with something like surprise, that I wanted to live.

I kissed Willy's forehead, smoothing his hair back, and smelled the sour metal of his breath.

Back at Dad's apartment, I began prowling in earnest. I hadn't seen him in four years and only rarely in the decade or so prior to that. He was the man in the hospital bed, and he was a voice on the phone. But who was he? Who had he become? How did he see us?

I invaded his privacy. I opened every drawer in the place, every box, every file. He folded his underwear in threes and stacked it in a single drawer. He collected antique pens and, apparently, used them. His spices included cumin and turmeric; two vanilla beans had a bottle to themselves. His slippers — a kind of frayed suede moccasin — were the same ones he'd worn when I'd visited from college.

There was little memorabilia in the house. His heart was in his bookshelves, and this heart was selective. Modern giants — Flaubert, Proust, Mann, Pound, Beckett, and Joyce — each had a shelf or more to themselves. There were fine, preserved hardbacks, though not necessarily collectible editions, of most titles. These were accompanied by reading/teaching copies, paperbacks distraught with notes, comments, and questions, penned every which way across fading, thumbed-up pages. Another section featured older copies of the American Renaissance writers, especially Melville, Hawthorne, and Emerson, looking a bit dustier and more standoffish than their twentieth-century heirs. A few dozen art books shelved about knee level had telltale tears and scuffs from use. His own books and those of friends occupied an alcove above the desk.

You might have mistaken his home for his office, not the final stopping place in a life that included two wives, five children, and God knows what else. There were files of course curricula, though not as many as you'd expect from nearly forty years of teaching, numerous metal boxes of note cards, obviously untouched for decades, and reference books by the typing table.

Personal effects were few. A three-by-five photo of Willy Jr. and Amanda was tacked to a desk bulletin board. A folder contained some of Erich's drawings, some stories I'd written in elementary school, and a half dozen photographs I'd sent from Madison. There wasn't much of Deborah here, a wedding invitation, a couple of postcards — a dearth symptomatic of the way she periodically dropped him from her life. He kept letters in file folders, too — from Mac, former students, notes from friends. This archive was crammed full.

I made one find that surprised me, and it changed everything. At the bottom of a brown metal filing cabinet I discovered a stack of three manuscripts, typed and captured in softcover large-ring binders. A carbon copy of his book of poems, published in the late seventies, lay on top of a detective novel he'd written since retiring. His most recent work was buried under them: an "anti-memoir" as he'd subtitled it, called "Speak Not, Memory," apparently a nod to Nabokov.

I flipped its pages. My stomach flipped in turn as the names fanned by: Erich, Lorna, Willy, Deborah. He had written this "fictional autobiography," his introductory note explained, in an attempt to forget. The book was heavy and limp in my hands, as though the pages longed to cascade to the floor and form a pool around my feet. The manuscript was typed, with arrows here and there and pages marked "insert A" and "insert B," stuck in at regular intervals. I grabbed a Coke from the refrigerator and didn't look up again until I'd finished the book, close to sunrise.

My father had written his partial life story in three "movements." The first, set just prior to my birth, took place in Graz, Austria; the second covered the period from our departure for Mexico to Erich's suicide, but focused more on Willy's own reactions to events than on what was happening to us. Finally, there was an epilogue of sorts, almost entirely in dialogue. Set at "A table in heaven," it featured a conversation between the characters "Willy" and "Lorna." Their talk begins with him trying to puzzle out their life together and devolves into a kind of Beckettian comedy routine, each remember-

ing doing things they couldn't possibly have done, each taking credit
for the memories of the other.

I read in greedy horror — greedy for detail and horrified by its
absence. Moreover, I was appalled by how bad the book was, not just
poorly imagined as fiction and incomplete as history, but badly written. "Speak Not, Memory" — what an atrocious title! — comprised
one giant mea culpa, cute and self-conscious, spun in a style wholly
out of keeping with my father's intelligence, literary skill, and previous writing. Its narrator — named Willy — groped throughout
toward some Ur-regret, the prime mover of everything that subse-
quently went wrong in his first marriage. It was drivel, written by a
man happy to let his love of sentences distract him from the emotional complexities of a situation that he distinctly did not love. It
was a pitch for forgiveness by a wisenheimer adolescent with a blind
eye angled toward posterity. It was the worst kind of history — the
kind that leaves everyone other than the author out.

The Mexican sequence consisted mostly of phone conversations, Willy begging Lorna to come home and making vague
threats about what he'll do if she doesn't. Meanwhile, he engages in
endless cerebration (fighting the impulse to write in her voice, I suspect) in an effort to get inside her nutsy, desperate head. This por-
tion ends when Willy consults a psychiatrist colleague who advises
him to stop funding his wife's flight. Willy weeps on the couch. He
and the shrink trace his feelings of guilt, and he grapples with the
pain of responsibility for what might happen. And there, "in the
plaguing nexus of responsibility, shame, and the need to get on with
it for God's sake in the face of precipitous abandonment, he experi-
ences father-and-child feelings all jumbled up. A drop of dye plinks
in a beaker of water. The dye spreads until the idea is everywhere in
him: 'Yes, something has to give. I'm the adult.'" And so he refuses
her money, one final time, until Mexico is behind her.

"'Money, Willy.' She demands, disgust seething from the backs
of her teeth.

"'It's time to come home now or to let them come home. The
bank's closed, Lorna. No more foreign currency.'" Did he actually
say that?

"And as her phone smacking the cradle beat a tattoo in his ear, he blurted, 'I need to see you,' when he meant to say, 'I need to see them.'"

On Erich's commitment to St. Elizabeths, Willy was positively self-abusive, a fussy little flagellation that ran on for more than forty pages, counterpointed by a three-page — one paragraph — description of the table he and my brother sat at in the asylum visiting room. He includes a lengthy rationale for his insistence that Erich sit up straight in his hospital pajamas. As I read, I began to feel pukey, hot-flash sick. Why can't they give me pills that make me feel better instead of worse, I thought?

The shocker, for me, was the stuff about Austria, a part of our common history that no one had bothered to tell me. It was the story of stories, his dark fable of my incipience, whose cast of characters included Willy and Lorna, their four-year-old Erich and two-and-a-half-year-old Deborah. Time: autumn, 1956; place: the land of his ancestors.

As part of a Fulbright grant, Willy'd contracted to teach a university seminar on Hawthorne and the American Renaissance while researching Wittgenstein for a burgeoning project. My not-yet mother had agreed. Following their endless, gut-churning first plane flight to Vienna and the rush of excitement that attended their arrival, Lorna, who'd never been this far from home, began behaving strangely, full of fear. She became convinced that they were being followed. The parks seemed to her to be minefields; the blinking of lamps from the hills, messages. She threaded her hair between the slats of a cellar coal bin, to determine if anyone tampered with the steamer trunk stored there. There was a corpse in the trunk, she claimed, though she wouldn't say whose.

My father, afraid for her and for Erich and Deborah, whom she'd begun to neglect, sought clinical advice. (This was the first of three times he sought such advice. He did it again before he cut off our money supply in Mexico and prior to locking my brother away at St. E's.) A new Viennese friend led him to a doctor who, in turn, guided him to Herr Direktor of the community hospital, the

Landeskrankenhaus. Lorna's sudden psychosis was acute and not uncommon, Willy was told, a form of culture shock, nothing that couldn't be undone. So, he committed her.

His intentions were the best, he promises the reader. At this point in the narrative, he still hasn't mentioned the most important fact of her condition: She was pregnant with me.

Lorna stayed inside for over a month, sad, scared, and doped up. One day the head doctor offhandedly refered to "the fetus." Here my father slips into the present perfect (Quel device!):

> Willy is — there is no accurate word. He tells the doctor, "I didn't know," but of course the doctor can see that. "If I'd known, I would never have subjected her to . . ." Suddenly naming what he'd subjected her to seemed to him in the worst possible taste, certain to offend the director's sense of decorum. "Of course not, of course not," the doctor says. He holds out a box of long cigars to Willy and says, "What man would?" He hands the American professor a small gold tool to cut the tip off the cigar and extends an engraved lighter, already flaming.
>
> They smoke. Willy sits there shaking his head, rubbing his brow. The doctor is at once his judge, his confessor. "She was raging, out of control," Willy explains, practically begging the lab-coated gentleman to understand. "She endangered the children."
>
> "Of course, of course," the doctor repeats in Freud's accent. "How can you know what she won't tell you?" He savors a great stream of smoke. "No cause for concern, my dear fellow, no cause for concern. Happens all the time. Indeed, six weeks here is enough for anyone. We will release her today. Take her home and the episode will soon be as if it never happened."

So, I knew. He'd given me the key, the piece you slog through years of therapy for. My mother's face pressed itself on me, not as she'd been in my lifetime but young, mournful, and beautiful. She was Joan of Arc, locked in a cell, carrying me, secretly, in the waters of her sadness, the still eye of her hurricane self. Why should she have wanted me to live? If I didn't directly cause her imprisonment and sadness, if I was just one of several precipitating factors, including lifelong depression and mania, culture shock, and hormonal unbalance, if everything that followed hadn't been catalyzed by my unrevealed presence in her womb — at least I would always be her reminder, the seed of our family's distress. There it all was, impending in fetal me. A story to end a story.

I can't say what felt worse to me, that no one had told me any of this, or how parenthetical Erich, Deborah, and I seemed in it. Willy spent his imaginative energy conjuring the ice cream he and Lorna sampled on the walk to the Landeskrankenhaus ("sweet vanilla and almond breaking over her tongue in a final unsuspecting pleasure"). By the time he got to the children, he'd run out of invention. What did Erich and Deborah see? What did they feel? What seeped into them or trickled down to me? As powerful as his explanations might have been for me — rife with new biographical fact — they were like Mexico: I could search for years and never find myself there.

I was furious, an angry Oedipal fire set to consume and kill the father, who, if his writing were any indication, was half dead already. (Never mind the near-corpse in the i.c.u.) I grabbed at the drawer of his desk, jerked it open, and thrust my twitching hand in search of pens. I came up with several. I threw myself into a chair at the dining room table and without thinking, overturned Willy's badly titled memoir so that only the backs of pages showed. I jerked the paper back until I was at the front (which was the end of his story) and let loose upon the blank underside of my father's "life."

I wrote: "When my brother hanged himself in a shower stall at St. Elizabeths, I took his name." And I continued to fill the flip side of my father's memoir, a hot attempt to write myself into history.

27

DEATH OF THE FATHER

Deborah called that morning. Her voice was nervous and constrained. "How is he?" she asked, clearly thinking he'd died before she'd reached the scene. "I've been trying to call."

"He's pretty chewed up," I explained. "They cut him open from the collar to the pelvis, and again on his leg to replace the arteries that collapsed. He lost so much blood; it ran down between the walls of his aorta for hours. They say he'll be all right, believe it or not, but he's barely opened his eyes, and when he did they just rolled back in his head."

"No, that's not true. I haven't called. I haven't been able to. You understand don't you Erich." And suddenly she was sobbing over the phone.

"It's all right, Deborah. There wasn't anything to see or do. You'll come up now. It doesn't matter."

She was barely articulate through her crying. "Oh, Erich, how did I get here?"

There was a strange pertinence to her outburst. I'd been sitting at the dining room table when she called, writing, or more accurately thrashing, my way across the back of Willy's manuscript and had just been remembering our first months in Venice Beach and the quick appearance and departure of Deborah's first love, Chuck. My sister's tears broke in waves across fifteen years.

"He kicked me out," she said. "He kicked us both out."

"That was decades ago, Deborah. And Mom left him; she took us away from him."

"No, Dave. Dave kicked us out. My father has a heart attack and he tells me to get out. We don't have anyplace to go."

Our conversation was happening on too many planes at once. I tried to focus on her words, to clear my head of everything I'd read that night and written that morning, to shake the thought of monster Dad, tubes and wires coming out of everywhere. I had a mental image of movable planes like infinite sheets of glass, pictures from our lives projected on them. We look through one surface to another and another. Long-focus, middle-distance, or near, our vision shifts and slides, as do the these parallel, simultaneous lives, past, present, future, imagined, real.

"Put our stuff into a locker somewhere," I told my sister. "And get up here."

I squirreled my father's manuscript behind a bookshelf, pen stuck inside. I showered and threw on some clothes. I stopped at the diner on the corner and loaded up on coffee before getting the subway up to Columbia-Presbyterian. I bought a *Times* and stared at it. I tried to distract myself from what I was thinking: today Deborah will kill herself and Dad will die.

My vigil continued. I waited for Dad to wake up. Intensive care seemed quieter than usual. They let me sit by him almost all day. In contrast to the peace I'd felt on the preceding days, I was now a ball of agitation, mind wired, body fried from lack of sleep. "Open your eyes, old man. Prove me wrong."

Deborah didn't arrive and she didn't arrive. I calculated the time it should take her to get here from Penn Station, trains pulling in every hour on the half hour, forty minutes for the subway wait and ride, another fifteen to find her way through the hospital to here. No one visited, though Hildy checked in by phone. Just sheer waiting.

Finally, around eight o'clock at night, as visiting hours were ending, a nurse tapped me on the shoulder. "Someone wants you," she said, tipping her head toward the lobby.

Before I could see Deborah's face, she had her arms around me and was sobbing in my neck. As I pulled back, I saw that she was wearing sunglasses and that her lip was swollen and split. I reached for the glasses and, without resistance from her, slipped them off. One eye was puffed up and purple. Both were wet with red heat.

Never-again Dave, she'd once called him.

She hid her face in my chest. All I could make out amidst her gulping and sobbing was, "sorry, sorry, sorry."

"He hasn't died," I said, though I knew she wasn't exactly crying about Dad. "He's starting to come to. He rolls his eyes and says, 'Wheee! Whoopee!' like a kid on a ride. The doctor says it's a response to the trauma. Acute psychosis. He thinks he's a little boy. Except when he's asleep, which is most of the time."

"Wheee," she echoed without affect. "Whoopee."

"Whoopee!" I said. She nearly giggled.

I could feel her settle in my arms. She took big breaths. When she spoke, her voice was deep and quiet. "It's not my life anymore; it's gotten out of my hands. I can't go on like this." I walked her to the handicapped bathroom in the hall. A desk nurse turned her head to look as I ushered Deborah through the door. I put the lid of the toilet down and eased her onto it. I folded a paper towel and ran cool water onto it. I patted Deborah's eyes and cheeks. She winced and bit the inside of her cheek, but she accepted my ablutions. When they were completed, I began washing my hands, more out of habit than need.

Deborah joined me at the mirror. "Boy oh boy," she said, "if Mom could see me now. . . ."

We caught each other's reflected eyes. Hers began to pool again. I felt like crying too, seeing her so sad.

Deborah moved into Dad's apartment with me. We played house, stocking the kitchen with food and collecting bills in a neat pile on the desk. Boxes arrived with her clothes. I shopped at the Gap for things I needed. We slept in the twin beds in the second bedroom — the kids' room — a continuous slumber party. We freshened the sheets on Willy's double bed, in anticipation of his eventual homecoming. We oversaw our father's slow recuperation.

I was full of memories at the time, or at least in search of them, and so the past lived in parallel to our exigent present. But, as much as we talked, and we talked constantly, we never went there. I brought it up only once. Deborah was mopping the hall floor in a succession of slaps, squeaks, and clicks. I stepped past her into the bathroom. I began to scour the tub with Comet and a coarse brush. When she reached the door, I looked over at her, her face laminated with makeup. She could be so defiantly superficial.

I sat on the edge of the tub and watched her mop. "Do you ever miss him, Deborah?"

"Do I miss who?"

"Do you miss Erich ever? Do you think about him?"

Suddenly Deborah looked young, surprised. She could be so beautiful, her face round and open with my mother's green eyes.

"Sure I think about him, but I don't *think* about him."

"Don't you wonder what was in his mind when he died? What he'd have been like if he lived. He might be standing here with us."

She pulled out a cigarette and lit it. She rested her back against the wall. "He did what he wanted to do. That's all. He did it. That's what he was thinking, if he was thinking at all. He's better off where he is. Better off than here," she said with a nasal laugh. "He couldn't be happy. You didn't know him like I did."

"What do you mean?"

"I don't know what I mean."

She flicked her cigarette into the bucket of Mr. Clean. "Poor Erich. Missed all this fun."

At bedtime I'd say good night to Deborah — I would literally tuck her in — turn out the light, and take my place at the dining room table, hunched over Willy's book, which was rapidly becoming my book as I wrote across the back. I was aware that my "story" was more speculative than factual. It was my impressionistic family archive, the kind of collage that memory, imagination, and twisted feeling assemble. I scribbled under a single lamp, surrounded by the dark weight of Dad's life. His books were quiet. I made my own soundless uttering in their company, the *shush* of a pen eddying across paper. I was scratching for my mortality, the kind that takes place in this body the world.

The process was nothing like fun. Each sentence I formed seemed to come from somewhere below the skin. Located, it needed

to be dislodged; dislodged, it left an abscess. Every night from midnight to five, I could be seen at my father's dining room table bobbing my knee up and down, hugging my ribs, twitching, squirming,
and grimacing, a mad mess of anxiety and relief, mouthing words to
myself, keening.

A couple of days after Deborah showed up, Dad came to. The
first time he saw her standing over him, he called her "Mommy" and
mumbled some gibberish about a baseball. As he opened his eyes
more often and for longer periods of time, he began to see us both
with something like clarity. I read sadness into his face at finding us
there. It may have been exhaustion or physical anguish, but I
thought his face said, "It's come to this."

At first Deborah didn't want to be seen, especially by him, and so
she made herself scarce. When she did appear, her face was caked
with makeup. She healed before long, but the bruise above her
cheek created a shadow under the thick base. The corner of one eye
pinched slightly, culminating in a small scab, the last vestige of
Dave's good-bye. Deborah pasted together this way, Dad holding on
by plastic threads, me, half emaciated and shaking from too much
coffee and too little sleep — our scars, our small monstrosities, had
become visible all at once. We were not a pretty sight.

Willy and I began to talk, mostly concerning the elaborate, prosaic details of his health. Illness became the world and the language
of the world. The doctors' pronouncements stimulated endless,
Talmudic analysis. So did the fluctuations of temperature, heart rate,
blood pressure, the play-by-play monitoring of the body's state, the
arrangement of oxygen tubes, catheters, IV, bed. It's remarkable how
much time you can spend discussing sleep or hospital food.
Everything is present and changing and in constant need of attention. How are your pillows now, and now, and now?

By the time he'd moved into a semiprivate room, in the week
prior to Christmas, we were able to add strings to our conversational
bow. We talked about the people who came to visit, we made a holiday shopping list for Willy Jr. and Amanda, we joked about what
we'd wear to Reagan's second inaugural. Deborah went looking for

work, and each day ended with a tremulous report from that front. My sister, who'd always displayed palpable anger on the subject of Dad, now seemed almost penitent in his presence. The three of us were unexcitable with one another, respectful intimates detained in the same cell at the end of a long day's protest.

We celebrated Christmas '84 around the foot of his hospital bed, four surviving offspring years apart in age, and one stiff-backed ex-wife. I'd bought Willy a Santa Claus cap, which he wore with sheepish glee. He sipped juice through a bendy straw while the kids opened books and games I'd had store-wrapped. Clearly, the five-year-old Willy was the apple of his father's eye. He and Dad pored over the pictures on his Lego box as the rest of us faded into the walls, waiting for the next gifts to come undone. Deborah and Amanda, now ten, stood in exactly the same position on opposite sides of the bed: hands clasped in front of them, eyes unfocused upwards, as though willing themselves to disappear. I made choppy conversation with Hildy, who was "so pleased" that I was "able to be here to tend to your father."

When they'd gone, Dad handed me the Santa hat and settled into the bank of pillows behind him. His eyes fluttered shut and he indicated sleep. I watched him breathe and sink back. He appeared to age with each breath until, finally asleep, he was as old as the world.

Deborah and I brought him home in mid-January and nursed him into the summer. There were several more hospital stays, and at least three more surgeries. Deborah took work as an administrative manager for a gay health-service network in the West Village. She puffed up a bit with being needed in what was becoming a national crisis. She could be seen bustling about the apartment at night like a matron hen. My job suited me; I was secretary and valet to Professor Emeritus Hofmann. I ordered his medication and colostomy supplies, shopped for his food, made notes to call this colleague or that insurance company, and then placed the calls. I held his pants when he slipped them on and his hand when he stepped into his shoes. I ushered him onto the handicapped seat we installed in the tub, hosed him down with the rubber hand-shower we'd bought, and scrubbed his back.

When the kids came by, I stepped aside, like a house steward at the ready. I'd present orange juice with cherries on a tray, whisk in to grab Junior if he got too physical with his ailing Dad, and compliment Amanda on her new dress. I had been raised to service by my mother, I guess, and I enjoyed my proficiency.

Dad and I were customary and familiar together, as if we'd lived in each other's company forever. When we read, in our adjacent chairs, he'd occasionally stop to read out a phrase or paragraph he loved and discuss it. The TV was on a lot, a background babble of baseball, neo–Cold War idiocy, and international terrorism.

He loved talking to the TV screen, playing the madman. "Atta girl, Maggie," he'd catcall at Mrs. Thatcher. "Hurry back to the orphanage; it's time for the children to be punished!" He smacked his palm to his forehead. "Oh, my god! She's what J. Ed Hoover dressed up as!"

As he strengthened, we took occasional bus trips to destinations throughout Manhattan. We bought a CD player and started collecting digital versions of his favorite classical albums, one at a time. He kept count of how many CDs he owned. "Thirty-four, five, and six," he'd enthuse to the sullen hobbledehoy at the cash register. We played chess at nights, but, unsatisfied with my challenges (though he never said so), he started up against a chess computer a friend had given him in the hospital. He beat it at every game until he got to level six.

We'd shoot pool at a place near Columbia, Willy going at it gingerly, all deference to his scarred-up, half-healed body. Every shot was a "trick shot" to him, and whenever he avoided sinking the eight ball, he made verbal note of his increasing prowess. We followed pool with late lunches at his favorite Italian restaurant on West Ninety-third. Once there, he'd drink too much — anything, according to his doctors, was too much — and rattle on genially. I could see that he missed, if not teaching, at least the collegial hallway chatter of faculty life. His innate sociability surfaced despite life's attempts to isolate him: distant parents, runaway wives, cost-cutting college administrators. He blabbed on about Willy Jr. and Amanda and downplayed any hostility between Hildy and himself. "Of course, they always want to overpower a man," he glossed cryptically, "but the regrets, those are all mine." We skirted mention of the two decades we'd spent apart.

I had always thought of Willy in isolation: a man at a screen door, watching his family leave; a father alone with his troubled sons; an aging academic hiding from lightning under the dining room table. He had a quotation from John Cheever's *Bullet Park* pinned to a corkboard that I'd thought of as a rubric for his life: "You're a lonely man and a lonely man is a lonely thing, a stick, a stone, a bone, a doormat, an empty gin bottle. . . ." I imagined him cowering under the table during a thunderstorm and thought I'd caught his essence. I hadn't. And I still didn't catch it, day after day, didn't piece this new information into a whole portrait until after he'd died.

My world was chronically unpeopled; his wasn't. He had dozens of friends, colleagues, former students. He had lived and worked as part of something larger than himself, larger than "us," and, as I stood in attendance on him, as he received visits, calls, and letters, I became part of it, too. His faith, however tentative, was other people. Jump into the void. Maybe someone will jump with you.

Moreover, for all Willy's razor intelligence, for all his unarticulated, inarticulate sadness and high Aryan reserve — put a couple drinks in him, get him talking about his children or friends, and you'd have a gushing, dopey sentimentalist.

"I love all my children," he announced, a sheet or two to the wind.

"You're not supposed to be drinking, you know," Deborah reminded him, swiping our glasses from the table and disappearing into the kitchen.

"And I love bowling," he added. "One of the happiest times of my life was when you and your brother and sister were little and we drove up to Toronto to spend the weekend bowling."

"We were never in Toronto, Dad," I said, dull protector of truth.

"And how we'd go sailing when I'd visit you in Madison. . . . What was the name of the lake there?"

"It wasn't a lake, Dad. It was the Mississippi River and we went down it on a raft." He'd never been to Madison.

"Little Willy and I are going to Dublin when he's older," said the leprechaun father.

I laughed a wee killjoy laugh.

"He's such a wonderful kid. All my kids are wonderful kids. Wunnerful wunnerful."

Deborah, passing through the room again, snatched the Jameson bottle off the table. "I'm going to tell the doctors on you," she said.

"So threatens Nurse Ratched," he replied.

I was principal witness to my father's sweetness. I was basking in it. I noticed but I didn't see. Or I noticed but couldn't believe it extended to me.

"He was a softy," Mac told me over the phone, after Willy had died. "And he was over-the-top proud of you kids."

I grunted politely in response.

"Sure," Mac added, "he was worried, too. Worried as hell, all the time. Worried *and* proud. That's what he was saying with all that rafting down the Mississippi blather."

Willy's good eye began to fail him. We didn't know what exactly was wrong. As time passed, though, it became harder for him to see things close up, which made reading nearly impossible. My father had always held books close, right up to his one live eye. One day I glimpsed him moving a book before his face, circulating it in the air, as if wiping a window an inch or two in front of his face. I suspect his range of near vision had begun to tunnel, to narrow or shutter down to a thin beam of sight. He was trying to place the passage he was reading inside the beam. He broke out in a cold sweat and put the book down.

I began reading to him. We pretended that nothing unnatural was taking place, that reading aloud, son to father, had ever been the family way. He asked indirectly, treating me like a research assistant on the trail of lost sources. He'd have me read passages, and only rarely whole chapters or stories. He'd send me to the shelves in search of a quotation or description. "There's that section on the sucking stones in *Molloy* I've been wanting to go over," he'd say, and I'd fetch. We'd spotlight great moments in literature, scenes, fragments, lines of prose. I'd read and he'd close both eyes, forefingers making a steeple under his chin while he burrowed inside. I wished I could listen as he listened, words playing off decades of associations, accumulated knowledge, and reference. A man, suddenly old after a lifetime in service to a single demanding god, at prayer. And his god was the word.

More and more, he wanted Flaubert. He had me poke around in *Sentimental Education* and *The Temptation of Saint Anthony*, reading passages over and over again. He'd ask me to read the French, but I was helpless there. His frustration swelled and he checked it. We stuck with English.

At first I thought he was memorizing, that he wanted to carry certain passages with him, word for word, through the rest of his dark days or to the grave. Then I thought he was punishing himself, second-guessing his choices: If he'd only chosen to study Flaubert instead of Wittgenstein and gone to France (as Lorna wished) instead of Austria, his life and everyone else's would have turned out otherwise. As I read a paragraph or page over and over, he'd settle down into the warmth of his guilt. Or maybe he was picturing himself, in his mind's eye — the only purely sighted one he had — moving through a different life altogether. Finally, after several days of plucking books and reading snatches out loud, I realized what he was doing. He was choosing an epitaph.

I don't know if he found it. I do know that I went over one sentence from *Madame Bovary* at least a dozen times. "Just repeat it until I tell you to stop," he said, after hearing it the first time.

I did as he commanded. "The truth is that fullness of the soul can sometimes overflow in utter vapidity of language, for none of us can ever express the exact measure of his needs or his thoughts or his sorrows; and human speech is like a cracked kettle on which we tap crude rhythms for bears to dance to, while we long to make music that will melt the stars." When I tired of repeating it, I looked up.

Willy's glasses lay in his lap. He was pressing his palms against both eyes and weeping.

I waited until his body's quaking slowed, and I said, "I found the memoir. I read it, Dad."

He rubbed at his eyes and sighed. Then, with a snort through his nose, part blow, part laugh, he responded. "Yes, I never got that one right."

Willy died on a bus on his way to the Strand bookstore on lower Broadway. It was his only solo junket since the first heart attack ten months earlier. I was not surprised, when he told me where he was going, that he hadn't given up the hope of being able to read again. You go where comfort is, where you are understood, even if it means standing, almost blind, among stacks of books.

To be precise, he didn't die on the bus, but in the hospital that night, most probably of another aneurysm. He gave a gargled shout and lost consciousness on the bus. In one of those unlikely turns of event that mark New York life, the bus driver veered from his path and headed to St. Vincent's in the West Village. Most of the passengers chose to stay aboard and see how it all turned out, rather than disembarking when the driver first discovered he'd been stricken. The bus headed to the emergency driveway, where driver and passengers loitered for more than an hour, giving statements to police, reporters, and whoever asked. The *Daily News* headline read, "Columbia Prof Fails on Bus."

Even after he'd died, my father's body remained, for me, almost palpable. My memories of him were details that conjured his physical whole. I recalled his oiled hair, flecks of dandruff along the strands, and there he was before me. Likewise, his sausage fingers coming to a point beneath his chin, the liver spots on his jowls along the beard line, the pink scar that zippered up his shaven body from pelvis to throat. There was always Listerine on his breath, and it carried the whiff of the whiskey and decay it masked. His eye, creamy and dead, even in life, appeared before me at the slightest suggestion, the magnified image of a waking dream.

He'd made clear his wishes for that body. Willy believed that life absolutely ended with death — no God, no hereafter, sweet or otherwise. So, he didn't want his body taking up earthly space, or his ashes assuming symbolic weight. For him, Beckett's ash heap was a literal one, upon which his cremated remains were to be shoveled. "Gone is gone," he insisted in a marginal note on his will, the pedant even in death.

28

The World's Room

Deaths bracketed the epochs of our family life. Willy's was the third to do so. For me it was the beginning of release from the prior two. Before long I had covered the empty page-backs of my father's memoir and moved on to his typewriter and new pages. I worked hard, would continue to do so for many years. As I wrote, I wanted to remain "on voice," as Lorna used to say. By this she meant sustaining a richness of tone that comes when breath and sound connect without tension. "If the sound is right, the singer is carried on it," she'd explain. "The notes are full of who the singer is." At twenty-eight, I was seeing what my father, with his milky, blind eye must have seen all along: You can't find the perfect word. You grope for it, struggle with two or three or twenty choices, but no word — no *name* — can hold all the meaning you want it to. ". . . We tap crude rhythms for bears to dance to, while we long to make music that will melt the stars." At most you can do what the singer does: vocalize, put sound into the world.

I stayed in the apartment, whose lease I'd inherited from Willy. Deborah roomed with me in between crises. We'd each received one-quarter of Dad's life savings, his TIAA-CREF teaching pension. With this inheritance I rented a small storefront on the ground floor of a mixed-use building on 112th Street off Amsterdam. It took more than a year to find the space and realize the idea I had for it, but I did. I stocked the store with books, specifically works of biography and autobiography. There was no end of books that suited the collection I had in mind: tales of political and sexual identity from around the world, stories of personal recovery —

from incest, addiction, McCarthyism — memoirs of shame and faith, emigration and displacement, grief and identity. An entire generation of writers, it appeared, was offering up lives on paper. We were earning the "I." That's how I thought of it.

I named my bookstore "The World's Room," of course, and kept Erich's "Ballad" in the safe. His unfinished lifework was the bookstore's spirit-object, a thing whose secret existence made concrete the goals and values of the business. During all the years I'd kept it close, Erich's mad, adolescent memoir had become my talisman, both reminder and protector. The notebooks embodied a failed attempt to do what all these other writers had done: write themselves out from under a life that seemed determined to bury them.

And I shed his name. It happened before the store or inheritance check. It happened in a moment. Dad died, was cremated and commemorated, and suddenly — without premeditation — I was ready.

I was preparing to leave for D.C., to tie up our loose ends there. I would arrange for Deborah's belongings, and the few of mine that remained, to be shipped north from their temporary storage. I would visit my shrink one last time to report that I'd weaned myself off the drugs he'd been prescribing for the past year. And (this I didn't tell Deborah) I would locate and visit Erich's grave.

Deborah and I were sitting at Dad's table making a list. She was writing addresses and phone numbers on a piece of paper, chain-smoking. I hadn't lived in Washington for long before moving in with Dad, so she wanted to cover me. She listed the bus and Metro lines; she made descriptive notes of the items detailed on her storage rental agreement for me to check on before the movers got their hands on them. She made me count my cash three times.

My sister's competent streaks alternated with periods of quivering desperation when she'd latch onto someone or something new. In years to come, she would fall into a consuming, sexless love affair with a dying man and, for several years in the early nineties, get drawn into a Manhattan-based theater and therapy cult, before it was broken up by lawsuits and scandal. For the moment, competence reigned. "This is Denise's number. She's an old friend of mine from Minneapolis, but she's lived in D.C. for years. If you need anything, if anything goes wrong and you can't reach me here, call her."

"I'll only be gone for two days, Deborah."

"I'll let her know you're coming, that you may call. Here's her work number, Erich."

"I'll be fine."

"Of course you'll be fine, Erich. I want to make sure you have backup is all."

"Deborah," I said, putting my hand on hers to stop it from writing, "Don't call me that anymore, all right? I don't want to be called by that name anymore."

She sucked in air, a reverse sigh. She stared at me across the table. Her eyes grew heavy and dark. Then she turned her attention to the cigarette in the ashtray. She took a drag and watched it burn down.

"That was his name," I continued. "It was very much his name. It's not mine. Not now at least."

Deborah tilted her head sidewise. She gave me an old Jewish lady look and asked, "What would you like I should call you?"

"I don't know," I replied. "Teddy, Ted, Theodore, some version of myself. Just not that anymore."

"All right," she said; "You want it, you got it."

We were quiet for a minute. Then she pushed the paper across to me. "Here. I think that's everything."

"Thanks."

"I gotta pee," she said, moving away.

She stopped near the shelf of art books. A half cry escaped her throat: "You just disappeared!" She looked back at me and her eyes were brimming. "One minute you were there with me in Venice, we were saying good-bye. Then you disappeared. I thought you were dead. I thought terrible things had happened. I thought you'd died a hundred different ways!"

I stood and moved to her. I held on to her. Her arms hung down. "I won't disappear. I promise. I'm back. I won't disappear."

—m—

I hadn't, since the funeral, seen Erich's grave. I didn't know where it was, and I doubted that Deborah had ever tracked it down. Mac knew, but he'd returned to New Mexico after the memorial, where he'd settled in the early eighties. I couldn't ask Dad.

I used a map and phone book at the library to locate cemeteries. I called three before I found the right one. I took the Metro to an office near Catholic University, where a man in a fine gray suit pointed out the spot on a legal-sized, xeroxed grid. Erich's body had, I discovered, a latitude and a longitude all its own, a section, a row, and a column. He was still where we left him.

It was one of those bright, sharp-focus autumn days that make D.C. summers worth slogging through. Sixteen years had passed since I'd stood at Erich's grave. I had only seen the cemetery at its rainy, mud-thick worst, but I remembered it as a beautiful park. Would it correspond with my memory? I didn't know, nor did I know if Dad had ordered a tombstone, or if some unseen stranger regularly, mysteriously, placed fresh-cut flowers on the spot. I only knew I wanted to say some words over his buried body. I knew I wanted this double life, this not-my life, to be over.

I rode two buses to the cemetery and, as I rode, I imagined myself there: kissing the stone, tracing with my thumb the engraved name — his name — Erich Wilhelm Hofmann. The stone I envisioned reminded me of my brother's cushy, baby white cheek. I recalled his kindness and saw myself grabbing a fistful of grass and dry soil and letting it pour from my hand. The texture of the earth, I thought, would assure me that nothing is too solid to change shape, that life remakes itself, even as it appears to be sifting through your fingers. I would take a deep breath, hunch close to the ground, and whisper, "Rest, Erich. Rest."

Erich's plot was not the island I imagined it to be. I had remembered a field of mud, cornered by towering trees. In fact, he was buried in a small strip packed into the middle of a row of such strips, a row within a battalion of rows. There were no trees nearby. Also, contrary to my expectations, there was no significant tombstone.

Instead, a small stone marker, engraved with Erich's name and dates, 1952–1969, confirmed his presence with minimal ceremony. Dwarfed by the odd-sized slabs and monuments around it, it looked more like a name tag worn at a business conference than a memorial — something stuck on a lapel to identify the wearer, rather than to confirm his stature in the world. Dad had probably ordered it when he bought the gravesite.

The grounds were well kept, mown, and litter free. The graves were so regular and the lawns so vast that I had trouble focusing on Erich's little property. It had no impact, no resonance, except what I could work up. I'd forgotten to bring flowers. There was no fresh earth to sprinkle on the grave. To kiss the gravestone, I would have had to lie on my belly and press my face almost into the ground. Even standing was a task, with no place to prop myself, no right way to hold my hands. I hung my head with my hands clasped in front of me to pray. I couldn't think of a prayer or a god to pray to. I said my brother's name a few times, like some two-bit conjurer. I wrote it in the air.

"Just stand around, dummy," I mumbled.

So I stood. I stood like somebody standing in line to use the john. I folded my arms for a while, then laced my fingers behind my head, then stuck my hands in my pockets. I watched my toe make divots in the grass. I looked at clumps of cloud overhead. Small brown birds darted by.

The breeze rose and fell. I could feel, as though just beneath the skin of my arms and chest, music pulsing — some mournful strain I couldn't quite make out, but which I knew belonged to my mother. I stood there trying to catch the sound, its sadness. I stood there, alone and missing everybody.

Everybody, even her, maybe her most of all. Some music won't leave you alone. Her songs were like that, pregnant with loss and hope. "O bonnie babes, gin ye were mine, / I would dress you up in satin fine. . . ." I could see her sing it, her face made of fine angles, chestnut hair pulled back, the tan ledge of her clavicle. I could all but hear her.

It is possible for the body to forget the feeling of love. And it's possible to remember.

I sat down, leaned against a stranger's headstone, and just cried. I pinched Kleenex from the small plastic pack I carried.

My father had ended his memoir with a scene set in heaven, at a table in heaven. Now I closed my eyes and pictured myself in such a place. A white, endless room with tables everywhere. Bagpipe music playing at a distance. Lorna was beside me, as was Erich. They both placed their hands on me, on my shoulders and arms. Not being a heavenly body, my skin resisted their touch. I could feel the weight of their hands, and the warmth of them, through my everyday clothes. As their fingers and palms bounded me, I became aware of my own body: its flesh, muscle, bone, organs, nerves, and the blood that coursed inside.

I watched their peaceful faces. Their eyes were serene, but I was afraid. Of them. Of what might happen next. Of giving in and losing myself to the pressure of their hands. I was afraid I would evaporate at their touch, but I didn't. I remained firm.

I opened my eyes with that yearning you have when a dream carries over into the waking morning. I didn't know what to do next, but my body seemed to know. My hand was sending me signals. Instinctively, it started groping around on the ground beside me, reaching for a tissue, maybe, or for something I might have dropped. My hand, with a will of its own, began patting the grass, confirming the earth over Erich's bones.